JUST US

He Calls me Harp Series

JUST US

HEATHER WHITE DRISCOLL

Copyright © 2023 Heather White Driscoll.

All rights reserved. No part of this book may be used or reproduced by any means, graphic, electronic, or mechanical, including photocopying, recording, taping or by any information storage retrieval system without the written permission of the author except in the case of brief quotations embodied in critical articles and reviews.

This is a work of fiction. All of the characters, names, incidents, organizations, and dialogue in this novel are either the products of the author's imagination or are used fictitiously.

Archway Publishing books may be ordered through booksellers or by contacting:

Archway Publishing
1663 Liberty Drive
Bloomington, IN 47403
www.archwaypublishing.com
844-669-3957

Because of the dynamic nature of the Internet, any web addresses or links contained in this book may have changed since publication and may no longer be valid. The views expressed in this work are solely those of the author and do not necessarily reflect the views of the publisher, and the publisher hereby disclaims any responsibility for them.

Any people depicted in stock imagery provided by Getty Images are models, and such images are being used for illustrative purposes only. Certain stock imagery © Getty Images.

ISBN: 978-1-6657-3199-7 (sc)
ISBN: 978-1-6657-3200-0 (hc)
ISBN: 978-1-6657-3201-7 (e)

Library of Congress Control Number: 2022919675

Print information available on the last page.

Archway Publishing rev. date: 3/6/2023

For Patrick.
For always respecting Harper & Scott.

For Willow.
For asking: What happened to them?

ONE

"I DIDN'T GROW AT ALL, HARPER," Leigh exclaimed while getting out of my mother's new Lexus RX300, a car that accurately represented my mother and her overwhelming sense of superiority. "I'm starting my freshman year of high school in a middle-school body!"

I felt content with myself as I entered high school. I didn't believe I was hot, or even sexy, but I could hold my own, and I was tan, which was a rarity among the population of the state of Washington. I had just hit five feet over that summer. My parents may have been slightly concerned that I had a height deficiency; looking back to that time, I realize this was a silly notion. I was growing, just at a much slower pace than, say, my ten-year-old sister, who happened to be the same height I was as I entered my freshman year.

The point is that in 1997, I felt like I finally measured up with the big girls. I had a great tan. My braces had just been removed, my teeth were freshly bleached, and I had grown out my dark brown, exceptionally curly hair. I was a high-school girl now, too! I felt that the young woman I had finally become on my own was good enough for high school. I wasn't sure what else I could have changed to make myself more sellable by high school standards, and I wasn't sure I actually wanted to be sellable by high school standards, to begin with. I didn't want a boyfriend; I just wanted to be accepted as part of the status quo and slip under the proverbial radar.

This was not Leigh's intended path.

Leigh had always embodied a high level of optimism toward high school and life in general. Her self-assurance is superior to anyone else I know. No matter what happens in life, Leigh will always find the bright side and push forward. Short like me with a cute childlike voice, the adorable blonde shoulder-length stacked bob she wore became her signature look. Unfortunately for her, Leigh anticipated her braces staying on for three years. I had pulled away with only two years of braces under my belt. She told me that she appreciated looking at my smile, as it acted as a reminder that her dental hardware would one day be removed, and she, too, would be left with an electrifying grill of her own. The big difference between us was Leigh wanted nothing more than to be noticed. I didn't feel comfortable embracing notoriety. She wanted to be popular, she wanted to be seen as a girl who had it all, and she really wanted not to be a virgin.

"I think Brett is the guy I'm going to do it with," she stated confidently as we walked between classes to Prairie Center, more conventionally known as PC. It was the only convenience store on our island and within walking distance of our high school, making it the place to see and be seen for high school students. Leigh demanded we go between first and second periods.

"Why does it have to be Brett?" I asked, knowing fully that Leigh was looking to brag about the potential demise of her virginity. "He's such a stereotype! Typical Seattle grunger, with his flannel and a guitar on his back. It would be embarrassing to admit you slept with a cliché."

"Well, all the really hot guys know they're hot and aren't interested in me."

"Leigh, you are gorgeous! Quit it with this self-deprecating act of yours and go after a guy you really find hot," I exclaimed. "Brett isn't hot. He's adequate."

"What is your problem with sex? You spent the entire summer disparaging the idea of sex and ignoring its reality!"

"Here is my stance on the matter: I'm going to save the deed for college." My attempt at holding back a smile was losing ground as I began a rant she'd heard more than a few times over the summer. Leigh couldn't contain her own grin, either.

"If Brett is typical of the pool of degenerates I have to pick from in the greater Seattle area, it's probably best to avoid sex until college, where the cesspool is much shallower. And in the end, what I'm really doing is saving my adult years from hours of sheer humiliation as I tell people about the things happening now. I mean, say I was at a cocktail party in my late twenties, yakking it up about my most embarrassing adolescent moments, and Brett was listed on the tally of men I had sex with. Just imagine!... Granted, people would understand—me being a Seattle native and all, they'd expect me to have a grunge-band boyfriend or two along my path to maturity—but in all actuality, I'd hate to be that cliché."

"Here's the problem, Harper," Leigh sighed. "You overthink everything, and your rant is tiring! Do you honestly plan on attending cocktail parties?"

"I don't overthink anything," I exclaimed. "And yes, I do. My parents always attend cocktail parties whenever someone my dad works with retires."

"You do too overthink," she exclaimed as we walked down the candy aisle. "Do you know why I picked Brett? He's probably a five, maybe a six if he cleaned up a bit, and he sits a few rows away in my first-period health class."

"Doesn't Ms. Tierney put you in alphabetical order?" I politely put my hand on her shoulder. "Your last name is Kimble, and he is?"

"Snyder."

"So, logically, you agree there isn't any chance of interaction over the space of a few rows. Plus, he's a senior in freshmen health. You really want to go with a guy in freshmen health as a senior?"

"First off, it's not *freshmen health*; it's just health—"

"That is required to be taken in the ninth grade—"

"Whatever! Secondly, I don't want to go with anyone. I just want to get laid before this year is over!"

"Calendar year or school year?" I grinned. "Leigh, if you can't laugh at the ridiculousness of this conversation, this year is going to be a long one."

"This is not ridiculous," she exclaimed. "This is serious business!"

"Uh-huh."

"Harper, I meant to ask you: What are you doing after school today? Wanna come over? We can watch TRL and try to call in."

"I have soccer practice from three to five," I told her. "Oh, and my dad says that we should stop trying to call in because we'll never get on."

"What do you mean? We're bound to get on Total Request Live if we wait it out!"

"Yeah, I think he was getting at that it might not be live for us. It's filmed in Times Square."

"Huh, are we sure?" She sounded perplexed. "Anyway, you find out this afternoon if you made varsity soccer, right? Shit, Harper, if you made it, we are in!"

"Leigh, I highly doubt that me making varsity soccer is going to increase our social ranking around here. No one ever goes to the games." I huffed. "It's only girls' soccer."

"Yeah, but more people might go if they find out a freshman made the team!"

Leigh continued to prattle on about climbing the high-school social ladder, and her obsession over Brett and his garage band of misfits for a bit before someone caught my eye. I found myself stopping my friend mid-sentence by nodding my head toward the boy walking toward us and asking her, "Who's that?"

The more I looked at him, the more I realized that this was not a "boy," as I so erroneously described him; this was a man. There had to be a significant age gap between him and me. He had a man's height, bone structure, and appearance, that's for certain. For the first time, a man actually caught my eye. I had finally found my potential better half. Of course, it happened only a few minutes after I decided to vocalize my disdain for the male population of my high school.

Luckily, my fourteen-year-old self's inability to stay focused paid off in this encounter.

This guy was tall, maybe six-foot-five, and clean-cut despite his intentionally messy sandy blond hair. He made me genuinely rethink my plan on abstinence. He had the most beautiful skin that was so tan it was as if his skin were made to soak up the sun, but it was not obnoxiously dark. It had an olive tone. He had blue eyes and perfect, exceptionally white teeth. He knew the importance of taking care of his appearance, and I respected that. He was clearly my better half in all physical matters. He was happy, too, as evidenced by the fact that he was laughing very loudly with eight of his friends. Of course, he was happy—with a frame and appearance like that, a person would have to be happy. It would be a crime to not be.

I had visions of my life with him. I could see us walking hand in hand, our classmates envious of us, and our beautiful, acne-free, tan skin standing out in a sea of pale mediocrity. Then Leigh interrupted my daydreams.

"That's Scott Pierce. He's a senior. Look, we only have five minutes before the second-period starts, so we gotta hurry!"

"Leigh, how do you know?... I mean, how do you know his name is Scott? More importantly, how do you know that he is a senior?"

I felt like I was talking too fast. It was as if my train of thought wasn't keeping up with the words coming out of my mouth, which I wasn't used to. I was so panicked that my vocal cords were working faster than my brain, so fast that I couldn't form the correct questions I sought to ask. I kept my eye on Scott. He was still laughing with his group of guy friends, but he was walking toward Leigh and me. Before Scott approached me, I wanted to learn as much from Leigh.

"He's in my health class." She stated.

"My God, Leigh, what freshmen health class are you taking that you have two seniors in it?"

I thought about which health class I was in and if there was any chance I could still hop over into Leigh's section. She could hear my voice's panic and see my hands' erratic motions. Leigh replied as fast as she could when she saw Scott was quickly approaching.

"Calm down! It has a mixed bag of students in it. Scott apparently didn't take the class when he was a freshman and needs the credits to graduate."

"Is Scott dumb? I mean, why wouldn't he have secured the credits four years ago?"

"What, you think Brett's dumb?" She barked. "No, Scott's not dumb; he just never took the class."

"Yes, Brett is dumb," I replied. "Maybe I should take first-period health with you."

"Scott is a senior! He's never going to notice either one of us. It's not even worth going on about, okay? Scott Pierce is not for the taking!"

"Not thirty seconds ago, you were entirely certain that Brett was going to be your boyfriend, and now you don't think I can get Scott?"

"Not boyfriend," she corrected me. "I never said, *boyfriend*. I just need Brett to take me to the homecoming dance so I can remove this dumb V tattooed on my forehead!"

"Are we back to this? It's like you're consumed with losing your virginity!"

"Also, Harper, there is an obvious difference between Brett and Scott: Scott is really hot! He's like a nine."

"A nine?" I exclaimed. "He's a ten! He's a full-on ten!"

"Nah," she replied, "I don't agree. His height bothers me. I think there is such a thing as being too tall."

"I don't agree at all! I think I like him more because of his height."

"Either way, he isn't yours for the taking!"

Leigh was right; the belief that Scott would even notice me was a complete farce, a delusion. It was something that needed to be put away. Scott would be nothing more than a crush. Leigh was right. There were differences between Brett and Scott. Scott appeared to wear clean clothes daily and probably disregarded youthful crushes; Brett might as well have had a V tattooed on his forehead. I was willing to bet he'd end up being a clinger after Leigh put out. Scott didn't walk like he had a big V tacked on him. He walked with confidence, and he certainly wouldn't be a clinger. Leigh was right—he was hot, and he knew it.

Sometimes, though, daydreaming does pay off. Scott and I passed by one another while I was still fantasizing about him and me, bumping into each other. Apparently, he wasn't paying attention, either, because his elbow hit my shoulder and the force of it knocked me to the floor. I swear, falling down was never an intentional act. I was so caught up in my fantasy that I abandoned reality, and reality knocked me to the floor. Perhaps it was fate that intervened and forced that collision in the candy aisle of my town's only convenience store, as if every teenage girl's dream rose and chose my path to cross Scott's, but at the time, it was embarrassing.

I was hoping and praying with everything in me that Scott wouldn't say a word about this. The fact that I was now on the floor in front of this gorgeous boy was embarrassing, and I mentally crawled inside my shield of freshman protection. If I were lucky, he would issue a quick, insincere apology, and we'd both be on our way. I was hoping that would be the most interaction we'd have—ever. I didn't need a senior banging up my day or, for that matter, year, especially with the inevitable clout of senior superiority that his group of 'boys' touted themselves with.

"Hey, Shorty," he addressed me while laughing with his friends. "You should look up while you walk."

In that split second between confusion and rationality, as he poked fun of my height, I emerged from my shell, my need for self-defense emerging. I didn't enjoy having my unprogressive height brought to my attention. No matter how attractive Scott was, how popular he may have been, or the age difference between him and me, he didn't have that right—just yet, at least. My fourteen-year-old mind regurgitated a response I'm not sure I ever wanted to say.

"Hey, Stretch," I said sarcastically.

As if on cue, his pack of senior pals all burst into laughter, apparently deciding that a person of my stature couldn't speak to Scott in such a fashion.

"Ah, we got ourselves a freshman smartass!" Scott smirked.

Scott offered me his hand to help me up. I was caught off guard by his gesture but took his hand nonetheless, taking a moment to examine it. His hand was long and lean, his fingers thin; he had a tan line on his wrist showing that an oversized watch once covered his already-dark skin. His nails were perfectly rounded, and managed to follow the contour of his fingers. Each nail ended in a perfectly toned crescent-moon shape, and I instantly wondered if he filed them or if they grew naturally in such a fashion. I stood up and quickly released his hand.

"Better than being a freshman dumbass, I suppose."

Even Scott laughed. He laughed in a way that suggested we could even possibly be friends.

"I'm Scott."

"Hi," I whispered. "I'm Harper."

"That's an interesting name. You don't really hear that name much, or…at all, now that I think about it."

"If you turn around and look at the magazine rack, you can see it again," I told him, my tone sarcastic.

"Huh… Harper's Magazine."

"And if you look a little farther, you'll see it once more."

"Wow!" He smirked. "And Harper's Bazaar."

"We can't all be fortunate enough to be named Scott, now, can we now?"

"I suppose not. It isn't really one of those cross-gender names." He smiled as he reached for my shoulder and wiped off some dirt from the floor. "I was thinking more along the lines of TKM when I heard your name."

"What's TKM?" I asked him, perplexed.

"You'll learn soon enough, Freshman. Are you alright?" He continued in his motions to wipe dirt off my shoulder. "I knocked you pretty hard against the floor."

"I'm fine," I whispered. "Thank you."

I started to wipe off my jeans, ensuring that no dirt was on them, while he continued on my shoulders. I was surprised at how flattered I felt that he continued to pay attention to the dirt on my shoulders. He stepped half a foot closer as he continued to brush my shoulder, and I could instantly breathe him in. He smelled of masculinity—or at least a drugstore version of masculinity that I wasn't about to criticize. My curls draped on top of his hand, and my body fluttered with excitement as I thought about how close he was to me.

"You smell nice," he whispered, his voice so soft that no one around us could hear.

I looked up at him, and he pulled his hand away, which I instantly regretted. He became nervous and fidgety, like he didn't know what to do with his hand as if he got caught. He rested both his hands on his hips and nodded, turning and following his eight friends as they walked off; he turned toward me and began walking backward.

"Take care, Freshman Shorty," he yelled, smiling.

"He said I smelled nice," I softly told Leigh. "Did you hear him? He breathed me in and said I smelled nice...."

"That was so weird," she replied, her voice quiet. "It was like he couldn't stop touching you."

"I know," I whispered under my breath as we both watched Scott head off with his friends, laughing, playfully shoving each other, and enjoying their senior year together as they headed back to the second period. "Did you hear the way he said my name?"

"He added that hard *per* at the end each time... We're probably going to spend the rest of the day reading into this, aren't we? I think we should examine the facts right now before we forget them and start to add to this."

That is precisely what we did. Leigh and I talked about my encounter with the man of absolute hotness. By mid-afternoon, the entire freshman class had gotten word of my encounter at PC. Whether her embellishments were intentional or not, Leigh made sure to add more to the story than what actually happened. My classmates' interest lasted for roughly two weeks. The first week focused on my encounter at PC: The details, words stated, any contact or touching, and so on. The second week, interest had turned toward any further meetings I may have had with the senior.

Everyone knew who he was, and his name was Scott, but defining him by only his class solidified me as a guide in the 'freshman-senior' bridge. Every one was so concerned with how things were progressing.

In reality, there was no progress to report. I had one literal run-in with a senior, who probably didn't even remember my name after he left the store. When the school year started, I just wanted people to notice the changes in my physical exterior—my longer hair, taller frame, and beautiful teeth. I did not want everyone to focus on my unfulfilling situation with Scott.

I spent every one of my waking moments thinking about Scott—where he was, what he was doing, what class he was in, where he planned on going to college. I became so consumed with how things were going in my head that I never made any progress in talking to him further in reality. I wasn't sure what I'd need to do to get him to notice me again.

I got so lost in my head when I rounded a corner before third period and walked directly into Scott, exactly three weeks after the incident at the store. I had nothing to say to him. I sat, momentarily shocked, on the hallway floor, amazed that this had happened again.

"Shorty!" He reached for my hand and helped me up, keeping hold of it. "We gotta stop meeting like this. I was in such a rush to get my latest edition of Harper's Magazine that I seem to have knocked you down again!"

"Funny," I breathed before I realized Scott was still holding my hand. "I'm sorry, though. I didn't mean to run into you like that."

"Shouldn't I be apologizing to you?" He pulled his brows together. "This is the second time I've knocked you down."

"So you admit the first time was also your fault?" I teased. "I'll be happy to take an apology for both events."

"Harper Whitmore, is it?" He grinned.

"Yes," I replied softly. "How do you know my last name?"

Before I could get an answer from the senior himself, the bell rang. He walked beside me, his chest rubbing against my shoulder as he leaned down and whispered into my bed of curls.

"I have my ways, Harper Whitmore."

"What do you mean—"

Before I could complete my question, Scott was gone, and the hallway was cleared out. All I had left was his smell and the giddy feeling I got knowing that not only did he remember my first name, but he'd taken the time to learn my last. He either liked to stalk women, or he truly was interested in me. I was hoping it was the latter, but I'd settle for either. He smelled of men's deodorant and another form of male fragrance. That smell stuck with me for the rest of the day. I'd sense a masculine scent and try to hold on to it, remembering that second encounter with my senior.

I walked around the rest of the day in a fog of euphoria over my encounter with Scott. I didn't care if I ended up on the floor again. I'd be comfortable with being knocked over once more if it meant I could see Scott again. I always seemed to happen upon him when I was lost in my own head and not actually looking for him, anyway. It happened again the same afternoon of my second encounter. I was walking back to the locker room, alone, after soccer practice, when I heard his deep voice draw me in.

"If it isn't my favorite little freshman!" I could hear his voice behind me and turned to see him lightly jogging toward me with a tennis racket in hand. "You're filthy, Freshman!"

"Yeah." I grinned and attempted to brush the caked-on mud off my forearms. This move was partly due to my nervousness, but it was probably more an attempt to make myself slightly more presentable in front of someone I found myself wanting to look good for. "Soccer practice in the rain will do this to you."

"I saw you play." He smiled. "You look good! You're quick!"

"Yeah? Thank you. I didn't know you played tennis. We don't really get a chance to watch the tennis team."

"Nah, no worries! Tennis is boring. I only play so I can do something in the fall—I'm not exactly built to play football."

"Oh, I see." I grinned. "Are you good?"

"Decent." He smiled. "I barely understand the rules."

I laughed at his joke, my heading coming back slightly and pulling my eyes off him for only a second. When I did, I saw a tall, dark-haired individual standing in the parking lot. He was watching us, looking at Scott, looking at me. He seemed upset, angry, and maybe even annoyed as he tossed his tennis racket back and forth between his hands, continuing to glare at Scott.

"I think someone is waiting for you." I nodded my head toward the tall tennis player standing afar. "Your friend seems like he wants your attention."

Scott looked over his shoulder, then turned his waist entirely and stared at the boy in return. After only a few seconds, Scott redirected his attention back to me.

"Huh." He waved his hand toward his teammate, his expression more serious. "We're all right, Kid. We're good here."

"Does your friend need you?" I asked.

"That kid is not my friend." Scott's grin returned as he stepped a half inch closer to me. He was close enough for me to smell him once more. He was close enough to reach into my ponytail and pull a blade of grass out of my mangled curls. "I want to have lunch tomorrow."

"As in, with me," I mumbled, "or just in general?"

"In general, I'd like to start eating lunch with you."

He walked away and headed into the locker room, not waiting for me to respond. I turned and headed into the girls' locker room, waving politely at the black-haired tennis player still standing in the parking lot.

I didn't sleep much that night. I couldn't tell you when I fell asleep, but it was much later than usual for me. I was filled with anticipation about what my lunch with Scott would entail. I clung to everything Scott: Every word, gesture, mannerism, and smell. I gave up a little before two in the morning and tiptoed downstairs to take an over-the-counter sleeping pill.

Just as my night dragged on, so did my morning. The following afternoon, Leigh walked me into the cafeteria arm-in-arm as an added means of comfort.

"Why is he sitting by himself," She asked. "Where are his friends?"

"I don't know." I panicked. "Is this lunch just the two of us?"

He slowly stood up from the cafeteria table. His right hand rested casually in the pocket of his light-wash jeans, and his gray t-shirt peeked out from under the white open-buttoned shirt he wore with the sleeves rolled up to just below the elbow and a small Polo emblem on the left pocket. He wore a large smile, more a grin than anything else, as he waved me over to his table.

"I think Scott wants you to sit down with him," Leigh continued as she released my arm. "Alright, you can do this! I'll sit at our regular table and watch. Just don't…..just don't freak out!"

"Little Harper Whitmore," he exclaimed as I joined him at the table, and we both sat down together. "I have been looking forward to this lunch for a while."

"Yeah?"

"Yes, I have."

"Why is that?" I asked, nervously chuckling.

"I wanted to talk to you. I feel like I don't see enough of you."

"Really? Trying to find me probably isn't that difficult. You could have tried rounding any corner a little tighter," I teased. "By the way, I figured out your little *TKM* reference: *To Kill a Mockingbird*, by Harper Lee," I gleefully informed him, a playful smile emerging on my face.

"Ah, but rounding corners more tightly would be too easy, Harper. I have to challenge myself every now and then, like trying to charge into you in wide-open cafeterias." He chuckled. "And you must be in advanced freshman English."

"Is walking toward me a challenge?" I pressed. "And did I pass your intelligence test?"

"It can be a slight challenge—my line of vision is so high that it doesn't see anything below six feet. Where do you fall?" He continued, "And it's my new thing—I only talk to intelligent women."

"Five feet," I answered. "And I'm glad you consider me intelligent."

"Yeah, see, that's why I kept running into you! I had to sit down to gain a better view of you."

"I didn't realize you wanted an eye-level view of me," I replied. "We could have done this much sooner."

"I'd prefer a different view of you," he whispered with a grin.

The sudden feeling of being in over my head started to loom. I wasn't sure if I wanted to continue sitting next to Scott if that was what he was interested in, but I was too scared to walk away from him, so I sat there, shocked at his statement. I had a feeling my face indicated such. I felt my body tense up. My arms pulled tightly against my frame as I crawled inside myself and kept my silence.

"That was uncalled for. I meant it as a joke—you know, with all the senior-chasing your class has been doing." He scrambled. "A joke. Nothing personal."

"I'm not like those freshmen," I mumbled. "Not even a little bit."

"I understand," he replied sincerely.

"Do you?" I pressed.

"Of course."

He looked over my shoulder as if something had caught his eye; he stared for a few moments. Probably a very hot, very tall senior girl with a killer rack, I thought, who owns a car, plays volleyball or basketball, and is going to the University of Washington to major in Pre-Med. She probably isn't a timid freshman like me.

"A blonde girl is staring at us," Scott sounded suspicious.

I didn't even need to turn around. I knew precisely which girl he was referring to—my archenemy and the bane of my existence.

"Yeah, that's Taylor. She doesn't exactly like me." And with a small influx in my voice and a sarcastic undertone, I continued to explain Taylor. "I'm pretty sure I know why, too. We used to be great friends in middle school. Best friends, even. Then high school started, and she dropped me."

"Oh." He moved his eyes back to mine. "And how do you know it's Taylor? You haven't even looked yet. Secondly, why wouldn't she like you? You seem like a very nice, cute, smart, quick-witted girl. Dropping you as a friend seems like her problem, not yours. Try not to beat yourself up over it."

"Really? You think I'm quick-witted...and cute? That's sort of the idea I wanted to give off," I exclaimed. "I think she dropped me because I don't look like her...*You know*?"

"She comes off looking like she's trying too hard."

"To answer your original question, I know it's Taylor because everyone likes Harper. Don't you know? I mean, you've wanted to talk to me for a while! After all, you just said you wanted a 'different view of me,' if I remember correctly."

"Geez, you are quick. No hesitancy about throwing my words back in my face—"

"Except Taylor!" I went on. "She is the only blonde girl I can think of that would stare me down like that." I glanced over my shoulder at Taylor, who was staring at me and looked back at Scott. "She's been sort of nasty the last few weeks, and I have a feeling it's going to continue."

"Why is she being nasty to you in particular?"

"Oh, well, that's easy. Because of you!"

"This is because I am a senior, and you are freshmen? And we are friends? I thought she decided before we became friends that she would drop you."

"Well, yes, it is partially because we're now friends, but I think it's more because she is consumed with what you are doing with *me*. Me, a short, ordinary freshman...." I had no idea where this was going, and rambling seemed appropriate, so I continued. "I am not exactly considered as hot as she considers herself...Wait!" I looked up at him, shocked. "You think we're friends?"

That is when I saw his smile. It was a half-smile that he had to tilt and turn his head to shield. It was a genuine smile; his eyes were as blue as ever, silver rims around the blue. He laughed nervously.

"Do you want to be friends, Harper?"

I looked down at the patterns in the laminate tabletop of our high school's generic cafeteria table. I bit the bottom of my lip before looking up ever-so-slightly and replying in a whisper that I didn't recognize as my own voice.

"Yes, I would like to be your friend—and hopefully more than that."

He smiled as he lightly pinched a runaway curl near my jaw and tucked it behind my ear. Scott effortlessly forced our conversation to continue, his voice serious.

"So, Harper, now that we are friends, why don't you tell me something about yourself?"

"Anything. What do you want to know?"

"You are very tan for a Washingtonian."

"Yes I am!" I grinned. "And I'm very happy you noticed it!"

"You must have gone away this summer?"

"You didn't need to go away this summer to get some sun. We had a record heat wave here with little to no rain."

"I wouldn't know. I went to eastern Washington for the entire three months."

"I've always wanted to go—mainly for the sun." I smiled. "My parents insist on going to Boston every summer, though."

"My parents have a place on the lake, and we spend the whole summer there." He smiled. "So…Boston?"

"Ah….Yeah," I mumbled. I was terrified to begin talking about myself. "My mother is from Boston originally. She came out here for graduate school and met my dad, and here we are, but we go back three times a year or so…You know…to visit that side of the family."

"I'm glad to hear it's not for the sun." He lightly laughed as he explained that statement: "I mean, the winters there are rough. I can't imagine you could pull out of winter as bad as they get and slide into a great summer."

"I'm already dreading Christmas!" I roared with laughter. "But the summers there are sweltering. I don't think people on the west coast actually realize that."

"So…your mom is from Boston and named you Harper?"

"Tell me about it!" I laughed. "The woman has a strong aversion to the letter R. It comes out Haapa!"

"Where did she come up with that name to begin with? It is a great name, but you are literally the first person I've ever heard of named Harper."

"That's not true!" I teased.

"That's right, the political magazine. I've been recently informed of the existence of this." He chuckled. "Oh, and of course, the fashion periodical."

"Have you ever heard of Harper romance novels?"

"Vaguely." His brows pulled together, and he slowly smiled. "It rings a bell."

"My mother had a strong affinity for them during her pregnancy."

I tried to contain my smile as Scott roared with laughter. His teeth were as white as mine and perfectly straight. His smile lines were blatant as he worked overtime to contain his laughter.

"By the way, *Haapa*," he interjected, mimicking my mother's pronunciation of my name, "your, ah, friend is here."

I looked up from the table, and there Taylor stood. I had hoped it was Leigh, but she was still supporting me from a distance.

"So, Harper, are you going to introduce me to Scott?" Taylor demanded.

"No, I won't, Taylor…Maybe another time!" I looked back at Scott. "This is the first time I've run into Scott today," I explained to her.

Scott was starting to stand. I was worried he'd heard what I said and decided that having a freshman "friend" full of freshmen drama wasn't appealing to him at first. He bent down at the waist and picked up my backpack from the floor. I stood up and began reaching for it.

"No worries, I got it." Scott touched the small of my back as he gestured with his other hand toward the cafeteria exit.

As we walked toward the central courtyard of our high school, we began walking side by side. My nerves were completely on edge. I saw Leigh in the distance, tracking my every move for later discussion. I thought for sure I'd blown it with that last comment to Taylor. Scott had to think I was a bitch, someone not worthy of his time. I had to think of a way to rectify this.

"Did you want to meet Taylor?" I quickly asked. "We can go back, and I can introduce you."

"Boy, Harper, you are short!" Scott changed the subject without answering my question. "Standing right next to you, it's *really* noticeable."

"Scott, you are really tall. Probably taller than most."

"So bright this freshman is," he teased. "I'm just shy of six-foot-six, so yes, I am taller than most."

I shrugged; I had nothing to say to that. I had nothing to physically hold onto. I was conscious of every movement I made. I swung my arms a little as I walked and decided to aim my hands into the back pockets of my jeans as we walked side by side. Before I could do this, I was caught off-guard as he swiftly scooped up my right hand

and held it while we walked. He saw me looking at our two hands and continued to talk to me, not even acknowledging that my life was balanced in his left hand.

"No, I don't want to meet Taylor; I've seen enough of Taylor," He confidently answered my earlier question. "She has made herself very apparent to my class."

"I don't know what that means."

"Don't worry about it." He smiled. "Tell me, Harper, how does it feel to be the only freshmen on the varsity soccer team?"

I let out a sigh and an awkward chuckle.

"I heard you were good!" he continued.

"Ah, you heard about that?" I cringed. "I thought no one paid attention to the girls' team."

"They used to not pay attention, but things have changed!"

"Nothing has really changed; I'll probably only play about fifteen minutes a game."

"I don't know about that. You ladies haven't had your first game yet—you might be surprised." He smiled.

"How did you know I made the team, anyway? I mean, the senior girls have barely noticed me."

"Most of the senior class is talking about you," he continued. "You're really good. I mean, I think you are. Your coach thinks you are, too, or she wouldn't have put you on varsity."

"Have you been asking about me?" I blurted.

"Um...." He took a deep breath, stopped walking, and stood in front of me, forcing me to a stop. "The truth is, you caught me off-guard that day in PC. My first attempt at trying to bang up a freshman's day, and that freshman didn't seem scared. That caught me for a minute. You've sorta been catching me off-guard a lot, that's all. So.... yes, I have been asking about you."

"Scott, are you my own personal stalker?" I teased, "If you've watched me play soccer, asked about me, and finally approached me, it sounds an awful lot like you're a stalker!"

"You want me to be your stalker?" He joked. "I suppose I'll take the job."

"Hired!" I kept a large grin on my face, and Scott saw right through it and laughed.

"Harper, you don't seem to be afraid of anyone. I am a bit confused about how Taylor can be getting to you like that—especially when she asked, sarcastically, I might add, to be introduced to me."

"Yeah, maybe you're right. The thing is, Scott, that she already knows who you are. She knows everyone. She was just playing a stupid game that I don't know the rules to. By blowing her off, I forfeited any participation in the game."

"Isn't that the truth," he whispered under his breath.

"How about you say hi the next time you watch me play?" I teased. "Then, we'll take *whatever this is* off campus."

"Hmm, *whatever this is*? I think I am pretty sure I know what this is," he said confidently.

"So, you think that this is *something*? I mean, I thought we were just friends. If it's not something, I am not sure I want to put a ton of effort into it. I have an assortment of freshmen guys with learner's permits to look into, you know. Also, if this doesn't work out, I might have to tell everyone that you're a stalker."

He set my backpack on the slick, wet ground near our feet. He leaned down toward me in the middle of the courtyard and kissed me. The first kiss of my entire life caught me off-guard. He held onto my right hand and used his other hand to carefully cradle my face, ever-so-gently guiding my head. The kiss was beyond words; the absolute enjoyment that filled my body would be impossible to describe. His lips were soft, smooth, and gentle. He was slow and methodical about the kiss. He knew how to kiss someone—he was patient and gentle. It was as if Scott knew this was my first kiss and took great care to ensure that it was good and, most importantly, memorable, as if he wanted all my future kisses to be compared to this one. When he pulled away, he pulled my bottom lip ever-so-lightly and momentarily rested his forehead against mine.

"Next time," he whispered, "we'll do it without the retainer."

"Oh, my God," I groaned. "I am so embarrassed."

He laughed a deep chuckle that I could feel through his chest before he pulled back lightly and looked up, noticing that the Seattle rain was here. It was not a hard rain, though, just the mist that only Seattle experiences.

"Well, that's unfortunate." He looked down at me and lifted my jaw. "I guess we should start heading into the building."

We lingered outside the freshman English classroom. I wasn't sure I wanted to walk in; I wanted to figure out exactly what Scott was to me. He handed me my backpack, then casually leaned against the wall as I proceeded to put my hands in my back pockets. He was casual and confident in his movements as he pulled my hand out of my back pocket and held it, absentmindedly playing with each of my fingers. To avoid the inevitable end of our lunchtime meeting, I kept the conversation going with unimportant questions.

"What class do you have now?"

"The perks of being a senior: You can work the system, so you have two study halls back-to-back; I'm done for the day."

"Really? Why don't you skip lunch and just go straight home?"

"My friend Brad and I usually do that," he quickly replied, "but I told you, I wanted to have lunch with you today. It just took me a while to figure out how to get you alone. You seem to always have your friend attached to you."

"Yeah, that's Leigh. I wasn't tied to her hip today at lunch, though, which should show you that we are capable of having a break from time to time. Oh, did you know she is in your freshmen health class?"

"It's not freshmen health; it's just health." He laughed. "And yes, I know Leigh."

"Maybe I'll switch into your section of health. That way, I can spend additional time with Leigh, and you and I can share a class together. Friends do that sort of thing."

"I think that's an awful idea. I need to actually pass health in order to graduate. With you in the same section, I'd never get any of the classwork completed. Please stay in your section, for my diploma's sake."

"Scott, please stop distracting my freshmen students," Ms. Marrow, my English teacher, instructed Scott as she headed into the classroom. "Harper has potential and doesn't need to be distracted."

"Okay, I should go, Scott; I have to work to get to my senior year so I can have the luxury of two study halls."

I attempted to pull my hand away from Scott's, but he pulled back, and I was flung into his chest. He held me there for a bit, locking his fingers with mine before he spoke ever-so-lightly.

"What are you doing after school?"

"Listen, I think I've said this before, but I think it's really important for me that I be perfectly clear," I clarified. "I'm not like most of the freshman girls. I'm not—"

"Harper, I was asking what your plans were for after school. Nothing was meant by it."

I could hear Ms. Marrow demand my attendance in her class and felt that my education deserved just as much attention as Scott was getting from me now. I didn't want to pull away, but the fear of being just like the rest of my class resided deep in my brain. I was also a fresh-faced freshman who was altogether terrified of getting into trouble with my freshmen teachers. In a panic, I gathered all my strength and pulled away.

"Um, I don't know…How about we discuss this later?" My voice was wracked with nervous fear.

I stormed into English and took my seat next to Leigh, who already had a post-it waiting on my desk, "DETAILS!" clearly written in bold glitter-pen ink. I looked to my left at Leigh, who was already pulling out a sheet of notebook paper and ready to start a novel's worth of notes on the recent events.

Thanks to the wonders of Scott's charm and ability to appease anyone, including faculty, Scott opened the door to Ms. Marrow's ninth-grade English classroom. He leaned against the doorway, looking toward the back of the classroom, where I sat. With absolute certainty, I knew that whatever he was about to do was going to change my existence in this high school.

"Harper," Scott asked again, "what are you doing after school today?"

"Scott! Oh, my God." I panicked. "Let's discuss this later. Leave."

"Nope!" He grinned. "Let's discuss it now. What are you doing?"

"Nothing. No, wait, that's not true," I mumbled, "I have soccer practice from three to five."

"Alright, I have tennis practice from three to five also. We can skip it today, though. You already made varsity soccer; you've proven to be good enough for varsity. You and I are going out, alright?"

"You just announced to the class that you and I are going out!"

"So?" He shrugged. "Ms. Marrow, I am sorry, but this won't take more than a minute. Harper, I'll meet you at the flagpole at two-thirty."

"Harper, quickly answer Scott's question so we can proceed with class," Ms. Marrow instructed.

"Alright, meet me outside the locker rooms at five. I am not skipping practice, and neither should you."

"Fine, five it is, and we'll both attend our practices."

As casually as a senior could, or as I learned, Scott could, more precisely, he walked over to Taylor, who was sitting in the front row, and put his hand out.

"I'm Scott, Harper's boyfriend. I think you know her?" Scott quickly snapped his head up. "Ms. Marrow, good to revisit ninth-grade English. I'll probably be doing it more often! I'll see you later, Little Harper Whitmore."

"Alright, class," Ms. Marrow called, reasserting her control. "Enough senior excitement for one day...."

TWO

I KNEW GOING INTO FIFTH AND SIXTH period that afternoon that they were going to drag. If not for Leigh and her note-writing capabilities, I am sure English, my fifth-period class, would have lasted much longer. We did what we always did when something monumental happened in our lives: We wrote about it. Between the start of English and the finish, we maintained a solid seven-page dialog about how I felt having a senior interested in me. The conversation was entirely one-sided; Leigh was obsessed with the idea that I could lose my virginity, which was something I had no intention of losing so quickly.

Sixth-period art dragged on as well, but it was an added help that Leigh and I had that class together. We sat side by side, attempting to be engaged with the pottery wheel, but I had the terrible feeling everyone in the school knew about my impending date with Scott Pierce.

"What are you going to tell your parents?" Leigh asked.

"I don't know," I mumbled. "I have to call them and let them know they don't need to pick me up. I might just tell them I'm going out with a friend. I'm not lying; he is a friend."

"Harper, he is more than your friend. He said so himself."

"*He* said that. I didn't," I corrected her, becoming slightly frustrated with the pottery wheel. "I hate this class! I am not artistically talented by any measure. Mr. Abbas will fail me if I don't get one item in that kiln."

"No one fails this class. Mr. Abbas is high all the time! I'll put something in the kiln with your name on it if it comes to that," she assured me. "Do you want to be more than friends with Scott?"

"I think I do, but I don't know. I don't know anything about him. I know he's a senior. I know he's hot and funny, and his parents have a place in eastern Washington, but that is all I know…He knows a lot more about me than I know about him."

"That is why you're going out with him tonight—to learn more about him and decide if you want to be his girlfriend…Not to mention he'll probably kiss you again!"

"Yeah, he might do that again." I slowly smiled. "I think I'd be willing to skip getting to know him and go straight to the part where he does that again."

"If you have sex tonight, I'll kill you!"

"Oh God, no," I assured her. "We're not doing that! No way—"

"You'd better start thinking about it. He's a senior. He's gonna want to." She smirked, pointing to the mass of clay I'd been spinning on the wheel. "Now, take that ashtray and put it in the kiln!"

"It's a jewelry dish for my mom," I whined.

"Julie Whitmore didn't buy that at Neiman Marcus. She's not going to use it."

After practice, I would typically help the coach round up the soccer balls and be the last one in the locker room, trying my absolute best to avoid any real conversation with the senior girls. I was always a bit intimidated by them. After my afternoon with Scott, that wasn't the case. I was the first in the locker room, skipping the routine ball shagging I did with my coach, and I was the first to be completely showered and dressed.

I was tying my Vans up while sitting on the locker room bench when Maureen, a tall, beautiful senior, looked over at me and asked, "What's the rush, Harper? Off to see someone?"

I had never actually spoken to Maureen off the soccer field before, so I nervously bit my lip.

"Yeah, I sort of have to meet someone."

"Really, anyone we know?"

Her voice was friendly, but it also had a sarcastic undertone, so I wasn't quite sure which direction this conversation was going. I had a sneaking suspicion she already knew who my date was and was trying to find a way to get me to say his name out loud. The only thing I trusted about Maureen was that she wouldn't physically kill me.

"Ah, you might...."

I tried with everything in me to keep the smirk off my face for fear of what Maureen might actually do to me. I knew full well she knew who Scott was. I opened my mouth slightly but quickly bit the end of my lip. A half-smile appeared despite my efforts, and the entire locker room quietly started to giggle.

"Shut up, everyone; I am trying to talk to Harper," Maureen instructed. "Now, Harper, is your date with a senior?"

"Um...I think he might be a senior, yes."

"Really?"

She said really like she was genuinely interested in my social life, but I knew better than to trust her next move. She walked across the locker room ever-so-slowly and sat down on the bench next to me as if, at any moment, her demeanor could change on a dime. She put her left arm around my shoulder and looked at me, though I didn't look directly back at her, and then looked back at April, another senior girl encouraging this hazing.

"April," Maureen asked her, "do you have any idea which senior Harper might have a date with? I can't think of anyone."

"No-o-o," April replied, smiling as she played along. "I can't think of a single senior that Harper might be off to meet."

"Harper," Maureen teased, chuckling. "We have no idea which senior you are talking about. Please, just tell me. I need to hear his name...Just say his name for me." She shrugged her shoulders. "Consider this... *Practice*."

I had no idea what Maureen was getting at. What was with her urgency to hear his name? She exhaled with fake frustration and looked down as if she was mentally getting ready for something before jumping into the crowd of girls forming around me.

"Because I am positive that you will be *screaming* his name real soon," she exclaimed gleefully.

My eyes flew wide open in sincere panic as she said this, out loud, in front of everyone in the locker room. The locker room was in absolute hysterics—not one senior girl could hold down her laughter. Passionate anger and embarrassment shot through me all at once, forcing out a screamed response.

"Are you kidding me?" I screamed. "You guys barely speak to me before, and all of a sudden, because of him—"

"Harper, he deserves a name," Maureen sneered.

"I am not a senior-chasing freshman," I screamed. "Not once did I engage in anything with him!"

"Oh, Scott! Oh, Scott, please. Scott," the entire team started chanting. The varsity girls were all making sexual remarks and gestures at my expense.

The anger filled me. I could feel the redness burning across my face.

"Oh, come on, Harper," Maureen pleaded jokingly. "You had to expect this. You knew this was coming. You couldn't have seriously thought we weren't going to find out you were with Scott." Maureen laughed. "Now, do us a favor and say his name, Harper! We're not going to stop unless you say his name."

Because of the sheer embarrassment that I was experiencing, I quickly threw my uniform, cleats, and shin guards all in my bag at once, never zipping up the bag and running toward the exit.

"Say it, Harper," Maureen commanded sternly, "or expect more tomorrow!"

I froze, stopping right before the locker room exit. I knew I couldn't go another day dealing with being hazed by the senior girls. I stood frozen for a few moments, not turning to face the girls. I looked down at my feet, still not moving my body, and acquiesced.

"Scott."

"Not good enough," Maureen replied. "Say it louder, and like you *mean it*."

"Scott," I yelled.

"Still not good enough." She walked close to me. "Say it like you *need* it."

"I don't know what you want, Maureen," I whined.

She stared at me, waiting; the rest of the soccer team stood behind her. I could feel her inches away from me, staring at the back of my head and just waiting for me. Her stare burned through me.

"Do it now, and we'll stop," she promised.

Letting the strap fall from my shoulder, I dropped my bag onto the tile floor. I turned and looked directly at Maureen, catching a glimpse of the entire soccer team standing ten feet behind her. I stared at her. Maureen was waiting to decide if I would fight her on this or make a joke about it. I knew I couldn't fight Maureen; I'd lose that one. She was powerful—she had pull, and people feared her. I opted to conform to her demands.

I took a deep breath and closed my eyes. I put my right hand on my chest; my left hand fixed itself into my full head of loose curls. I bent my knees slightly and began moaning loudly, lightly moving my hand around my hair. I breathed heavily and lost my hand deeper into my curls. At one point, I squeaked for the thrill of her expression. I rolled my eyes back and pushed myself up against the cold wall.

"Oh, Scott, please! Please, Scott! Do it," I moaned. "Scott! Please do it! I need it!"

I dropped my hands and looked directly at Maureen, watching her casually bend a piece of gum into her mouth as if she experiences this sort of thing daily.

"Good enough?"

After a moment of silence, the entire soccer team burst into laughter. Maureen glared at me, her eyes piercing and drilling through me. Her lips pouted, and then a slow smile emerged across her face.

"That's all I wanted to hear, Harper." She walked closer to me and whispered words that would stick with me for a long time: "Don't give him anything, Harper. I don't want to hear about you becoming another dumb girl."

At that moment, I didn't know what she meant. I looked at her, not responding. I took in her words, absorbing them. I wasn't a dumb girl; I never wanted to be a dumb girl or be known as a dumb girl. I stared at her for a few moments. She nodded her head toward the exit and walked back to her locker. I froze again at that moment as she trailed back toward her locker.

I was startled to see Scott leaning against the hood of his truck, waiting for me, as I ran out of the locker room. I caught my breath. I felt exhausted from both the weight of my soccer bag and being picked on by Maureen. He slowly moved toward me until he stood only inches from me.

"That was nice, Harper. I enjoyed hearing my name coming from your lips. Thank you."

"You heard that?" I smiled nervously. "All of it?"

He grinned and nodded.

"Scott, you have no idea what I just had to go through."

"Harper—" He stopped and tapped his index finger against his teeth. "I see you removed the retainer. I thought it was very.... *adorable*."

"Yeah, I am never wearing that thing again. If I end up with banged-up teeth again, we can blame you," I said sarcastically.

"No, no, you should wear the retainer." He laughed. "I was only making an observation at the time that it felt different kissing someone with a retainer."

"You've kissed a lot of girls, have ya?" I smirked. "They all have bad teeth?"

"Ah, funny." He nodded his head toward the door of the girls' locker room. "I, ah, have a pretty good idea of what you had to go through in there. I ran into a few seniors from your team as they were walking back from the field. They asked why I was waiting around the women's locker room, and I told them."

"You knew?" I asked, accusation heavy in my voice. "You knew Maureen was going to haze me like that?"

"No. That I didn't know. I didn't even think she would find it interesting that I was with you."

"Oh, that part Maureen found very interesting. She was near-insulted that I didn't share this willingly with the team," I stated. "I also find it interesting that you consider yourself *with* me."

"I sort of heard part of your performance...It was *very* good, I might add. And I do consider us being *with* one another."

"I think I hate Maureen," I whispered. "Why don't we see how this afternoon goes before we start throwing the word *with* around?"

"Nah, you don't hate her. She's just being a senior captain." He was trying to comfort me, I think. "I agree about this afternoon, though. How about you see how the rest of the afternoon goes, and then you'll start using the word *with*?"

"That sounds like something a stalker would say!"

"You did hire me for that."

"And you are exceeding expectations," I joked, feeling very cheered. "Tell me, how much did you hear?"

"I heard your polite manners—a few pleases, which was very nice. It's good to use your manners," he teased. "Followed by my name, a few more pleases—again, excellent manners." He grinned at my lack of similar glee toward his recitation of my own words. "Oh, Harper, don't worry about it. I don't care. By the way—"

"Hmmm?"

"Did you call your parents to let them know you would be home later than usual?"

"Oh, my God!" I stepped back from him. "You think I am a little kid, don't you? I wear a retainer, I have a sense of urgency about getting to class on time, I don't skip practice, I get hazed by seniors, and I need to call my parents."

"And you're deeply worried about what people think," he added, "as well as afraid of seniors."

"I'm starting to rethink the word *with* right about now," I groaned.

"Ah, now that's not fair," he pointed out. "I'm not really on the clock yet. And I don't think you're a kid. I just assumed your parents would pick you up after practice, and maybe I'd get to meet them. That's all!"

"Not likely! But I did call them. I told them I was going out with a friend after practice and that I'd be home later."

"Oh, just a *friend*?"

"Yes, a *friend*." I laughed. "I'm not ready to tell them the specifics of my older male friend."

"By the way, I'm on the clock." He grinned as he quickly picked up my bag and walked toward the parking lot. "Could a male friend tell you that you looked unbelievably sexy in your soccer cleats and shin guards at practice? That's something a friend can do, right? A friend can notice you were skins today during your scrimmage, and it was really hot."

"Are you teasing me? I can't seem to tell," I asked. "And you watched me practice today? You know, I had a sports bra on. I wasn't naked or anything! Maybe we could skip over the me-being-naked talk."

"I didn't say anything about you being naked; a friend wouldn't say anything about you being naked."

I smiled and tried to hide my laughter.

"Tennis practice got out an hour early because of the rain. I had to do something with my time. I am not teasing you, either; you looked really hot out there."

"Do you think you might have too much time on your hands? I mean, you've got two study halls back-to-back, and you have time after school to watch me play soccer. That's a lot of free time."

"Another perk of being a senior—I get whatever I want." He shrugged. "So, tell me what other sports I can see you at. You know, for future hours spent stalking you."

"Not many." I laughed. "I only play soccer in the fall and run track in the spring."

"No winter sports?"

"No winter sports. I don't think they allow five-foot girls to join the basketball team," I teased. "I think the minimum requirement is five-ten."

"It's good that you don't play winter sports because I do, and I need my fan base to grow!" He smiled. "I am kind of a big deal around here when it comes to basketball."

"Really, you play basketball?" I teased. "I wouldn't have guessed!"

"Is it that obvious?" he asked sarcastically.

"Yes, your height is very obvious."

I leaned against the side of his truck and watched him gently set my bags in his backseat, enjoying the comfortable silence between us as Scott stared at me and I stared back. I nervously bit my lip. The feeling, and the silence, lingered between us. He leaned in until his bottom lip was nearly touching my top lip. I was ready for this. He lightly touched my waist, lifting my shirt slightly, and I could feel his fingers on my skin. The kiss earlier that day, though my first and very good, caught me off-guard—I wasn't ready for it. This one I was prepared for; this one I wanted to happen.

His lips had just touched my lips when I heard screams and shouts coming from the distance. I pulled away from Scott and tried to look over his shoulder, my shirt still slightly raised. The touch of his fingers still tingled against the bare skin of my waist as he, too, moved over to see what the commotion was. He ever-so-lightly started running his fingers up and down my lower spine; as he did this, a feeling of absolute pleasure that I'd never experienced grew in my body. I could barely think straight as his long fingers hit each vertebra on my lower back with precision. When I first heard them, I should have realized that the screams were from Maureen and four other seniors, all making catcalls and panting my name. With a smirk and a light wave of one hand, Scott continued to draw imaginary circles over each vertebra with the other.

"Oh my God, Scott!" I turned toward him and examined the asphalt at his feet. "They will haze me for this tomorrow at practice; it will never end. I really thought I'd flown under the radar with these girls until you noticed me."

"Give Maureen a month; she'll move on." Scott stared at me. "She'll get bored."

"I'm not sure I can put up with this for a month."

He slowly began another journey toward my lips. I decided that perhaps it would be beneficial if I met him halfway. I was screaming inside for my lips to reach up toward his, but my feet didn't do as instructed and move forward so my lips could reach his properly. I desperately wanted to lightly press my hands against his biceps, but I felt fortunate enough that my hand rose even to the point of resting on the side mirror of his truck. I was still touching something that was part of him that way, even if it wasn't him directly. Just as I could feel the skin of his lips, my name was shouted from behind me, startling Scott and me out of our moment.

"Harper!"

I flinched and quickly looked behind me. A tall boy with jet black hair and dark eyes was jogging toward us. He looked familiar, and when he saw me look at him, he stopped jogging toward us and began running for us. I looked back at Scott, who appeared annoyed, aggravated, and slightly angered.

"Hey…. Harper," he breathed. "What's up?"

"Ah…Hi?" I was confused and looked up at Scott for direction before looking back at this boy, and as a means of politeness, I asked. "Ah…How are you?"

"I'm Barrett," he proclaimed. "We haven't met, but we're in the same class."

"Ooh…It is nice to meet you." I politely smiled and nodded. "This is my friend Scott. He isn't in our class, so you might not have met him before."

"Just a friend?" Barrett pressed. "Nothing more?"

"Ah, well—" I looked up at Scott as I scrambled. "It's new—"

"We're seeing each other, Barrett," Scott thankfully interrupted. "It's new, but we're seeing where it goes."

"Ah, yes! That's exactly what we are doing," I exclaimed, relieved that Scott knew precisely what we were doing, after all. "We're seeing one another."

"Oh." Barrett sighed. "For how long?"

"Um, well, like I said, it's new," I mumbled, knotting my fingers nervously. "Can I help you with something? I mean, is there something you needed from me?"

"Scott," Barrett barked, "can we have a minute?"

"No," Scott replied.

"You've had all the minutes in the world with her; let me have mine."

"So have you, and you've wasted them," Scott informed him. "Now you're scrambling to talk, so talk."

"I just—I don't know—I just wanted to say hi, and see if you would be interested in hanging out." He stumbled over his words, directing them at me. "Maybe we can eat lunch tomorrow or see a movie tonight?"

His eyes were shifty as he looked everywhere but at me. He dragged his right toe in half-circles around his left foot and kept his hands tucked deep into his dirty black jean pockets. I took in his physical features; his feet, posture, hands, and shifty eyes. I wanted to know what he was looking at, and I suspected the answer to that question was "anything but me." He seemed nervous, but more than that, he seemed annoyed. Everything about him made me uncomfortable. I looked at Scott for direction, and he was no help. He maintained the same confident posture and only raised his eyebrows when he saw me looking at him, as if he, too, was waiting for an answer. I could feel my heart race as the awkwardness and uneasiness of this moment got to me. At that moment, there was one thing I was sure of: I wanted to spend my evening with Scott Pierce. Despite my coy wordplay and, at times, witty banter, I wanted to be more than Scott's friend.

"Oh.... Ah, well, that's very nice of you," I stuttered, "but, see— Maybe if I had known a while ago—or maybe even before lunch today...I guess—well, maybe if I had known before a few weeks ago that you were interested, I might have said sure. But—"

"But what?" Barrett pressed.

"But like I said...I'm *seeing* Scott."

"Oh, I get it!" His voice was clipped. "You're into older guys with money."

"I didn't know—I didn't say that," I stammered while looking directly at Scott. "I really don't know anything about money, honest. I'm not here for that—"

"Hey," Scott interrupted, "time's up! Now quit being a dick."

"You're the one being a dick," Barrett snapped. "You knew, and you had to do this! I'm too late, right? She's already fallen for you. Fuck you, Scott!"

"Why are you doing this in front of Harper?" Scott argued. "She's not interested! She told you nicely. Now be a man and move on. Quit being a prick."

"Yeah, whatever," Barrett snidely remarked. "Have fun."

Barrett quickly moved backward before turning and jogging back into the locker room.

"Do you know that guy?" I asked. "That was weird, right? That was a weird thing he did? I've never experienced anything like that."

"He's an ass," Scott replied. "Are you alright?"

"He seemed very angry with me, but I wasn't lying. If he had introduced himself to me a few weeks ago, I would have been interested in knowing him. I could still eat lunch with him, though. You know, be his friend?"

"Harper," Scott counseled me, "you are way better than that kid!"

My first time sharing a meal with a man was an experience in itself. Scott watched me with a smile while he engaged in the first of what would be many verbal analyses of my most endearing qualities. Sitting across from him at Louie's, a generic "townie" pizza establishment, I realized he was much more than he projected himself to be.

"Harper, you can get more than water and a single slice." He grinned. "I'm getting a large plain cheese with a soda, so you won't break the bank by getting a drink that's not water."

"I don't drink soda," I whispered, conveying a lack of confidence in my personal life decisions.

"What?" He roared with laughter. "What do you drink?"

"Skim milk or water." I smiled. "Occasionally juice, but only if it doesn't have a high acidic value."

"Can I ask why?" He grinned as the waitress waited patiently for my confirmation on the water.

"Soda will rot your teeth out—"

"I should have known!" He laughed. "You and your teeth!"

"And some juices have high acidic values that can do the same harm as soda. Milk is good because of the calcium, though."

"But only skim milk," he added.

"Yea..." I shrugged, embarrassed.

"But you'd order a soda if you drank soda?" He smirked.

"Yes," I stated.

"Good, I just want to make sure you're not ordering less because you fear the bill," he teased before looking over at the waitress. "She'll have water, and we'll have a large pizza."

"Oh, and can I have a straw with my water?" I smiled as she nodded. "Thank you."

"A straw?" he questioned.

"I drink everything through a straw, and it doesn't have anything to do with my teeth." I grinned.

"Do I have good teeth?" He smiled.

"They are really good," I replied, complimenting him. "No stains or brush lines, even though it looks like you had braces."

"How can you tell?" He pulled his brows in and smiled. "I try to pass it off as natural."

"I can't; you just told me!" I grinned. "I hope to do the same thing once I get out of high school, myself—I don't want anyone to know that I wore braces for as long as I did."

"Good to know!"

We shared a moment of laughter, followed by a small moment of silence between us, during which we only looked at each other. I was nervous and wanted to look elsewhere, but I remembered how uncomfortable I was when Shifty Eyes talked to me and wouldn't look at me, so I simply resorted to chewing my straw.

"So, that guy in the parking lot was weird," I stated for conversational value.

"I don't want to talk about him," Scott stated. "He doesn't deserve to be spoken about."

"Ah, I see."

"We should talk about *us*," he suggested. "You need to decide if you will use the word *with*."

"This is true...."

"Oh, by the way," He handed me a piece of paper that had been folded up in a diamond shape. It was one of the notes that Leigh and I had written in English.

"Did you read it?" I mumbled as I slowly put the note back in my pocket.

"Harper, I think that if you are ready, you can go ahead and start referring to me as your boyfriend." I bit the corner of my lip again and looked anywhere but directly at Scott.

"So, you did read it?" I asked again.

"Not all of it," he replied. "I was curious as to what it was. It must have fallen out of your bag; it was on my truck floor."

"You know, then?"

"Ah, that your friend Leigh is a little too obsessed with your sex life?" he teased. "Yeah, I figured that out."

"Yeah, well, Leigh hasn't done it, either…."

A flush of panic raced through me as I realized that I had openly admitted my own lack of experience. I covered my face in embarrassment, hoping he'd drop the subject altogether.

"Maybe she's hoping to live vicariously through you," he joked.

"I think I should go."

"No—Nah, don't go anywhere!" He reached across the table and lightly pressed down on my forearm. "I didn't mean anything by that. I…Well, I sort of already figured as much," he said nervously. "What I mean is, I sort of figured you were a *virg*—You'd never had sex before. I mean, earlier today, I figured it out. Before you admitted it or before I read that note, I figured out that today was probably your first kiss."

My eyes widened as he brought up the apparent state of my virginity.

"Okay, this isn't going well." He stumbled over his words. "I assumed you hadn't really gone any farther. I don't care. It's really not a big deal."

"Scott," I barked, interrupting him before he could continue this embarrassing train of thought.

"Yes?"

"It's true: I've never had a boyfriend. A guy has never expressed interest in me before. I've never even held a guy's hand. Today was my first kiss. I've never had sex. I've never even had a crush before. I am very nervous around you. I have a hard time calling you my boyfriend because I know that you are a senior, and I am a freshman, and you are probably going to want—"

"Whoa! Whoa! Whoa! That's where you're wrong," he interrupted. "If that's all I wanted, I could get that. Trust me on that, Harper. Whenever you are ready to have that talk, I am open to it, but I am not rushing it. We can go forever without having that talk, and I'd be fine with it, but don't think I am only interested in you because of that."

I sat still, wearing a straight face and taking in everything he just said. Then his statement hit me; I started to laugh; my head was thrown back with hard laughter. The kind of laughter hurt my lower back and made it hard to catch my breath. I made eye contact with Scott. His face looked confused, but he still managed to keep a smile shining through.

"What is it? What's so funny?" He kept smiling as he watched me laugh. "Tell me!"

"Really? If that's all you wanted, you could get that?" I mimicked. "That is the most conceited statement I've ever heard. You're openly admitting that your popularity and good looks allow any woman to throw herself at you? Please note, Scott, that I have not thrown myself at you once. If anything, I'd say that you've kinda been throwing yourself at me. I mean, you're the one that threw me to the floor at PC a few weeks ago. Then there was that time on the second floor of the main building—remember that?"

"Are you done?" He grinned. "Anything else you want to add? Maybe you'd like to add something more about my *good looks*?"

"Oh, my God," I gasped.

"Harper, you said it, not me. I think you're the one throwing yourself at me."

"You know what, Scott?" I smiled and shrugged my shoulders. "I'm not sure how I would feel about having sex with my friend, anyway. I mean, having sex for the first time with a *friend* might be weird."

"Unbelievable," he exclaimed.

"I'm just saying it might be weird—*for you*."

"No, seriously—unbelievable."

"Oh, so you don't want to have sex with me?" I grinned. "At least we got that cleared up...*friend*!"

"Hey, when are you going to start calling me your boyfriend?" He laughed. "Have you figured that out yet?"

"Scott, you didn't ask me if I wanted to be your girlfriend. You just asked me if I wanted you to be my friend." I smiled. "I just met you! I mean, who's throwing themselves at whom now?"

"I think it goes without saying, but if that's how you feel, Harper, we'll probably have to stop kissing. I'll need to stop holding your hand, and I'll probably have to stop enabling you when it comes to not telling your parents the absolute truth about your whereabouts. I mean, friends don't do these sorts of things, right? Friends are supposed to be good influences."

"Nah." I shrugged. "As for the kissing, you've only done it once. I'll be fine...I'm sure that another boy will want to kiss me. That guy in the parking lot seemed like he might be down with kissing me—"

His lips were forceful and aggressive; they matched the force behind his hands as they cradled my face. The table was still rattling from the force he used when he quickly and abruptly pulled away from it to kiss me. I had no idea where to put my hands, so I rested them on his forearms and enjoyed this new method of kissing. He was forceful, and it attracted me to him in a whole new way. I enjoyed the moments our lips shared as he towered over me while I sat, enjoying him.

"That guy in the parking lot wouldn't be able to kiss you like that."

"No," I breathed. "I-I imagine he wouldn't—"

"Have you thought about the word *with*?"

"It would be easier to just refer to you as my boyfriend. You are a boy, and you seem like someone that could be my friend, but we'll see how the rest of this date goes, and then I'll decide."

"Don't do me any favors," he breathed. "I think it was you this afternoon who said you'd like to be more than my friend."

"Wow," I giggled. "Use my words against me!"

"I learned that trick this afternoon." He smirked and sat back down.

"Then, if anything, you're a fast learner."

"I highly doubt you're nervous around me." He grinned. "You seem very at ease with putting me in my place."

"Well, I don't know about that." I rolled my eyes. "Maybe it's because I don't get a chance at school to exercise my quick wit."

"I do enjoy this banter."

"So, who are all the girls you can get that from?" I sneered. "Anyone I know?"

"Well, your gal-pal Taylor seems ready, willing, and able," he teased as he watched our waitress set our pizza on the table. "I just gotta say the word."

"And what word would that be?"

"Yes."

"Really?" I exclaimed. "She's asked you outright?"

"Well, not in so many words," he explained, "but the implication has been made."

"And she is just waiting for the yes on your part?"

"I assume so, though I imagine she might expect me to be her boyfriend. I'm not interested in being that freshman's boyfriend."

"Ah, that is a very nice save." I cheered at him. "*With* is starting to sound better and better."

"I try."

"So, it's safe to say you've done…*it*," I emphasized. "With a girl—"

"Well, I've never done it with a guy!" He laughed, his mouth full. "But yes, I have."

"Oh." I nodded nervously. "Interesting."

"Is *with* starting to sound bad?" He smiled. "I can retract my honesty."

"No. You're older than me—it was expected."

I saw Scott smile while he chewed on the end of his straw, my eyes on his lips, and his eyes following mine. After only knowing him a short while, I think I already had him figured out on some level. I knew something was brewing on the tip of his tongue, and I knew he wasn't sure if saying it would hurt my feelings.

"You can say it."

"Harper, there is a lemon in that water." He grinned. "I won't be held responsible for your damaged teeth!"

"That was good." I cheered him on. "I'm impressed!"

"You know, I'm just trying to win you over."

My first date with a boy was the sort of date most girls would keep close in their memories. He made me laugh; I made him laugh. We quickly arrived at a space where we were teasing one another openly and casually. I nearly forgot that he wanted to be my boyfriend and not just a friend. The conversation was easy and comfortable, like talking to an old friend. That feeling vanished as we left the restaurant, and he scooped my hand up in a way that forced me to stop and look at him. I smiled. It wasn't a nervous smile, though; it was a sincere smile. We both stood facing one another.

He slowly stepped forward. I was fixed on his deep blue eyes. We didn't say anything to one another for the first time. He leaned down to meet me face to face. He slowly moved both hands onto my ribcage and pressed his bottom lip against my top lip. I instinctively closed my eyes and stood on my toes. My shirt lifted slightly around my waist. I was finally able to raise my hands to his arms. He pressed harder against my lips and pulled me closer against his body.

My skin was burning hot through my shirt; I felt the outline of Scott's hands against my ribcage. I wanted to feel Scott's skin, to know what his skin felt like. I wanted to know what a boy's skin felt like. I wanted to know if his skin was as hot as mine in that moment. I knew there was no way I was making Scott feel the same way he made me feel. I slowly ran my fingers down the sleeves of his T-shirt; I pressed my fingers against his bicep, very timid about my movements. I was hoping Scott wouldn't notice my hands, that he'd be too focused on other things to mind what my hands were doing. I gently touched his skin with my fingertips. I could feel the definition of his biceps through his warm skin. Immediately, Scott's kiss was much more forceful. He clutched me closer to his chest.

"What time do I have to get you home?" he whispered.

"I told my mom I'd be home by seven."

"Alright." He nodded.

Scott pulled into my circular driveway; I sat on my knees in the passenger seat, facing him and not ready to call my evening with Scott over. He leaned toward me and kissed me again. It was a soft, gentle, and carefully executed kiss—and I enjoyed it.

"Harper," he asked mid-kiss, "do you want to take the school bus tomorrow morning, or do you want me to pick you up?"

"My mom usually drives us. How about we stick with that?" I whispered. "That way, I can postpone having to tell my parents about my much older boyfriend."

"So I'm your boyfriend," he teased. "*With* has the Harper seal of approval."

Waves of excitement coursed through my body as his lips re-locked themselves with mine. He was slow and careful about his movements, as if this was new for him, too.

"Harper?" He pulled back. "I thought you didn't play basketball."

"I don't." I smiled. "Why?"

"Why do you have a hoop in your driveway?"

I pulled far enough away from him that he could see my smile as I turned quickly to examine the never-used hoop in the driveway.

"Ah, yeah, we do have a hoop." I lightly laughed. "Morgan is the only one that uses it, though."

"Come on."

I watched him quickly unlock the doors and hop out. I realized just as soon that our kissing was done for the evening. It appeared as though we were shooting hoops in my driveway, which was something I didn't recall ever doing before.

"I don't know where the ball is—" I refrained from finishing my sentence as I watched him open his backseat. "I should have known that you'd have one."

"Harper, I told you. I'm kind of a big deal at basketball." He laughed. "Of course, I carry a ball with me."

I stood on the driveway's edge and watched as he dribbled, dunked, and did outrageous spins. I was utterly amazed. He was unbelievable. I grew even more surprised as I watched him hang from the hoop. The backboard never broke or shattered from his weight.

I was floored as he stepped back to the edge of our large driveway and flicked the ball from his fingers. He sank it from the farthest point of the driveway. I knew nothing of the sport except the general principles of the game, and the first guy I'd ever dated was making outlandish moves right in front of me.

"You're unbelievable," I exclaimed. "I have never seen anyone as good as you— certainly not in my driveway!"

"I told ya." He cheered. "Varsity since ninth grade!"

"Yeah, but there is a difference between being told about someone's talent and seeing it on display in front of you!"

"Hey," he exclaimed.

He continued to dribble between his legs, then spun the ball on the tip of his left index finger. He shot from the farthest point of my driveway, chasing his shot before it even hit the rim.

"Who is Morgan?" he continued. "You said Morgan is the only one that uses the hoop."

"Morgan is my sister."

"Older or younger?"

"Younger." I smiled. "Ten."

"Yeah," he exclaimed. "Shorty like you?"

"Not at all!"

"Really?"

"She's the same height, with short blonde hair and fair skin—very thin…She'll probably grow to be very tall."

"Your height bothers ya?"

"Slightly," I stated. "My family is very tall. Both my parents are tall, and seeing Morg outgrow me feels defeating."

"I can relate."

"Doubtful!"

"No, I can!" He bounced the ball to me. "Being reminded of my height is exhausting. And being reminded of the height of my family is just as annoying."

"Well, I won't make any comments about your height." I grinned. "But I would like to know how tall your family is."

"My dad, Jack, is around the same height, and my older brother

Jared is a little shorter than me. My mom, Marie, is probably a little taller than you. She failed at passing any short genes along to her kids! And finally, my nephew Ethan is the same height as me."

"How old is your nephew?" I questioned. "If he's in fifth grade and the same height as you, I might be able to sympathize."

"No," he said quickly.

I focused on dribbling the ball as best I could without looking too awkward as I stumbled over my feet. I could sense that he was watching me, already examining my footwork and looking for ways to offer suggestions to improve my basketball athleticism before I had successfully completed a single bounce pass across the driveway.

"Do you know how to play Horse?" he asked.

"That's the one where I shoot from a spot, and if I make it, you have to shoot from the same spot...Right?"

"Exactly, until you spell out H-O-R-S-E," he spelled. "You wanna play?"

"I may be a freshman, but I know how to spell horse," I teased. "I'll play, although I can only shoot from one spot."

"Doubtful, freshman—very doubtful!" He smirked. "You might surprise yourself."

"Alright, I'll go first."

He lightly bounced the ball to me. I stood directly under the hoop and did a simple layup, the only shot I knew how to make. As he watched from afar, I could hear his smile transform into a grin.

"I have a feeling you intend on standing under the hoop all night."

"Yeah," I chuckled.

"So, maybe this game isn't in our near future." He grinned. "Ethan, my nephew, is nine months older than I am. He graduated last year. My brother Jared, his father, is a health-class cautionary tale. Sexually active at fifteen with no condom will make you a father quickly!"

"Oh, I see." I nodded. "And would I be able to hear this tale in freshmen health or just health?"

"Oh, freshman, you are quick," he teased.

"Well, I am sure everything turned out fine. He graduated high school, so it can't be so bad."

"No, Jared is fortunate enough. He finished high school, went to college, got a job, and married Ethan's mother, Stacy."

"I'm more surprised you have a brother fifteen years older than you," I exclaimed. "The Ethan stuff happens. No one is to blame for it."

"I'm very surprised at your reaction. Most people hear the Ethan Pierce story and jump right into judging—they figure it's a Pierce family trait!"

"What's the Pierce family trait?"

"Ya know." He shrugged before doing what he would consider a simple layup.

"Having kids at odd times in life?" I smiled. "How old was your mom when she had you?"

"You really don't know about the rumors, do ya?" He dribbled. "My mom was thirty-eight when she had me."

"Oh, well, that's not too old. Your mom just had her children spread out, I suppose. That's all. I wouldn't consider that a family trait."

"That's not what I meant."

"What did you mean?"

"It doesn't matter." He did what I would learn to be a correct bounce pass. "What about you?"

"Oh, well, my mom's name is Julie. She's from Boston, as I said earlier; she is a stay-at-home mom who did not spread her children out." I smiled when I saw him smiling at my dribbling capabilities or lack thereof.

"And my dad is Jay," I continued. "He is a ferry boat captain—has been for nearly twenty years."

"When you dribble, try not to look at the ball," he suggested. "Trust your hand."

"Yeah...I don't trust myself to learn how to do that." I laughed. "I don't play sports that require my hands."

"You'll get it!" He cheered me on. "By the way, do you ride the ferry for free?"

"Why do you ask?"

"I figured that since you were the daughter of a ferry captain—"

"Well, I don't drive yet. Anytime I go off-island, it's with my mom, but I think she has a sticker on her windshield."

"That must be nice. The fares went up this year."

"By chance, are you related to the Sheriff?"

"I am," he informed me. "He is my father."

"I knew it!"

"How did you 'know it'?"

"You have a sticker on your back window with the sheriff's symbol."

"Yup!" He grinned. "Provides me the luxury of never getting snagged by cops."

"How old are you?" I blurted. I was embarrassed that it came out. "You don't have to answer, but I figured I'd ask. You know how old I am."

"How old do you think I am?" He quickly caught my attempt at a bounce pass, despite the pass taking two bounces. "Any guesses?"

"Seventeen…Or are you *eighteen*?"

"If I said eighteen, would it be a problem?" He shot a beautiful three-point shot.

"Not with me," I mumbled, "but…Maybe…I don't know—maybe people would start talking."

"I can assure you, Harper, that they are already talking. Being eighteen has nothing to do with what they are saying." He dribbled. "People have been talking for a few weeks already, and we gave them a ton more to talk about today. I get talked about a lot."

"You do?" I was surprised to hear this. "Why?"

"Harper…." He leaned against the hoop's pole and stared at me. "I've been…I'm just going to say this, and you can ask anything you want afterward, alright?"

"Alright."

"So, you're a freshman, so you probably haven't heard anything about me. Maybe you're a freshman that didn't think to ask about me. You seem like a genuinely nice person that doesn't believe in gossip—"

"Oh, I hate gossip!"

"Yeah, see, I figured that much. Alright, so it's probably better you hear it from me. Like I said, ask anything you want after I say this."

"Alright."

"I've got sort of a...track record of being associated with a lot of the girls."

"Oh, you date a lot?"

"Well...Harper, I wouldn't say date."

"So, you're—you're saying you've slept with a-a lot of girls?" I stammered. "That's what you're saying?"

"I wouldn't say slept with, either," he corrected me. "I'd probably say *fucked* would be more correct."

"What?" I gasped.

"Maybe that was a bit blunt—"

"Is that what you're planning on doing with me?" I panicked. "Are you trying to do...that with *me*?"

"No!" he snapped.

"How do I know that's true?"

"Because you're not the type of girl that would let that happen."

"Then why are you here? I mean, if you don't date girls and you only...whatever it is you called it, why are you here with me now?"

"Well, maybe I want to start dating a girl."

"But why me?"

"What do you mean?"

"Are you only interested in dating me because I'm a freshman, and I don't know anything about your past?"

"But I just told you about my past."

"I know, but maybe that's your charm," I exclaimed. "Maybe you use honesty in your story. Maybe that's how you slip your way into a girl's life! Next thing you know, she's put out!"

"Well, thank you for thinking I'm a master manipulator, but that's not how I do it." He laughed. "I've never had a girlfriend. I've never dated a girl, and I've never let a girl think there was a possibility of that."

"Really?"

"Every time I ran into you on campus, I thought about how I

could run into you again! That is how I knew I liked you; I don't just want to use you."

"You used these girls?"

"We used each other," he claimed.

"Oh, that's how it works." I smiled. "So you see sex and relationships as being mutually exclusive?"

"I'd say that I used to see it that way."

"Because of me?"

"Harper, you didn't throw yourself at me that day in PC," he explained. "Most girls seem to do that. You seem content in just challenging me. You had no problem putting me in my place tonight at dinner."

"And that turned you on?" I teased. "I'll put you in your place all day long if you want."

"That is what drew me in!" He laughed. "You're really not afraid of me."

"The attraction isn't entirely one-sided." I dribbled. "I find you charming, exceptionally good-looking, funny, and confident."

"So, I've got a shot?" He smirked.

"I think I already agreed to start referring to you as my boyfriend," I teased. "Things are already favorable for you."

"Really?"

"Can I ask you something?"

"Shoot!"

"Does it bother you that I've never done it?"

"Why would it bother me?"

"Well, I don't know." I rambled a little bit. "Maybe because you've done it before, and I might be a drag to be with if...*You know.* Especially since if we were ever to do it, you'd be the first guy I ever did it with. A lot of guys might think that would be a burden. But mostly because I am slightly—"

"Slightly what?"

I stammered while standing in my driveway, so I started walking around in circles, avoiding eye contact with him. I stopped before I began dragging my foot, creating imaginary circles on the concrete with the toe of my sneaker as a means of distracting myself from the heavy conversation. I was hoping to avoid saying the words he was now asking me to say. I've never said them out loud, even to Leigh. I heard him drop the ball. The sound of it dribbling off the concrete and onto the gravel worried me because I thought he'd decided to leave. Instead, I could feel his hand on my back. He was slyly pulling me toward him.

"What were you going to say?" he whispered.

I pulled away and sat on the steps of my porch. I was somewhat surprised that Scott sat next to me, but I was more surprised when he easily reached for my hand and interlaced his long fingers with mine.

"I really don't want you laughing at me...."

"I won't laugh. There is nothing funny about this discussion."

"I mean—alright, listen. I'm not like most of the girls in my class, let alone the girls you've been with."

"Maybe that's good. Maybe it's good to not be like everyone else."

"Does everyone in the school know about your history?" I whispered under my breath. "I mean, is what you've done common knowledge?"

"I wouldn't say 'common knowledge,' but I think I am seen as a dick—that gets girls talking," he informed me. "I think many of the girls I was with thought I was into them. They wanted to be in a relationship, but I didn't. The time I spent with those girls was time I enjoyed, but I knew it wasn't something that would last. I was honest with them about what the situation with them was, but some of them didn't believe me, or they didn't like it."

"And then there is me."

"You...Well, you caught me off-guard." He grinned. "I never wanted a girlfriend—until you."

"What?" I laughed. "You're joking!"

"No. Most girls don't stand up for themselves around me. In fact, no girl has ever stood up to me like you did that first day. Then you did it again in the main hall at school. Today at lunch, I was impressed with how uninhibited you were of me. It's like you didn't care that I'm a senior, like you weren't intimidated by me at all. It was the easiest conversation I'd ever had, and it was...with a girl. I typically don't have conversations with girls."

"Don't laugh at this, but I was going to say I am slightly intimidated by it," I said honestly. "Not you—"

"How so?"

"I'm one of those girls who puts a ton of importance on her first time," I whispered, my voice barely louder than my breath. "I think I'll only be able to do it if I have a boyfriend. The thing is, I never thought I'd have a boyfriend, so I never had to worry about it, and I think you're my boyfriend now, so I'm afraid that you're going to expect me to do it, and I don't think I can."

"Ah." He looked straight ahead. "Alright, since it seems we've already established our titles, I think we should now make some rules and clarifications about our relationship. Here goes: I'm Scott Pierce and Harper Whitmore's boyfriend. I had had sex before and enjoyed it, but I will leave the decision of if or when we do it up to my girlfriend. If she wants to, we'll do it; if she doesn't, we won't."

"Really?" I asked, unable to keep some uncertainty out of my voice. "No pressure?"

"You may very well be a relationship person, but I sense that you are probably also the sort of girl who has to be in love before she has sex."

"I might be." I smiled. "And this doesn't bother you?"

"This is your decision!" He grinned. "I find it slightly refreshing to know that I'm going into a relationship in which what I say about sex won't factor into anything."

"If I tell you something, you won't tell anyone?" I smiled. "Promise? I mean, I've never had a boyfriend before, but I think it's a rule that we don't tell anyone anything that goes on between us, right?"

"Who am I going to tell?"

"Scott," I exclaimed, "you're the most popular guy on campus. Everyone loves you! Girls want to sleep with you...They want to have your babies!"

"Ah, babies? Probably not," he stated. "In fact, I know they don't want to have my babies— but the first three are true. I won't tell anyone anything that goes on between us. I'd like to keep this part of my life private. You'll be my first girlfriend, and I'd like to keep us out of the rumor mill."

"Alright...I really enjoy kissing you," I whispered, "but I don't know what that says about me."

"I had a feeling you did. It certainly doesn't say anything bad about you."

He leaned in slowly. His perfect, white smile was the last thing I saw before I closed my eyes. The kiss was better than this afternoon, better than anything I'd ever experienced. I felt as though my heart would fly right out of my chest as the blood raced through my body.

"Can I ask you something?" he whispered as he pulled away from my lips.

"Yes."

"Why does your house look so different than the rest of the homes in this neighborhood?" he asked. "Actually, it looks different than every house on this island—this state, actually."

"When you kiss me, you're thinking about architecture?" I whined. "I don't think that's a good sign."

"Oh, trust me, architecture is the furthest thing on my mind. Per our recent agreement, however, I can't discuss what I'm really thinking!"

I roared with laughter at his words; Scott's laughter rang just as loudly as mine.

"But seriously," he continued. "Your house doesn't look like any house around. You have to admit that."

"Alright, my parents built this house fifteen years ago. They bought the land, had blueprints drawn up, and hired a contractor to come out and start building a custom Cape."

"What's a Cape?"

"It's this style of home. They are traditionally built in New England, which, as you know, is where my mother's from."

"Ah, I got it! Everyone in New England lives in a Cape, and everyone in the Pacific Northwest lives in—"

"Shit."

"What?"

"That's what my mom says," I smirked. "She says people in Washington wouldn't know culture if it shit on the front doorstep of their modern, eco-friendly homes."

"Has anyone ever told your mom that thoughts such as this are why people think Bostonians are elitist assholes?"

"She embraces it. Just listen to her notable accent!"

"I can't wait to hear your mother!" He laughed. "I'm actually looking forward to it."

"Just don't tell her she sounds like a New Yorker." I laughed. "She hears that everywhere."

"I'll try to refrain from saying that…Your house definitely stands out, though. It's huge!"

"It's not entirely a traditional Cape," I explained. "The floor plan is wider and a bit more open. Capes in New England have a smaller, tighter floor plan to conserve heat because the winters are so bad."

"Ah. Which do you like better?" he asked. "New England or Seattle?"

"Well, I love Boston in the summer, but I'll take a Seattle winter over a Boston winter. I'll admit that when Seattle gets those hard rains, I enjoy them."

"Good to know. If you decide to run away in June, I'll have an idea of where you went."

"If I did run away, I'd snag your truck!" I laughed. "It's an unbelievable ride."

"Yeah, that was my sixteenth birthday present from my parents," he told me. "A please-be-good present."

"Were you not good?"

"Freshman year was tough— not as tough as my sophomore year, but still rough. I'm past those days, though. You don't need to worry about them."

"I see," I sighed. "Because of the girls?"

"Sort of…A lot of the guys I was playing ball with at the time got into some pretty hard stuff—I went from hating needles to embracing them," he said sarcastically. "Took me the summer after tenth grade to get over and even."

"Oh, I see. I am sorry to hear that, Scott. That is very sad," I said with sincerity. "That must have been awful. But hey, you got a beautiful truck to keep your mind off those days!"

"Yes, a mint-condition 1996 white Nissan Pathfinder." He smiled. "Brand new when it was delivered."

"You seem to really enjoy it."

"It's better than Brad's ride."

"Brad is your best friend, right?"

"He is a very good friend of mine. He's a senior, too," he explained. "He's about six-three, wide build, jet black hair. He was with me the day we first met."

"Oh, I don't know him. I didn't really notice anyone that day except you." I shrugged my shoulders. "Actually, except for the seniors on my soccer team and you, I don't know any seniors."

"He drives this white piece-of-shit Honda Civic. It's got blue and green lights on the undercarriage and those ridiculous rims that spin in the opposite direction than the one that the car is moving in. You've probably seen it in the parking lot. Oh, and you can hear him coming from miles away. He's got an obnoxious sound system."

I smiled and nodded my head.

"Yeah, you know who he is!" He laughed. "I refuse to be seen in that atrocity of a car."

"Should I tell him that his mode of transportation is absurd?" I smiled.

"Oh, Harper, please, could you?" He placed his hand on my shoulder. "Make sure I am around for that, though. I want to be sure to tell him that you had no idea who he was until I described his POS Honda."

"It's a nice car. It's just very…noticeable. I can't complain, though. I don't have a car. I don't even have a learner's permit." I pouted. "But I am getting one next month when I turn fifteen!"

"You're fifteen next month?" He exclaimed. "That brings our ages closer together than I thought—only three years. When is your birthday?"

"Halloween." I smiled.

"Really?" He laughed. "Well, that is not scary at all!"

"And your birthday?"

"September fifth."

"Isn't that Labor Day weekend?"

"Usually."

"Hey, do you want to come in?" I offered. "It's getting kind of cold out."

He looked down at his wrist. His watch was enormous; the face was chrome, and an impressively masculine band was attached to the large, exceptionally detailed face.

"Your watch is very nice."

"Thank you." He smiled. "It's a Tag. I got it for Christmas a few years back."

"It's nice." I smiled. "So, did you want to come in?"

"Well, I was going to say yes, but…When do you plan to tell your parents about your older boyfriend?"

"I'll probably tell them around the time they start to notice that I'm continuously staying after practice with a *friend*."

"If you're planning on using the word *with*, that's probably going to be real quick."

As if Scott could read my mind, he slowly leaned toward me. Ever-so lightly, he placed his left hand on my jaw and kissed me, immediately putting my parents' inevitable concern out of my mind. I leaned in toward him, putting both my hands on his jaw. Slowly, gracefully, and at my own speed, I moved my hands and arms back until they were wrapped around his neck. I felt his hands drape along my waist and pull me toward him. I fell into him.

Immediately after passionately kissing on my front porch under the dark fall night, I pulled my head back to look at him. He held me close as I looked into his blue eyes, trying to freeze-frame this moment in my life. I wanted to remember this. I looked at him and ran my left index finger over his cheek, noticing the thin lines there. They were deep and in the shape of a crescent moon. It seemed they were meant to be a part of his personality and character. I watched his eyes and followed them as they moved to watch his finger spinning one of my curls around his index finger. I was focusing on everything that made him up, and he was doing the same. He wrapped that curl entirely around his long index finger. I still couldn't believe that I was Scott's girlfriend. Scott, the most beautiful guy in our high school, wanted me to be his girlfriend—not just his girlfriend, but his *first* girlfriend.

"Harper." He continued examining his finger as it tangled in my messy curls. "I really like your hair."

"Thank you," I whispered. "That's very nice of you to say. I was thinking about maybe trying something different."

He shook his head and mouthed 'no.'

"Maybe I'll rethink that."

He simply nodded.

"You wanna go to the football game Friday night?" he asked.

"Really?" I exclaimed. "'Cause I really want to go. I was planning on going with Leigh."

"Tell you what, Harper, how about I pick you up Friday night, and Leigh can come with us?" He smiled. "I was supposed to go with Brad, but I'd rather go with you."

"Scott, if you're going to pick Leigh and me up on Friday night, you'll probably have to meet my parents." I cringed.

"That's fine," he said casually. "I'd assumed as much. I'll drop you off tomorrow after practice, and we'll do it then."

"You'll really do it?" I smiled. "You'll meet them both?"

"Sure!" He nodded. "I'd prefer it if you told your folks about me beforehand, though. I don't want to walk into a situation where they have no idea who I am."

"I'll tell them tonight."

I looked down, thinking about how I would tell them about Scott and his driver's license. I also thought about how and when I'd tell Leigh about my relationship status. Poor Leigh's relationship status was stagnant.

"Hey Scott!" We looked up at each other. "Do you know Brett in your health class? He's a senior also."

"Sure do." He nodded. "What about him?"

"Nothing." I shrugged. "I just heard about him and was wondering if you knew him."

"Harper, are you interested in going out with him?"

"No!" I shook my head. "Not at all! Not even a little bit!"

"Alright, then. Why do you ask about him?" He smiled.

"Don't tell anyone this, alright?" I giggled. "I am about to let you in a huge piece of insider information, and after I tell you, you can't repeat it.... especially to Leigh!"

"Promise, I won't tell." He made the Boy Scouts symbol with three of his fingers. "Not a soul. I don't even know anyone who would find Brett gossip interesting—the kid is a major burn-out, but if you know something I don't, please tell."

"Leigh has an enormous crush on him. She has a thing for grunge guys in garage bands that have no gigs lined up and insist on walking everywhere with their guitar on their backs." I shrugged. "She finds him just adequate enough to have sex with him, and she is dying to lose her virginity! On her list of top items to complete before the end of ninth grade, having sex for the first time is number one."

"No one is going to find that piece of Brett information interesting, but the second part many would find worth knowing."

"See, that is exactly what I told her, but she thinks she can only get dirty grunge guys. She is so pretty."

"She's hot. That's what she is."

"Good to know," I said sarcastically, "that you think my best friend's hot."

"Only second to you, Harper," he recovered. "But in all seriousness, she can't do that. That kid is such a waste. He failed health; that's why he is taking it his senior year. How do you fail health? And the whole band thing? Come on! It'd be one thing if he were actually good, but this guy isn't good. There was a battle of the bands, like, three years ago, and Brett's band was invited. The kid's band had a missing drummer, and his bass player was high through the entire thing. Convince Leigh to pick another guy to lose her virginity to."

"It doesn't matter. Leigh hasn't even spoken to him. She's too afraid. I think she's waiting for him to make the first move."

"Won't happen. Brett is unaware of most things that occur around him. She'll be waiting a long time."

I smiled at Scott for a moment before saying the words I was dreading: "I have algebra homework, and I have to finish a book for English."

Like before, he leaned toward me and lightly rested his hand along my jaw, moving slowly. I felt his kiss on my lips, and, instinctively, as if I'd been kissing Scott for ages, I wrapped my arms around his neck and pulled myself toward him, feeling his hand release my face and move to my waist.

"I should go," I breathed.

"I really miss the retainer. Will I be feeling it tomorrow?"

I tossed my head to the side and smiled, watching him let go of me and head to his car. I watched him as he pulled out of my circular driveway. When he had gone, I ran into my house and straight upstairs. There, I firmly seated myself in front of the full-length mirror of my bedroom. My skin was hot. This was the first time I knew with absolute certainty that Scott had changed me on the inside as well as the outside.

I anticipated that the discussion with my parents about my older boyfriend would be painful, and I decided that thinking about that conversation just then wasn't worth the time. I decided to simply be prepared for it and deal with it when it arrived. As easy as it would be to worry about telling them, it was easier to stop thinking about telling them. I washed my face and put on my pajamas—a white camisole with white shorts—and examined myself in the mirror, wondering what exactly Scott saw in my short, barely developed body. I believed him when he said he liked me and my personality and loved our banter. I believed everything he said.

THREE

"HARPER!"

Scott quickly sat next to me in the overpopulated cafeteria. At that point, we'd been together for nearly a month, and I think he only kissed me on the cheek because he knew my fear of public displays of affection.

"Hey Scott!" I bit my lip as a means of holding back my grin. I wanted his lips on mine in the open cafeteria. I wanted the elation I felt when he kissed me to be present in every moment of my life, including a routine lunch in the large cafeteria. I wanted more than to just see him, talk to him, and listen to his deep masculine voice tell me about his life and how he saw me fit into it. I wanted his touch to go beyond my knee or hand. Leigh knew it as she sat across from me at the table that day. She had begun experiencing the same feelings toward Brad, who was a recent addition to our lunch table.

"Harper, we still on for the tennis match tonight?" Scott asked. "It's at five-fifteen."

I had to pull myself out of the trance; the feeling of Scott's thumb casually rounding my kneecap under the table made it difficult to answer.

"I'll be there!" I answered cheerfully. "I might be a little late because soccer practice gets out at five, and I have to shower up, but I'll rush to get there."

"You will always be such the responsible freshman," he teased, "never thinking to either skip practice or ask to leave a little early."

"No," I groaned. "As the only freshman on the team, I'm afraid to ask for anything special."

"Leigh," Scott said as he tried to contain his laughter, "you coming?"

"Nope," Brad replied. "Leigh's hanging with me tonight until the football game at seven."

"I am?" Leigh asked, perplexed.

"Leigh told me she has never heard of PlayStation," Brad informed Scott, "which makes my Friday night pretty much laid out for me."

"I think I said I'd never played it, not that I'd never heard of it," she corrected him. "Do you want me to come over? I have CCD tonight, so I might not be able to hang out."

"You have what?" Brad inquired. "What is CCD?"

"It's a class we have for church," I offered. "It stands for Confraternity of Christian Doctrine."

"Shit, Harper," Leigh exclaimed. "You really do pay attention."

"It's written on the cover of the book they gave us, Leigh—" I reminded her.

"Either way, I'll see if I can skip," she informed Brad.

"I'm skipping." I shrugged. "I don't care—"

"Harper." Scott tilted his head and pulled his brows together tightly. "If you have something else planned, we don't have to hang out tonight."

"No, I want to watch you play. Then we'll go to the football game. It's fine."

"Are you sure? I mean, this seems like an important thing—"

"Not to me." I shrugged, dismissing his concern. "I'll just have reading to catch up on. I don't need to go to the class."

"Alright, if Harper is skipping, then I'm skipping, too!"

"Great," Brad exclaimed as he leaned toward Leigh's lunch and started picking at it. He was so close that she could no doubt feel his breath on her neck. "I'll pick you up after school, Leigh."

"Oh." She looked directly at me with wide eyes. "Harper, I have to go to my locker to get my book for English. Wanna go with?"

"I'll go," Brad offered. "I gotta walk that way, anyways."

"Alright, I'll see you in class then, Harper!" Her face was full of panic as they both walked out of the cafeteria side by side, so close that their arms rubbed against one another.

"Is Leigh alright?" Scott casually asked. "She seems a bit jumpy."

"Hmm, I'm not sure." I smiled, quickly shifting the attention off Leigh and onto us. "So, I'll be at the game tonight."

"Match," he corrected me.

"Hmm?"

"Tennis isn't played as a 'game,' it's a 'match.'" He smiled. "A very boring, slow 'match.'"

"Oh, well, I'll be there either way."

"Great! We'll head straight to the football game afterward. But I gotta tell you that my parents are attending the match tonight."

"Are they prepared to meet me?" I contained my panic as best I could under the disguise of intrigue. "I mean, they know about me, right?"

"They do, but." He stammered and pushed his fingers through his hair. "It's...more. It's more than that. I've never had them meet a girl before."

"But a month ago, you met my parents. They'd never met a guy I brought home before, and it went pretty smooth." I smiled. "Actually, it went pretty well. My mom really likes you, and my dad was excited to have someone to talk about basketball with."

"That's different." He sighed. "My mom is going to ask a million questions, and I think she might bring up stuff that happened before, and I really don't like the idea of you suffering through that."

"Hey!" I flashed him a reassuring smile. "It will be fine. I've already heard most of it from you, and hearing it from your mom won't change how I feel—"

"And how do you feel?" he interrupted. "'Cause I'll tell you how I feel."

"And how do you feel?" I panicked.

"I really like you." He smiled. "You're honest. It makes being with you easy. I can tell you anything, and you won't judge."

"I'm glad—I mean…I'm happy," I stammered. "I guess—I figure if you're going to tell me something difficult, it's better for me not to judge because that's only going to add to your difficulty." I shrugged. "And since this is my first relationship, I figure being honest is best. I'm already overthinking so many different things. Adding dishonesty into the mix will probably ruin us."

"I can't even picture you lying." He grinned. "You're probably horrible at it."

"I'll be fine meeting your mother tonight," I reassured him while flashing him my most adorable smile. "I don't know your mother, but I do know that if she brings up anything uncomfortable, I'll most likely be able to brush it off."

"Alright…I'll probably play poorly tonight because of this." He laughed. "Then again, I'm not very good at this sport, anyway."

And then he did it. It was like he could read my mind. He must have known that if he applied a smidge of dominance to our relationship, he could push me in the direction I wanted. His kiss was soft and slow initially, and then he pressed into me with force. I became more and more receptive to his intense embrace. I was demanding more from him in this end-of-lunch kiss. I suspected Scott was demanding more from me, also. He had done more than this before and was probably teetering on annoyed with my slow progress in giving more. He had never said anything after I'd pulled away from him out of nerves, though.

"I'll see you at five," I breathed.

"Does that mean you're leaving practice early?"

"I'll see you at five-fifteen."

"Ah…." He released a long breath through his teeth and looked at the ceiling, mainly muttering to himself, I suspected. "She is so responsible."

"Scott." I grinned. "Can I—"

I threw myself into him without thinking about it first. I kissed him on my own, with no provocation from him. I feared he wouldn't be receptive, but he was. His large right hand cradled my jaw while the long fingers of his left hand got lost in my curls. He directed the last of our time at lunch. Just as I'd become enamored with my boyfriend and his kisses, the panic set in when I felt his left hand move onto my ribs. His thumb was just grazing the outline of my breast when I instinctively flinched and pulled away.

"I should get to class," I breathed.

"Yeah," he breathed, "I'll walk you."

A test in fifth-period English prevented Leigh from having the chance to discuss her confused state. Sixth-period art arrived, and I knew exactly what to expect. Art appeared to be a canvas for her confusion as she threw a large piece of clay onto her wheel and stood over it.

"What is he doing, Harper?" She inquired. "You gotta find out!"

"I have no idea." I winced.

"Then ask Scott!" Her demanding tone held much more than an order; it also held a threat.

"Leigh, I'd like to help, I really would, but the thing is that I have my own confusion to sift through. I need to sort that out. Before I can ask Scott what his friend Brad is doing, I need to know what Scott is doing first."

"He treats me like his best friend," she exclaimed. "I don't need a best friend! I have a best friend!"

"Hey!" I gently rubbed her back, leaning into her so only she could hear me. "Leigh, come on. Maybe he just likes hanging out with you. Maybe he is interested in being something more but is trying to figure it out himself, first."

"Harper," she whined, "is that what Scott did?"

"Scott flat out told me he wanted to be with me."

"I need Brad to tell me what we are before something happens," she roared. "Maybe we shouldn't skip our Confirmation class tonight. Maybe we need to go and confess—"

"Do you anticipate something happening while hanging with him tonight?" I grinned. "Are you telling me something?"

"Harper," she promised as she leaned over her wheel and smiled, "if he kisses me, the panties are coming off!"

"Leigh," I groaned, "try to pretend to be a good Catholic."

"I do not trust myself around him," she whispered. "If he was Brett, I wouldn't care about what happened afterward, but this is Brad Avery! I care about what happens afterward with him! I care if he sits next to me afterward. I care if he continues to pick at my lunch, play with my watch, or lightly shove me when I make a stupid comment. I need that to continue afterward, and if he doesn't tell me what we are, I can't be certain that will continue!"

"O-oh…This is a problem," I affirmed. "Well…Alright, if he kisses you tonight and you enjoy it, ask him if anything has changed."

"What if I kiss him?"

"I didn't think of that," I exclaimed. "If you kiss him, you make the rules."

"Scott kissed you," she reminded me, "and it seems like you are making the rules in that relationship."

"True," I told her, perplexed, "but there really aren't any rules—more like boundaries. Maybe just make out with him if you feel the urge…You know…."

"Good idea! I can easily make out with him." She giggled. "And that's easy? No thinking?"

"I don't know," I mumbled. "We haven't really done that."

"Have you gotten to his hand under or over bra?"

"Hand nowhere near bra."

"Oh, Harper," she sighed.

"We've come close," I explained, "but I always get really shy and pull away. His hand will start on my shoulder and progress down, and I'm fine with that, but by the time it ends up on my ribs, and I feel his thumb glance over my underwire, I pull back. The entire time, I'm screaming at myself for pulling away."

"That has to stop!" She threw a ball of clay on her pottery wheel in hostility toward the situation. "Right now! No more of that! Ignore whatever you're telling yourself, and let him touch you!"

"Is that what you're going to do tonight with Brad?"

"I don't know what I'm doing with Brad. Don't take any advice from me."

I showered after practice quickly and thoroughly, ensuring I smelled clean. I lightly spritzed myself in perfume and scrambled to leave the locker room before my teammates' commentary could begin. I'd successfully gone a substantial amount of time avoiding their thoughts on my relationship, but that doesn't mean I was immune to the gossip slowly eating its way through to my core.

For a brief moment, the thoughts of gossip stopped. I saw Jack and Marie Pierce at their positions on the cold steel bleachers alongside the tennis courts. I recognized them from afar. He was still in his sheriff's attire while she was dressed casually; she still looked immaculate, nonetheless. He was tall, and she was short; it was a reflection of Scott and me as we strolled together on campus.

I feared this moment; I feared her not liking me. I was worried that she'd find something she hated about me, some small quality she found distasteful, and would find it necessary to bring that to light. She'd hate my age or my grade or think Scott was wasting his time with a girlfriend. I walked a little faster and decided it was best to get this over with. Like a bandage, I'd rip it right off and introduce myself. If they didn't like me, I'd back off and make myself scarce. I'd let Scott deal with his parents.

"Hi," I said quickly, with a light wave. "How are you?"

They both stared at me. Neither moved. They looked down at me from the high bleachers—it was probably a metaphor for how they saw me. His father sat on the edge of the bleacher, watching me as I fiddled with my fingers. I was a live wire as the silence droned on. I kept waiting for them to acknowledge me.

"Hello," his mother replied with a raise of both her eyebrows.

"Yes." His father nodded. "Hello."

"It's nice to see you." I smiled, nervous. "You know, at a tennis game...I mean *match*."

"Well, our son is playing," she offered as a reminder. "We do enjoy seeing our son play."

"Oh, I do too," I exclaimed. "This is the first time he's had a match that wasn't during soccer practice."

"Excuse me, darling." She leaned forward, her hands on her knees, and examined me from above. "Do we know you? Does my son know you? Are you one of those girls bidding for my son's attention? You should know those girls annoy me."

"Oh, my God." I released a small breath as panic took hold. "You have no idea who I am. Scott didn't tell you—"

"Darling," she sighed, "I don't know what my son has told you, but he isn't exactly reputable with the ladies. I'll save you an embarrassing moment. You won't ever be coming to our home for dinner—you will most likely never come to our home. He won't take you to a dance or any other social function whatsoever. Introducing yourself to his parents isn't going to win him over—it will do the exact opposite."

"Oh, my God." I was near tears. Her words weren't for me. Those words were for the girls before me—the ones who were never his girlfriends. The fear that maybe I was somehow dragged along through some game Scott was engaging took hold. Maybe his parents really had no idea who I was. I remembered lunch, though, and all the conversations we'd had together and realized that maybe his parents were new to this, too.

"It's alright," she continued. "I get annoyed with it also."

"I'm Harper," I whispered, "Harper Whitmore. I've been dating Scott for a little over a month."

"Marie, you'd better apologize," her husband blurted out. "She's going to tell Scott all about this one."

"You're Harper." Her words were stern, but she breathed them out of concern and panic. "You're his girlfriend?"

She casually stood up and stepped down each bleacher before stepping softly onto the moist, dewy grass. I extended my hand but found she felt this occasion deserved a hug as she proceeded to engage in one. I inevitably received a handshake, but it came from his father.

"It is so wonderful to finally meet you," she stated with a large smile across her face. "Scott has told us all about you—three days ago, to be exact! You can understand my earlier words. If I had met you earlier, I never would have said what I did. I am truly sorry."

"Oh," I nervously laughed, "that's weird."

"That's Scott," his father informed me. "We tend to be the last to know anything about his life."

"Harper, trust us—our lack of foreknowledge is no reflection of you," Mrs. Pierce added. "Come and sit by us. I want to hear more about you. And please, please accept my apology."

"Alright." I followed her lead and sat down. "And it's fine. I understand where you were coming from."

"You do?" She pulled her brows together. "I'm surprised."

"Oh, well, he's told me as much as he's comfortable with." I politely smiled. "And I'm fine with that."

"Scott didn't tell us how beautiful you were," Marie exclaimed as she reached for my hand and held it tightly. Her red acrylic nails shined and complemented her gold jewelry and large diamonds. "Your hair is incredible. It has so much volume; it's as if you can make out each curl. Natural?"

"Yes." I nodded, attempting to hide my smile as I looked down at my hand, which was being held by both of hers. "You sound just like Scott."

"You are a very attractive young lady—unlike those other permed girls we've seen around." She smiled. "And from the sounds of it, Scott seems very taken by you."

"That's nice to hear, though our relationship is very new. We've only been seeing one another since September."

"Well, at least now I don't have to worry when he comes home at eight on school nights." Her short-left arm reached over my shoulder and pulled me close to her body. "You chilly? We can share a blanket, and you can tell me all about yourself."

"Did you know that I am a freshman?" I laughed lightly and rolled my eyes as I nodded at her expression. "I bet Scott forgot to tell you that."

"He told us you were younger but didn't elaborate on the exact age difference."

"I'll be fifteen next week," I offered. "Three-year age difference."

"Who's counting?" She chuckled.

"Seniors are counting."

"Good thing you only have to worry about one senior." She winked.

"I wish it were that simple." I took a small breath and smiled.

We sat together for over an hour, laughing and smiling through the matches while Scott's father asked questions about my soccer season and what it was like to be the only freshman on varsity. It wasn't as stressful as Scott had made it out to be. My relaxed state vanished when a group of girls came to watch the tennis match, and the gossip I'd been trying desperately to avoid and pretend didn't exist started in. They were loud, vocal, and unaware that I sat only a few bleacher seats behind them as they went on about Scott and his freshman girlfriend. They were cruel and oblivious as they questioned what a freshman wasn't willing to do. They continued getting louder as they began talking about what services they would offer Scott without any wait.

I lowered my head and focused on my knees. I tried to remember how just a few hours earlier, Scott was casually holding my knee under the lunch table and letting his thumb swirl over my kneecap. I focused long and hard on my knees before I saw Marie's acrylic fingers interlock with my fingers and gently squeeze. Her thick gold ring, sporting a large, single diamond, shined on her ring finger as she reassuringly squeezed my hand.

"Girls," Marie announced, "there is nothing glamorous about the way you speak. It's sad and unattractive."

"What's it to you, lady?"

I grew tense; my left hand grasped her hand out of fear and nervousness. Her large diamond ring poked through between my fingers as I laced them tightly with hers. I straightened my posture and moved closer to Marie as a means of hiding. I let my curls act as a curtain between me and the rest of the world. I would never have dreamed of addressing a woman of Marie's age in the way these girls just did. Their lack of self-awareness only meant their juvenile discussions about Scott continued.

"That's my son you're talking about." Marie tilted her head toward me and nodded. "And this is my son's girlfriend. You'll note that she doesn't talk like that. She is the one who became Scott's girlfriend, not a girl who talks freely about oral sex in a public venue. The way I see it, you could learn something from my son's girlfriend."

"Thank you," I mumbled.

"You know what the problem is with this game, Harper?" Her burgundy lips drew back in an endearing smile, revealing beautifully white teeth as she changed the subject. "Scott not only has to play a few singles games tonight, but he also has to play a few doubles. I have no idea if he won or lost any of them at the event's end!"

"Do you think Scott keeps score while he plays, or do you think he keeps playing until they say stop?" I asked her, grateful for the subject switch.

"I have no idea." She laughed, flashing her deep laugh lines. "The game goes on forever, darlin'!"

"No, it doesn't, Marie," Jack added in a stern tone, "the match is almost over when they get to forty and say 'match point.'"

"They've said that a few times, Jack," Marie exclaimed. "Harper, I hate this sport. I've sat in these bleachers for four years, and I couldn't tell you if Scott ever won or not."

"I'm sure you don't really mean that." I smiled. "Scott told me he wasn't that good, but he seems to be playing really well."

"Harper, you're a sweetheart." Her tone made it clear that she was going to redirect this conversation. The circular motions of her right hand on my back confirmed it. "Please, ignore those girls," she said sincerely. "They're trash. It comes from being born into trash, and you're better than that."

"I don't think I'm better than anyone."

"That is something a girl born into class would say," she added. That same radiant smile reappeared on her face. "I'll need to meet your mother now."

"She's from Boston." I smiled. "She won't openly admit she is better than anyone."

"Ah, so she knows she's better than everyone but is sophisticated enough to not brag about it." She chuckled. "Instead, I bet she dresses better, looks better, and takes better care of herself than most."

"If by taking care of herself, you mean getting her hair done every six weeks, nails every two; driving a Lexus; never wearing flats; and, as Scott pointed out, owning a home that doesn't look like any home around here, then yes, you have described Julie Whitmore."

"Harper, do you live in that Cape off Parker?" Marie queried.

"I do."

"The ferry captain's house?" his father asked.

"That is my home."

"Island living!" She sneered. "You may not know everyone, but you know their business...I can see myself really liking you."

"I'm glad! Scott was afraid you were going to embarrass him." I chuckled. "I don't see how you could ever embarrass him."

"Oh, I could," she assured me, "easily! But I like you, Harper. You're his first girlfriend, and I think I'm gonna try to keep you around for a while."

"That is very nice of you to say." I gave her my huge grin before looking up and seeing Scott's smiling face strolling toward me, his racket spinning in his hand. "Did you win?" I asked him. "I honestly have no idea."

"Three out of the four matches." He chuckled. "I lost my doubles match, but I was partnered up with that jackass Barrett."

"Be nice," his mother warned.

"Scott!" I watched as Jack stomped down the bleachers and marched toward his son, noticing they were about the same height as Scott had told me. "Harper's a very charming girl. Your mother is taken by her."

"Thank you." Scott nodded. "She is very charming."

"Your father is right, Scott." Marie smiled as she looked at me. "I want you to do your best to keep her around."

"No pressure, right, Mom?" He laughed before looking up at me. "We still on for tonight?"

"Do *you* still want to go to the football game?" I asked. "It starts in fifteen minutes."

We were late, but not late enough for anyone to notice, and the people who did take note of such things were people that gossiped about us already. His hand was warm, and his fingers were smooth as they interlaced with mine. I could feel something happening inside me, and it forced me to pull myself closer to him. I was quiet as he directed us toward his group of friends. I clung to him, holding his right hand tightly with mine at first and then encasing it in both my hands. As the circle of senior guys all laughed and lingered in the smell of flat beer, I wrapped myself in Scott's arms.

"You alright?" His smile was sincere as our faces tucked closely toward one another. "Are you cold?"

"A little." I smiled and stood high on my toes, reaching for him and entirely prepared for his hand to move into my curls and guide my head toward him. He was warm as he pulled me closer into his black fleece jacket. "Not really anymore," I informed him.

"You want to sit in the bleachers? We can discuss what we'll do for your birthday next week."

"Maybe later." I grinned and pushed myself into his kiss, ignoring the yelling in my head. "I'm comfortable like this."

"But Harper, this will be your first birthday with me as your boyfriend!" He pulled back slightly, his deep blue eyes full of surprise. "I've gotta plan something huge! It's gotta be so huge that I'm going to need to tell your sister I won't be able to simply be a fan sitting next to her at Monday's game because I'll be too busy planning for this first major event in our relationship."

"I'm sure she'll survive." I laughed and slowly pulled away from his arms. "Plus, Monday's game is an away game, so you'll be in the clear."

"We were going to travel to the away game. I'll have to make a call this week to your little sister."

"Are you sure you need to plan something this huge for my birthday?" I laughed. "I mean, you'd have to give up a truck ride to and from Mt. Vernon, as well as the opportunity to listen to boy bands—"

"I do love your sister's taste in music!"

"Let's keep the original plan; we can go to dinner for my birthday. Keep it simple. It's only my fifteenth."

"Your sixteenth, I'll be sure to make a blowout event."

That's all I needed to hear. I was back clinging to his every word.

FOUR

I WAS ROMANTICALLY HANDICAPPED.
Allowing a pat on the ass was about as comfortable as I had gotten in nearly three months. Scott never said a word about it. Though I had a sneaking suspicion someone as well practiced as Scott would probably be getting annoyed with only kissing me and occasionally patting my ass.

Leigh always quickly reminded me that Scott and I hadn't made out yet. She cleverly asked every morning before first period, "Have you been felt up yet?" The answer was always no. The answer was also no for Leigh, but Leigh still didn't have a definition of her relationship with Brad. Subsequently, she had to live vicariously through the precise definition of my relationship with Scott. I felt at this point in our relationship, Scott was no doubt eager to skip making out and head right into sex. The only trouble with this was I wasn't. I hadn't become comfortable with the thought of having sex or being felt up, but I had arrived at the possibility of it all. I say 'possibility' because I was terrified of actually initiating any physical intimacy. Numerous times, I'd catch myself staring at him, thinking that perhaps I could just tell him what I wanted and let him do all the work. I was easy game as long as he initiated things. Alas, I remembered that Scott looked at me as a girl he respected and wouldn't objectify. All I wanted was to be objectified...as long as he physically initiated it.

"So," I stammered, examining anything but Scott and his deep blue eyes, which would inevitably pull me in. "Are you still going to the game tonight?"

"Absolutely," he asserted as he stood casually with his hands in his back pockets. We were outside by his truck in the student parking lot, and he was looking as unintentionally gorgeous as ever. "If not because I want to see you score a hat trick, then certainly because I promised your sister I'd sit with her."

"You really think I'm going to make three goals tonight?" I smirked. "I'll try, but no promises!"

"Harper, it hasn't been done this season by anyone in the league. You've gotta be the girl that does it! You're the fastest in the league!"

He smiled before he leaned down slowly and kissed me. The force of his kiss gently drove me back into his truck's empty bed. He leaned over me. I wrapped my arms around his neck and encouraged whatever we were doing to continue. His lips were soft and smooth as he parted my lips with his tongue. His kiss was enough of a distraction that if he wanted to do more, I'd have no qualms about it—despite being in the middle of the student parking lot. I enjoyed the aggressive nature of his tongue invading my mouth, and I hoped his hands would take the same initiative across my body.

"I have a feeling that's not what you really wanted to ask me." He smirked as he broke the kiss, resting his forehead against mine.

"What do you mean?" I pulled myself out from under his arms. "What do you think I wanted to ask?"

"I don't know." He shrugged. "I just don't believe your mind was entirely focused on whether I was really going to the game. I've done nothing but talk about the game all week."

"Why are you calling me out like this?"

"Harper," he declared in a low groan.

"Alright," I mumbled and shrugged myself out from his light grip. "I've been going crazy over this. I might as well tell you. I am completely unable to think about anything but this one topic, even when we're watching television or doing our homework together. Sometimes, I'll spend the entire period in class thinking obsessively over this—"

"You're talking about the rumors? I'd assumed that if we just ignore 'em, it would be like they didn't even exist, but I imagine that since you're a freshman girl, gossip is pretty intimidating."

"No, it's not the gossip." I sighed. "I mean, I hate the gossip, but… This isn't about the gossip."

"Well, what is it?" he asked, a little perk in his voice.

"Scotty," I groaned. "It has to bother you—"

"What?" he breathed, his beautiful half smile shining through. "What has to bother me?"

"You know," I emphasized my idea with my hands. "The slowness of it all."

"You mean?" He nodded in agreement. "Ahh…Well, why are you spending so much time thinking about that?"

"I don't know," I whined. "I think it's because I know you've done all that stuff with other girls—girls I see every day—and now you're with a girl that hasn't done *any* of it, and I might be a drag."

"Absolutely not," he snapped out before taking a shallow breath. "Listen, I don't want you to spend any more time freaking out over this. It's not a race. You'll figure out when you're ready, and we'll go from there. Everything in our relationship is great. I love it all. That part will happen when it happens; it can't be forced."

"Organically?"

"Exactly!" He grinned, clamping his hands onto my hips. "Just like the rest of our relationship. Organically."

From there, Scott returned to kissing me. The force of his kiss continued to press me to the floor of the bed of his truck. I gently placed my hands on his shoulders, hoping he would take that as an invitation for more.

"Harper, we can't stay here," he whispered while we pressed our foreheads together. "Not like this."

"Will we get suspended?" I teased. "Will this get me kicked off the soccer team?"

"Not suspended, but we'd probably get a firm warning from the principal and probably a phone call to our parents." He chuckled lightly. "Basically, something I'd like to avoid."

"Gotcha!" I stood high on my toes and kissed him. "I'll see you and my three other fans later tonight!"

"You didn't eat lunch today," he reminded me. "Wanna skip the rest of the afternoon and head to my house?"

"Sorry, I can't." I groaned. "I won't be able to play if I skip."

"Ah, that's right! My girlfriend is a responsible little freshman. No variety in her day," he whispered into my neck before quickly lifting me up, catching me by surprise, and hugging me, tickling my ribs. "Isn't that right, Harper?"

"Quit it!" I laughed. "I like to follow the rules."

"You won't when you're a sophomore." He laughed. "I look forward to being with you when you're not so responsible."

That's all he had to say; my trust in myself was complete. He'd thought about us being together beyond just the here and now. It was a trivial statement on his part, but I decided I could force myself into much more for me.

"Alright, I'm headed home. My day is done."

"I'll see you tonight," I cheered. "Wait, Scott! Do you have plans after the game?"

"Nope, nothing," he yelled across the parking lot. "Why?"

"No reason," I hollered. "We can figure something out later if you're interested!"

"Of course I'm interested!" He laughed. "We'll hang out after the game!"

I waved goodbye and watched him pull out of the parking spot. He stopped one more time before he headed home.

"Hey Harper," he yelled out his window, "you're getting that hat trick tonight!"

"Whatever!" I kissed him through his window, standing high on my toes. "You're stressing me out over it."

"Hey Harp," he yelled. His new nickname for me caught me off-guard. "*You* and only *you* are allowed to call me Scotty! Got that, Shorty?"

73

"*You* and only *you* are allowed to call me Harp," I smirked. "Got that, Stretch?"

It was fifty-three degrees in late fall, and I sat stretching in the center of the field. I saw Scott arrive at the game, fresh, clean, and wearing white sweats.

"Harper, Scott told me in calc that you would get a hat trick tonight."

Maureen started becoming nice to me after that incident in the locker room. I'd dare say she became a friend. I'd like to have thought it was because she respected me, but I had a feeling that Scott had words with her shortly after the locker-room incident. Either way, she and I had arrived at a place filled with mutual respect and slight admiration for one another.

"I am going to try," I responded. "This could be our last game, and I'd like to end it with a hat trick, but that's not why Scott is excited about it."

"Why is he excited about it?" Maureen moved closer to me while we stretched.

"Scott doesn't believe that if I do it, I'll slide into the mud pit midfield."

The seniors on the soccer team had perplexed faces as I tried to explain the two-sided bet Scott and I had made. There really was nothing to win with the bet; it was more just a game between the two of us. It boiled down to a game of who knew whom better. I wanted to prove that Scott didn't know me as well as he thought.

"I told Scott if I ever got a hat trick, I'd rip my shirt off and slide in the mud pit with just my sports bra on."

"That would end up in the yearbook. You know that, right?" Maureen started to smile as she switched to stretching her right hamstring. All of us followed. "I tend to agree with Scott; you could probably get a hat trick—no doubt about that—but I don't think you would slide into midfield! Then again, you have been surprising the senior class this year…Most of all me!"

"Really? I have?" We all lined up the midfield to get our shin guards checked by the ref. "How so?" I asked as we stood in line.

"You're still with Scott, even after everything people have said about you and your boyfriend."

We quickly spun around to look at the backfield while the ref inspected our cleats.

"Everyone thought once you found out about what kind of guy Scott was, you'd bail," Maureen informed me.

"Was?" I asked as we walked off the field together. "He's not anymore?"

"The guy Scott was before is not near the guy he is with you. Not by a long shot."

"Explain." I grabbed Maureen by her arm and looked at her. "What does that mean, exactly?"

"It just means that you're Scott's first girlfriend ever. You've been together for almost three months, and I know you haven't done anything with him yet. He seems to not be an asshole about it. A lot of girls liked to do things *for* Scott, and maybe that's always been the problem. He's used to getting what he wants. Whatever you're doing—or not doing—keep it up."

"Harper," April chimed in as we walked off the field together, "Scott isn't even a little bit like he used to be. I think the fact that you don't seem to appease every need of Scott's is impressive. Combine that with the fact that you are still with him despite the rumors, and it might very well impress Scott enough to actually love you."

"Scott doesn't love me." I rolled my eyes as we huddled up. "He cares for me, but love isn't a topic of conversation yet."

Our team circled up, and we gave ourselves a quick cheer and a pep talk before taking our positions on the field. April and Maureen were on either side of me, towering over me.

"Harper," Maureen explained as the circle broke up, "If Scott *only* cared for you, he wouldn't stay. Scott is the all or nothing kind of guy."

"And he's *all in* with you, Harper," April added as the referee's whistle blew.

We took our positions on the field, and I shook Maureen's words out of my head to focus on the start of the game. Maureen took the center field as she began the kick to me, left-wing, and we began our three-way progression against King's High School. While running the left-wing course, I was body-slammed twice by a girl from King's. I kept waiting for the ref to card her. I ran the central drill, kept the ball half-field on King's goal side, and quickly snagged my first goal. As a team, we collectively felt confident that repeating the same drill could secure the upper hand in this game. Our opponent would never suspect us repeating the same play.

We reran the same exercise, and I got my second goal, which forced me to think of Scott and how he was no doubt on the edge of his seat and waiting impatiently for my third, and the subsequent slide into the mud pit he thought I wouldn't do. I got what I considered to be fouled twice more by King's, and each time, I got up and screamed at the ref, "Are you watching these girls? Their cleats are showing! I can see them!"

As we walked off the field for halftime, Morgan caught my attention, and I went over to her. "I think you're going to do it, Harper," she assured me. I looked at Morgan and her enormous bag of mixed candy from PC and then looked at Scott, who had guilt on his face, and all I could do was smile.

"She wanted some candy," he explained. "What could I say?" He smirked. "And I think you'll get your hat trick, though I still don't think you'll slide into the mud pit."

"Harper," my dad interjected, "Keep your temper to yourself." My dad always had opinions about good sportsmanship, though he never got slide tackled by girls twice his size.

We circled up as a team on the sideline, where I vented how my knees were a disaster from those girls. After we broke from circling up, I sat on the grass and pulled my sock down, taking in my knees' disastrous state. Scott walked up to me and knelt.

"Harper, how bad is your knee?"

"I'm super pissed, Scott! They aren't calling *anything*!" I pulled my shin guard down and saw the bruises where cleats had slammed into me. "The ref told me there is 'no special treatments' for girls my size." Scott had the decency to look upset. "You know what that is, Scott? That's bullshit! I'm not asking for special treatment; I'm just asking that he starts paying attention."

Scott placed my shin guard back on and pulled my sock up. I adjusted my sock to make sure it was securely on and took Scott's hand to help me up. "Harp, you'll be fine! Just keep playing your game."

I got my third goal immediately into the second half. I could feel Scott get out of his chair and watch me strike the ball into the goal. I turned around to face my fans and looked directly at Scott, who was already standing. He kept his hands in his pockets and looked down at the ground, hiding his smile. I felt my team pat me on the back, but I gave most of my attention to Scott, who looked up at me and waited. I knew I was going to do it; as I looked at Scott, I knew that Scott knew I would do it.

I immediately ran with all the speed I had. As I ran, I pulled my shirt over my head and held it in one hand. I continued at full speed, bent my knees, and slid into the enormous six-inch-deep mud pit that filled our high school's midfield. The mud raced up my thigh as my knees cut through it. I fell slightly forward, completely covering my chest and body in mud. I slowly got up, pulled myself out of the deep mud, and walked back toward my left-wing position.

The ref and a yellow card greeted me on the left outside. "Unsportsmanlike behavior, number twelve," he told me. "Please put this in your sock."

"Really? You can get yellow carded for *that*?" I pointed to the pit. "But my right knee doesn't warrant a card?"

"Keep it up, twelve, and you'll get yourself another one." The ref looked down at me and walked back toward midfield.

Scott and Morgan slowly walked toward where I was standing on the sideline, putting my yellow card in my sock and making sure it could easily be seen by all despite the mud on my once-blue sock. Both stood, each eating a box of Junior Mints, utterly amazed at my behavior.

"Wow, Harp," Scott exclaimed. "You really just did that. You are completely filthy! I am amazed that you did it and got yourself a little yellow card for your sock! That's nice. You should be proud. I think the yearbook caught that slide."

"Hey Scotty!" I gave him the biggest hug I'd ever given him, leaving the imprint of my muddy body on his clean, freshly showered body. Maybe it was the game or Maureen's and April's words, but whatever it was, I felt a sudden eagerness to begin letting go of all my inhibitions and clouded worries. Our lips pressed together, and his long arms wrapped around my waist, allowing him to embrace me and the mud I was caked with. "Don't ever think I won't come through," I promised. I glowed in the happiness of our matching grins as I pulled away. I put my jersey over my head and finished the game.

We beat King's. Afterward, I met up with the fans—my parents, Scott, and Morgan—and we all discussed my achievement and Scott's now completely filthy T-shirt.

"Harper, you are not getting into my new car with this on you." My mother said as she ran her finger up and down through the air.

"I'll take her home, Mrs. Whitmore." Scott smiled at me and pulled one of my curls, removing a large chunk of mud. "Shower before you get into my car, please," he requested of me.

"Thank you, Scott, and please stop calling me Mrs. Whitmore."

"I'll try to remember that." Scott smiled through the slight nervousness in his voice before looking back at me.

"Harper, we're going to head out," my mother added, taking a step toward me. She wouldn't get close enough to take a chance of getting mud on herself. "We have to drive Morgan to her friend's home, and then your father and I are going to Seattle for dinner." Mom slowly leaned in to kiss me on the forehead before pulling away. "I'm not going to kiss you, Harper, but you had a fantastic game! I am so proud of your goals." She ran her hand along Scott's arm. "Be safe," she told him. "I'll see you two later."

"So," I mumbled as I moved my attention directly to Scott. "Did you still want to do something tonight?"

"Definitely."

Of my own initiative, I kissed him. He kissed me back, placing one hand on my jaw and ignoring the mud I had splattered across my face. His kiss deepened, and I welcomed the feeling of his tongue in my mouth. His hands casually lifted the hem of my jersey, and his fingers rested on the skin of my waist. I intentionally collapsed onto his chest, inadvertently pressing him against his truck. I rested my forehead against his sternum and felt his breath on the crown of my head.

"What's up?" He lightly panted.

"Do you want to come over tonight?" I examined the asphalt outside the locker room, terrified of Scott's answer. "To my house?"

"Yes." His smile radiated. "What do you have in mind?"

"I don't know," I shrugged. "I was hoping you'd have an idea."

"I do have an idea...."

"Yeah," I whispered nervously. "We-we could start with maybe getting dinner, like pizza, and then we could rent a movie or something." I looked at the mud on my arm, pretending to be distracted by the dried, caked-on mud. "I know it sounds like a lame Friday night...."

I knew he must have had thousands of Friday nights that had been spent in better fashion with thousands of better girls, but I was too scared, too nervous, and, most of all, too embarrassed to share what I really wanted to do—rather, what I wanted him to do. I was relieved when his large hand cradled my face and pulled my mouth up to his lips.

"It doesn't sound lame at all," he reassured me with a large smile. "It sounds great."

"Um, do you...?" I bit my lip and looked at the mud on me. I didn't look appealing at the moment, and what I was about to ask was going to need to sound appealing despite my current appearance. "Well, would *you* want to...Only if you want to." I tugged at the hem of my muddy jersey out of sheer panic.

"Harp, whatever it is, I'm sure it will be fine," he reassured me. "What do you have in mind?"

"Okay, don't laugh."

"Harp, unless it involves playing in that mud pit, I'm sure it will be fine."

"Would you want to go into my hot tub with me?" I pointed at myself. "Only if you want to, though—you don't have to. You won't hurt my feelings if you say no—"

"Hey! Hey, Harp, I think I'd like to go into your hot tub." He smiled. "I wouldn't say no to that. Ever."

"You would?" I asked anxiously. "With me?"

"Oh, wait! Wait! Wait, with you? Shit, Harp, I thought you would just turn the hot tub on and let me soak by myself." He pulled his brows tightly together and shook his head. "Yeah, now I don't know. This changes everything."

"Scotty!" I roared with laughter. "Seriously!"

"Go shower. We'll have to stop off at my house first."

I smiled and ran off into the locker room.

"Harper," he yelled. "Seriously, the tub is all mine tonight. I'm not sharing it!"

"Hilarious."

I showered, utterly silent in response to all the euphoric cheers I received about my hat trick and our miraculous win over King's. I had bigger things on my mind. I couldn't believe I'd suggested that I share a confined space filled with water with Scott. I couldn't believe that he'd agreed to it. Finally, I couldn't believe that he was going to see what I looked like in a swimsuit. I didn't own a one-piece swimsuit. I owned two bikinis, and I regretted purchasing them now. Looking back, the purchase was entirely driven by my need to have an even tan on my midsection. It never occurred then that I'd have a boy look at me in those bikinis and perhaps enjoy what he saw.

Scott had never seen me dressed with barely anything on, and I wasn't sure I was entirely prepared for that to happen now. I was not wholly confident that Scott would enjoy what he saw as I looked down at myself in the shower. I stared at myself for the longest time in that shower stall, terrified that Scott had seen much better. There were girls in this school that had much bigger breasts than me. There were girls in my class that were already a full D-cup. I was at best a small C, but in reality, I leaned more toward a large B. Some girls wore low-cut shirts and showed their midriffs. I routinely wore shirts that showed my belly but never shirts that emphasized or embraced my breasts. I didn't have breasts that I felt it necessary to embrace.

I shampooed my hair vigorously, completely ignoring the loud girls in the locker room, who were all cheering about the win over King's. I ran my hand over my legs, ensuring they were still smooth from my shave last night. I checked my underarms, which were still smooth. I lathered up repeatedly and rinsed my body, doing this over and over and making sure the smell of mud didn't linger.

"Harper!" Maureen and April called from outside the showers. "Get out here!"

"Yeah?" I grabbed my towel, wrapped it around me, and walked out, holding the knot very tightly. "What's up?"

"'What's up,' you asked. You tell us. You've been in the shower for the longest time. We know you were covered in mud, but come on," Maureen implored. They looked at each other. "What's going on with you?"

"Nothing."

I was noticeably quieter and somber as I snuck by them to head to my locker; I couldn't even fake sounding chipper. I looked down at the locker room's tile and my red toenails. I realized that not only would Scott see me in my bikini, but he'd also see that I loved having red toenails.

"Harper, what's on the agenda tonight for you and Scott?"

"Nothing." I carefully walked between the two girls and headed for my locker. "We're just going to hang out at my house."

"That's it?" April said—not to me, but to Maureen. "Harper, are your parents out tonight?"

I nodded and smiled.

"Was it his suggestion to hang out tonight?" she continued.

"No, I asked him."

"Are you two going to...You know?" April asked.

"No!" I said sharply. I wasn't afraid of the topic, but if I ever did get to the point where I could do that with him, I didn't want anyone to know about it. I didn't even want people to have a slight inclination that we might be the type of couple that had a sexual relationship.

"We're just going to hang out," I informed them.

"So, what's wrong?" April asked, concerned. "You seem upset."

"Nothing's wrong," I answered, looking into my locker for my tear-away pants and a hooded sweatshirt. "Nothing's bothering me;

I'm just on edge about the night." I got dressed and tried my best to hide the fear and annoyance growing inside me.

Maureen sat down next to me, and April sat across from me. "Harper, if you're just hanging out, leave it at that. If something happens, then something happens. You don't *have* to plan everything out."

I nodded in false agreement to placate Maureen into silence. I had to force myself into moving forward with Scott, or I'd stay stagnant in my relationship.

"Harper," April whispered, "you'll push through this fear and come out fine. Don't be afraid of Scott." She put one hand on each of my knees. "Everyone notices it, Harper."

"Notices what?" I looked up at Maureen and April. "What do they notice? Tell me!" I felt panicked.

"Harper, you probably don't notice it," Maureen chimed in. "Remember what I told you before the game? Scott's not the same. Before, girls would try to talk to him as he pulled into the parking lot or walked the halls, and he wouldn't even notice them unless he thought he could get something. It's like he was in some sort of self-absorbed coma before. Now, if some girls try to talk to him, he'll tell them he's with Harper Whitmore."

"It's true, Harper," April added. "We never tried anything with him, but a ton of girls around here got fucked over because they didn't know how to play the Scott-Pierce game." April looked at Maureen and then back at me. "Everyone knows his old game, but for some reason, he won't play that game with you. He insists on being your boyfriend. Every senior girl that got burned by him, Harper, hates seeing you two together. They all wanted Scott to be their boyfriend."

Maureen looked at me. "We thought you were upset because maybe someone from our class said something to you again."

I shook my head. "No, no one said anything..." I looked at them both and spoke in a panic, "But we haven't done that—"

"Oh, we figured as much," April said.

"You're not going to run around telling people this, are you? I know you two can be major bitches." When I said this, they both laughed. "And Scott told me about how he did some bad things before me."

"Oh, he admits that much, does he?" Maureen laughed. "We wouldn't ever tell anyone anything. Some chicks have been formulating an opinion about you, but trust me, we come correct with those bitches!" All three of us laughed. "What do you plan to do tonight?" Maureen asked.

I took a deep breath. "I think we'll get a pizza, rent a movie, and hang out at my house. There really isn't much else to do tonight. The first basketball game is in two weeks, so I figure we might as well enjoy the last free Friday nights before the season starts." I shrugged my shoulders.

"Harper, you can do that. That's nothing!" April assured me. "Don't waste your time being nervous."

I nodded; I didn't want to let either of them know that anything more than a simple evening was being planned. I certainly didn't want either of them to know we were going into my hot tub. Coming to Monday's practice and facing both these girls might be a painful experience if they knew I had shared a confined space filled with warm water with Scott Pierce. I slowly got up and made sure I was put together. I grabbed a hairclip, clipped my mess of curls onto the top of my head, grabbed my bag, and exited the locker room. I saw him as soon as I opened the heavy push door. He was slouched against the side of his truck, but he pushed himself upright when he saw me and headed toward me, reaching for my large bag.

"Little Harper Whitmore!" he yelled loud and jovial enough to make me laugh. "Lord, that was the longest twenty-five minutes of my life!"

"Do you know how much mud I had on me?" I tilted my head and grinned. "I had mud in places no one should have mud."

"Come here!"

He latched onto my sweatshirt and tugged me closer to him. I fell against his chest, and he resumed leaning against his truck. He wrapped both his hands around my waist and held me tight. I stood on my toes, my feet between his, and reached for him as he kissed me.

I moved my hands around his neck and let him pick me up. This kiss was passionate, a kiss much deeper than the one before my shower. I pretended I didn't notice it, feigning ignorance to that nudge on my thigh during our kiss, but I knew what was happening to him. I wasn't about to pull away from him and bring the very noticeable appendage between us to light.

"So, what do you want to do first tonight?" he breathed.

I shrugged and went back to kissing him, losing my hand in his hair.

"I think I have an idea," I informed him, and we continued to rest our bodies against one another, kissing in the empty, almost-dark parking lot.

After sharing a pizza at Louie's, where I watched Scott eat six slices, we stopped at Scott's house for his swim trunks. His room was as messy as always—his clothes were on the floor, and his bed was unmade. You could barely see the floor through the scattered clothes and numerous pairs of sneakers. I tiptoed through the mess and sat patiently on his large bed. I wasn't intentionally snooping. I meant to sit quietly, waiting for him to locate his shorts and clean clothing. But sitting there, I tugged on his nightstand drawer just a bit. I had no intention of caring about what was in there. I told myself that the drawer was ajar, and a quick tug wouldn't hurt anyone. Then I saw what I'd always suspected.

"Those were from before!" The force behind him shutting the drawer startled me. "Those have nothing to do with you, Harper."

"Uh-huh." Panic grew inside me, and it must have shown on my face.

"Those were there well before we ever met." His brows rose with determination. "They're probably expired."

"You've had girls in here before?"

"Well…Actually, no," He forced out. "I've never had a girl in here until you."

"Oh."

"Does that factor into anything?"

"No, it's just interesting." I shrugged my shoulders. "That's all. I'm not mad—"

"You're not?" He perplexed. "I thought you would be."

"Why?" I looked up at him. "You said they were from before me."

"And you believe me?"

"Are you lying?"

"No," he snapped. "Honest, they were from before we started going out."

"Then I'm not mad."

"Why do you believe me so easily?"

"What would be the point of you lying?" I asked, not giving him a moment to answer. "You can easily get any girl you want whenever you want, and you know this, but you want to be my boyfriend. You want to be with a girl who hasn't done any of it, a girl you gave all the cards to."

He was silent as he looked down at me; he dwarfed me in comparison. Other than that, the only difference between us was his experience. In that room, though, we shared in total honesty.

"I really care about you, Harper," he breathed. "I don't care that you're a virgin. It means nothing to me."

I believed him, so I smiled, stood up, and reached for his hand. "Well, that's where we differ," I mumbled. "Come on, let's go."

Once we arrived in my driveway, I knew it was D-day. He would see more of me than I'd ever voluntarily showed a particular guy on purpose. There is a difference between wearing a black bikini to the beach and wearing a black bikini in front of a *specific* guy; the guys at the beach don't have names. Wearing one in front of a guy that does makes me feel much more vulnerable about the entire experience.

I'll never forget how I felt walking up the path to the front door and knowing that Scott was right behind me. I held firmly to the door handle. While attempting to focus on sliding the key into the lock, I lost my grip on the key and dropped it. Scott casually and without judgment picked up the keys and opened the door himself. He could no doubt feel my nervousness as it radiated through my skin and filled the entryway to my home. Standing in my large, empty house, I set my soccer bag down and spun around, looking at him. I reached for the two videos and set them on the hall table as he shut the large red front door and locked it.

"You want to?" I pointed to my room upstairs. I was thrilled that he nodded and didn't suggest anything more. The nerves continued to discharge through my pores. I walked slowly up my staircase; Scott kept the same pace behind me, despite his large legs. I tripped over the second step from the top out of pure anxiety. I felt Scott's hand grab my waist. Even though it was a reflex on his part, I still felt the nerves pick up their pace as he touched me. He'd touched me a thousand times on the waist, but for some reason, this time, as we were walking up to my room and I knew I was going to get undressed, his quick, reflexive action caused my stomach to flip all over again.

"You okay?"

I nodded.

"You sure?"

"Yes," I breathed.

I knew his question was about more than just me tripping over a step; I wanted to do this. I was tired of being scared and wanted to no longer be afraid.

"I'm good." I stopped at the top of my stairs and looked back at him. "Thank you."

I headed into my walk-in closet and found my swimsuit hanging exactly where I left it at the end of last summer before Scott came into my life. I looked over my shoulder at Scott and saw that he was looking at our homecoming picture and its frame, which had the year etched on it.

"Harper, I have the same one framed." I nodded at his enjoyment. "But I didn't get a frame with the year on it." He looked at me, smiling.

"I'm always shocked at how clean your room is." He grinned at me as he walked the perimeter of my room. "Not to mention how cheerful it is. It's such a *girl's* room!"

"Scott, have you never been in a girl's room before?"

"Nope!" He grinned at me as he continued to examine my bookshelves, desk, and nightstand. "Just yours."

He was right about my room being girly. My light purple walls, pink crown molding, and the beige carpet looked good with my white bedroom furniture. A soft green bed skirt with matching sheets and pillowcases graced the bed. A full-size white feather-down comforter sat on the bed, and a few plush teddy bears were securely tucked along my footboard. I watched as he picked things up off my desk to examine them: Pink- and silver-framed pictures, postcards, and makeup. He picked up a bottle of pink nail polish and carefully read the label before replacing it and moving on to an equally pink tube of lipstick.

I bit my lip and smiled at how happy he seemed to actually be in a girl's bedroom. I realized that this experience must have been equally as new for him as it was for me.

"Harp, I'm really proud of your hat trick—not because you slid in the mud, but because you actually scored three goals. You'll probably get a write-up in the Seattle Times."

I looked down at my bare feet on the beige carpet, focused on my red toenails. "I doubt I'll get a write-up. I mean, a girl from the worst team in the league scores a hat trick against the second-worst team in the league?" I shook my head. "I don't see it as being that big a story."

"Don't cut yourself short. You're unbelievable at soccer." He crossed the room to stand in front of me. He ran his fingers along my jaw and leaned in to kiss me quickly. "Plus, you're on the team that is the best of the worst. Be proud!"

"Okay, now you're sounding like Morgan. I'm good, nothing more." I stepped lightly around him and headed into my closet.

He wrapped his arm gently around my waist before I could step away from him. "Nope, you're much more than good, Harper," he whispered in my ear. I looked up at him and then enjoyed his much firmer and longer kiss.

"Thank you," I whispered.

I let go of his half hug and walked to the bathroom. I grabbed two beach towels, pranced back into my room, and handed one to Scott. He took the towel, and we faced one another. I had a feeling that one of us had a much faster heart rate than the other. If Scott's heart rate was accelerated, it was only because he may have been concerned for me and where this evening was headed. This was the difficult part for me to handle—the being-in-charge part. Whatever happened in the next moment was entirely on me; I'd invite it. I'd start it, and I most certainly would have to generate enough energy to have it, whatever it was, continue. My breathing was shaky and slightly erratic; the silence was becoming deafening.

"Harp, I'm going to...." He pointed to my bathroom, stammering through his words. "I'll be right back." He nodded and looked at me before walking into the bathroom I shared with Morgan.

I quickly ran into my closet and took my pants off, pulling my black bikini bottoms on and ensuring they were secure and not revealing anything I wasn't prepared to show. I quickly unzipped my hooded sweatshirt and took off my bra. I covered my depressingly small breasts with my forearm as if their sheer presence was enough to make me gag as I grabbed the top of my swimsuit. I pulled my bikini top over my head and tied it in the back, ensuring it was tightly secured.

I stood in front of the full-length mirror next to the bed and examined myself, running my hands over my waist and the curves of my hips. I turned, looking over my shoulder at my backside. I tugged lightly at the top's bow, ensuring it was secured. I noticed that my bikini top was a bit snug. It appeared as though I may have filled out a bit since August. I wasn't exactly overflowing in my top, but there was a noticeable difference: I had more of my chest showing than I'd usually had when I wore this top. Maybe this is how it always looked, and now I was a bit more cognizant of this fact since a specific someone would be looking at me. I examined myself a bit longer than usual, running my hands over my curves and losing the self-deprecating feeling I usually had about my body. I studied each fundamental fact about myself. I was short and small, but I had a great body. I was in shape; some might say I was more in shape than the average female athlete my age. My teeth were terrific. Despite my breasts being smaller-sized, they fit well with my size and frame. I decided to stop attempting to hide my chest and let the bikini top adjust as it would naturally. If I bubbled out a bit, so be it. I looked good.

"Are you ready?"

I turned around and saw him as I quickly grabbed my towel off my bed and wrapped it around me. All my recent self-certainty had been startled out of me the moment I realized Scott was actually looking at me.

"I didn't mean to startle you. You seemed ready." His eyes drifted up and down my body not once but twice. "You look good! Real good."

"Yeah?" I took a deep breath and held it as my eyes locked with his. "Thank you."

I looked at his bare chest and noticed he was incredibly fit. He was in such excellent shape. You could make out the indent of each of his abs, and his oblique muscles were exceptionally cut and noticeable. His white board shorts were cut low enough to see the V-shape that cut down his torso. He had an even tan throughout his entire visible body and not a single hair on his chest. I wanted to touch his chest. I wanted to know what it felt like to run my hands over each bump of every muscle that strived to push through his dark skin. Then, I suddenly realized I was more nervous about being near Scott's body than trapped in my own. I was nervous about the body of a half-dressed man who would soon be in my hot tub.

"Are you ready, Harp?" He pulled me out of my trance.

"Yes." I caught my breath. "I'm ready."

I walked toward him and lightly brushed up against his chest on purpose as I tried to squeeze by him to exit my room. It was a sly move that I am sure didn't go unnoticed by him.

"You've been sticking to the name *Harp*." I smiled. "Doing a good job at it, *Scotty*."

"It's our thing."

We walked side by side down my long staircase, and Scott gently laced his fingers through mine. We rounded the corner at the bottom of the stairs toward the long hallway to the kitchen. I stopped at the media shelf and began examining our CD collection.

"Scott, what do you want to listen to?"

He looked through the stack of CDs that our family shared. "Do you have any Hanson?" he asked.

I laughed, the laughter calming my nerves.

"Maybe some N'sync, if you got it?"

He wrapped his right arm around me as I laughed and leaned

back into his chest. He moved in front of me and thumbed through the stack. "I mean, it's been about a week since I've gotten my boy-band fix." He filed through each CD. "Oh, shit, Harper. Look! You've got some Backstreet Boys." He looked down at me. "Please, Harp, for me, would you?"

I clung to his chest from behind him as I tried to keep control of my laughter.

"Harp, it would really make my evening," he teased.

I moved to stand in front of him, feeling his hands wrap around me. "Are you good with this one?" I pulled out Live's *Throwing Copper*. He took it out of my hand without saying anything. "Maybe this one?" I handed Dishwalla to him and was surprised that he took it and put it back on the shelf. "Really?" I asked him. "I kinda like that album."

"No, that CD only had one good song, and it will get stuck in my head for days," he said. "And I know you, Harp. You'll play that one song over and over."

I pulled out the Foo Fighters' self-titled album. "Yeah," he agreed, "that one's good." He took it out of my hand and pulled Sublime out of the stack of CDs. "I'm convinced that this CD will never get old. We'll be in our thirties and still talking about how great this album is."

He lightly ran his fingers down my ribcage. The move was entirely absentminded, but I was tensely aware of how his fingers played with each bump of my ribs through my towel. I leaned my body against him and forced myself to embrace the feeling.

"Sometimes I wonder what people outside of Seattle listen to. You know, Harp?"

He asked this question as if it was a question of philosophical proportions. It very well may have been, but my mind was elsewhere. I was focused on Scott's long fingers on my ribs through a somewhat thin beach towel. I had to force myself out of my trance before my state became apparent.

"Scott, Sublime is considered rock rather than alternative or grunge. Foo Fighters and Live could be considered alternative, too, and I am sure that people outside of Washington State enjoy grunge also. We don't own it." I smiled.

"You're wrong, Harp. People outside of Washington are not obsessed with grunge like we are. I've seen it. Haven't you seen it? Think about Boston. Do you think they have a strong connection to April of 1994?"

I shook my head and tried to rein in my grin. It was teetering on a smirk as I watched and listened to Scott begin his rant about the Seattle grunge-music scene.

"That's right," he began, "they probably think the demise of Nirvana was just a blip in history. If they *do* listen to grunge, it's purely because they want to have a connection to Seattle. We should consider ourselves fortunate to live where we do." He continued, "And speaking of Boston." He pulled out a CD from the stack. "Why the hell do you have the Mighty Mighty Bosstones?"

"That was a gift from my cousins." I turned around and saw that his face was full of absolute disgust. "Before you get all high and mighty in your strong opinions of grunge music, I have to tell you something, Scott."

He stared down at me while holding me in his two very long arms and stretching against the wall.

"Don't change your musical opinion of me because I am telling you this, okay?" I laughed. "I'm being honest here."

He nodded, trying to placate me.

"Last summer, I saw the Bosstones in concert."

"Harper Sage Whitmore," he roared, pulling away from me, his towel in his hand, and heading toward the front door. "I'm leaving."

I couldn't stop laughing. He was nearly halfway in our hallway when he spoke next. "Seriously, I am out, Harper. I can't be with a girl who spent an entire evening listening to plaid-wearing Ska punk rockers playing live."

"Scott," I yelled, "I didn't pay for the ticket!" I couldn't catch my breath; I was laughing too hard. "Scott, don't go! It gets worse before it gets better!"

"Harper, I have no idea how it could get any worse than that." He turned and smiled at me. "You are a Seattle native and need to stay true to your roots." He walked toward me. "Tell me how it can get worse."

"Scotty, I actually have a favorite musician that isn't grunge. This artist isn't part of a band at all."

He leaned against the wall and looked down at me. "Tell me, Harp. I can take it."

"You won't leave?" I asked teasingly.

He shook his head and mouthed no.

"I'm not telling you." I laughed. "I'm going to put the CD in and let you figure it out when it comes on. I have to make sure you'll stay!" I winked.

"It better not be anything Celine-Dion related. I swear, I won't be able to deal with being with a girl obsessed with both *Titanic* and Celine Dion."

"Oh, but Scott, you promised to take me to see *Titanic* when it comes out," I pleaded.

"I might be breaking that promise." He shrugged his shoulders. "If I keep my promise, we'll be seeing it off-island. I don't want to run into anyone we know."

"Oh, we're seeing it." I laughed and pressed my hands against his chest, pushing him away. "Go start the hot tub while I put my favorite non-grunge-related music in—and I don't want to hear any comments from you while—"

He waved his hand toward me sarcastically.

I placed all the CDs in the carousel and grabbed the remote before following Scott outside. I opened the patio doors just as my favorite singer started. Scott slowly looked up from the water and stared at me, taking a deep breath and sighing. I took the remote and used it as a microphone as I sang along to Mariah Carey's "Fantasy."

"Really, Harper?" He smiled. "This is your favorite?"

"Really, Scott, she is." I put my hand up in the air, pointing toward the speaker. "Wait! Hold on—my favorite part is coming." Scott looked at me and smiled, I believe out of embarrassment for me. "I know all the words. Wait for it…."

"I want to hear it, Harp. I really want to hear it all." He encouraged me to continue singing, containing his laughter. "Tell me, Harp, when I walk by, do you get *kind of hectic inside*? I mean, Harp, *I am so into you.*" He spoke the song's lyrics, ending his little spoken-word jam with a smile so broad that his smile lines were showing themselves.

"Only when you're *talking sweet and looking fine.*" I recited the lyrics just as quickly as he did. "And you know the song, apparently, so no making fun of me!"

"Here it comes, Scott." I pointed to the speaker, "*Images of rapture/Creep into me slowly/As you're going to my head/And my heart beats faster/When you take me over/Time and time and time again—*"

"I gotta tell you, the dance moves are what really sold it. The voice was just shy of being spectacular," he said sarcastically, "but your dancing is what sold it, Harp. That did it for me!" He pointed to the speaker. "Did you happen to put the other CDs in? I'm curious to know if we'll hear more of your vocals tonight."

"Are you disappointed in me? I've loved Mariah Carey since I was in elementary school...It's similar to Morgan's love of boy bands. She learned to listen to other genres, but she'll take her boy bands with her where ever she goes."

"Fine, you can have your Mariah Carey, but I don't want any more musical surprises while we're together," he joked as he casually wrapped his arms around me for another hug before getting into the water.

He slowly stepped into the tub, skipping the three small steps leading into the tub, and turned around to face me. I could hear my heart pounding, and my pulse raced through my entire body. As I stepped up onto the fiberglass steps, I could feel the grips on the steps rub against the bottom of my feet. I focused all my attention on my tiny, red toes. My feet climbed down slowly while everything else inside me was racing. I usually raced down these steps—I'd done it hundreds, thousands of times—but tonight, I was going down them like I'd never been in my own hot tub. I arrived at the middle step and began to slowly unwrap my towel.

All the self-esteem I had gained upstairs, in my bedroom, was gone. I had nothing left. I was back to thinking that my body was less than satisfactory. I was back to assuming that Scott had seen better—much better. I was back to wishing that I had larger breasts.

I ensured my swimsuit was in its correct place and nothing was showing that shouldn't be before I completely unwrapped the towel. I carefully folded it twice and draped it over the heated towel bar, avoiding all eye contact with Scott. I immediately placed my palms against my bare stomach, overanalyzing each movement I made. I spent a few moments going over the best ways of actually entering the water without drawing any more attention to my less-than-perfect fifteen-year-old body.

I stepped down each step slowly, watching my red toes immerse themselves farther into the water. I slowly took each step into the hot water, keeping my eyes focused on the water level as it crept up to well above my now-bruised knee. I instinctively reached down to my knee to cover the bruises. I was startled when I felt Scott's hand touch the backside of my thigh and pull my knee out of the water.

"Does it hurt?"

I was relieved that he was looking at my knee, of all things. That way, he wouldn't be looking at any other part of my body. I quickly placed both my palms back on my stomach before answering him.

"No." I kept my eyes on his. "I think it will soon, though."

I had no time to think before Scott slowly ran his hand up the back of my thigh and wrapped his long fingers around one side of my waist. I stood, looking at both of my feet, flat on the floor of my hot tub, paralyzed by fear of his new touch. I was now only inches away from him; he slowly and gently moved both hands on my waist. I didn't say a word; I kept my eyes locked on my red toes. He pulled me closer to him. I felt his smooth, tan, chiseled chest against me as we pressed against one another. He pulled my hands to his waist and then moved his hands to my face and kissed me.

"You are beautiful, Harper." Of course, he'd known how nervous I was about this and how terrified I was of him seeing me in barely anything. "You've got nothing to worry about."

I clung to him, my forehead pressed against his chest. I was still staring at my red toes. "You really think so?" I whispered.

He pulled me closer, gently cutting through the water backward and pulling me with him. He sat down with his back against the corner of the hot tub, and I floated between his legs. I faced him, my breathing ragged. He ran his hand up and down my spine, looking at me.

"I really do."

"Scott?" I slowly pulled away from his touch. "Have you done this before?"

"What?" He looked at me, confused, and pushed closer to me. He reached for my waist, and I put my arms around his neck. "Do you mean hot tubbing with a hot girl I'm really into?"

"Sort of." I rolled my eyes and looked away, biting my bottom lip to the point of tugging at it.

"No, I haven't. Actually, I've never been in a hot tub with a girl before." He kissed me quickly and gently pushed me away into the corner. "So there!"

I floated away from him slightly, pressing my hands against his chest. I made every effort to keep only my neck above water and my feet from touching the floor.

"Really?" I smiled. "Never?"

He shook his head.

"That's amazing." I lightly splashed him. "I thought you'd done just about *everything*."

"No." He grabbed my waist. "See, Harp, if I was in a shared space—like a hot tub, for instance—I imagine that would spark conversation, and you know how I felt about conversations with girls. Also, the whole hot-water concept seems to be very romantic for women. Here now, with you, I'll agree it is a *very* romantic moment."

"You think this is a romantic moment, Scott?" I teased as I floated closer to him.

"Oh, I do, Harper," he exclaimed as his eyes widened with laughter. "I find going out to get pizza with you a very romantic moment. I suspect seeing *Titanic* with you will probably not be a romantic moment. I might have to draw the line there."

I threw my head back in laughter. "Oh, we're seeing it, Scott," I promised as I pushed myself closer to him. "We can see it off-island—that's fine, but we are seeing it!"

"God, you are hot, Harper," he breathed, causing me to catch my breath. He looked at me, cutting through the water and focusing on my body. "Unbelievable."

As he said that, all my fears of having a lesser body faded away, and I was back upstairs, thinking about how fantastic my small frame was in my bikini. I stood up in the hot tub and walked closer to Scott, who sat patiently watching me as I came toward him. I pressed my body against his, wrapped my arms around his neck, and sat on his lap.

"We're seeing it," I said under my breath.

He pulled me closer to him. I felt his hands exploring my body and realized we were making out. I felt slightly inclined to pull away, but I ignored that feeling as I continued to enjoy his hands on my ribs, back and waist. I enjoyed it all. His lips pulled away, and he kissed my neck, letting his lips run the course of my neck and jaw.

He pushed toward me, and we floated to the other corner of the hot tub. I felt his hands run over my thighs, and I slowly wrapped them around his waist. I hung onto his neck and kissed him. I paid attention to his every touch; he was aware of this and subsequently cautious. He ran his hands along the safe parts of me, the parts he'd touched before. I wanted him to journey to more parts, but I knew he wouldn't. I knew he'd wait until I said he could. I wanted to say it—I wanted to tell him to touch me wherever he wanted to, but I didn't have the words. I didn't know the words. I just knew I wanted him to feel me, to touch more than just my back, my ribs, my thighs, and my legs. I wanted him to know that he could go farther. I finally pulled away from his lips, and he went beyond my safe parts—he felt me from behind. He didn't slap or hit it like he usually did at soccer games or in the high school parking lot; he clung to it as he pulled me onto his lap.

I ran my hand down his chiseled chest and wrapped one arm around him as we continued to kiss. I felt him lace his fingers onto the elastic of my bottoms, not going any farther than that. I ran my free hand down his abs and around his waist, never unlocking my lips from his.

I continued to get lost in Scott's touch. I wasn't the same Harper.

I somehow got lost in the moment and enjoyed everything around me. My back against the hot tub, I felt him pull closer to me, and there it was. For the first time in my life, I felt the full extent of what I could do to a man, to Scott. I looked at him again before I kissed him, pulling myself closer to him. I felt him against the inside of my thigh, and I knew then that I wanted to do it. I wanted to see it – him, right there. I was nowhere near ready to go beyond making out, but I was curious about what it would be like to feel it in places other than my inner thigh. I continued pulling myself closer to him, forcing my need to feel him subside.

He slowly pulled away from me and glided back to the opposite corner, smiling as he sat down and looked at me. I smiled at him, biting the corner of my lip. I looked down into the bubbling water around my chest and quickly spun away from him, embarrassment taking hold. I fixed my bikini top again to cover my now exposed chest and dropped my head into my palms as embarrassment flooded through my body. I wasn't embarrassed just because he saw me, though that would be embarrassing enough; I was also embarrassed because he'd seen me wanting him, wanting more than what he was giving me. Scott had felt me touching him both directly and indirectly. He had felt me wanting him, pulling at him for more, and because of that, I was humiliated.

"Harper." I felt Scott's hands wrap around my waist and run down the front of my thighs. "It's not a big deal."

"It's a big deal to me, Scott," I whispered. "I'm not like—"

"Stop it!" He spun me around. "Harp, I'm not with those girls anymore. I'm with you. I don't want to hear about how you don't think you're as pretty as other girls or how you don't feel like you amount to much. You are unbelievable, Harper."

I ran my finger along his smile lines. "You really think so?" I whispered. "I was so nervous about tonight—you have no idea. After I asked you if you wanted to…I immediately wished I could have taken it back. I felt like I was in way over my head."

"Harper—"

"No, it's true," I barked. "A million things ran through my mind just after I asked you to come over, one being that I didn't exactly stack up to the other girls you'd seen or been with."

"Harper, you need to stop thinking that," he assured me. "I was never a boyfriend to any of those girls. They meant nothing to me."

"It's really hard not to! Everywhere I look, people are telling me about this girl or that girl who was once linked with you. I look those girls up in old yearbooks and, yeah, they're kinda hot, Scott!"

"But they're also kinda slutty," he said very matter-of-factly. "They've been around—a lot! They've not just been with me."

"Scott! I popped out of my bikini tonight," I reminded him. "I might be considered slutty."

"Not a chance," he assured me. "You'd have to have popped out in a large group on purpose while completely drunk repeatedly throughout your high-school career. I'd also have to tell you repeatedly that I don't want to be your boyfriend, and you'd still have to throw yourself at me." He shrugged his shoulders. "I was the only one that saw anything tonight, and I am your boyfriend. I'm not going to tell anyone, and neither of us is drunk." He leaned in and breathed in my ear, whispering, "I am also the one that really enjoyed seeing it."

"I was all over you just now. My behavior might be up for question!" I covered my face. "I am completely embarrassed about that, Scott. Oh, my God! You have no idea how humiliated I am about that."

"Are you kidding me?" He pulled my hands away from my face. "That was hot, Harper! I thought it would take us much longer to get here. Don't be embarrassed about that. That was not slut behavior."

"The definition of a slut isn't exactly cut and dry," I explained. "One minute, I am completely shy, and as soon as you tell me I'm hot, I am all over you. That seems slutty to me."

"Well, Harp, if you want to be my slut, that's fine, but I don't share." He slowly kissed my neck and gently ran his tongue up to my ear. I enjoyed the feeling of his breath as it tickled along my neck. "I thoroughly enjoyed you being all over me, and if telling you you're hot gets you hot for me, then I think I found what it takes!"

"You did?" I asked, surprised. "Was I good at it, Scotty?"

"Harp, you were a natural—especially the part when you tried to ride me." He smiled and pulled away. "I think I might be done for tonight, though, unless we are having that *talk* now." His face looked pained.

I pushed myself toward Scott. "Scott," I whispered as I floated between his knees, "what if I told you I was thinking?"

"I'd say I figured as much." He grinned. "But it's up to you...."

I splashed him and pushed him away. "I know, and sometimes I wish it wasn't. It would make things a lot easier."

"What, you want me to tell you when we're ready?" he teased, "because in that case, I'm ready to do this."

"I know you are." With ease, I climbed onto his lap. "I felt it very clearly on my thigh."

"Look, who's not afraid to touch me now!" He laughed.

I got out of the tub, reached for my towel, and wrapped myself up, keeping the towel only around my waist and allowing my bikini top to show.

"Look what one hot-tub session with Scott Pierce does to my little Harper!"

"What's the point of hiding them now?" I laughed. "You've already seen them."

"No, I didn't," he groaned. "I saw one, and let's be clear, Harp, it just made me want to see both at the same time."

"Are you joking?" I asked. "I can never tell."

"Come on, Harp, tell me: What are my chances tonight?"

"Scott," I sighed. "I'm kinda—"

"I know, babe."

We entered my room. I felt Scott's hand along my waist again and knew our evening had changed our relationship. We found ourselves in a much more open space. After the hot tub, I was capable of reciprocating Scott's touch without a feeling of inadequacy coursing through my body. I pulled loose from his grip and headed into my walk-in closet to get dressed.

I put on a white camisole and pink satin pajama shorts. I felt somewhat shy about how I looked in my ordinary pajamas but not nearly as nervous as I would have felt if our first hot-tub session hadn't happened. I left my closet and saw Scott tying his sweatpants. I immediately felt saddened inside. I wanted to at least "accidentally" see what I had done to Scott. I could have spun it as an accident when it would have been entirely on purpose.

"Harp, do you want to make out?"

"Why?" I smiled as I leaned against my closet doorframe. "I thought you couldn't because it was too *hard*?"

"It is," he emphasized, "but that pajama ensemble you got going on is worth the aggravation."

"Scott! I wear this every night." I posed for him and spun around, sashaying toward him. "It's nothing special."

"It is when you've never seen it before."

"Let's put our movie on, and then we'll make out while pretending to be interested in what we're watching." I fell into his arms and watched my hands run along his chest. "I can feel myself becoming a make-out queen, Scott!"

I pulled away quickly and raced out of my room and down the long flight of stairs, crossing the hallway and into the large living room. I laughed as I heard bare feet patter on the hardwood floor behind me, knowing that Scott was immediately behind me. I knew I'd won when Scott caught my waist and picked me up, lightly tossing me on the oversized sectional and crawling over me.

"Scott!" I pointed to the television. "You have to put the movie on. That's how it works!"

"Is that how it will work when we see *Titanic*?" He pulled away and picked up the video. "Huh? Is that how it's going to work during a three-hour-long movie? We're going to pretend we're watching it while I make a play to feel you up?" He turned on the television and pushed the tape in. "'Cause if that's how it will work during *Titanic*, I might be good with seeing it!" He returned to crawling over me. "Hmm?"

"You can take me to see it off-island in two weeks, and I'll tell you then what might happen afterward." I beamed at Scott, becoming more and more at ease with him. "But in the meantime, you can feel me up right now."

"Will do!"

I realized then how I could get Scott to do more than just play it safe with me. I relaxed on my back in my nothing-special pajamas and watched him crawl on top of me. In one motion, he ran his hand over the course of my body, starting mid-thigh. He fell over me and kissed me hard, aggressively, his kiss containing purpose and determination. I pushed my hand into his hair, pulling him into me, and wrapped my legs around his waist as I embraced my newfound sexuality.

"I have something to tell you," he whispered while he ran his lips over mine. "I've wanted to say this—"

"Tell me," I demanded anxiously, a vast amount of excitement in my response, "but only if it's good."

"It's very good," he replied between kisses. "I've never said what I have to say before, so I'm a little unsure what to do."

"Is it about how much you're enjoying this evening?" I pulled my head back and looked up at him. My smile was enormous, much larger than Scott's. "Because I'm hoping you've never enjoyed yourself as much as now."

"It's much more than that," he replied as the movie flashed behind him. I could see the images from the television flash across the side of his face and along his back; the colors from the television were vibrant against his skin in my dark living room.

"It's about how much you mean to me. It's much more than just this evening."

"Oh, Scott." I held his face and ran my thumb across his lips as I smiled. "That means so much to me!"

"You honestly don't care about the drawer and what you saw?"

"Nope," I quickly replied, looking up at Scott's eyes. "What happened before me has nothing to do with me. You've never had a girlfriend, so I think you value certain things in your life and certain titles, and your girlfriend is one of them."

"You've figured me out," he mumbled.

"If you were just going to use me for sex, you wouldn't have put so much effort into us. You'd simply try to focus on getting me alone in places where people wouldn't notice us. You probably wouldn't even come to my house."

"That's true," he whispered as he pressed his forehead against mine, our lips gently brushing against one another. "I'm not proud of those days, Harper, and I only recently started to not be proud of them."

"I care what those girls say when they start to use my name to hurt you or when they start to say mean things about me," I whispered. His lips gently touched my face, and he leaned over me. It was sensual, intimate, and, most importantly, honest. It was the closest we'd ever been, both physically and emotionally. I was feeling him directly and indirectly again, but it was pure in its emotion this time. "Scott, not sleeping with you has more to do with me than you, and I'm not proud of how slow I am on this subject."

"I know that, and I understand why," he whispered, "but don't change because of me."

"You do?" I asked with shock. "You really do?"

"I've never met a girl who both wanted to be with me and was terrified of being with me at the same time," he whispered as he tucked a damp curl behind my ear. "Most girls don't care how they feel afterward. They just hope that I'll hold their hands on campus."

"Oh, Scotty," I declared gleefully, "*I really care about holding your hand on campus*—not for anyone else's sake, but because *I* love it!"

"It pisses a lot of girls off that we hold hands," he said flatly, "but that doesn't mean I'm going to stop holding your hand."

"I've heard they're all pissed off," I whispered, "and they all want to destroy me."

"They won't," he replied. "Maureen and April both seem to find enjoyment in scaring them off."

"I don't know about that, but those two seem to enjoy knowing what goes on between us."

"Trust me, Harp—those two have never had anything to do with me. They are very into each other." He smiled. "I learned that in the eighth grade."

"Is that when you lost it?"

"Lost what?" His brow pulled together tightly.

"You know! The first time you *did it*."

"Fourteen. Eighth grade. Mia Jones. Back of the school bus, underneath the seat. The ferry ride home from a field trip."

"Where was the field trip?"

"The Seattle Science Center."

"Were there people on the bus?"

"Yes."

"Did people know?"

"Only because she told people."

"Where is this 'Mia Jones'?"

"You ask that like that is allegedly her name." He smirked and rolled his eyes. "She dropped out, I think, halfway through tenth grade."

"Was it her first time?"

"Oh, God, no," he groaned.

"Fascinating story."

"You're not freaked out by it, are you?"

"Not at all. That was before you knew me years ago, so why would I care? You experienced that—I can only listen and learn."

"Is there anything else you're interested in knowing?"

"You know what I'm interested in?" I whispered as I let my hands run down his bare chest and latch onto the waistband of his sweats. "I'm very interested in *you*."

"Oh really, Harper? Tell me what you're interested in me doing." Scott ran his large hand under my shirt and locked his lips on mine. I wrapped my legs around his waist. "God, you are hot, Harper."

I wasn't ready to commit to a sexual relationship yet due to my underlying fear of almost everything related to sex, but it was my issue alone. Scott hadn't pressured me in any way. I focused my attention on the feeling of Scott's hand under my shirt as he was feeling my breast for the first time. I slowly moved my hips in response to Scott on top of me. I'd have removed my camisole if I hadn't had such a handicapping fear. A voice in my head was screaming for Scott to take it off himself. All the emotions running through me, the thoughts, and the internal commotion were exhausting. The end result was both of us asleep on my sofa.

My mother woke us up at one in the morning by rubbing on both my arm and Scott's. "Guys, we're home. Harper, why don't you go upstairs? Scott, I'll get you another blanket. It's way too late to drive home."

Scott slowly started to get up. "No, I can drive home, Mrs. Whitmore."

"Please stay. It's fine. And please stop calling me Mrs. Whitmore. I prefer Julie!"

I looked over at Scott and smiled. While my mom went to the linen closet, I slowly got up but was pulled back down. "Harper, goodnight." He leaned over me and kissed me goodnight. "I still have something to tell you."

"Hmm? Tell me," I said anxiously. "Is it about how you're taking me to see *Titanic*?" I pressed my forehead against his and whispered, "Or is it about feeling me up *under* my shirt?"

"I gotta say they did feel really nice!" He laughed softly before he looked toward the linen closet and saw my mother returning. "I'll tell you later."

Just then, my mom appeared with a bundle of blankets in her hand.

"Okay, tell me tomorrow," I demanded, still giggling at his comment.

"What's so funny?" Mom looked at us as we sat on the sofa next to one another. "Did I miss something?"

"My girlfriend has become completely obsessed with seeing *Titanic*." He nudged my ribs and smiled. "She's losing her cuteness."

I thought I would have immediately fallen asleep when I got into bed, but the thought of Scott sleeping downstairs kept me awake for most of the night. Restless thoughts about Scott's hands running over my body kept me awake; the excitement of wanting more with Scott kept me alive and vibrant.

It was well after three in the morning when I finally resolved to sneak downstairs, quietly passing my parents' room and slipping into the living room, where Scott slept. His right arm was bent over the top of his head, and his left arm casually draped across his now-bare chest. The white sheet and heavy blanket were pulled only as far as his waist, escalating my earlier thoughts. I slowly tiptoed toward the large sofa where Scott slept. I watched him; he was even beautiful when he slept. His soft skin was in the shadow against the bright, moonlit sky. I decided to attempt to be aggressive.

I gently pulled the heavy blanket and sheet up and rested my ninety-eight-pound body against his, facing him. I pressed my palm against the sofa above his shoulders and delicately kissed him, my bottom lip meeting his top lip. I was slow, barely touching him. He was still very much asleep when I began kissing him, though soon, he slowly became more receptive. One of his palms rested flat on the bare skin of my back as his other hand slid underneath my shorts, grabbing me from behind as if he'd never needed permission to take what he wanted. His kiss was forcefully aggressive; he pulled my body against him, and I finally felt what I wanted again.

I woke up late in the morning to Scott sitting on the edge of my bed and softly touching me. The feeling of his deft index finger as it traced the length of my arm woke me up fully.

"Harper," he whispered into my ear, his breath dragging down my collarbone as he showered me with kisses. "Harper, I know you're awake."

When I didn't respond, he stopped touching me softly and decided to wake me up by forcefully tickling me. I decided then I wanted to lose my virginity to Scott Pierce.

FIVE

WE'D GOTTEN GOOD—REALLY GOOD.
We'd arrived at a place in our relationship where we couldn't keep our hands off each other. Scott had gotten better at pulling away before our make-out sessions went too far. We were inseparable. We weren't nervous around one another any longer. We didn't fear the unknowns in our relationship. We embraced what we meant to one another. A few days before Christmas, on a Friday afternoon, I decided to tell him I was tired of being a good Catholic girl.

Our Friday night was planned: He had a basketball game against Shoreline High School. He intended to break the league record for three-point shots. I was sitting in the center of his bed, watching him prepare for his game when I chose to tell him. It did not come out exactly as I had planned.

"Scott, I have something I need to say," I mumbled.

"So do I. Brad told me he's going to some ceremony for Leigh." Scott's brows were pulled tight. "It's at her church, which is also your church…."

"Yeah, I know about it." I shrugged. "It's not for a few months."

"You have the same ceremony, right?" Scott pressed. "It's some sort of confirming or something?"

"Scott, do you go to church?"

"Never." He grinned. "Not by choice, anyway. My parents are agnostic. I really have no idea who Jesus is or what he did, but I imagine it must have been something pretty major."

"Ooh." I giggled.

"What's so funny?"

"Nothing, it's just kinda funny; I mean, you use his name all the time."

"Is that a problem?" Scott immediately got serious. "Do you think of me differently now because of my beliefs?"

"What are your beliefs?"

"I have none," he stated flatly. "I don't even think about it."

"Hmm." I thought about it. "I don't think of you differently—not even a little bit."

"Good. I'd hate to see us break up over something trivial like beliefs."

"No, we won't break up." I chuckled. "The ceremony is called Confirmation. It's something Catholics do to dedicate themselves to the religion for the rest of their lives."

"I gotta be honest; I'm slightly hurt that you didn't invite me. I heard about this from Brad, who's not even Leigh's boyfriend," he exclaimed. "You don't sound exactly thrilled about the experience, so I suppose I'm not exactly hurt anymore."

"I haven't been talking about it because I feel like I've been trapped," I stated. "I feel like I've been manipulated into this! Someone my age shouldn't be forced to make decisions like this! I really don't care about it."

"Harper!" He grinned. "I've never seen you upset like this."

"I'm not upset. I'm just not excited about my Confirmation," I clarified. "I feel like I'm being tricked, and that's not fair."

"What exactly is a *Confirmation*?"

I took a deep breath and slouched into Scott's bed. "I have to dedicate myself to the Catholic religion. I'm essentially confirming my life to Christ by way of Catholicism."

"Why does this bother you?"

"It bothers me because I spend my days thinking about *other* things at fifteen. I'm *not* thinking about whether or not I want to be Catholic for the rest of my life," I exclaimed. "I am convinced the nuns know I'm not taking this seriously. They are boxing me into a religion I might not want."

"And at fifteen," he asked me, "what are you spending your days thinking about?"

"Mainly?" I sighed and rolled my eyes out of embarrassment. I knotted my fingers together and avoided any eye contact with Scott. "*Us*. I'm not going to be a very good Catholic with the thoughts I've been keeping."

"Leigh isn't a very good Catholic. She hasn't been for some time." He grinned. "There must be some additional rules in Catholicism to cover *her* thoughts."

"Yeah, it's called confession." I smiled. "I haven't done it in ages, though, and I don't want to. I'm expected to go to confession before I'm confirmed, and I'm worried I might be in there the longest."

"What could you possibly have to confess about?" He laughed. "You are the most wholesome girl I've ever met."

"Um, the constant making out with my boyfriend, for one." I laughed sarcastically while Scott rolled his eyes. "There is also the constant *thinking* about making out with my boyfriend and me *touching* my boyfriend, and then we slide right into me *thinking* about touching my boyfriend!"

"Hey, it's through the pants!" He grinned and chuckled lightly. "Since when does *thinking* about anything require a follow-up with confession?"

"According to the Church, *thinking* is the same as doing." I laughed. "Which isn't true at all! I can vouch for that."

"It all comes down to what you do with your thoughts," he teased. "Most of *my* thoughts have been taken care of on my own time."

"Now you can see why I hate the church," I screeched. "I want out of this thing!"

"What does Leigh say about all this?"

"Leigh said she's just doing it for her parents' sakes, but what's the point, then? I mean, you're supposed to be doing it for yourself because you believe in the religion. If Leigh is just going through the steps to make her parents happy, if she doesn't buy any of it, then it's a meaningless experience. I don't want to have a meaningless experience. I'm *not* going to get boxed into this."

"Can you tell the Church that you're not ready to do it? Maybe you could suggest that you'll be in a better place next year."

"I've thought of that. I even sat down with one of the sisters at the church. She told me that I should speak with the priest, which is basically boxing me into a confession. The sister said that my heart may be filled with sin."

"What sin?" He roared with laughter. "You haven't done anything!"

"Um, yes, but I've *thought* about doing something."

"Harp, it sounds like this thing has you boxed in at every corner," he exclaimed. "You can't win!"

"I could *not* do it and then live with the supposed guilt of not being Catholic."

"Harp, babe, I'm not Catholic, and I don't have any guilt." He smirked. "I seem pretty content."

"According to the Church, that's because you haven't been enlightened yet," I said sarcastically. "See, the Church has got you pegged even if you *aren't* Catholic."

"What does your mom say?"

"Oh, that's the other thing," I roared. "No one in my house even takes this church crap seriously. I mean, we barely go except on holidays and…Really, we only go on holidays. Even at weddings, my parents skip the church part."

He casually crawled onto his bed and relaxed next to me, his hand carefully spinning a curl around his long index finger. I slyly pulled myself closer to him. "Harper, I'm going to ask you something, and I want you to be totally honest. I know this goes against the original rule—"

"It has nothing to do with sex," I snapped. "I've never associated being a virgin with growing up Catholic."

"How did you know I was going to ask that?"

"Because you never get serious in a conversation unless the subject is associated with a problem we're having, and the only problem we're currently having is my virginity."

"Harp, it's not a problem."

"It is for me," I exclaimed. "I've never believed in saving myself for marriage, which is the whole idea in Catholicism. It's another reason I'm rethinking this whole Confirmation business. Please, don't feel insulted that I didn't mention it or invite you to it."

"Harp, I'm not insulted. I wish you had told me sooner that this was something you were dealing with."

"You really wanna hear about this sorta stuff? You're not even religious!"

"I don't need to be religious to care about how you feel about this."

"Thank you." I smiled softly.

"You seem to know exactly what you believe in and what you don't." His fingers slowly dragged down my arm, distracting me from our discussion. "I think you have an argument for getting out of this, and I'll support your decision. If your parents go insane and kick you out because of your decision, just know that you can always move into my spacious bedroom."

"Yeah?" I laughed. "You'll take a virgin in?"

"You? Yes!" He grinned.

"Good to know." I smiled and lifted his chin up toward me. "My non-religious fear of sex is fading away."

"Is it?" he whispered as he kissed my cheek, gently moving over to my ear. He knew what he was doing and how I'd reciprocate. "It was never the actual act?"

"No," I breathed.

"I gathered that much," he whispered. "I remember when you snuck downstairs last month—"

"Yeah, and that took a lot of guts on my part." I grinned at the memory. "My fear has been about how I'll feel and how *you'll* feel afterward. Will we be different?... That sort of fear."

"Harp, I'm not going to answer any of those questions because this is something you need to figure out. I can't tell you how you'll feel after, but I can tell you that I won't feel differently about you."

"See, that's why I needed to come over here right after school," I exclaimed softly, gently pulling back from his touch enough to keep a somewhat safe distance between us while I explained. "I've been wanting to tell you how I feel for a while."

"How do *you* feel, Harper?" He emphasized his words carefully. I knew exactly what he was getting at, and he was right. I needed to start telling him how I felt about things. "We've gotten very serious in a very short time, so I hope you feel good about us."

"It's not bad!" I chuckled. "It's good. Well, *you* might not take it as good. It's probably good for me, but it won't be if you don't consider this good."

"Is this about the ashtray you made me in art? I didn't throw it away; I left it on my nightstand," he teased to ease my nervousness. "I'll keep that for the rest of my life."

"It's not an ashtray!" I chuckled. "It's a jewelry dish."

"It's something you threw in the kiln for a grade!" He laughed and pointed to his nightstand. "I left it on my nightstand, and you'll notice hair-elastic thingies in it. Sometimes I'll wake up and find one on my pillowcase."

"That's cute!" I giggled. "Maybe I should remind you how the hair elastic got on your pillowcase—"

"I know how it got there; your hair gets tossed around while I am feeling you up pretty aggressively."

His lips pressed firmly against mine, the force of his kiss pushing me into the pillow and deeper under his control. His lips found my neck. His hands became distracted, and I encouraged it. They had a path, a routine journey they took down my body, but this time was anything but routine for me. Hopefully, it was anything but routine for him. My body screamed with excitement as I breathed in the smell of Scott, enjoying his touch.

"I have to tell you this, Scott," I breathed.

"Tell me," he groaned into my neck.

"I always think about how much I enjoy being this close to you."

"You can't really get any closer than me being in only my boxers," he mumbled, losing his hands under my shirt. "I already know how much you love *this*—"

"How about *me* in your boxers?" I breathed.

He stopped. He didn't move; he simply looked at me. His hand remained frozen on my ribs. His face was full of surprise—his virginal girlfriend had offered herself up.

"Are you surprised?" I panicked and scooted a bit out from under him. "You must have realized that I would eventually come to this point. The way we've been this last month has been incredible, which is why I had to rush over here today."

"Honestly, Harper, I thought it would be in the New Year, maybe in February, you'd finally believe that I loved you, and we'd do it then!"

"You what?" I panicked. My face must have reflected my shock as a slight fear grew inside me. "What did you say?"

"Fuck." He sighed and collapsed next to me. "That's not how I wanted to tell you. I had a whole plan about how I'd tell you, and this wasn't it."

"I don't care about your plan," I exclaimed. "I want to hear it again!"

"Harper," he breathed heavily. "Was it too soon? I assumed you knew, but you weren't open to hearing it. Isn't that why you never pressed me when I told you I had something to tell you?"

"I never pressed you because I don't press you on anything," I told him, defending myself. "I would never demand anything of you."

"Was it too soon?"

"Scott," I whispered quietly, my heart rapidly increasing in speed. "That is what I wanted to tell you. I wanted to tell you that I love you."

"Harper—"

"Scott, I'm sorry." I could feel tears behind my eyes. I just said the hardest thing I could imagine.

"Harper, please don't cry. You have nothing to be sorry for. This is a good thing!"

"I do! I didn't think you loved me—it never occurred to me that you loved me. I kept my feelings to myself for so long. I decided to tell you I wanted to sleep with you because I figured that would be easier than putting my feelings out there."

"Harp, I've never said that to anyone, myself." He softly wiped a tear away. "I'm not upset that you didn't say it sooner."

"You're not?" I dabbed at my eye and smiled. Scott pulled me closer. "You don't care that I didn't say it first?"

"I don't care at all," he assured me. "I'm just glad that it's out there."

"But the way you wanted to say it for the first time—"

"It doesn't matter. I'd probably get the same reaction," he teased. "You'd probably still cry. At least this way, I got to see it rather than visualizing your reaction to reading it on a card."

"I do love you, Scott." I smiled. "I really do!"

I clung to him. He hadn't hugged me this tightly before. I could feel the warmth of his breath on my neck. Demanding more of it, I kept my arms tightly wrapped around his neck. I fought his release of me but lost. I accepted the feeling of his forehead pressed against mine. His kiss was gentle and reassuring.

"Now stop crying." He laughed. "We're fine."

"I know."

"Harper?" He grinned as he dragged my body to the center of the bed and let his hands get lost. "About the wanting to sleep with me? *That* is news to me."

"Ah." I chuckled. "We're past the emotional stuff?"

"*Way* past it!" He forcibly kissed me before he dragged his lips along my neck again. "I'm ready to start having meaningful sex."

"Don't," I snapped, quickly placing my finger over his mouth. "Don't ever remind me of your past. I already remind myself enough."

His head drooped, and shame took hold of his face. His comment had been meant to be innocent and harmless, perhaps even self-deprecating, but my reaction was a clear reminder that I didn't ever want to hear about *them*—his girls. His soft blond hair tickled my face. He kept his head hanging, avoiding eye contact. I kissed him slowly, gently, and sincerely on his lips but found him to be not as receptive. I saw the guilt in his eyes.

"It's alright," I whispered. "It's my problem."

"I won't ever do that again," he assured me.

"Hey!" I smiled. "Don't be like that! We're good."

"I want to say this, but I'll only say it once: This is the first time where it matters. This counts! I've never had this before, and I'll be having it with someone who will value the experience and taught me to value it."

"You made this easy—"

"Harper, you made this easy," he corrected me. "I've never said that before, but I've wanted to say it to you for a long time. I wanted to tell you a few times, but I wanted to tell you in a way that you'd remember."

"I'll always remember the first time someone told me they loved me. I'll never forget this—"

"I don't want you to think of this as the first time *someone* told you they loved you; I want you to remember this as the first time *I* told you I loved you."

"Scott," I sighed, "I'll never forget this moment."

"I'll never forget this moment, either." He grinned. "This is when my girlfriend offered to come into my boxers."

"Every time we hot tubbed together, every time we were alone, every time we watched television together…Even when we went out to dinner, I thought about it," I explained. "I'm always thinking about being *that* close to you, which was how I knew I was ready. I've fantasized about the experience a million times, and I'm ready to actually live the experience."

"Harper, no one has ever been as close to me as you are."

"I know."

"You matter to me. I've told you things about myself that I've never admitted to anyone, and you made it easy to do that."

"I've told you things about me—"

"Harper?" He smiled. "Stealing from bulk candy at Safeway isn't exactly criminal behavior."

"I still never told anyone about that."

"It proves that you're better than me," he declared. "You'll always be a better person than me."

"That's not true," I argued. "You know that isn't true! You are an unbelievable person! Just look at how we are together."

"I've only been that way with you."

"And that's all that matters," I told him. "All that matters is how we are with one another."

"And you made it so easy for me," he breathed. "I never thought I'd find anyone as understanding as you. I never thought I'd find someone I'd fall in love with so easily."

"And that's why I want to…." I let the rest of that statement hang before going on. "I've thought about this so much, and I'm tired of thinking about it. I'm ready."

He lowered himself onto me as I opened my legs; instinctively, his hands crawled up my shirt. He moved carefully, methodically, and with purpose. He peeled the white long-sleeve cotton shirt over my head before lowering his lips to mine again. Suddenly I felt it again—he was present and against my hip. I smiled as he kissed me forcefully, and I pulled the blue comforter over his body, closing us off.

"I've wanted us like this for a long time," he breathed into my neck. "Just us…"

"Scott!" I beamed with excitement. "This is happening…."

I followed the movements of his hands. He was forceful and aggressive, unlike any other time we were this close together. I knew where each finger was going as it traced and outlined my entire body. I fell deeper under his control as I sunk farther into his pillow. I had no idea where I was or what I was doing, but I knew that I was under a power greater than my own, and I didn't care. I embraced it. I assisted him in unbuttoning my pants and tugging, pulling, and yanking them off my hips. He tossed them onto the floor.

"Harper," he informed me, smiling, "button-fly jeans are not allowed anymore."

Like the time in the hot tub, I could feel him pressing against me. This time, though, I was feeling it in places I wanted to feel it. While enjoying his kiss, I dragged my fingers down his chest and latched onto his waistband. I slowly tugged at his elastic band as Scott worked on my generic white department-store bikini-cut panties. I wanted them off, mine and his; I wanted to release the shame of my ignorance about fashionable undergarments. I could feel his middle finger slip underneath the band on my hip, latching onto it.

His hand released the band, still in place, and my panic ensued. He didn't take my panties off; he slid his hands up my back to the back of my bra and quickly, with one hand, undid my white department-store bra. We'd never gone any farther than this. The soft tickle of his fingers brushing the straps off my shoulders caused me to remain in a trance of Scott's power.

"You're so beautiful, Harp." He looked at me, and I watched him staring at me, at my body. "It's like I'm looking at you totally differently. We're in a totally different place right now."

I draped my arms over his shoulders and pulled him tightly against me, preventing him from seeing me. I felt embarrassed as, yet again, the realization that he had seen better fluttered through me.

"No, don't," he instructed me. A slow smile emerged on his face. "I want to see you."

"You do?" A different flutter occurred in my stomach when his hands touched me again, and I transformed into the only girl he ever loved. He saw how I openly accepted his touch. While my eyes stayed locked on his, his hands explored my vulnerabilities.

"You're so soft," he breathed as he delicately touched and caressed me, working his way down my body and under the waistband of my white panties. "I want to feel all of you."

He traced, outlined, and touched me softly in a place I'd never explored. I fell farther into his pillow as my body moved in ways it never had before. The excitement of his touch roused me into pressing my lips firmly against his. My tongue entered his mouth as he continued circling his fingers slowly. He plunged his long middle finger inside me.

"Ahh!" My head rolled back from the sheer shock and intensity of his action. "Scotty!"

"You're into this." His lips moved along my neck as his fingers moved faster in and around me. "Say you want it, Harp...Say you need it."

"Scotty," I breathed, "I want this."

Biting my lip, I smiled and watched him reach into his top drawer. This was happening. We'd built ourselves up to a place in our relationship where reaching into his nightstand drawer was a welcoming gesture. We both snapped our heads toward the window when we heard the sound of two doors slamming shut and a single car alarm, followed by a masculine voice.

"Who is it?" I panicked as he pulled away from me and maneuvered off the bed, untangling himself from the sheets and heavy blue comforter before tripping over to the window. "Someone's here?"

"Fuck," he roared. "My mom—"

"Oh, my God!" I rifled through the covers, looking for my shirt, jeans, and bra, and not finding them. I panicked as I tripped out of his large bed. "I can't find my shirt!"

"Shit, Ethan's with her. Damn it!"

"Oh, my God." I panicked again. "Where's my bra?"

"Harp! Harp, babe, come here." Scott pulled me close to him. His body was warm as I came to rest firmly against his bare chest. "I want to feel you once more before I go into the bathroom and calm down."

His hands dragged down my spine, and then he began teasing his lips down my collarbone and farther along my chest, working his way down until he was kneeling in front of me. I draped my arms softly over his shoulders and laced my hands into his hair.

"She's in the house, Scott," I panted as I knotted my fingers into his hair, physically demanding him to continue his attention to my chest.

"I don't care," he mumbled. "This is the first time I've seen you like this."

"Scott," I breathed, "you gotta stop!"

"Fuck..." He groaned and rested his forehead on the space between my still-exposed breasts. "I want to be inside you."

I knew what he was doing in the bathroom. I wasn't ignorant. I've always known what happened in there every time we got that close. I was lying on his bed, dressed again in my jeans and long-sleeve white cotton shirt, trying to slow my heart. I could hear Marie downstairs talking to her grandson, and all I could think about was

Scott locked in his bathroom, quickly "calming himself down" with his right hand—and all I wanted was to participate.

I couldn't stop thinking about what he was doing in there, and I was anything but relaxed by that thought. I idly flipped through a *Sports Illustrated* magazine as I sat cross-legged on his now-made bed. I filled my mind with useless basketball statistics to avoid thinking about opening that door and helping him "calm down."

"Hey Harper!" I snapped my head up and saw Marie standing in the doorway, looking cheerful and perfectly put-together. Her voice was perky and enthusiastic when she said my name. "I wasn't expecting you! Where is Scott?"

"He's in the bathroom—" I nearly blurted out what Scott was doing but stopped myself just in time and remembered the basketball statistics. "—gearing up for his basketball game tonight, you know?"

"He's going to do wonderfully," she exclaimed. "I'm so excited that we're going together. Ethan's downstairs. I'll send him up to say hi!"

Before I could wave goodbye, she was on her way down the hall and stairs, yelling for Ethan.

"Harper!" Scott leaned against the bathroom doorframe and smiled as he dried his hands. "That was good, but it better have a different ending next time."

"Scott." I smiled. "You're…calm. You took care of yourself, and I am left completely high-strung!"

"Harper," he whispered as he leaned into me, "you could have done the same."

"I've never done that." I shrugged. "I wouldn't know how."

"Really?" His brows pulled together tightly. "I haven't stopped since I was thirteen. But you…*Really*? So this afternoon was the first time—"

"Yup!" I smiled. "First time ever."

"I like it." He leaned toward my lips. "I like that I was the first ever to touch you."

"That, I believe." I laughed. "What are we doing after the game?"

"It's up to you." He grinned. "Do you want to get drunk at the bluff again, come back here, or go to your place?"

"Well, I was wondering if *everyone* was going to be there?"

"It's always the same crowd," he said as he sat beside me on the bed and casually held my hand. "Is that a problem? I figured you liked Brad, and the other senior guys seem to like you. I like Leigh—"

"No, I like your regular friends, and I know you like Leigh," I mumbled. "I'm just more concerned with the guys that hang around you—the ones that don't like me."

"Who doesn't like you?" he snapped. "Has someone said something to you? Harp, no one can upset you and claim to be my friend. No one can upset you...*period*!"

"That guy Barrett—Barrett Hudson," I clarified. "I know he's your friend, and I try to be very nice to all your friends, especially Brad and the guys you've known your whole life, so I'm not starting anything. I just stay away from *him*, usually. I don't think he likes me."

"Barrett Hudson is *not* my friend," he declared. "He follows Brad and me around because he thinks he needs us."

"Oh, I thought he was a friend." I shrugged. "I never said anything because of this. I mean, you two played tennis together, and now you play basketball together."

"What has he done? What do you know about?"

"What do you mean, 'what do I know about'?"

"Harper, I just need to know exactly what he did."

"Well...Nothing, really. I mean, aside from how he speaks. He doesn't speak to me, but he'll say things about me knowing I can hear him. I am also having a difficult time with how he looks at me. He stares."

His lips were pulled tight as he nodded, but it was clear that he was fuming inside. This reaction of his was one of the reasons I was reluctant to continue my concerns and worries about Barrett.

"He likes to stare...A lot," I clarified. "I can handle it, but tonight I'd rather it just be you and me. I'm not in the mood to deal with him."

"I know what he's been up to," he whispered. He leaned over, putting his upper-body weight on his knees, and examined my small hand, which was firmly between his two very large hands. "He's said a few things when he thinks I'm not around, but he knows I know what he's been saying. He wants you, but he only wants to fuck you."

"Scott!"

"He doesn't want you as a girlfriend, either. He may have initially wanted you as a girlfriend, but he's given up on that. He just… *wants* you, and I stand in the way of that."

"Maybe I should tell him I'm all in with you." I smiled and shrugged cutely. "He might back off."

"He knows that already, and he doesn't like what he sees," Scott informed me. "That's why he's watching you. He wants to see you alone."

"He doesn't bother me when you're around."

"Exactly," he snapped. He punched his mattress with enough force to cause me to bounce. "He's tired of seeing me, Harp. He used to go to your soccer games and scream your name; I tolerated it then, but now…I mean…Now, I play on the same team again with him, and I will not tolerate him commenting about you!"

"What does he say?"

"It's less about what he says and more about what he does. I assumed the situation was manageable as long as you were never bothered by it, but now you've noticed it. When you meet me outside the locker room, he's watching us. He's watching my hands on you and memorizing what your hands are doing on me, and it bothers me. On the way to an away game, I'll sit in the back of the bus and mention you, and suddenly, he'll start to listen in. I'm not even mentioning anything really important."

"Scotty?" I showed a very large smile in hopes of getting him back in a good mood. "What are you mentioning about me?"

"Last Friday, the guys asked if I wanted to hang out on Saturday night, and I mentioned—" He cleared his throat and tried to hide his smirk. "—that I was going to the movies with my girlfriend."

"Did you tell them what movie you were taking your girlfriend to see?" I grinned. "Out loud? Did you name the movie title?"

"I said I would be seeing a long film about a sinking ship!" He laughed, but it sounded bitter. "The guys started laughing and making bullshit comments about 'who kidnapped Scott Pierce.' I laughed, too. I mean, I'm not exactly the same guy I was last basketball season. That Barrett kid just had to chime in, though. He's a freshman on varsity basketball; he needs to keep his mouth shut!"

"Well, I don't know about that." I groaned. "I was on varsity soccer as a freshman and didn't always abide by that rule."

"I bet at the beginning you did! Once it got around who your boyfriend was, the seniors probably started thinking of you differently."

"I mostly stayed to myself, even after it got around who my boyfriend was. I was terrified of being around all those older girls, but there were times that I'd goof around on the bus with the seniors, I guess."

"Barrett doesn't understand that concept and has consistently butted into conversations and situations he doesn't belong in. During the last away game, he decided to tell me how whipped he thought I was. He said I'd better get a hand job in the theatre."

"He what?" I snapped. I jumped to my feet, tearing my hand out of his. "Why would he say that? He doesn't know anything about us. He doesn't know anything about *me*!"

"He said it once, but he'll never repeat it," Scott promised. "I nearly beat the shit out of him on the bus. Not one senior laughed, and he knew he fucked up."

"Oh, my God, I'm so mortified." I groaned. "The guys on your team, for a moment, had an image of me doing that. I'm so embarrassed; I *can't* go to the bluff tonight."

"Harper! *Harp*! It's alright. Calm down! It's alright." He reached for my hand and pulled me into his chest. "I can assure you that no guy thinks about you doing that for me—they think about it being done to them."

"Scott, that doesn't help."

"It's true, Harp. They look at me with you and are pissed—Barrett especially. That's why he watches you and memorizes what your hands are up to. He wants to replay it later for himself," Scott explained. "But Harp, listen: He won't say that to you because he knows I'll beat the shit out of him."

"Scott," I whined.

"Hey guys!"

We turned and looked at the door and saw Ethan standing against the doorframe. He could have been Scott's twin, his exact clone. Ethan had the same hair, same skin, same blue eyes, and same perfect grin. He even had matching jeans and sneakers. I could have quickly fallen for his soon-to-be nineteen-year-old charm if Ethan had been at PC back in September.

"I'm here to see you break this bullshit 'record'," he teased Scott.

"It's not bullshit," Scott explained to him. "I'm the only player in the league to come this close to breaking it, so even if I don't nail the two necessary three-pointers tonight, I'll still go down as the only player to come this close. Plus, I have like nineteen more games to play this season, so I don't even have to hit them tonight!"

"Scott," I groaned. "You average five three-pointers a game! You can casually walk into this and take your time. You don't have to rush out and hit them both immediately."

"Harper," Ethan coaxed, "he does. You'll hate sitting next to me through the whole game if he doesn't. I'll catch you both downstairs!"

"Scott?" I leaned into him slowly and gently kissed him. "I think we should skip the bluff altogether tonight."

"Couldn't agree more!"

I wore his blue away-game jersey. He was number twenty-two. I always looked adorable at the games, wearing whatever jersey he wasn't; my hair was done in two French braids, ribbons in the school colors tying the braids off. I even used blue glitter hairspray. Like always, I sat next to Marie, Jack, and Ethan on the second bleacher from the floor.

"Harper!" Marie sat very close to me, as she always did. She pointed toward the main entrance of the gym. "Your friend Leigh is headed this way. You don't have to sit with us if you don't want to."

"Oh, no, Leigh likes you guys," I exclaimed. "She'll sit with us!"

"Is she Brad's girlfriend yet?" Marie teased. "I'm just...curious."

"She'd like to know the answer to that also!" I laughed.

"Leigh," Marie addressed her as she neared us. "Is Brad your boyfriend?"

"I have no idea," Leigh stated. "At this point, I'm fine with whatever we are. It's not like he has any other girls hanging around him, so if we're anything, we're exclusive."

"Leigh!" Ethan leaned in toward her and winked. "I'll be your boyfriend if that's what you're looking for. I don't know you that well, but you seem like my type."

"Ethan, you're nearly nineteen," Leigh countered. "I'm fifteen. It wouldn't look good."

"So?" He scowled. "Scott's eighteen and Harper's fifteen."

"It's different, Ethan," I explained. I tilted my head and smiled. "We're both still in high school."

"What happens next year?" Ethan pressed. "He'll be a freshman at some other school."

"Ethan," Marie snapped, "be nice to Harper."

"I am," he groaned. "I'm just saying that Scott will be nineteen next September. Harper is still going to be in high school, and he doesn't even know where he's going next year. How solid is this relationship, *really*?"

"Ethan," Marie snapped. "We spoke about this! Be nice to Harper."

"We'll be fine," I assured both Marie and myself. "We'll figure it out."

"You absolutely will." Marie's hand casually rubbed my back. "And Leigh, *I* think Brad's your boyfriend, but just to be sure, you should ask him. Better yet, I'm going to speak with his mother."

"I'd rather see how long this continues," Leigh told Marie.

"Leigh," Ethan started, grinning. "I'll be your boyfriend. The title is secure!"

"Seriously, you're old," she teased him.

The topic of my future with Scott consumed me. I was fixated on Ethan's words and newly concerned with Scott's reliability. The reality was very real at this point—Scott would graduate this spring. I was now worried that every feeling, emotion, and desire Scott and I shared was purely temporary. He would leave while I stayed and grew up.

I was so consumed with this new worry my mind blocked everything around me. The mindless chatter continued between Leigh, Marie, and Ethan.

Scott's voice rang through the crowd, and the shield lifted. When I saw him standing on the sidelines, the ball balanced between his arm and hip. His blue warm-ups were still on, and beads of sweat already rolled down his temples. I smiled at him as he waved me over. I ignored the discussion of Leigh's relationship with Brad, and Ethan reminiscing about his high-school basketball days, and walked toward my boyfriend. My mind and senses were back, and I was clear about my present with Scott, if nothing else.

"It's almost tip-off, Harp," he yelled into my ear.

"You're going to shatter this record," I cheered at him, "well before halftime!"

"You made tonight's game a lot harder for me to concentrate on this afternoon." He smiled and pulled my body to his chest, kissing me right there in the crowded gym. His hands slid down my back and into the back pockets of my jeans. He never removed his lips from mine. He pulled me closer to him, letting the ball drop and roll onto the court. Apparently, he was too busy engaging in a generous public display of affection to worry about the ball. "God," he whispered against my mouth, "I had a great time this afternoon."

"Even if we didn't have the best ending?"

"Doesn't matter. This game is gonna be tough, even if we did have the desired ending."

"Scott!" I grinned. "Your parents are ten feet away; they can see what your hands are doing!"

"My *hands* should be the least of their worries." He grinned. "You *had* to tell me you wanted to sleep with me three hours before tip-off. I might just start chucking three-pointers into the air to wrap this game up!"

"You're going to do this! This record is yours!"

With the cheerleaders, the pep band, and the game itself, the gym was filled with loud noise as I sat between Marie and Leigh. Sitting on that hard wooden bleacher, I had to tell someone the excitement that brewed inside me, and I knew that Marie wasn't an option.

"Leigh—" I yelled in her ear.

"I already know."

"How?"

"You two are different," she yelled. "It's like a weight has been lifted between you two! You seem to be able to touch each other however you want."

"Really?"

"Who said it first?"

"I was going to, but he beat me to it!" I chewed the straw for my water with a large grin and nodded. "I wanted to say it—I think about him, about *us*, all the time. I'm consumed with being his girlfriend."

"Are you in love with him or in love with being his girlfriend?"

"Him," I stated without hesitation. "More than anything."

"Did he tell you why he loves you?"

"He says that he sees me as someone that makes him feel like he can be loved."

"Can you imagine being eighteen years old and already thinking that sex is only about the act and nothing more?" Leigh rolled her eyes and shook her head. "Do you know how many he's had...like his...*number*?"

"I do." I nodded.

"Well?"

"It's not exact, and he doesn't like to talk about it," I mumbled. "There are a few he doesn't remember exactly, but he knows something happened."

"Brad told me... Not his *number*, but that there were times Brad had to go get him. Do you think anyone on the team still uses?"

"Scott thinks a few freshmen use on the junior varsity team, but for the most part, he thinks varsity is clean."

"I think that Barrett kid uses," Leigh mumbled, "but I'm not certain. He's the only freshman on varsity—I think Brad and Scott don't really like him."

"I don't know him personally." I shivered. "Scott told me all about him this afternoon, though. I told Scott today I don't feel comfortable when he is around, and he clued me in."

"Harper, darling?" Marie's hand suddenly resting on my back was enough to startle me out of my quiet conversation with Leigh. "Do you want anything from the concession stand?"

"No, I'm good." I beamed. "But thank you."

"Alright." She rubbed my back once more, quickly, before leaving.

"I think Marie is obsessed with you!" Leigh laughed. "She's always rubbing your back, smiling, or holding your hand."

"I know," I chuckled. "I think she's afraid I'll leave Scott. The reality, Leigh, is I don't think I could run away even if I wanted to. It's like he has a hold on me. Take how he looks at me right after they announce his number, for example. It's hard to explain. The gym is absolutely insane with people, but Scott always runs through the tunnel before the game and manages to find me. In this huge crowd, he finds me. He looks right at me, and it's like no one else is in this gym at all, just us...I think maybe I've always loved him. It's like, throughout our entire relationship, I've been working toward loving him, but I didn't know it was love until I actually said it!"

"Ah, shit!" Leigh's eyes shifted toward the exit to the gym. "Heads up. Taylor's here."

We both looked to see if Taylor was coming at us now. Sure enough, she walked right up to us. "Harper, are you going to the bluff tonight after the game?" Taylor asked snidely. "Actually, I want to know if Scott will be at the bluff tonight *without* you."

"Honestly, Taylor? What are you doing? I don't get it. What did I do to you? Did Scott do something?" I figured if I played nice, maybe she'd be willing to cease her hostility toward me, and I could enjoy the rest of my freshman year. "I just don't understand—we were friends last year, and now you hate Leigh and me."

"She hated us for about a *week*, Harper," Leigh corrected me, "and then her worst nightmare was realized, and she found out that her ex-best friends were getting the attention she wanted!"

"If Scott did something," I continued to Taylor, "let me know, and I'll try to fix it. Scott's very understanding."

"Hey, Taylor!" Leigh leaned toward her conspiratorially. "We were just discussing something you might be interested in."

"Highly doubtful," Taylor snapped.

"No, you'll probably find this is something you'll really want to hear," Leigh coaxed. "It's real interesting!"

"Fine, tell me." Taylor seemed less than interested in hearing Leigh's news.

"We were just discussing how much Scott loves Harper and how much he dislikes you. Stop asking about him!"

"Leigh," Taylor asked, "Don't you get tired of riding Harper's coattails? And Harper, don't you get tired of riding Scott's coattails?"

"Hey!" Ethan leaned toward Taylor. "Blondie, I was just reminded this evening, from my grandmother, of all people, that we're not supposed to be mean to Scott's *girlfriend*. I took that to mean Scott isn't fucking easy broads anymore. Apparently, he's found a girl good enough to be *with*. My point here is you missed your shot with Scott. Last year would have been the year to try to hook up with him. This year, though…This year is different. Sorry."

"I never wanted to *fuck* Scott," Taylor seethed. "And who are *you*, anyway?"

"Oh." Ethan stretched his arm out to shake Taylor's hand. "I'm Ethan, Scott's nephew. Whether you wanted to fuck him or not, it doesn't really matter. Even if you didn't want to, you would have—they all do. Well, except Harper, and I can see why."

"Harper?" Leigh looked at me and touched my shoulder out of concern. "Taylor's just pissed because she's not riding anyone."

"Leigh, fuck off." Taylor snapped her head toward Ethan. "And you, too!"

"Oh, that's right, Taylor," Leigh corrected herself, "you *are* riding a few seniors, but none of them are Scott!"

Leigh and Taylor were about to get into it when I stood up. Scott was on the edge of the three-point line, and his feet were already in the air as the buzzer went off. The ball was already in the arch position. If he made it, it would count. I held onto Leigh's hand, but Leigh didn't notice. She was about to get into a complete blow-out with Taylor.

"Taylor," she shouted, "you're never going to have him!"

"Leigh," I screamed, "he's going to do it!"

I squeezed Leigh's hand tightly as the ball arched. Scott had already landed, back on his feet. As he moved back to catch his position, he watched it sail. His eyes never moved from the ball. His face lit up as he watched that three-pointer sink through the hoop. I screamed, and it was as if Scott could hear only me. He stared at me as I cleared a single tear off my cheek. Fans behind me patted my shoulders and arms as they screamed for Scott. I never took my eyes off him; I squeezed Leigh's hand again tightly, never moving my eyes from him. Ethan pulled me into a hug.

"He did it, Harper," he yelled. "He did it!"

Scott smiled at me as I embraced his nephew, and then his eyes moved behind Ethan and me and looked at the people beyond. Crowds of fans were looking at him, their faces full of excitement and congratulations. Our school was only leading by a few points, but that three-point shot broke the record for Scott. I stared at him as he walked backward into the locker room, smiling, his arms in the air.

Suddenly, the excitement was over for me. Leigh and Taylor were still arguing, and Taylor's following words shot through my chest, producing the most intense pain of my fifteen-year-old life.

"I've already been there," she proclaimed. "Wasn't even that good. I turned him down."

Leigh was still holding onto my hand. She turned ever-so-slowly to look at me. The people in the stands filed out toward the concession stand until halftime was over, but I stood there, staring at Taylor and holding onto Leigh's hand. I felt like my entire life was hanging in the balance.

I wanted to hit Taylor. I wanted her to feel the pain that I felt and the agony those lies created. The halftime show was beginning. The cheerleaders were already running onto the court, but I stood there staring at this girl who used to be my friend.

"Harper, no, she hasn't," Leigh whispered. "Don't believe her."

"You're still here, little girl?" Ethan interrupted. "Why? I thought Leigh told you to screw off. I thought *I* told you to screw off. Harper, where is my grandmother with the food? I'm starving!"

"She is on the sideline talking to Brad's mom," I stated with no emotion. "Taylor just said Scott has been with her. Why would she say that?"

"I heard that." Ethan dismissed her words. "She's lying to get under your skin. It's obvious. I'm going to see my grandma."

Taylor stood there looking at me; she had to be able to sense the rage that was coursing through me. I stepped down onto the lower bleacher, closer to Taylor. I felt that she was starting to get scared. Her words were losing power with each inch I moved toward her.

"Say it again, Taylor," I dared her.

"Oh, Harper," Taylor said, "you thought you were the first freshman to catch his eye? That's cute but untrue."

"Scott doesn't like you," Leigh yelled. "You know this, Taylor!"

"That's because I remind him of what he can't have anymore."

"Harper," Leigh assured me, still holding my hand, "Taylor is lying. Even if she wasn't, which she is, you know what? It doesn't matter. Scott is with you, not Taylor." Leigh turned to look at Taylor. "Isn't that right, Taylor? Scott is with *Harper*, not *you*."

I nodded my head in agreement with everything Leigh was saying. She was right—Scott wasn't with Taylor; Scott was with me. I wasn't going to forget that and start listening to Taylor now.

"You're right, Leigh. Scott is *with* me." I grinned. "He told me before the game that he loved me, Taylor. Did he tell *you* that he loved you?"

"It wasn't about love, Harper."

"No, it's not about love with you, Taylor." I grinned. "That's what makes me different. *You* aren't the girl that gets told she is loved—you're a commodity, nothing more. I'll be at the bluff tonight, and Scott will be there, too. With me."

"Ya hear that, Taylor?" Leigh laughed. "Harper and Scott will be going to the bluff *together*. Maybe you could make an appearance."

"Taylor," I asked her, "Even if what you said was true, why would you tell me? Talking about it makes you look like the senior-chasing whore you are."

"Good luck with Scott, Harper," Taylor seethed before storming off. "It won't last."

"That girl almost ruined your night," Leigh proclaimed.

"Almost," I agreed.

It was nearing the end of halftime, so I jumped down the bleachers and stood on the sidelines to meet Scott.

"You did fantastic," I cheered at him. "You got them before halftime!"

"What are you and Leigh gossiping about?" He grinned. "Anything worth repeating?"

"That's private girl talk." I attempted to hide my smile but failed. "I do have a tip to pass along, though."

"All ears!"

"Brad better put a definition on what he is to Leigh," I told him conspiratorially. "Real quick, too! Enquiring minds want to know."

"How many minds?"

"Three."

"Who's the third?"

"Your mother."

"Yikes! Brad had better put a label on it, then. That woman will press him!" He laughed. "Hey, was that Taylor girl bothering you two?"

"No, but she was spreading nasty rumors about you," I smirked. "It was not nice at all!"

"About me?" His brow raised. "She doesn't even know me—"

"Well, that's a relief!" I interrupted him. "From the gossip she was trying to spread, it seemed like you two had a *thing* in the past!"

"Ah! No...*thing* ever existed between her and me," he declared. "I can assure you."

"So, I'm your *only* freshman?" I squirmed closer to him and into his arms while he dropped his ball and kissed me. We ignored the family-friendly catcalls from the stands as he pulled me closer. "Good luck," I wished him.

"Thanks."

He won the game against Shoreline. I say *he* because he made four additional three-point shots from the deepest point of the arch, adding to his new record. He was good; he loved to play, and it showed. He dominated the court, acting just as a senior captain should act. I watched the second half with intent and dedication. I took everything in as he listened to his coach on the sidelines and then spoke with his hands as he communicated everything to the rest of the team. He deserved the two scholarships he was offered. I was saddened that one of them was in Arizona, but he hadn't decided upon a school yet, so I didn't let it get me down.

"See you at the bluff tonight, Harper?" Leigh reminded me. "I don't care what you and Scott have planned tonight; you are *both* going to be in attendance at the shore."

"Is Ethan coming?" I teased as he stood just as Scott does, with his hands in his pockets. "Hmm?"

"Nope." He smiled. "I'm going to dinner with my parents and grandparents, and then I'm starting my weekend plans of doing nothing before heading back to Central on Sunday. But...ah...Maybe Leigh, here, would like to join me? I am free until Sunday at noon."

"You know Brad, and I are—"

"Are what?" He grinned. "No one else knows, so tell me."

"You're going to be nineteen," Leigh whined. "My parents would kill me!"

"Is my age the only reason you're not interested?"

"I'm not answering that."

"You're scared!"

"Harper, see you and Scott at the bluff," Leigh ordered, "or else!"

"Scott and I will be there!" I smiled as I watched Leigh trail behind Ethan as they worked their way out of the gym. I waited patiently at the edge of the first-row bleacher for Scott. I began dribbling a ball before I walked it over to the hoop and made my only shot.

"You're solid on that shot, Harp!" Scott's voice echoed. "Now, make that same shot a foot farther away."

"No." I grinned. "I can't!"

"You might surprise yourself!"

"I won't...I have no follow-through."

"If you've got anything, you've got follow-through."

"If you say so."

"Are we headed back to my home or yours?" he asked while speeding by me and stealing the ball mid-dribble. "'Cause I gotta tell you that getting drunk at the bluff is the last thing I wanna do tonight."

"I sorta got corned by Leigh and promised we would at least show up." I attempted to guard him while he made routine shots from all the angles of the key. "And if we make an appearance," I reminded him, "we can easily disappear."

"Harp, trying to guard me isn't working for you." He dribbled around me and quickly spun before making a layup. "We'll show up, and then we can do our own thing."

"Good idea." I snagged the ball and dribbled to the top of the key. "We just have to say hi, and you just have to have one beer with Brad."

"You'll never stop looking at the ball while you dribble." He laughed. "I swear, you're gonna trip over your feet."

"Nah, I won't trip." I dismissed his idea. "You guard me *way* too tight for me to fall on my face."

"I never guard you; I stand there and follow your footwork to the hoop. I don't even need to anticipate your footwork—it's always the same pattern." He laughed. "If you want, I can really guard you. You won't make it past a single dribble!"

"Thanks for giving me a fighting chance, Scotty."

"It's your height that does you in!" He laughed. "And your size."

"Off to the bluff, then?" I dropped the ball and stood on my tiptoes, waiting patiently for his lips to meet me halfway. "We'll stay for a little bit and then get out of there?"

"Harper!" He said as he kissed me. "Your manners are what got us into this. We *should* be skipping the bluff tonight."

"Coulda, woulda, shoulda," I exclaimed. "We'll go for a bit and get outta there."

We arrived at the bluff much later than everyone else. About five different bonfires were already roaring down the length of the shore. If I knew Scott, he'd probably want to sit by the fire with the fewest number of people and leave quickly. I had figured that tonight Scott would want to hear over and over about his remarkable record, but he seemed pretty content with having just me and a few of his close friends praising him.

With the ease that only a small person could have in the situation, I hopped over the front seat and settled in the backseat to change into comfortable clothes before we gathered around a bonfire. I rummaged through my running bag, looking for weather-appropriate attire, and located some black sweatpants and one of Scott's oversized hooded sweatshirts. It was hardly sexy, but I wasn't really concerned with being sexy when I was packing.

"Scott, are you going to give me some privacy?"

"Harper," he promised as he smiled and continued to face me. "I'm going to watch."

"Scott," I whined, tilting my head and smiling out of embarrassment. "Alright, try to keep your hands to yourself."

"Babe, that is an impossible task."

I pulled my jeans down and tried to pull the cuff over my heel. Scott climbed over the front seat and landed on me, knocking me onto my back. He grabbed the cuff of my jeans and pulled them off with ease, tossing them onto the truck's floor.

"Thank you, Scott!"

He kept looking at me—not at my face or my eyes, but at me. I felt like he could see through everything I had been afraid of when he looked at me like that.

"Harper, you and your manners! Ever since that day in the locker room, I knew you had *great* manners. Here they are again, distracting us from what's really important."

He ran his hands up and down my thighs and played with the elastic on my white bikini panties. His middle finger dipped under the elastic while the rest of his fingers tightly gripped the band. I was screaming inside for him to take them off. I watched his hand as it tightly, yet very gently, held the elastic. I wanted nothing more than for him to quit being gentle and be the way he was earlier, back in his room.

I reached into his bag and pulled my black sweatpants out of panic and fear about what I wanted him to do. I was simultaneously screaming at myself for grabbing my pants and Scott for not taking my panties off. I never took my eyes off his as I held onto my sweats;

I was terrified of what would happen if I looked away. I may have looked calm on the outside, but the internal struggle and turmoil were killing me.

"When are you going to take them off?" My voice cracked.

"I love the anticipation." He smiled. "I love seeing it in your eyes."

"I don't think we can do it here." My voice cracked again. "Everyone will see."

"I have tinted windows."

He pressed himself against me, kissing me harder than before while his hands remained locked on the elastic of my panties. I was thankful that he kept pushing the sex issue. I wanted him to be forceful and take charge, to be aggressive. I enjoyed the feeling of him against me so much that I used my legs to intensify the message I was hoping to send—I wrapped both my legs around his waist and urged him to continue grinding against me.

"Plus," he added, "even if we plan to do it, you still won't be ready for it."

"What's that supposed to mean?" I asked indignantly. "You still think I'm a kid? I was ready for it this afternoon!"

"I didn't mean it like that! I mean, this isn't something you can prepare for. It's not a test that you can study for. It just has to happen." He pulled me up, continuing to play with the elastic of my panties. "Listen, Harper, I know you very well, and you would never want your first time to be in my backseat. No matter what signals you might be sending now, I know that would royally piss you off later."

"Oh, you think you know me so well, Scotty. You think you've got me all figured out?" I teased as I pulled myself up and pushed him off me. "Okay, let's do it here. Right now."

I climbed onto him and reached for his jeans, laughing uncontrollably.

"It's on, Scotty," I promised, laughing and teasing. "I am going to destroy you. You think you've got this all figured out? You think it's all sewn up, and you're in charge now?" I giggled at his glowing grin. "You'd better watch out—I will obliterate you!"

I couldn't catch my breath; I was laughing so hard. Scott managed to pull my shirt off and wrestle me down to the point of not breathing at all. I continued to be unable to catch my breath as Scott's quick grip, and nimble fingers kept me laughing uncontrollably. I let out occasional screams as Scott's hands journeyed across my body to all the exact locations where he knew to tickle me.

"You really think you could destroy me?" he questioned, laughter causing his already wide smile to widen further. "I have a foot and a half and well over a hundred pounds on you, and you're going to destroy me? Harp, I'm barely touching you! What's so funny? Harp, why are you laughing?"

"I can't breathe, Scott! Stop it!" I roared with laughter as I tried to squirm out from under him. "Quit it! I give up!"

"Are you done, Harp? You give up?" he teased. "Or am I still taking your breath away?"

"Scott!" I laughed. "Is this how you want to do it? Me in my bra and panties, and you holding me down?"

"Harp," he continued, laughing and trying to hold his smile back, "are you getting smart with me?"

"Calm down, Scott," I joked. "You don't want to find yourself in a situation where you'll need to 'calm down' later on."

"Harp, that ship has sailed! I have a partially dressed hot piece of ass in my backseat!"

"Oh, pinning partially dressed girls down is what does it for you?" I giggled.

"Oh, Harp, you're about to wish you hadn't said that!"

He laughed as I continued to squirm away from his grip, laughing uncontrollably. Scott continued to move his hands along my body. I finally caught my breath when he let me go. He reached over and gave me my sweatpants, which I had dropped in our tickle fight, and his hooded Mariners sweatshirt. He watched me get dressed, but he wasn't just a passive voyeur. He rubbed my thigh as I put my foot through the leg of my sweats, and he touched my back as I leaned over the seat to get my sandals; he wrapped his arms and hands around my stomach as I pulled on his sweatshirt. I pulled the hood up to my face and took a deep breath. He must not have washed it because it smelled just like him—the smell of freshly applied Old Spice deodorant and soap wrapped around me. I felt him touch me and looked over in time to see him watching me.

I climbed over the backseat and unlocked the hatch of his truck from the inside, waiting for Scott to meet me in the back. I dangled my legs over the edge while Scott sat down next to me and started to unbutton his jeans. He was utterly immodest. He really didn't care who saw his baby-blue boxer shorts. I watched him. I made no pretense of eye contact; I just looked at his blue boxers.

"Take it all in, Harper!"

"Oh, Scott." I hopped down and faced him. "After what I felt this afternoon, I don't know if I can."

"O-oh Harp, I don't know about *that*," he groaned. It sounded very sexual; he spoke those words in a way I'd never heard from him before but knew I wanted to hear again. "But if you wanna see more, I'll show you," he promised. "Just say the word."

"The word."

"Such a smart-ass!" He smirked.

I kept my hands in my pockets, though it took all my strength, as he pulled his pants up his legs. I so badly wanted to see *it*. I wanted to know what one looked like right in front of me. I wanted to see *his*, but I was never bold enough to admit it. He slid his Adidas sports pants up and quickly pulled me close to him into the truck's bed. He spun me around like a rag doll and pulled the hatch down, tapping the dome light of his truck. He gently pulled his waistband down.

I couldn't speak; I just stared. I was nervous and afraid of what to expect. I'd never seen one in my life outside of the health textbook, and that image had tarnished my vision of *it*. I'd hoped that's not how most of them looked; I needed to know that Scott wasn't as ugly as the health-class image. Scott was too beautiful to have something as ugly as the image in our textbooks attached to him.

Suddenly, there it was. I didn't even have enough time to really get anxious. I sat cross-legged between his long legs and looked at it. This was the first time I'd seen a real one in my life, and it was nothing like I imagined, nothing like I saw in health class. I couldn't imagine it being inside of me. I gasped like a child and pulled myself closer to him. Now, more than ever, I wanted to get my first time over with and experience being with Scott. Instead, my virginity shined through.

"Scott?" I breathed.

"Hmm?"

He held my hand and pulled me closer to him. His lips meeting mine just then was almost enough for me to forget my juvenile question. I knew I couldn't look at him when I asked the question on my mind—the only logical thing was to keep kissing him and ask through the kiss. I knew the answer was probably something obvious, something I must have missed. The question was probably something only a naïve virginal girl would ask, but I had to know why.

"Um...So," I mumbled, "why does *yours* look different from the picture in health class? It looks...*prettier.*"

He didn't laugh. Instead, he touched my face with one hand and pulled me closer with the other. He kissed me, and then his lips ran along my neck up to my ear.

"The one in health class isn't circumcised."

I could hear his smile. In typical Scott fashion, he made a joke about the situation as he pulled my face away from his. "I imagine the one in health class would give anyone nightmares. Fuck, it gives me nightmares, and I have one! I think they show that one to girls on purpose to try to scare them off from ever having sex."

"Oh."

"You gonna stop staring?"

I shook my head but mouthed, "yes."

"That's my Harper."

"I've wanted to see it for so long," I whispered. "Each time, we were close. I was terrified—"

"Hey," he reassured me, "don't be terrified anymore. It's just us."

"Can I touch it?" I blurted, unsure where the bravery to ask derived from but trusting at that moment he wouldn't judge my asking.

"You can do whatever you want with it." His confident smile grew wide as his eyes remained fastened to mine, and he reached for my small hand, never removing his eyes from mine and placing it on him. His lips returned to mine and became much more demanding, and I never let go. I simply gripped; the length and girth didn't seem plausible, but I was too enamored with the moment to question it or even focus on anything more than how much I loved Scott.

"Can we skip the bluff tonight?" I pleaded, enjoying the feeling of his lips on mine and his hands running over my body. "It was such a bad idea to come here. We need to leave."

"Where ya want to go?" he asked as he started to unzip my sweatshirt and move his lips to my chest. "We can go anywhere. Just tell me."

"Can we go to your room again?" I breathed. "I know your family went out to dinner."

"Harp," he whispered, focusing on my bra hooks, "do you want to do it tonight?"

"I think I do," I breathed. "I wanna pick up exactly where we left off this afternoon."

"I agree," he breathed between forceful kisses. "Tonight would be perfect."

"I leave for Boston on Sunday," I reminded him. "I'd like to leave for Christmas looking forward to doing it again."

"Harp!" He sighed and pulled back to examine my face. "I forgot about that. That reminder just destroyed my night."

"Oh, poor Scotty," I teasingly sulked, pouting my lips. "You'll survive Christmas."

"You're back before New Year's, right?"

"I'll be back before the New Year! If only because I demand my New Year's kiss." I promised. "And you'll survive for seven days without me."

"No, Harp," he groaned, "I won't. I'm going to stay at my house, bored out of my mind!"

"What did you do last holiday break?" I asked. "Did you stay at home, bored?"

"Last Christmas was different. I would have found someone to entertain me and occupy my time for the break. I don't want to do that this year. I want *you* here entertaining me."

"You're so selfish," I teased. "What would we be doing if I stayed here this Christmas?"

"Oh, geez, I don't know. We'd probably hot tub in the rain every day, then order take-out. I'd probably take you to see Titanic *again*." We both laughed at the idea of seeing it again. "We'd probably go running together. Of course, I'd give you your Christmas presents, and then we'd probably hang out all day, laughing. Then we'd do it again the next day, *and I'd enjoy it*."

"Is that what you did last holiday break?"

"No. Last holiday break, there was no hot tub, no laughter, and no take-out—mainly because there was no Harper."

"You always know exactly what to say!"

"Whomever it was that occupied my time last year didn't have a name!" He smirked. "This year, she has a name."

"*So* smug…"

"Please stay," he pleaded. "We'll exchange gifts and spend all our time together!"

"Do you want to exchange gifts before or after I return from Boston?"

"Neither," he demanded. "I want you to stay here for Christmas."

"That's not an option, Scott." I gave him a patronizing smile. "You gotta pick from the two options I gave you."

"After," he groaned. "It will give us something more to look forward to."

"Scott, the windows are all fogged up."

I examined each window in his large truck before settling in front of the back window and writing a message in the fogged glass. I was sure to write it backward so people outside the car could read it.

"Harp loves Scotty," Scott read out loud. "Is that a reminder in case I bring a chick back here while you're away?"

"Well, it wasn't supposed to be; now that I think about it, it might be." I chuckled.

"So, are we headed to my house?" he asked. "I'm into abandoning the bluff!"

"Let's do it," I nearly yelled. "But Scott, listen to me on this: I am really excited about doing it, but when I really think about doing it, I'm sorta terrified. I am.... *small*."

"We'll go slowly," he whispered. "We're not in a rush. It's just you and me. Now that I think about it, I'm sorta glad we didn't do it this afternoon—we were rushing into it. What if we did do it, and my mom came home in the middle?"

"Yeah, you're right."

The truck started to shake from both sides, and I heard the pounding fists against the glass windows. The truck started rocking side to side. I fell deeper into Scott's chest, feeling the vibrations of the rattling truck through it.

"Harp, they'll go away," Scott breathed. "If we just ignore them, they'll stop."

I didn't answer; I wanted to stay with Scott in his somewhat private truck. I wanted to continue feeling his hands along my waist as he kissed me. I wanted Scott's hands to find themselves under my shirt again. I wanted Scott to go back to unhooking my bra.

"Scott, I don't think it's going to stop," I forcefully groaned.

"Fuck!" He yelled loud enough for everyone outside to hear, and his fist pounded lightly against the glass. Screams for his attention echoed from the people outside. "I just want to be left alone with you," he told me. "Do me a favor and sit in front of me."

"We'll make this quick," I snapped, "then we're outta here!"

Scott opened the hatch and sat on the edge of the truck, letting his feet dangle; I sat between his legs as we were met with Brad, Barrett, and Leigh.

"Leigh," I exclaimed. "How long have you been here?"

"Not long," she chirped, staying glued to Brad. "Brad drove me back to my house to grab a few things before coming out here."

Her eyes were wide as if screaming as Brad stood behind her, rubbing her shoulders for added warmth. Her eyes got even wider when Brad draped his arms around her from behind and squeezed tightly, gently lifting her off the ground.

"Warm, babe?" Brad's lips nearly touched her ear as he leaned into her.

"Yup!" She smiled before looking directly at me and mouthing, "What is he doing?"

"I have no idea," I mouthed back. "He called you *babe*?"

Barrett Hudson stood alone, like always. He'd simply tagged along with Brad. As a freshman, like me, he was lucky to be on a varsity team and hang with Brad and Scott, though he didn't see it as luck or a privilege to play varsity as a freshman. He saw it as entitlement and a gateway.

"You two ever consider getting a room?" Barrett asked. "It's like you two are *always* on one another. If your hands aren't all over Harper, Scott, it's because Harper's practically riding you!"

Scott immediately shot a glance at Brad, and on cue, Brad shoved Barrett and shook his head at him. Since I was sitting between Scott's legs, I could feel that he wasn't in a position to get into Barrett's face. I was thankful that Scott had Brad there to correct Barrett. Scott's face held a warning, and I appreciated it.

"Harp," Scott promised as he kissed my ear, holding his lips close, "he won't say anything like that again."

"It's fine." I shrugged my shoulders and fell deeper back into Scott's chest. "He doesn't know anything."

"Nah, he's just being a dick." He whispered into my ear, "I'll take care of it later."

"Thank you."

"Listen, guys," Scott addressed everyone at the truck. "I think Harp and I are going to skip the bluff tonight. We've already done this scene this season, so I think we'll head out."

"No, you're not," Brad ordered. "You broke a league record; you're gonna get fucked up with me tonight!"

"Nah, I really don't think I'm going to." Scott tilted his head and shrugged Brad's words off. "Harp leaves for Boston on Sunday, and I just wanna hang with her before she has to go."

"You're blowing off your bros to hang with a *chick*?" Barrett exclaimed, his voice cocky. "Fucking weak!"

Scott abruptly set me down on the gravel, startling me from my semi-relaxed state, and walked toward Barrett while flexing his arms. He shoved Barrett against Brad's Honda.

"Don't ever say shit like that to me again, Barrett—especially in front of Harp. You don't know *shit* about my girlfriend or me." He pushed himself off Barrett. "And I'm not your fucking bro. If you piss off Harp, you piss me off, and it sounds like you've pissed her off quite a bit already."

"Bitch doesn't know what she's talking about."

"That *bitch* is my girlfriend," Scott yelled, pressing against Barrett again. "You lost. Move on!"

"Hey, hey! Just ignore him," I breathed as I clung to Scott's bicep and pulled him off the kid. "He didn't mean anything by it. He's just trying to impress you."

"I'm not your fucking *bro* Barrett," Scott barked, shoving his finger into Barrett's face. "You better quit it with that shit! You call her a bitch again; you're done!"

"Just ignore him." I guided Scott back toward his truck. "It's just us."

"God, I fucking hate that kid," he groaned into my ear. "*Hate* him!"

"Scott," I suggested, pressing my body against him and forcing him against his truck, "you need to cool off before we go back to your room."

"You're probably right." He leaned into me, whispering, "I don't want to get home and still be pissed at that clown. I gotta be in a great mood."

"You just gotta show up." I giggled.

"Oh, Harp." He smiled. "I guarantee you it's a little more involved than that!"

"See, Scott? You're already back in a great mood!"

"That freshman *pisses* me off," he said emphatically, nodding in Barrett's direction.

"Hey!" I smiled and moved myself into his line of vision, straining to reach some sort of eye level with him. "Maybe you should focus all your energy on *one* freshman and forget the rest."

"I should be doing that!" He grinned and placed his hand on my jaw, pressing his lips against mine. "Alright, let's cool off and head back to my place. This will buy us some time to ensure my parents are asleep!"

All the fires had been created lining the shore with a view of the Sound. The bluff had a massive drop down to the beach, which, unlike most beaches, was covered in rocks and large pieces of driftwood soaked in salt water. I've never found any beaches outside of Washington state similar to the beaches I grew up with here. The water here was constantly freezing, but the temperature in the air was bearable, not freezing like it would be during most Decembers in the country.

Most of my high school would go to the bluff after every game. Some people would come before the game was over and set up, which means the bluff was a fantastic view for those showing up late. The rows of fires ran the length of the beach, and when you were high up on the bluff, you could smell the smooth breeze of the Puget Sound air pull-in off the shore.

"Let's just stay for a bit," I suggested.

"Alright, sounds good," Scott agreed.

Scott held me firmly against him as he helped me down the narrow edge of the bluff. The path was steep and overgrown. Even if I were in sneakers, I wouldn't have been balanced enough to make it on my own. He held my waist from behind as I stepped lightly down the steep path, picking me up, lifting me over driftwood across the path, and setting me back down on the other side. I slipped only once. I nearly fell over the ledge before Scott firmly grabbed my bicep with only one of his hands and pulled me back onto the path. The trail's end had a five-foot drop to get to the beach. I knew to stop at the trail's end and hang onto a branch growing out of the bluff while Scott jumped down. He turned, wrapped his hands around my waist, set me down, and patted me on the butt.

"Nice job, Harp! You only nearly died *once* this time."

I wrapped my arm around Scott's waist as we waited for Brad to help Leigh. Barrett followed, not saying anything to me. He stared at me, and I followed his eyes as they examined my arms wrapped around Scott. He continued to say nothing. I was convinced at that moment that Barrett hated me. His face was unresponsive. He was clearly not my biggest fan, so I pulled myself closer to Scott and turned my face away.

"You got a staring problem, Barrett?" Scott snapped.

"Just checkin' Harp out," Barrett said calmly.

"No! No! No!" Scott pulled away from me. "*You* don't get to call her Harp. You don't *ever* get to call her Harp. Her name is Harper, and I know *all* about your staring. Got it, Freshman?"

"She's a fucking freshman too, Scott," he countered. "You never seem to give her shit about her grade."

"Jesus, kid," Scott groaned. "Shut the fuck up!"

"Barrett," I said both softly and reassuringly, "maybe you should lay off a bit. Maybe you and Scott should keep some space between yourselves. You have to play together for another few months, and you don't want to be fighting with each other like this, so…just… maybe…. You know…Separate for a bit."

"What's it to you, Freshman?" Barrett snapped at me in a near growl. "I earned *my* status; you're just another girl that Pierce started fucking!"

"Oh no," I gasped. In slow motion, I watched Scott's hand let go of mine. I could see each of the fingers on his right hand pull away as I watched his lefthand flex open. Each of his fingers stretched full and pressed firmly against Barrett's chest. In a quick snap, Barrett's body was pressed against the ledge. All of Scott's weight pressed against Barrett, and it appeared he had no intention of letting up.

"I told you," Scott intimated in a low, raspy voice. "You upset Harp; you upset me. My girlfriend doesn't like to hear about that shit."

"Christ, Scott!" Barrett gasped for air and tried to push Scott off him. "Get off me!"

"I know what you're doing, Barrett." Scott pressed his weight down harder and kept his face inches away from Barrett's. "You keep watching us. You keep watching her. Everyone knows what you're doing, and in turn, everyone is watching *you*—and everyone is telling me what they see."

"You're leaving next year, Scott," Barrett mumbled.

"Stay away from her."

"Scott?" I tugged on Scott's free arm, pulling him far away from the scene to have a moment to ourselves. "Let's go." I turned back to Barrett. "And Barrett, please stay away from me."

"Stay away from *us*," Scott told him.

"Scott," I whispered into his chest, "he says whatever he thinks, and what he thinks isn't real. He had to mention *that* to upset you to this point. He had to throw *that* in my face."

"Honestly, Harp, he doesn't know anything about us. He sees us together and thinks he has us figured out, but not one person knows what goes on between us. He thinks he can try to hurt you by reminding you of stupid bullshit gossip from the last three years. You gotta ignore him."

"I don't like people talking about *that* part of our relationship." I clung to his sweatshirt. "They can talk about anything else but *that* I want to stay between us."

"I know." He smiled and pulled me closer to him. "Are you alright?"

"I'm alright, but I'm not in the mood to cool off here any longer."

"Hey, Harpy," he teased, "I'm all about getting out of here, but babe, I don't want you in a bad mood because of that asshole! He's nobody. He's just some dick who needs Brad and me to help him get laid!"

"*Harpy*? Really?" I tilted my head and smirked. "Wait, he needs *you* to help *him* get laid?"

"Apparently, he doesn't have much game with the girls, but he's heard rumors about me and thinks I'm the guy to help him. Sadly, for him, this year, those rumors don't apply. I have my little *Harpy* to keep my attention. Brad has his freshman—"

"Well, Brad's freshman is searching for a title, and he seems oblivious to that need." I grinned. "Your little *Harpy* wants to leave now so she can be alone with her *Scotty*."

"Are you alright?" He pulled my body into his and buried his face in my neck. His hands tickled me, causing me to giggle. "She seems alright," he assured nobody in particular.

"I'm fine!" I laughed uncontrollably. "I can't breathe."

"There it is again! I'm taking your breath away."

"Stop," I whispered. "He's standing there." I stared at Barrett while I enjoyed having Scott's arms around me. "Maybe we shouldn't flaunt our relationship anymore?"

Barrett stood casually, holding a beer in his right hand and watching Scott...More accurately, he was watching Scott's hands. He looked both angry and annoyed. Hatred was sketched across his face. I felt violated somehow, even with the safe distance between him and me. I feared him for some reason. I was safe with Scott, but I wasn't always with Scott. Barrett was my age and my grade and on the same progression through high school as me.

"Ignore him," Scott directed me. "He just wishes he was me right now. I'm definitely gonna continue flaunting!"

"I'm tired of him. I'm tired of the things he says."

"Hey, they're just words." His hand felt soft as he lifted my chin and kissed me. I was back to ignoring Barrett. "Let's skip this crowd. He'll be here all night, just staring at us and wishing my hands were his."

"Your hands aren't doing anything." I giggled as I leaned back and embraced him, holding my own weight. "They're just on my waist."

"He'll take my most routine physical gesture and get excited about it. He is that desperate!"

We walked over the difficult terrain of the beach, stepping over the enormous driftwood and uneven rocks. We made our way through the large crowds and back up the steep hill to the Pathfinder. He held my waist tightly as we walked up the length of the worn path. No one seemed to have noticed that Scott and I were continuing to walk away. No one said anything as we separated from the crowd. Once we were high above the beach, we got into the truck and drove off.

"Scott?" I leaned over the center console and began kissing his ear, letting my hand wander on his thigh. "Would you rather hang out with the crowd?"

"I've been drinking with that crowd since I was a freshman. I'd rather enjoy my last year here with *my* freshman."

"Oh, so you won't be here next year?" I teased.

"Sorry, babe, I won't be here next year."

"I'm glad we decided to leave," I breathed. "We really only have tonight and tomorrow afternoon before I have to leave for Boston, you know."

"Oh, we *will* be hanging out tomorrow, Harp!" He winked.

"God, what have I agreed to?" I exclaimed jokingly.

"The best, Harp," he promised, only half teasing, "you agreed to the best."

Behind two oversized vehicles parked on the Pierce's steep driveway, Scott and I participated in what we were really good at. When it was time to go in, it took great strength on both our parts to pull away from one another and run up the steep driveway. We laughed loud enough that our screams of enjoyment echoed through the heavily wooded property. He caused me to howl with laughter as he picked me up and carried me up the front steps. I couldn't contain my excitement; Scott's smile radiated. We were happy and knew what we wanted to happen as soon as we were in his bedroom.

Scott quietly shut the front door, and I heard the lock click. It was then that we realized our night was never going to go as planned.

"Harper? Scott?" Marie yelled from the kitchen. "That you?"

"Why are they still up?" I whispered, leaning into Scott.

"Yes," Scott yelled toward the kitchen. "We're home."

"Come into the kitchen. We're all in here."

"I'll be back the morning of New Year's Eve," I whispered. I pressed my head against his chest. "I guess being a virgin for one more week won't kill me."

"It'll kill *me*," Scott groaned. "Knowing that my hot girlfriend is three-thousand miles away and *wants* me to take her virginity will be enough to drive me insane. I'm going to hate this Christmas."

"Let's put our pajamas on and watch a Christmas movie," I suggested, hoping to cheer him up. "That way, we can at least pretend we're spending our Christmas together."

"What time do you have to go home?" Scott mumbled. "It's a little before eleven now."

"It's Friday, so I don't really have a curfew—"

"You'll spend the night?" Scott instantly perked up. "Harp, babe, love of my life, I'm going to go an entire week without you! I need all the time I can get with you now."

"Spending the night isn't going to happen." I sighed and tilted my head. "My parents will flip if I sleep in this house."

We had our romantic evening. We cuddled on the oversized sectional sofa in his living room and watched a black-and-white version of a holiday classic. My body rested against his chest as I sat in my usual position between his two very long legs. I pulled the large patchwork quilt over my chest and enjoyed feeling Scott's chest slowly rising. His hands were wrapped around me, and his lips frequently grazed my ear as he murmured my name. Seven days without Scott would eat me alive. I wished for Christmas to be over quickly so I could fly back here and be just like this.

"Harp," he breathed. "I'm going to give you one of your Christmas gifts now."

I spun around in his arms and smiled at him; this smile was more significant than any I had ever had with Scott.

"Harper," he announced, "It took so long for me to decide where I am going to college because of you. I've been given two options to play basketball, and I haven't made my final decision because I *want* to be near you, but I wanted to tell you that I loved you first. I wanted you to know *that* first and foremost. I wanted to see how you reacted to that, and then I was going to decide." He took a deep breath. "I'm leaning toward the University of Washington."

I looked up at him and then threw my entire body weight into him; I was so happy. The unexpected force of my body threw Scott off balance.

"Really? You'll take the in-state option? You'll stay? You won't go off to Arizona? You'll play for Washington?" I kissed him before he could answer. "You're not taking it just because of me, are you? Do you really like Washington? Do you like the campus and the business program, all of it? There are other reasons for you to stay, right? Not just me?"

"Yes, Harper, I do like the campus. I like the basketball program and have a good shot at going pro. They also have a good business program if the professional thing doesn't work out."

"Oh, Scott, you'll be drafted into the pros. I know you'll make it! I love you so much! You have no idea. You don't have to do anything for New Year's. I won't freak out over the midnight kiss, I promise. This is all I needed." I held his face in my hands as I kissed him. "It's not a waste. It's not a waste at all," I murmured, mostly to myself.

"Harp?" His brows pulled tightly together. "What's not a waste?"

"Oh, never mind. Forget it."

"Harp?"

"Ethan mentioned that we really didn't have a future, 'cause you're going to college, and that—"

"Whoa! Whoa! Whoa!" His face turned serious, and he started to examine mine. "Ethan says whatever comes into his mind without thinking about it. He never stops to reflect on who is listening to him. Don't listen to him. He's a jackass."

"I won't ever listen to him again," I blurted, dismissing Ethan's words because of the sheer happiness and joy I felt about his gift to me.

"Harp, I love you!"

"Not nearly as much as I love you, Scott—not nearly as much as I love you."

"Harp, I'm *not* playing that game." He grinned. "And please don't listen to Ethan anymore, alright? He doesn't have an original thought in his head."

SIX

I'D HAD ENOUGH OF *SEVENTEEN* magazine and its ongoing preaching about safe sex, its tales of abstinence, and its ways to improve your winter wardrobe. I decided immediately before boarding my flight at Seattle-Tacoma International Airport that I would graduate to a big girl periodical—*Cosmopolitan*. I wanted to read about being sexy and sultry and having an outstanding sex life. I wanted to read the article entitled "101 Best-Kept Sex Secrets" twice. I wanted to know about dressing in order to have great sex with a great man. With all this in mind, I bought my first *Cosmo* magazine at the duty-free shop.

After taking secure ownership of my new periodical, I opened my carry-on bag and was hit with deep-seated guilt. My religious studies book for Confirmation stared up at me. The one-inch-thick book was labeled with words like "catechism" and "salvation." It haunted me, undermined my confident decision regarding my sex life, and gnawed at me. I did the only thing I could do, though it was impulsive. I rushed to the ladies' room, ignoring the lines. With haste, I slid through the crowds of women and threw my Confirmation book into the wastebasket. The white dove flying through a perfectly clear blue sky on the cover of a book entitled *Confirmation: A Life with Jesus* looked up at me from the bottom of the wastebasket of a women's room in the Seattle-Tacoma International Airport. I stared at the book, which contained the rules for a safe existence with Christ, until a woman casually tossed her used paper towel into the bin, covering that white dove. I grinned. I would be everything that book didn't want me to be. I was going to be dirty with sin, and I was going to be dirty with Scott Pierce.

I ignored the Christmas cheer pervading my grandparents' home. I ignored the repetitive questions from each of my older cousins about my freshman year of high school, my soccer performance, and my friends from school. I didn't, however, ignore the opportunity to discuss my boyfriend when asked if I had one. Though I enjoyed the astonished faces I saw when I explained Scott's age, grade, and popularity, I didn't enjoy the faces of concern on my aunts and uncles. I chalked those up to conversations that must have been happening behind my back with my parents. My mind was entirely focused on what would happen as soon as I returned to Seattle. My stomach was in knots. All I wanted was for this holiday to be over so I could face the source of the excitement building in my core.

I spent a substantial amount of my downtime during my Boston holiday thumbing through my very-mature periodical. I flipped through the magazine many times that week. By the middle of the week, I had grown slightly frustrated that I would have to wait a few more days before I returned to Washington and tried all the things I'd been reading about. I loved Scott more than anything. I realized on this trip that I wanted to be one of the girls on his list of sexual experiences, but I wanted my name to have a star next to it—a star that meant I was the only girl he ever loved.

The day before my flight home, a group of my older cousins suggested we venture to the Back Bay of Boston for shopping. I jumped at this opportunity and knew precisely what purchases I intended to make. I had a general idea of what I wanted to look like during my first experience with Scott, which meant that I also had a general idea of what changes I would need to institute into my wardrobe.

Arriving off the train at Copley, in the Back Bay of Boston, I counted my holiday cash quickly as I trailed behind my cousins. I felt confident that three hundred fifty dollars was more than enough to spend on my new, more sensual undergarments. I parted ways with my six cousins as they headed to the food court of the Copley Mall, which was ideal for guy-watching, while I walked into La Perla, a shop that immediately leapt out to me. Words like *French* and *lingerie* caught my eye. La Perla was the sort of shop that usually intimidated me, but I found my skin prickling with growing excitement as I came across it in the mall directory.

The shining white floor was tile, and the female associates, dressed in all black, their hair pinned up, and measuring tapes draped over their necks, seemed well-trained and highly professional. I continued into the shop with slight hesitation. I began to feel like I was in a bit over my head, like my virginity was calling me out in a place like this. Every small step into this non-virginal shop seemed to point me out, as if each step was a neon arrow pointing straight at my department-store undergarments.

The low grumbling of electronic music played in the background. I immediately thought of Scott and how much he loathed the new computerized techno music genre. His refusal to enjoy any music that wasn't grunge always made me laugh. The thought of Scott reminded me of my inadequacy. With my four layers of clothing and one bulky winter jacket protecting me, I felt relieved as I thought of Scott in that lingerie store.

Under my four layers of clothing was my generic white department-store bra and panties, which did very little to accentuate those parts that Scott seemed drawn to the most. I stepped farther in and was thankful when a young associate walked toward me. I suspected she could see right through me and knew exactly what I was—a virgin.

"Can I help you find something, Miss?"

"Well," I mumbled, chewing on the side of my lip. This wasn't a good time to start getting anxious, but as I looked around, that is precisely what happened. "Would it be alright if I looked around first? I could come back to you, right? You're not going anywhere?"

"Absolutely," she assured me. She had a tight, flat smile that somehow comforted me. "Come find me when you're ready."

Her friendly, calming demeanor had me betting that she was knowledgeable, and she seemed like the sort of person who wouldn't judge me for my lack of experience, the kind of experience she knew I didn't have. Her chirpy voice seemed reassuring. I felt that she wasn't going to venture to the back room of this very sultry store and tell her associates about the adorable curly-haired virgin mucking around in the black-lace section of her store. It seemed like she genuinely cared, like it wasn't just an act she put on because she made a commission.

I examined the lace and silk in reds, blacks, and even outrageous lime green. I discovered the bras and thongs, even the one-piece sets, and finally arrived at a black bra that added a more manipulative lift without taking away from what I already had. It had a matching thong with a small, red, delicately placed bow on the back. I didn't care much for the bow, which seemed juvenile and *cute*. I didn't want *cute* built into the picture I was trying to create. I wanted sexy and hot; a cute red bow didn't fit the night I wanted with Scott Pierce. I searched high and low for a thong that lacked the offensive bow but found none and decided that Scott would probably barely notice.

Before I entered the red, curtain-drawn dressing room, the sales associate from earlier carefully and professionally wrapped the tape measure around my torso and said words I thought I'd never hear directed at me.

"Thirty-four C," she chirped.

"Really?" I shyly replied. My eyebrows were raised high in astonishment. "I didn't really—"

"Most women wear the incorrect bra size," she interrupted, sounding comforting. "You get comfortable wearing what you know."

I stood in that mirrored, closed dressing room and felt empowered and sexy as I thought of Scott. I felt like someone who should be desired. I stood examining myself in that mirror. I held my curls behind me and turned my body around to see my back and sides. I dropped my curls and knew, again, that I was ready to do this. I had spent the entire holiday vacation thinking about that Friday night with Scott before I left. I was tiptoeing toward obsession over that night. I thought about the fantastic long-distance phone conversations we shared, but I was hanging onto everything we did that night and wanting nothing more than to repeat it.

I left La Perla that afternoon with three bras, seven thongs, and an intense desire to take on this next chapter of my relationship. I decided instantly that my department-store undergarments would no longer be a part of my existence. A sensual, more sexually aggressive Harper was now taking necessary steps toward being desired even *more* by her boyfriend. At the last minute of that shopping trip, I decided to skip out on my original plan to wear jeans for our New Year's Eve date, and I spent my remaining Christmas money on a phenomenal dress at Sak's Fifth Avenue.

We landed in Seattle late on the night of December thirtieth. Between waiting for our luggage and waiting for a ferry, I didn't get to see Scott that night. I unpacked as soon as I got home, delicately setting my La Perla bag on the top shelf of my closet. I carefully hung up the beautiful form-fitting, shimmering gold dress on my door, removing it from the plastic garment bag. I leaned against my closet doorframe and stared at it, watching as the light from my closet caught each gold sequin's reflection, and I thought how this dress would always be in my mind for the rest of my life. This would be the last thing I wore before I was no longer a charter member of the dreaded "virgin club."

"Harper!"

My eyes flew open, my gaze landing on that dress on the morning of December thirty-first, 1997. I woke to a substantial amount of anxiety. I flipped the covers off my body and flew out of bed as my father's voice echoed up the stairs. It was well after eleven in the morning, and my anxiety about this evening demanded that I fill my day with activities that didn't involve daydreaming about Scott and my new undergarments. I ran out of my room with only an oversized T-shirt that belonged to Scott, looking forward to whatever my father was going to demand of me. Whatever he wanted me to do, I'd do it. It meant that I would be able to keep my mind occupied. For all I knew, he wanted me to wash the windows and the cars and power-wash the house. Wouldn't he be entirely surprised to learn that I'd be eager to do it? I needed to keep my mind occupied until tonight.

Scott was standing at the foot of my staircase with my father. He had his hands in his slightly faded jean pockets, casually standing in basketball shoes that were not laced up and a purple T-shirt that was not tucked in, a white button-down shirt with its sleeves rolled to three-quarter length covering the T-shirt. He towered over my father, who was not short, attempting to hide a half smile. His smile lines were just as I remembered them.

My father stood with his back to Scott at the bottom of the staircase, holding the Dunkin' Donuts coffee mug that my uncles purchased for him as a jab at the fact that my father, being a native Seattleite, had no tolerance for anything other than Starbucks. He looked at me as I began the race down the long staircase.

"Harper, Scott's here," he informed me needlessly, adding, "and why don't you put some pants on?" He turned and walked back to the kitchen.

I was barely down the long flight of stairs before my father was out of sight. I stood on the second-to-last step and smiled as I looked into the eyes of the love of my life. As I stood there looking at him, I realized I could never go for another extended period without seeing that smile and those blue eyes.

"Harp!"

I jumped into his arms, tightly wrapping my arms around his neck. I clung to him tightly, and he reciprocated. His arms were tight around my waist. He smelled exactly the same as he had last week. His cheeks were smooth, and his hair was soft, completing the picture of my boyfriend/obsession, Scott Pierce.

"Harp," he whispered into my messy curls, his breath sending chills down my spine, "I think you should put some pants on."

I couldn't contain my laughter. I felt a cool breeze go up my T-shirt and realized it fell just an inch below my behind. He set me back down on the second-to-last step, and we both intuitively sat next to one another and started kissing, both of us equally aware that my parents were just down the hall in the kitchen.

"Did you miss me?" I asked between forceful kisses, attempting to climb onto his lap without anyone getting suspicious about how quiet we were.

"More than anything," he breathed. "I was bored out of my mind. I'm already dreading next Christmas."

I was filled with even more elation as I hung on every one of Scott's words. We kissed on the staircase that late morning for quite some time. His hands remembered what they were allowed to do as they ventured under my T-shirt and hooked onto the elastic of my underwear. We cut it shorter than I would have liked because we heard the clearing of my father's throat from the kitchen and had reached just shy of the point where it would have become too *hard* for Scott to stop.

"Scott," I panted between his aggressive lips, "I was wondering what the plans are for this evening?"

"What do you want to do?" he replied, equally out of breath. "We can do anything you want."

"Had you thought of anything?" I breathed against his lips.

"I have. I have a whole night planned." He quickly pulled back and grinned. "If you have something else in mind, I am more than open to alternative suggestions."

"No, no suggestions," I told him, flustered. "Nothing—"

"Harper?"

"Alright, well, there is this one tiny little thing I kinda wanted to do this evening." I knotted my fingers anxiously and winked, bringing my mind back to my newly purchased undergarments and how desperately I wanted to share them with Scott. "But only if you're still interested."

"Harp!" He leaned toward me with a smirk on his face. "If you're suggesting what I think you're suggesting, I can say with absolute certainty that I am still very much interested in keeping that on the agenda for this evening."

"Oh, good!" I took a deep breath and exhaled, a small smile appearing on my face. "I was worried you might have forgotten about what we almost did or maybe you weren't interested anymore."

"No, no, no!" He emphatically ensured me. "That Friday night has not been forgotten! I'm still burning over the fact that we didn't get a chance that Saturday before you left."

"Scott," I reminded him, "I packed for fifty-three-degree weather. My mother made me repack my entire suitcase. There was no way I was getting out of the house that Saturday."

"I know, I know! I made reservations for dinner tonight on the mainland, and then I thought we could walk around the city before returning to the island. But if you're interested, Brad is having a party—"

"No party," I breathed. "Just us tonight."

"I couldn't agree more."

I couldn't stop kissing him. I couldn't let go of his jaw. He continued to pull me closer to him until I was on his lap. He carefully pulled his face away from mine when we heard my father clear his throat again.

"Harp, can he see us?" Scott whispered. "He's down the hall. How does he know?"

"I think it has to do with our whispering!" I smiled. "It could also have something to do with the fact that we have extended periods of silence, or maybe—"

"No, I think I got it!" He chuckled.

"I was just going to add that maybe it's because I'm only wearing a T-shirt that belongs to you, and we haven't seen each other in over a week." I smiled. "He's probably figured out what's going on!"

"I'll take it as my cue to leave, then. I do have to go." He sulked. "I'm not exactly happy about it, either."

"What?" I looked at his large watch. "Why do you have to leave? You just got here!"

"I have basketball practice from noon to three. It's been like this over the entire holiday break."

"Oh, that's awful," I sulked as I pulled myself onto his lap. One of his hands moved up my back as his other thumb gently outlined the side of my right breast. His lips were gentle on mine at first, but they became increasingly forceful and demanding as he continued to stroke the side of my breast.

"Please?" I breathed.

"Nah." He smiled softly. "Not when he's just down the hall."

I felt it on the apex of one of my thighs; it wasn't as obvious, but it had potential. I slowly slid off his lap and sat next to him on the step, reaching for his forearm with one hand and lacing the fingers of my other hand with his. I held his forearm for a moment before I saw them—roughly quarter-sized bruises in the bend of his elbow. I brushed his sleeve up and examined them before he tugged the sleeve of his button-down shirt back down.

"It's nothing—"

"Scotty, what happened?" My voice was filled with panic. "Hon, tell me! Are you alright?"

"Babe, it's just a little blood I had taken." His hand cupped my jaw as he pulled my lips to his. It was a passionate kiss that we usually would have shared when my father wasn't down the hall. It was the sort of kiss in which his tongue explored my mouth in the most erotic sense. He expounded on his answer as his lips drew me in: "Just a physical; don't worry."

"Alright." I forced a little smile onto my face and nodded. "I just worry about... *You know*... And I hate needles, myself."

"Hey," he assured me as he lifted my face to his, "you've got nothing to worry about."

I nodded and smiled before quickly kissing him.

"I'll pick you up at six?" His brows lifted as he asked. "We'll go straight from here."

"Yes," I exclaimed. "Absolutely!"

"I imagine tonight is going to be one of those events you spend all day getting ready for, anyway."

"You know me too well."

I reached for a hug goodbye, and he tucked my curls behind my ear and lightly smiled.

"I love you," he said in such a way that it seemed he'd become capable of saying it with even more ease like it was second nature for him.

"I love you, too." Even if he couldn't see my lips, I think he knew I said it with a smile.

"Just us," he reminded me before opening the front door and looking back down the hallway toward the kitchen. "Happy New Year, Mr. Whitmore," he called.

"Uh huh," my father grunted back from the kitchen.

I spent the entire afternoon in my bedroom, sitting cross-legged in front of my full-length mirror. I sculpted my eyebrows, became obsessed with my virtually unseen pores, and spent time trying to apply eyeliner perfectly. I took a break around three for lunch and a discussion with another human being. I realized I had been locked up in my room for three hours, thinking about nothing but my black bra set and my virginity. I needed human interaction, even if it was only with my family.

I saw my mother in the kitchen. She had her make-up done in such an immaculate fashion that I assumed she had her own New Year's plans, and those plans didn't involve being a mother to two daughters and a dedicated housewife.

"Harper," she exclaimed when she saw me, "what are your plans for this evening? It's your first New Year's Eve with a *boyfriend*."

"Yes it is," I cheerfully agreed. "Scott is taking me to dinner in Seattle."

"That is very romantic of him! I'm sure he's excited about having a girlfriend to spend New Year's Eve with."

"I think so, too!"

She looked at me, watching me as I sat down and began on a small plate of leftover pizza from my father's lunch. I wasn't hungry; though I didn't eat breakfast, I needed to maintain the appearance of being somewhat normal. I didn't want my mother to know that I had a reason to be anxiety-ridden or nervous, so I picked at my pizza and sipped at a glass of milk for her sake. She, too, was working on her hair for the evening, and she was also in a bathrobe. She had in hot rollers; she dreaded having to use them. She often said that she wished she had her daughter's hair.

"You look very beautiful," my mother said in a very small, encouraging voice.

"Thank you!" I grinned. "Even in a bathrobe?"

"I'm sure Scott would say the same."

"If I know Scott, he probably would."

"Harper, do you remember that conversation we had when you first started dating Scott?"

"Which conversation is that?" I asked, hoping it wasn't the one I thought it was.

"The conversation about letting me, your concerned mother, know when you become *close* with Scott. Do you recall?"

"Mom...."

"I'm only reminding you that we don't want you to be another teenage statistic—"

"Mom, we're not there yet," I interrupted. I felt that the word *statistic* was as good a place as any to interrupt her parental concern.

"*Yet?*" she repeated. "Am I to assume that this is something that will happen?"

"Mom," I groaned, "please leave it alone. We're not there."

"Your father and I are not ignorant of what teenagers do—"

"Mom," I interrupted again. "Please...."

"Alright," she conceded the end of this conversation. "Have fun tonight!"

She quickly kissed me on my forehead and left the kitchen. I was beyond thankful she had left it at that and didn't press me. As I watched her head back down to her bedroom, I couldn't help but wonder if I looked different somehow now that I'd decided what I was going to do. If anything, it was probably a look of both anxiety and eagerness.

Just before six, after my hair was pinned up and my dangly gold earrings were on, I stepped into my closet and closed the door. I reached high and pulled the La Perla bag off the top shelf. I clipped the tags off the black lace push-up bra with only slight hesitation. It was mine now. I did the same with the thong with the bow on the back and began to journey down my self-endowed sex appeal. I wasn't brave enough to look at myself in the full-length mirror. I was terrified to do so, in fact. When I was three thousand miles away, I felt secure in my choice. Now, I looked at myself, knowing that my boyfriend was less than six miles away, and felt less secure in my choice. Scott was never late, either.

I reached for my gold dress and gently stepped into it. With only a slight amount of fear, I slipped my arms into the dress and struggled to zip the back up. I took a moment to acknowledge that the only thing that would be standing between Scott and me was roughly eight inches of shimmering fabric around my waist, hips, and butt. My heels were four-inch gold stilettos. I had snagged them on sale. I felt put together, striking, and much older than fifteen. At the very least, I felt as though I was teetering around eighteen. I looked like I belonged at Scott's side. I wasn't a kid he was toting around in this outfit, but his girlfriend. In that outfit, there wasn't a noticeable three-year difference between us.

I stepped out of the closet and was surprised to see him sitting in my oversized reading chair. He was leaning over, his arms propped on his knees, reading a running magazine before he looked up and saw me.

"You're early."

"I'm on time," he corrected me.

He looked handsome; he wore black pants and a crisp white shirt with gold cufflinks. He casually stood up and stepped toward me. His long legs afforded him the luxury of only having to take one step. He slid his hand along my waist and pulled my face toward his lips in a single motion.

"You look unbelievable this evening, Harper," he whispered. "You look better every time I see you!"

"That might be true this time," I teased. "The last time you saw me, I was wearing one of your old T-shirts."

"Trust me; you looked good then, too."

I could only express myself with a smile; I had nothing to say. I had no words to express how excited and nervous I was about this evening. I wanted him to know exactly how much this evening meant to me on so many different levels.

"You're very handsome this evening, Scott. You look the best I've ever seen—"

"Night's not over, babe!"

He took me to the Space Needle. Our reservation was early enough that we wouldn't have to fight through crowds later for spectacular views of the fireworks show. We would see the fireworks later that evening once we got back on the island, or maybe not, and I would be alright with that. But for now, we could simply enjoy a meal. Scott couldn't keep his hands to himself. I wasn't sure if he was initially excited about our evening plans or if it was the dress, but I think it was because we both arrived at a place where we knew what was going to happen.

I couldn't tell you the details of what we discussed during dinner. We discussed so much, ranging from my flight to Boston to the fact that all my cousins would be attending universities in Massachusetts in the fall. He looked confused when I told him I enjoyed Dunkin' Donuts' coffee. Scott talked about hating to have basketball practice during the holiday break and how much he missed playing ball with his nephew Ethan. We came to a moment of silence in which we smiled at one another. There was a brief moment when I pulled my shawl across my chest to hide the added boost I'd purchased.

Our dinner was over, so we walked through the Science Center to Pike Place Market and down toward the ferry. The boat was empty as we returned home, and there were no cars but our own. We opted to rush upstairs and experience an empty boat. We broke the rules of the ferry and ran through the vast open area. The only sound was that of my heels clinking against the steel floor. I had run halfway up the staircase before I felt Scott's arms wrap around my waist.

The wind blew hard that night across the observation deck. My stray curls blew in the wind. When I reached that deck, I walked backward to the railing and watched Scott as he casually strolled toward me, slowly removing his hands from his pockets.

We broke every ferry rule that night. We ran through the vacant car lanes and up the stairs, and now we were forcefully, passionately, and aggressively kissing on the observation deck. I didn't care that there were cameras on deck. I didn't care that the entire crew could see Captain Whitmore's daughter making out on deck with her boyfriend. My father wasn't here to clear his throat, and I wasn't about to encourage Scott to pull away. The crew could, if they wanted to, watch a video of the Captain's daughter being felt up by her boyfriend. His hands ran over my exaggerated chest while I dragged my hand down his starched shirt and past his belt. I felt what was pressed against me. That was all on a piece of black-and-white videotape somewhere, and I didn't care.

Unlike any other ferry ride I'd been on, the ferry actually blasted its horn, causing our make-out session to stop abruptly, and we smiled at one another.

"Is this your father's boat?" Scott grinned. "I'd take a clearing of his throat over a ferry horn."

"Not tonight! He's out with my mom." I grinned. "The horn was either because we're close to docking or the crew knows Jay's daughter is making out with her boyfriend on deck."

"Are you known for making out on deck?"

"I am now!" I laughed. "And it's all on tape!"

"Oh, Harp, tell me where I can get this tape!" He laughed. "I imagine it's black and white—real artistic."

"I'll see what I can do. There is no mistaking the fact that it was us." I chuckled. "No other couple has such a height difference. We're one in a million!"

"Did you have a good time tonight?" he whispered in my neck. His hands were straying again. "Was it a good first New Year's as a couple?"

"It's not over yet," I reminded him.

We raced downstairs and into the Pathfinder. The crew waved when we disembarked, mouthing both my name and my boyfriend's.

"Harp," he asked, "can I make an observation?"

"Please do."

"You look unbelievable this evening. You look like a different person!"

"Thank you! I wasn't really trying to look like a different person; I was just trying to bring out my best."

"Babe, your best is unbelievable!"

His house was empty, silent. The only light was coming from the beautifully lit Christmas tree and mantle. The house smelled of Christmas—the smell of a real tree and holiday candles. I walked toward the living room and took in all the holiday decorations. There were three now-empty stockings over the mantle.

"Where is everyone?"

"The house will be empty until tomorrow morning." He nodded. "No interruptions."

"Ooh." I smiled while I casually walked toward him, looping my fingers into his belt loops when I got to him and reaching high on my tiptoes for his kiss.

"Harp," he whispered.

"Yeah?"

"Would you mind staying here for ten minutes?" he asked. "Ten minutes at most, I promise."

"Alright," I replied, slightly confused. "I'll just sit next to the tree."

He didn't say anything. He simply nodded and stepped backward, casually going upstairs with a slight smile on his face. I sat next to the tall Christmas tree and admired it. I loved the real needles and the natural smell of pine. I admired each perfectly placed Christmas bulb and ornament. Marie had placed each with precision. I fell in love with her tree. It looked as though it fell out of a Macy's storefront window. Her tree was beautiful, with its ribbon and white lights.

Deep within the pine needles was an ornament unlike the rest. It was a small, thick wooden ring with fading red and silver glitter around it. In the center was a picture of a young boy. His hair was a sandy blond color and spiked in the front. His eyes were a vivid blue. He wore a red sweater with thick blue stripes and a white turtleneck. His smile was large, almost goofy, and showed two disproportionate front teeth thrusting in opposite directions. He looked like a happy boy full of life. The year was written in green glitter below the picture—1985.

"I was six." He startled me. "First grade."

"I was three," I whispered. "In 1985, I was three."

"That's the only thing that separates us," he whispered. "Our age."

I didn't want to be the one who brought the obvious to light: There was much more than age that separated us. Our age was the least of my concerns. Age would probably bother me when he graduated and I, alone, was in high school, but right now, age wasn't a factor. However, his number of sexual partners and my number—zero was a factor.

"Your shoes are sparkling." He nodded to my feet. "The lights from the tree are reflecting off the gold."

I examined my shoes and smiled, still seated. He strolled toward me and knelt in front of me. He was still above my vision as he sat on his knees. He appeared nervous, as though this was his first time. I was filled with twice whatever Scott was feeling - I simply showed it differently. The best way to approach the situation was to abandon the elephant in the room and focus on something else entirely.

"Is Brad going to be angry that we missed his party?" I whispered, grinning nervously. "Leigh called this afternoon and begged me to come."

"What did you say?" He smirked. "To Leigh's invitation, that is."

"I asked her if she'd spoken to Brad."

"Brad begged me to come, too. He said that we should at least make an appearance." He smiled. "I told him we might, but not to be pissed if we don't."

"Brad seems to enjoy trying to pressure us into things." I giggled nervously. "Does he know?"

"Know what?"

"*You* know! What we're *doing* tonight?"

"Of course." He grinned. "He knows I'm spending my New Year's Eve with my girlfriend, alone."

"Ah." I laughed. "You're good!"

"No one knows," he whispered. "What happens between us tonight stays between us."

"Scott," I sighed, "we could have done it that night after your record, and I would have been fine with it."

"I don't want you to be *fine* with anything; I want you to be more than fine," he exclaimed. "I didn't want to rush anything with you."

His usually boyish room was not "boyish" any longer. He had

made the bed. His floor was vacuumed. There wasn't a single article of clothing on the floor, chair, or bed. He had placed three off-white pillar candles strategically around the room and lit them. The number of candles wasn't obnoxious, and they didn't smell. Each candle had one framed four-by-six picture of the two of us next to it. I didn't recall the pictures being taken. One was taken early in our time together—late September, during a football game. Another was taken in the student parking lot, where we sat side by side in the back of his truck. The last framed picture of us was taken after my hat trick by my mother. I was covered in mud and standing next to Scott, wearing his previously white sweatpants.

I turned around and smiled as Scott slowly walked back and shut the door. I was still nervous, still anxious for this to begin. I was also beyond naïve about how to even start things. We were always in the moment when we started; now, we were trying to get into the moment, knowing fully that we were going further than we'd ever gone. I did what I did best, which was pretend to be distracted. I walked his room perimeter and examined everything I'd already examined multiple times.

I walked the room until I got to Scott's bed again. He was already sitting on the edge, leaning over, his elbows on his knees. I stood between his knees and ran my fingers through his hair, dragging my fingers behind his ear and feeling his dirty-blond hair between my fingertips. His left hand ran down the contour of my right leg to my foot. He gently took my heel off. He did the same with my left shoe with smooth, confident movements. This time, his hand did not leave my leg; he moved back up my leg. When he reached the top, his thumb began circling around the inside of my thigh and continued inching farther and farther up.

He'd touched me *there* once before; just like the time before, my heart began racing. I needed to get distracted by something, focus on something, or I'd simply stand there looking at Scott, my fingers running through his hair, while his thumb kept inching up my thigh. I looked at his hand and saw the shiny gold cufflinks, and then found enough courage inside myself to sit on Scott's knee and encourage him to keep his hand on my thigh. I focused on his gold cufflinks.

"You know you're beautiful, Harper," he whispered into my hair. He dragged his lips across my neck and up to my ear. He found the zipper on the back of my dress and took charge.

"I know you tell me I am," I whispered softly.

"You don't know what you look like, Harper?"

"I do—"

"You don't know what people see when they look at you," he breathed. "You have no idea how unbelievable you are or how lucky I am."

Our foreheads pressed together, and my fingers traced the lines on his face. I could tell that Scott wanted me to remember everything from that night; he went so far as to ensure I remembered that specific kiss. It wasn't forceful or intense like the one on the ferry—it was soft and delicate. His bottom lip met my top lip, and he guided the movements of my face with his. I reached for his jaw. In a single motion, Scott brushed my dress off my shoulders.

I pretended I didn't notice my dress sliding down to my feet. I played ignorant and unobservant as my straps followed the course of my body down to the floor. His fingers tangled into my bra strap before my dress had fallen entirely to the floor. His long fingers snuck under the straps. All the while, I thought about my new black thong and its bow on the back. He was distracted and, I hoped, unaware of how my fingers were shaking as they undid each one of the buttons on his shirt.

He pulled me tightly to his chest and ran his lips across my newly purchased, exaggerated chest. His hair tickled my jaw, neck, and throat as he continued to kiss my torso. My heart fluttered; if he knew it, he was too gentlemanly to make any reference to it. He made no reference to the fact that I mimicked his moves as I brushed his white shirt off his shoulders, either. He was cooperative—he pulled his arms from his sleeves before I tugged his undershirt over his head and dropped it onto the floor. When his shirt was off, I discovered something else to be distracted by—his beautiful, tan chest and his kisses along my neck.

"Is this new?" he whispered, speaking of my bra, as he trailed his fingers down my spine. His fingertips lightly grazed the skin on the small of my back and traced imaginary circles that caused me to melt into his control.

"Do you like it?" I whispered into his hair.

He didn't respond. He sat on the edge of his bed and continued to feel me. Before I could settle into the feeling of Scott's touch, he stopped being coy and started taking charge. He gripped my hips and pulled me onto the bed. We picked up exactly where we left off on the ferry.

"Harp," he breathed into my ear, his body grinding against mine, "I'm only taking this off because I'm dying to see them again."

"You like *them*?" I breathed.

"Your tits! Christ, Harp!"

For some unexplained reason, that word didn't bother me. I think it was his honesty. In fact, his vulgarity turned me on more than I thought it would. Perhaps it was the complement, or maybe it was the fact that he felt comfortable enough to say it to me.

His hands unapologetically explored me in ways that he once stopped them from doing. I decided that everything I read last week about taking charge would happen that night. I wanted to be an equal participant in this. I felt him against my thigh, so I found my courage and reached for his waistband.

He pulled back but continued leaning over me as I tugged, pulled, and yanked his pants off. Scott returned to aggressively kissing my neck, moving down past my collarbone and onto his favorite part of my body. I used my feet to pull his pants down around his ankles. The first time I saw *it* suddenly seemed very distant. Looking at it now, it seemed new, fresh, vibrant, and eventful. I reached for it; I didn't ask this time—I simply gripped it. I realized again just how misleading the size really was. It was long, and the girth didn't seem plausible. Then I sounded naïve again.

"It's very large, Scott." My voice cracked, but my smile matched Scott's; it started small and grew into a large grin. "We'll go slow?" I asked him. "I mean, it doesn't look like it's going to fit!"

"Harp, there's no rush," he assured me. "We just need to go slow."

"I'm very small—"

"Harp," he told me, smiling. "It's fine."

He continued to lean over me as he kissed and felt me. I lost myself in the feeling so completely that I nearly forgot that sex was actually going to happen. He had me completely naked, and he was just the same. The blue comforter draped over him. With each forceful kiss, I loosened my grip and enjoyed the feeling of him. Scott was direct and to the point, reaching for my hand and placing it back on his member. I remembered then that we were done with only making out. We were onto something new now. His fingers circled slowly and then suddenly much faster. I unexpectedly gasped in amazement at how aggressive and yet so caring Scott could be at the same time.

"I can feel how much you want it...." His voice was a dark, low grumble.

"I really do," I breathed, pulling his lips against mine.

"Are you ready?" he breathed in my ear, pressing himself against me.

"Yes."

He tore the condom wrapper open with his teeth and lightly tossed the then-empty wrapper onto the floor. He then did exactly as he promised. He went slowly and repeatedly reminded me how much he loved me. He continued telling me how beautiful he thought I was and how much he loved me and my body. He kissed me constantly leading up to the moment, and when the moment came, he was gentle, gradually working his way in with intense focus. All the while diligently careful of my enjoyment and pleasure before he slammed into me.

"Ahh...." I screeched with pleasure. My back instinctively arched, taking in all Scott had.

"Harp, are you alright?"

"Uh-huh," I grunted. "I'm fine."

"Tell me if you're not," he whispered. "We can stop at any time. You just gotta tell me."

I clung to his back and buried my face into his neck. I tried to hide my painful expression from Scott's eyesight, but he pulled my lips up to his, forcing me to look at him. I focused on his soft lips instead of the feeling of pain that quickly coursed through my lower body.

"Harp, it's midnight," he whispered. "Happy New Year."

We pulled apart slowly; my head fell back onto Scott's pillow, and I looked into his blue eyes. I let go of his back, and we both shared the same smile.

"Happy New Year," I whispered.

Scott kissed me. He did nothing else; he didn't move, he didn't push, and he didn't force. He simply kissed me. It was a soft kiss, but I progressively pulled it into something more.

"You remembered!" I whispered.

"I remember everything."

"I love you so much, Scott."

He resumed his slow, cautious pace, never taking his eyes off me. For a brief moment, I smiled and watched him. We'd found a rhythm. I bit my lip to hide my growing smile. My smile grew larger and larger. Each time I tried to restrain my grin, Scott smiled broadly back at me.

"I love you," he breathed. "God, I love you so much."

I pulled his jaw toward me and kissed him passionately. He'd stopped and kissed me at midnight and reminded me that he loved me. He had made this night special not just for me but for us. I couldn't stop smiling at him. He continued kissing me, watching me, and rocking in a steady motion.

"I love you, Scotty," I told him. I knew he enjoyed our first time, and I knew I enjoyed being this close to him. His lips moved back to my neck, tracing a line back up to my lips, where he softly and gently kissed me again.

"You're smiling."

"I'm enjoying myself." I grinned and wrapped my arms around him.

"Yeah?" He glowed. "That's good!"

I pulled his lips back to mine and enjoyed the remaining feelings I experienced being this close to Scott. I watched and examined his movements. When he was finished, he rolled onto his side, and we looked at one another. I pulled the sheet up to my shoulders, holding my head up and smiling at him. I had smiled so much during the encounter that I forgot I was smiling, and I felt so good that I forgot to restrain my grin before it became silly.

"Was it alright?" he whispered. "Did you enjoy it?"

"I loved every minute of it."

His fingertips traced the outline of my body, starting at my ribs and continuing down to my hips before journeying back up. I did nothing but watch him; I held my head up and looked at him, taking in everything that was happening.

"Harp," he pleaded into my ear, "Stay…."

"You know my curfew! I nearly had to sign a promise in blood that I'd be back no later than two."

"Ohh," he groaned.

"We have a little time." I smiled. "Now, tell me your New Year's resolution."

"I'm going to give you everything you've given me."

"Wow," I exclaimed. "I haven't given you anything."

"Harper," he whispered, "You've given me everything, including you. Give me one more thing, and stay."

We fell asleep entangled with one another. My sleep was a surprisingly deep sleep for the short time it lasted. I wasn't sure if it was fear of my parents or the suspicion I knew they had about my sexual change that caused it, but my eyes flew open at half past one. I felt his arms around me; our legs draped over one another. He looked peaceful. His eyes softly shut, and his sandy-blond eyelashes made him look more beautiful than I'd seen him before. I moved carefully out from under his weight. I looked at him and felt a sudden weight lift off me. I'd done it. I was no longer some little girl following Scott and daydreaming about her first time. I'd finally found enough courage to move forward sexually in my relationship. Sex was still new, but I was a brand-new fifteen-year-old girl. I recharged as I watched him sleeping that night. I felt a little more grown-up now—not just because of the act itself, but because I'd made the choice to do it, the conscious choice I had made regarding the reality of my sexual fate. It had been something I'd only read about, heard about, and talked about; now, I'd finally done it.

"Scott," I whispered in his ear as I pressed my body against him. "Can you hear me? Please wake up."

"Hmm," he lightly groaned while he pulled me against him. "Do you have to go?"

"Can we do it again before I leave?"

SEVEN

IT WAS MID-MARCH, AND THE SENIOR class had just started releasing fliers reminding students to purchase prom tickets. The pink fliers were on corkboards in the main hallway, taped to some lockers, and hanging in the girls' locker room. There were even a few taped to the cafeteria door. It got to the point where one would have to be blind to not notice the prom reminders. I started to suspect Scott had zero intention of ever asking me, so my use of subliminal messages ensued. I began attaching fliers to the Pathfinder's front and back windshield wipers daily. I used multiple fliers at a time—some days, he had six or eight fliers on both the back and the front of his truck.

On a moderately cold Thursday afternoon in March, my afternoon of wallpapering Scott's windshields had already started. While he was off doing boy stuff with Brad before track practice, I had roughly fifteen minutes to complete my task. I was more excited this afternoon while papering his windshield because my parents were chaperoning Morgan's field trip, and it just so happened that it was an overnight trip. As promised, I informed Scott we had plans that evening. It was to be an evening free from interruptions.

I was nearly finished when I felt a light tap on my shoulder. As I turned slowly, I could only hope it wasn't Scott asking me what exactly I was doing. I was amazed to see the person staring back at me. I hadn't seen Taylor since our run-in back in December. I wouldn't say I was avoiding her; I would say that my obsession with my boyfriend had blocked out all other individuals—minus a few close friends, of course.

"Harper." She said my name like she'd never said it before, testing it out as if she were making sure it was actually my name. "I heard a nasty little rumor about you." She smiled a nasty smile. "Not nice at all."

I looked up at her. Her somewhat tall pack of girlfriends stood behind her. I had nothing to say to her, and if I did, I was sure I wasn't about to say it with a pack of girls standing around me. I may have been naïve, but I wasn't dumb.

"What, you're not interested in knowing what it is?" she asked. "Or, maybe you already know?"

"Is it just a freshman rumor, or is the whole school talking about it?" I questioned. "I need to narrow this down."

Taylor reached for a curl and pulled it condescendingly, checking the elasticity. Within a second, my hand instinctively swatted her hand away.

"Oh, Harper, you think the whole school knows who you are? That's adorable." She turned to her pack of girlfriends and lightly chuckled. "No, Harper, this is being talked about by the seniors and the freshmen. I doubt sophomores and juniors care about you."

I leaned against the truck, looking at these girls who had me scared. I was worried that things were going to go badly for me. The parking lot was nearly empty, and I was alone on this one. I was faced with a pack of girls housing one female who hated me more than anything.

"Harper, you think you're cool because Scott lets you drive his truck? You think you're popular because Scott's your boyfriend?" Her tone was sarcastic and patronizing. "Everyone knows why Scott is still with you."

"Why is Scott with me, Taylor?" I pressed. "Tell me. You seem to think you know Scott better than anyone, so please, enlighten me."

"Harper, everyone knows that you're a slut! Word is you get passed around among Scott, Brad, and the rest of the senior guys." She laughed as she looked at her girls. "That's probably why Scott lets you drive his truck—he's thankful he's getting it regularly. No girl is going *near* him!"

They all started laughing at me.

"Apparently, that's all Harper needs," exclaimed a girl in the back of the pack. She was hateful, and her words hurt me, so I refused to give her enough attention to learn her name.

They stood there laughing at me, laughing at a rumor about me that wasn't true. I was only a freshman. I'd have to live the rest of my high-school life knowing that at one time, a rumor like this existed. I, Harper Whitmore, was being thought of as a slut. I thought I was anything but, especially since I waited so long with Scott and I'd *only* been with Scott. I thought that made me the exact opposite of a slut—I was being monogamous.

"Ah, Harper Whitmore's going to cry," Taylor mocked. "Come on, girls; I don't want to have to explain to Scott how we made his precious *Harper* cry."

After sitting in the locker room for more than thirty minutes, I finally remembered my responsibilities as a sports team member. I arrived to practice late. I apologized to the coach for my tardiness and decided that sprinting wasn't something I intended to practice that day. I wanted to run at my pace, so I moved to the outer lane of the track and started to run. I ran six miles that day, and I thought of one thing the entire time—Scott. I knew he'd made it a point to keep our lives private. He never shared anything, he told me, but I couldn't help but wonder how something I considered so special and personal got out.

I believed Scott when he said he never told anyone, Brad included, and I believed Leigh when she said she'd stay quiet about it. I had never considered myself a slut, but I concluded that I could easily be viewed as one, if only because of my age. I was a fifteen-year-old girl with a very experienced eighteen-year-old senior boyfriend with a track record of getting whatever he wanted whenever he wanted. I was proof of that. I had pressed through my final lap when I heard large footsteps trailing behind mine. I felt the palm of a hand against my side just as I crossed the finish line. I knew he'd tracked me down.

"You all set?" He laughed. "Or do you have another six miles to run?"

"What?"

"*What?*" he exclaimed. "Are you kidding me? Babe, I've called your name every time you rounded the bend by the discus cage! What's going on? Why were you late?"

"Scott, have you been listening to what people are currently talking about?" I sighed. "I mean the rumors about us?"

"Harp, I never listen to what people are talking about. If I did, I would have become completely paranoid in the ninth grade!" He chuckled. "I can see that whatever is being said is upsetting you, so tell me what you heard. Is it about me, or is it about us this time? We talked about this, Harp; if it's about something I did in the last four years, it's probably true. You just gotta push through it!"

"No! That's the thing! It's not about us; it's not even about *you*," I roared, still angry after my run. "It's about *me*!"

"Well, whatever is being said, I highly doubt it's true!" He laughed. "I see you every day for nearly the entire day, and you haven't done anything worth gossiping about."

Scott stepped into me, wrapping his hand along my waist and pulling me close to him. His fingers started working in those imaginary circles against the skin on the small of my back, and his lips reached down to my ear. I knew what he was up to.

"I mean, Harp, I know some things you've done in the last week to *me* that I'd love to discuss openly," he whispered teasingly in my ear. "Then again, I'd also like to keep the mystery going."

"Did you, Scott?" I whined. "Did you discuss anything openly? Because if you did—"

"What?" He pulled away from me. "Are you *kidding* me? Harper, absolutely not! I never discuss that with anyone. I keep our relationship quiet, especially that part of it!"

"Scott," I sighed.

"What's the rumor?" he asked. "Harp, you gotta tell me."

"Scott," I mumbled, "people are saying I am a slut."

"Whoa! What?" His brows pulled together tightly. He was starting to get upset. "Who said this?"

"That's not all, though. They're saying that you're only my boyfriend because I put out and that I get passed around among Brad and your other friends."

"Harp, I know you hate rumors and gossip, but you gotta ignore this," he warned me. "This *will* pass, especially if we give it no attention."

"No, something like this will stick. I'll have it follow me the rest of my high-school life! I'll always be looked at as the freshman girl with a senior boyfriend because she put out!"

"Harper," he assured me, "absolutely not! This won't follow you."

"Scott—"

"Harper, if we weren't together next year, I could see this rumor sticking, but do you really think something like this will still be sticking around when you're a senior in high school, and I'm a junior—"

"You really think we'll be together that long?" I interrupted him. "I had no idea that you saw us together for that long."

"Babe, I see us together for a long time! Come on." He reached for my hand. "Let's get out of here. Are the plans still on for tonight?"

"Yes!" I grinned as he picked me up and walked toward the locker room. "My family is already gone, but I'm worried about tomorrow morning. What if they come home before we've left for school?"

"It's doubtful. If they do, I'll explain that I just arrived to pick you up."

"Alright." I nervously bit my lip as I thought Scott's words through. "I trust you, but I still have a lot of anxiety about this whole thing."

"See, Harp? You've already forgotten about the rumors. You're back to freaking out about me spending the night!"

"What did you tell your parents?"

"Harp, this will be the first time I've exercised the legal adult right of not having to tell my parents anything."

"Really?" I pulled my brows together and frowned. "What was your reasoning for the last seventeen years?"

"I was teetering on delinquency." He smirked. "I'll meet you back here in five minutes, babe."

He lightly patted my butt and kissed me quickly, and then looked toward the parking lot and rolled his eyes at the sight of his truck and the slew of pink fliers gracing its front and back.

"I will *not* miss high school committees next year," he groaned.

We parted ways as we walked into the locker rooms. Scott always had the ability to help me forget my worries, and that is precisely what he did. By the time I was inside the locker room, I had forgotten about the rumors and was back to thinking about Scott staying the entire night in my bed for the first time. I had added anxiety over this particular first-time experience.

I had only just walked into the locker room when I saw a group of older girls on the team, seniors, I thought, talking. They all took notice as I walked in.

"There she is!"

I looked up at the small pack as I pulled my bag out of my locker. One very tall blonde girl was gliding from the pack toward me. A continuous murmur of "ask her" followed her.

I kept looking at my bag, trying not to focus on the blonde senior approaching me.

"Harper?" she asked. "Harper Whitmore?"

I refrained from looking up at her. I focused on my bag and my warm-ups, spinning my lock. I knew these girls, and they certainly knew who I was. Her question was trivial at best and served only as a means to open a dialogue with me.

"Yep," I informed her harshly. "I'm Harper, and you're a senior who *already* knows who I am."

"Harper, don't be mean. I heard what people are saying about you. I just told those girls over there all about it."

I finally pulled my eyes up to her. She had a beautiful frame. Her height and lean figure served her well. She looked almost like a doll. Everything was perfectly symmetrical, right where it should be.

"Do you know who I am?" she continued in a very pressing manner. "I mean, really know who I am?"

"Yes, I know who you are," I replied with hostility. "You're Lindsay Paul. You're a senior, and you run the thirty-two hundred. Could you please tell me why you told those girls a lie? Do those girls *need* to know a rumor about me? Really?"

"I guess you do know a *little* about me. Tell me, Harper, did Scott tell you about me?"

I looked slowly into her eyes; she was probably one of those girls Scott *had* before me.

"No, Scott didn't tell me about a Lindsay Paul. Should he have?" I picked up my bag and prepared to leave the locker room. "Should I go ask him? I have to tell you that I really don't care what went on before me."

"Harper, ask him. Have him tell you. Let me know he told you, and I'll be sure to have this rumor stopped." She turned and began to walk away. "Maybe you should start caring about the guy he was before you," she warned me.

"Why?" I asked her, my voice raised so she could hear me. "Why do I need to know about you? Why should I care about who Scott was *before* me? I only care about the Scott I'm with *now*."

"Harper, Scott has changed since he's been with you." She stopped and turned back toward me. "He has changed a *lot*. He loves you, and that's not exactly fair to me." She turned her head to look at me again as she walked away. "Or to the rest of those girls."

I ran out of the locker room, nearly stumbling over my feet. The anger behind Lindsay Paul's words to me had me worried. Her words were so cryptic. She said she could stop the rumor; I had no idea what that meant. I pulled my key out of my bag and opened the Pathfinder's hatch.

"Harper, I just heard some disturbing news about you." I recognized the voice.

I snapped my head up and saw Barrett, then rolled my eyes and returned to putting my belongings into the back of the truck.

"I am sure it's not pleasant to be thought of as slut," he continued. "By the way, your love is in the locker room beating the shit out of that guy Justin from the baseball team."

If that were true, Scott was looking at a suspension. I jumped—high enough, for once in my life—and pulled the hatch down without Scott's assistance. I made sure to slam the hatch down with all the force I could gather.

"You know what, Barrett?" I roared, finally having had enough. "This is the sort of shit I'm going to run and tell Scott about."

My anger was back and stronger than ever; all the pleasant calm I'd achieved from running six miles had faded away. All the comforting words Scott recited to me had vanished. I was angry. I was mad at Lindsay, and I was now angry at Barrett. Part of me was getting angry at Scott for having a life before me that was now causing me pain.

"Say it again, Barrett," I screamed. "Call me a slut one more time, and I'll run into the men's locker room right now and have Scott out here. Say it!"

"Harper, your boyfriend is beating the shit out of some senior right now in the locker room. I doubt he's going to pull himself away to beat *my* ass." His grin was evil. "Plus, if Scott gets caught hitting me, he's looking at a suspension right before graduation, and that's not smart. He won't touch me."

I opened the truck and stepped up on the rail, angry enough that I was determined to ignore him. I felt someone's hand on the small of my back, the palm flat against my back and long fingers wrapping around my waist. If I hadn't known better, I'd have said it was Scott, but the way the hand was placed on my back wasn't the usual method Scott employed. The fingertips didn't lightly tickle or draw imaginary circles down my back before the palm went flat. This was different. The hand felt unwelcome and unnatural, and I pulled away.

"Scott's right to keep you around," Barrett whispered. "You are tight! This is how Scott does it?"

"Don't touch me, Barrett," I screamed as I pulled away from his touch. "You touch me again, and Scott and Brad will *both* be here."

Barrett kept his posture loose and calm as if he had me right where he wanted me. He thought his unwarranted touch could pull me in. He removed his hand, but only momentarily. I caught him shifting his hand toward my knee and moving it up to my thigh. His eyes followed his hand, entranced by his movements. He pulled his eyes up my thigh. His hand moved for half a second, giving me time to kick him squarely in the chest. He fell backward against an old Toyota Camry.

"Soon, Scott will be gone," he grunted. "You'll need someone to replace him. You'll need *me*!"

"Don't touch me, Barrett," I screamed. He laughed. "You think this is *funny*?" I raged at him.

"Harper, Scott taught you well. He must be terrified of what will happen to you next year. I'll bet he's terrified you'll *keep* getting passed around."

"I'm telling Scott everything you just did and said," I warned him. "You won't get a fight from me, but you'll get it from Scott!"

I got into the truck. Before starting the engine, Scott emerged from the locker room not wearing a shirt. I had nothing to say when he got into the Pathfinder. I was so angry that saying anything would result in tears. I simply pressed the stick into reverse and then quickly shifted into first, leaving the high school parking lot.

"You're getting a lot better at first," he encouraged me. "You don't jerk forward anymore. It's impressive how quickly you picked this up."

I could only look at him and nod. I sat quietly, focused on keeping the truck in the correct gear as we got onto the main road toward my house. Lindsay's words flooded my mind, and I could not decide if anger, confusion, or sadness was the correct emotion to express to Scott. Maybe it was time for him to experience what I was like when I was *really* angry. At the moment, I figured silence would be the best thing.

"Harp, you can go into fourth if you are comfortable with going faster."

"I'm fine in third," I whispered.

"Harper, we'll get through this. Just, please...Please don't shut me out on this one. We'll get through it. I know you are very sensitive about what is said about us. Despite my apathy about gossip, I know you hate it."

After parking it at the top of my driveway, I hopped out of the truck. I figured we'd talk it through and Scott would find some way to put me back in the mood I was in when we left the track together, but he hadn't gotten there yet. All I had on my mind were Lindsay's words and Barrett's touch.

"Harp," Scott sighed as he met me behind the truck, "are we still going to have a good night together?"

"Is that all you can think about?" I countered.

"Harper, I figured once we got into the house, we'd be alone again. It would be just us! I wasn't thinking about *that*; I was thinking about the entire night. I had it all planned out—"

"What did you have planned out, Scott?" I asked him, hostility in my voice. "What's going to happen?"

"Harper, we talked about this last night. I told you what I wanted out of tonight. I told you I'd been looking forward to this night for three weeks."

He began to itemize his list of expectations for the night, slowly stepping toward me.

"I wanted to shower with you, to feel you there before I took you back into your room—"

"Scott," I huffed and pushed him away just as his fingers began their route along the small of my back. "If you want to come in, then come in!"

I tugged and dragged my bag out of the Pathfinder and marched up the walkway. I knew Scott had spent a substantial amount of time planning this particular Thursday night, and here I was, unable to remove any of the anger I had inside me. I marched right by him. He stood there and only shifted his body ever-so-slightly to watch me.

"Are you coming in?" I roared. "I'd like to know your plans before I shut the door. If you want this night to happen, get in the house so we can get it over with!"

"I don't know, Harper! Are you going to continue being a bitch about this all night?" he yelled. "If you just want to *get this night over with*, I'll just head home. Screw spending the night together!"

"What did you call me?"

"Harper..." He backpedaled.

"No! What did you just say?" I walked slowly toward him and lightly pushed him repeatedly. "You just called me a bitch!"

"Harper! I didn't mean it." He stepped back lightly with each shove. "I meant that you were acting like one."

"That's better? I'm not acting like anything, Scott, except for a girl who is pissed that her name is being dragged through the mud because of her boyfriend!"

"Harper!" He quickly grabbed my wrists, preventing me from shoving him again. "How is this rumor my fault?"

"I'm not having this argument." I yanked my wrists away from his loose grip and stormed back up the walkway and into my house.

"The hell we're not, Harper! You just blamed me for this; I deserve to know why you think this is my fault!"

"That's the thing, Scott. I don't know why it's your fault, but according to Lindsay Paul, it is!"

He took a deep, long, and exhausted sigh. His shoulders drooped, and his hands followed. His face spoke of guilt and remorse at the same time. It was like watching a slow crash; his body collapsed on the inside as well as the outside. His eyes followed his body.

"Harper," he whispered.

"Did you, Scott?" I panicked. "Please tell me that you didn't. Tell me it wasn't because I was a virgin. Tell me that had nothing to do with any of it. Please tell me you still love me. Tell me you're still into me!"

A chain reaction had started. Seeing Scott's crumbling exterior tore me from the inside out. I felt abandoned and neglected, as if no one in this world could pull me from the isolation I was just thrown into. I watched him as he stood there and looked blankly.

"Harper," he whispered, "it isn't like that."

I had no energy to fight him or anyone anymore. I stepped aside and let him in the door. I looked like I felt—tired and worried that the worst thing I could possibly imagine was happening to me. I never would have assumed Scott was capable of being with anyone other than me while we were dating, and I was now headed to my room, desperate to hear him deny it. I was nearly halfway up the stairs before I looked down and saw Scott still standing in the doorway, not denying anything.

"Did you?" I pressed. "Just tell me now, and we can move on."

He casually started up the stairs and to my room. "If I did, would it be easy for you to take me back?"

"Before or after we started—"

"Would it matter?" he pressed.

"To me, it would."

"You'll stay with me after I tell you this."

"Don't ever tell me what to do," I demanded. "I have every right to be angry and decide what happens after you tell me."

I marched into my closet and began getting ready for the night. I had my night planned, and those plans had involved a beautiful red lace number I recently bought, but as I saw it in my closet, I realized those plans were being shelved. I was angry at everyone and everything for taking my night away from me. I pulled out an oversized shirt that I'm sure was Scott's at one point or another instead.

"I'm taking a shower," I mumbled. "I'm not sure I want to see you when I get out."

"Harp," he breathed.

"No," I said, saddened. "I was looking forward to this night. I went out and got a great item to wear. I even had it planned—we'd never leave my room. We'd watch a movie in here and eat take-out. I'm so angry right now! I trusted you! I thought you weren't like what everyone said."

"Harp, it's not like that...."

He stepped closer to where I stood in the doorway of my bathroom. His hands reached for my waist. Before I realized what he intended to do, his lips were pressed against mine. I squirmed, pushed, and pulled myself away from his grip.

"You called me a bitch! You don't get to kiss me," I yelled. "You slept with Lindsay Paul! You don't get to kiss me!"

"Harper, I want to explain everything. Why are you being so incredibly difficult?"

"Oh, *I'm* being difficult?" I roared. "Scott, things will be *very* difficult for you in a minute if you don't get the hell out of my house!"

He didn't acknowledge me. He walked the perimeter of my room and examined everything related to my relationship with him.

"You know we're done, right?" I shouted at him. "Take it all in, Scott, because you won't be seeing any of these things again!"

"Quit it, Harper!"

"Scott, did you sleep with her?" I glared at him. "Just admit that before I shower."

He didn't answer. He continued to look at my bedroom walls, picking pictures up from my bookshelf and examining all the things that were stored on my desk and dresser.

"Goddamn it, Scott! Goddamn it," I screamed. "I told you I loved you, and you do *this*. I feel like a dumb girl for believing you could actually change!"

"Harper, it's not like—"

I didn't bother listening to the rest of that sentence. It inevitably involved him saying that it wasn't like that—that she meant nothing to him and that it was just a one-time thing. I imagined he might even say it happened during the four months we weren't having sex when I hadn't been offering it up. He probably couldn't even go four months without doing it. He had to find some backseat broad to give him the hook-up.

I could really only imagine that was how it worked. I had no idea how Scott would have found the time. I literally spent all my time with him. I could only conclude that he wasn't sleeping; instead, he was going out trolling for easy broads. I stood in that hot shower, wondering if I really wanted to know about Lindsay Paul. I finished shaving my legs and let the water pound on me before I left my steamy bathroom wrapped in my towel.

I walked into my bedroom slowly; I placed my razor back on my vanity, never making eye contact with Scott, who was sitting on my oversized pink-and-green floral-print reading chair, looking at my scrapbook of our relationship. I walked into my closet, certain to close the door, and reluctantly pulled one of Scott's oversized T-shirts over my head before remerging with my hairbrush.

"Why are you still here?" I roared. "Are you at least going to put a shirt on? I don't want to see your chest, and it appears you have no real intention of leaving."

I pretended to be focused on combing each one of my curls thoroughly. I checked each curl for elasticity and proper bounce, wanting to avoid eye contact with Scott. I was sure he was inevitably planning his method of pulling me back to his side, and I wasn't sure if I was ready to smooth things over just yet. I had a strong desire to sit and mull over how angry I was.

"Are you going to bed at six this evening?" he mumbled. "It's unlike you to go to bed so early."

"Leave!"

"You are quite the scrapbooker; I didn't realize that you saved *everything* we ever did together."

He didn't move from my oversized reading chair, though the chair didn't look oversized with Scott sitting in it. He kept his eyes on me while I continued to brush my hair. I could feel his eyes as they burned through me.

"You're not going to speak to me, are you?" he asked. "How long can I expect you to ignore me?"

"You could probably take that scrapbook home. I don't think I'll have a boyfriend after this evening, and I'm not sure I will want to remember the one I had," I stated. "I can't believe you called me a bitch!"

"Harper, I asked if you were going to continue to *act* like a bitch."

"Exactly!" I pointed my hairbrush at him. "You called me a bitch! We've been through the semantics a couple times now—you called me a *bitch*."

"I am sorry for that," he pleaded with me. "I shouldn't have said that!"

"So you admit that you called me a bitch?" I shrugged. "Great."

"Harp—"

"Do you really want to get into this? What do you want me to say?" I tossed my hairbrush condescendingly onto the vanity. "Whatever happens between you and Lindsay shouldn't concern me, right? You fucked her, but it was probably before we were fucking, so I should just learn to deal with it, right? No matter how bad it is or how much it hurts me *now*, I should accept what happened and deal with it. Is that what you want me to say?"

"Harp—"

"Or did you fuck her between the first and second time you fucked me? Maybe you did it between the second and third time!" I roared, my anger reaching its zenith. "I have a feeling you did it in the beginning, though. Things are starting to get a little easier for us in the sex department, and you're finally enjoying it with me. You don't need Lindsay now!"

"Harp, I don't consider our sexual experiences *fucking*! Trust me, I enjoy every minute of it with you. I always have." He bent down and untied his shoes. "Just so you know, Lindsay Paul started that rumor about you."

"But what you do with Lindsay *is* considered fucking?" I glared. "Your precious *Harper* doesn't get fucked, but your side project does? Why are you taking your shoes off? You'll be leaving soon, remember? This *magical* night isn't happening...And no *shit*, she started it; I may be a freshman, but I'm not slow."

"That rumor she spread about you actually happened to her."

Scott slowly stood up from my chair and walked to me. Both his shoes were off; it appeared Scott had no intention of leaving anytime soon. It seemed as though he had every intention of settling in this evening. He was not leaving at all. I slowly walked backward, away from him, and fell back onto my bed. I got comfortable, draping the comforter over my legs and keeping a safe distance from Scott so he couldn't physically pull me into him.

"Harper, what I did to her in tenth grade wasn't something she deserved. Until you said her name, I never thought about the fact that the current rumor going around about us was a reality for Lindsay."

"*Me*," I corrected him. "The rumor is about *me*, not you. Not *us*."

"Harper!" Scott's voice was stern. "If you are going through something like this, *we* are going through it. You're not alone in any of this. And I swear to you that I have not slept with anyone but you since I met you."

"This isn't a recent thing?"

He shook his head.

"This is something that happened two years ago? It happened before me?"

He nodded.

"How do I know you're not lying to me?"

"I don't have anything to lie to you about. *I* know I've never cheated on you, and I think you know that, too," he whispered confidently. "I know you trust me; if you didn't, you wouldn't be so quick to use the break-up card as a weapon. That's the only card you can play to actually hurt me, and you know it."

"Why didn't you tell me sooner?" I whispered.

"Harper," he breathed, "you are entirely driven off emotion. When you argue and are really angry, you go one of two ways in expressing it. This afternoon, I was caught off-guard. I didn't know which direction you were planning on taking. I also wanted to explain everything to you when you were calm enough to listen to the explanation. And to answer your earlier question, yes, I consider what Lindsay and I did to be fucking. I wouldn't do that to you."

I picked up my hairbrush and started to lightly brush out my curls. I brushed through each curl, focusing on the ends of my hair. I didn't look at him; I kept my focus on my hair, terrified that if I spoke, I'd get myself into more trouble by jumping to more conclusions.

"Most people don't realize how long my hair really is," I said out loud to make conversation. "The curls disguise the length." I examined the ends of my hair while Scott began outlining my legs over the down comforter. "Maybe I'll cut it and wear it straight."

"Please don't do that," Scott whispered. "Please don't cut your hair. I love your hair. You know how much I love your hair. I love how each curl is its own curl; it's not a mess like some girls' hair."

"A lot of girls are wearing their hair straight."

"I love putting my hand into your curls and seeing how easy it is to get it back out." He smiled. "You take such good care of your hair."

He was sullen, almost dark-spirited, but he was sincere. He kept his focus on tracing my legs through the comforter.

"Harp, please don't change your hair," he continued. "It's one of the things I love about you."

"I know you didn't cheat," I mumbled under my breath. "I don't know when you would have had the time. I spend every waking minute with you, and if I'm not physically with you, I'm on the phone with you. You're not exactly capable of sleeping with someone and talking on the phone at the same time."

"I am very good at multitasking." He smirked.

"Scott, you talk a lot during the act," I reminded him. "You always tell me about how beautiful you think I am. Sometimes you go on long tangents about how much enjoyment—"

"Before you, there was no dialogue."

"Oh," I breathed, caught off-guard. "It's hard for me to imagine that—"

"Harper, you have a right to know what happened with Lindsay—"

"No, I don't," I snapped. "What happened between you and someone else before our relationship is none of my business."

"Yes, it is! You mean *everything* to me. I honestly didn't think my relationship with her then would affect you in any way. I just assumed she was over what happened in tenth grade because she never said anything to me about it until recently."

"I thought you'd never had a girlfriend before?" I asked, confused. "I thought I was your first girlfriend, and that's why I meant so much to you."

"You *are* my first girlfriend," he assured me. "That's not why you mean so much to me, though. You're the only girl I ever fell in love with, and you just so happen to be the only girlfriend I've ever had."

"What was your *relationship* with her, then?"

"Listen, Harp, I hadn't spoken to her since tenth grade, but a few weeks ago, I was caught off-guard when she approached me. After what happened a few years ago, she seemed to keep her distance. I know *I* kept my distance. I didn't intentionally avoid her; I just never had anything to approach her about. I never wanted to give her the wrong impression. That was the problem from the beginning—I gave her the wrong impression. No matter how clear I thought I was with her, she didn't go by what I *said* but what we *did*."

"What did she say when she approached you a few weeks ago?"

"She asked about you." He rolled his eyes. "She asked if I was in love with you. Something was weird about the way she asked. She didn't look at me. She glanced my way after she asked, but she kept her eyes focused off into the distance. I have no idea what she was staring at, but she wasn't looking at me. I was hesitant to answer her question because of the way she asked, but I decided that I should tell her the truth. I mean, what was I supposed to do; lie to her to spare her feelings? I told her the truth, I love you."

"Why would she care? How would she not know? That whole stupid high school knows you love me. You yell it across the track at least once a week. You sneak up behind me, pick me up, and then yell it right before I scream. I mean, everyone knows!"

"I make no secret of how I feel about you; it's true. I think she didn't like seeing what everyone else sees." He closed his eyes and breathed a heavy sigh. "She finally looked at me, and I could see it in her eyes: It took everything she had to say these things to me, ask me that question, and go on to say what she said next. She looked me in my eyes and said, 'So a freshman is good enough for Scott Pierce's love, but not someone he's known his whole life.' Harp, the way she phrased it, it wasn't a question so much as a statement. That was it. She left. She didn't even wait for me to respond."

"What did you do then?"

"I walked to your fourth-period algebra class and waited for you to come out," He replied. "Harper, that morning, you had told me about your parents going on Morgan's field trip. I was beyond excited to have an entire uninterrupted night with my girlfriend, and I would be damned if Lindsay was going to take me down from that high."

"She must have known," I mumbled to myself. "You were so excited when I told you about them going away. I remember, in the main hallway, you started talking about the hot tub and it being just us. The whole hallway must have heard you."

"Harper?" He inched closer to me. "Harp, I told you I was an asshole before we got together. I think I still am. For some reason, you refuse to believe I ever was or could be an asshole, though—"

I interrupted him. "Scott, I know what people see you as, but I—"

"No, Harp," he quickly cut me off. "Don't explain your perspective of me. I know what I am. I know that I *am* how other people see me. Harper, I intentionally forgot about that incident in the tenth grade because I think that even as it was happening, I wasn't happy about being in that situation. It was an easy situation for me to maintain, though, so I kept at it."

"You don't have to tell me if you don't want to." I breathed. "It happened well before me, and the rule has always been, what happened before *us* doesn't count."

"You let me off the hook for so much that I'll own up to this. I can't see you suffering through a rumor about what *I* did to Lindsay."

I nodded, allowing Scott to move to the center of my bed. I felt sudden relief at the thought that perhaps our night together could be salvaged. He took a deep breath, no doubt as a means to prolong this enjoyable moment before he delved into his story. He reached for the small, plush, purple Beanie Baby his mother had bought me when she visited the university. He tossed the small bear back and forth between his hands.

"Harper, I think Lindsay wants me to tell you this because she wants to make sure that you think I am a dick. That way, you will leave me. She probably thinks I have you believing I have always been this great guy."

"You don't have to—"

"Here goes…I got the Pathfinder that year, and it was a huge deal. I became popular just for having that car! I mean, I was popular my freshman year, but only because I was a freshman starter on the varsity basketball team."

"And, Scott," I teased to ease the tension, "I've seen your yearbooks; you were a very attractive fifteen-year-old freshman!"

"Thank you." He smiled. "But I think that goes without saying."

"Continue…." I gave him a reassuring smile.

"Apparently, over the summer, I'd gone from being a really great basketball player to being a really popular sophomore guy with a great car. Either way, a lot of girls wanted to date me. I didn't want to date anyone, though; I'd been clear about that when I was a freshman. I just wanted to go to school, play basketball, hang out with Brad and Ethan, and go to the bluff. I did not want to be bothered by being anyone's boyfriend. Lindsay Paul certainly wasn't the first girl I'd had, either. I'd taken a few up to the bluff before, but she was the only one who couldn't be...*Contained*."

"Contained?"

"She ran her mouth!" He shrugged. "She was the only girl I'd had who would talk about what went on up there."

"Oh." I sighed. "I never told anyone about the time we were up there in your car. I never even told Leigh."

"You're different, Harper. You're better than those girls. You hate it when people even suspect what might be between us. Some girls enjoy people knowing about their exploits. It's like a goddamn competition among who's been with me. Lindsay wanted people to think there was more than just *that* between us."

"She wanted people to think you were her boyfriend."

"She was the only one of those girls who wanted that," he added. "She was a cute girl, but I told her up front I wasn't interested in being a boyfriend."

"There was probably some confusion—"

"I told her, Harp. You gotta believe me on that. I told her outright that I didn't want to be her boyfriend. I'll take responsibility for everything else, but that is the one thing I stand clear on. I told her!"

"Scott, I believe you."

"She was *always* there! By the time basketball season started up, she was following me around. I thought we were just friends. I honestly don't believe I led her on! We'd talk during classes that we shared, and she'd meet me after class, but it was nothing serious. She was barely a friend. She'd always ask to come over to my place, but I wasn't going to allow *that* to happen."

"She thought she was more than just your friend. She may not have believed you two were a couple yet, but she certainly believed you were on that path," I explained. "If she asked to come to your home, she wanted to meet your family. She wanted to introduce herself to people as someone in your life, someone more than just a classmate. If she met you after class, she wanted people to see you walking and talking with her."

"I know...." Scott slowly reached for the bottle of water on my nightstand. He focused on spinning the cap off and gently setting it on the corner of my nightstand, taking his time before returning to the story. "How long has that water been sitting there?"

"Since you left it there on Sunday." I smiled. "Would you like a straw, Scott? I can get one for you."

"No, I'm good." He tucked my wet hair behind my ears and carefully moved closer to me. "Thank you, though."

"Let me know."

"Harp," he breathed. "Are you alright hearing this? I swear this all happened well before we were a couple. You gotta believe me. You and I mean a lot to me."

"I know. Thinking back, it doesn't fit—you cheating, I—"

"I'd never do that to you," he whispered.

"I think I always knew that," I mumbled, "but you seemed so guilty. You seemed so upset."

"I was upset because I never wanted anything I did before us to affect you, and I remembered that the gossip, in the beginning, upset you so much."

"I'm fine. I can deal with the gossip. I couldn't handle it if you did something like that to me; I couldn't handle any of that, but I'll find a way to deal with Lindsay and her rumor."

"I guess the rest of the story is pretty simple," he reassured. "I mean, we started making out at the bluff after the first basketball game, and she seemed eager to do more. I don't even remember how we got separated from the crowd that night. It happened so quickly. I remember walking with her but not really listening to anything she was saying. It was like I was following her."

"Hmm...." I nodded.

"Are you sure you want to hear the rest?" he asked. "Should I stop? I could just tell you the cliff notes version. I mean, this probably sounds familiar."

"No," I whispered. "It doesn't sound familiar at all. We've walked together to the end of the bluff, but I can remember everything we've ever discussed up there."

"After seeing your scrapbooking capabilities, I can imagine you would remember everything pretty well," he teased light-heartedly. "You seem capable of remembering everything."

"The night we went up there and wrestled in the backseat?" I smiled as I thought of the memory of him telling me he loved me and me being ready to give all I had to him. "It's one of my favorite nights."

"That night, I wanted to pick up right where we left off in my bedroom earlier. I wanted to take your braids out and have that moment again. You were so soft. Your legs were so smooth, and you had that huge smile I love so much. All I could think about in the truck that night was how you're too good for me because you don't care about anything before—"

"Scott," I interrupted, "anything that happened before me doesn't count. You know that."

"I knew I was better than her! That was the problem. I was better, and she was easy. I don't really remember anything with her or any of them, for that matter. I remember her reaching for my hand to hold it as we walked. I did hold her hand briefly, but then I pulled my hand away and put them both in my pockets. She didn't say anything about that. I think she just kept going about how great the game was and how spectacular I was."

"Scott—"

"I remember," he mumbled to himself. "She turned toward me and kissed me. I don't know how she could think we were anything; that kiss wasn't anything like our kisses. She is taller than you, so there was no slow progression; there was no bending over to meet halfway like there is with you. I look forward to kissing you. I look forward to that smile you have when you see me from a distance because I know that when we finally meet one another, your smile will be the last thing I see before I kiss you. There was nothing like that with her. There was nothing at all with her."

"You mean this smile, Scott?" I leaned up and over his lap and smiled.

"Yes, that smile!" He rested his hand on my waist and pulled me into a kiss. It was a long kiss, requiring him to gently guide me with his right hand. "This is the smile that reminds me that Harper loves me. I forget everything when I see Harper's perfect teeth."

"They are perfect," I whispered in agreement, my grin getting wider. "Absolutely perfect!"

"The rest of the story isn't good," he whispered. "I've always just blocked it out. Now that I'm with you, I don't have to block it out—it doesn't register with me; it's as if it had never happened. I am ashamed now because I couldn't imagine doing that to you. I can't imagine anyone doing that to you, but I did it to her, and now it is affecting you."

"Sometimes, when you talk to me, you make it sound like I'm a fragile girl. You make it seem like I'm so delicate, and you're terrified of hurting me. You don't give me enough credit, you know."

"Harp, I'm terrified you'll hit your limit with me and leave," he corrected. "I don't want you to leave me, so I need to make sure you feel secure in *us*."

"I won't leave you, alright?"

"Thank you. Anyway, Lindsay and I were so far off, Harp. She continued to kiss me, but I don't recall kissing her back. She pulled me toward the bluff's edge, and we did it on the part of the bluff with the tall grass. I didn't know she was a virgin until we were there and doing it."

"Scott," I exclaimed in shock. Scott held his hand up for me to stop talking.

"She never told me ahead of time. I was so in the moment that I wasn't going to stop, though. I'd never stopped with any of them, and I wasn't about to stop just because she was a virgin. I kept going; it wasn't like it was with you. I wasn't gentle; I never told her I loved her. I never kissed her during the act. I wanted it to be different for you because I cared. I was caring; I made sure that you knew I loved you. I made you feel safe. I was like that with you because I knew how much that moment meant to you, and I knew how much you meant to me. I knew you wanted to feel more than just my weight on top of you. With Lindsay, I didn't care about any of that."

"Did she ever say *no*?"

"Harper, it wasn't like that. She wanted it. I guess she thought that was how it went."

"Good thing she isn't a relationship person," I added, explaining, "Some girls can only have sex if they are in a relationship. Others have no problem with it either way, which is not bad! Lindsay is apparently the type of girl who doesn't need to be in a relationship."

"Harp, Lindsay is a relationship person," Scott informed me. "She thought we were something more than we were and allowed something to happen that didn't mean anything to me. It still doesn't mean anything to me as I look back on it now. Fucking her was the exact opposite of making love to you. We didn't talk about it ahead of time and discuss if she was ready. I didn't do that with any girl. I didn't care about her feelings during or after the act. It just happened."

He abruptly went silent. He tossed the Beanie Baby to the floor and slowly reached for a framed photo of the two of us at the State Championship in February that I kept on a shelf. He was facing me and holding his league MVP trophy, leaning in and holding me close while he kissed me. My left hand rested lightly on his face, and confetti fell around us.

"Where did you get this picture?"

"I got it from the yearbook committee. Leigh is on it." I shrugged. "Do you like it?"

"Yeah, I think this might be one of my favorite pictures of us," he whispered. "It looks like neither of us is aware that our photo is being taken. Those seem to be my favorites, you know? When we don't know our picture is being taken."

"Yes," I whispered with a smile. "I know exactly what you mean."

As he examined the picture, he looked as though he remembered the entire evening—before, during, and after winning that basketball game.

"Do you want the picture?" I asked him.

"I do, but I don't want to take your copy. Maybe the yearbook committee has the negative. You know, we could get another copy that way."

"Sure, I can try to do that for you. I am sure Leigh can track down the negative," I assured him. "You can take that one in the meantime—you know if you really want a copy."

"No, I couldn't take yours. You love your pictures. I'm over here all the time, anyway; I can see it as much as I want."

"That's true."

"I'm still going to be coming over, right?" he mumbled anxiously.

"Scott," I sighed. "Of course you can continue to come over."

"But can I come over as your *boyfriend*?" He stumbled over his words. "You know because you said—"

"Scott, you are still my boyfriend."

"I just need to make sure that we're the same as...*before*."

"We're the same," I assured him softly. "I get it."

"Harp, I should have stopped when I figured out she was a virgin. I know that. I should have realized *before* the bluff that she was a virgin." He groaned. "I finished and left her there. None of the others were ever virgins; I never had to worry about that sort of stuff before. I couldn't spend time with her afterward. I didn't want to hold her, and I couldn't tell her how great it was. I couldn't do any of that. I just left her there to get dressed...*alone*. I climbed the path back to the truck and saw Brad. I didn't even stick around to talk to him; I split."

"Scott, this isn't—"

"I kept going to the bluff with her," he continued. "The following Monday morning, I pulled into the parking lot, and she was waiting for me. She went on and on about how she had a great time with me on Friday night. I didn't call her after that. I didn't reach out to her; I pretended it didn't happen. I spent that entire weekend *not* thinking about her. I avoided her for the rest of that week; I'd walk right by her all week as if she didn't exist. We did it again that Friday night. I thought I could do it differently—you know, stick around, maybe. I did exactly the same thing, Harper. When I was finished, I went back up the bluff and into my truck, all alone. I couldn't figure out why I kept running away from her."

"You couldn't have kept this up. How long did you keep running?"

"Until the end of the season." He rested his head in his hands. "I only stopped it when someone asked me how things were going with her. I didn't want a relationship."

"Scott, that's like three months—four if you include playoffs."

"She'd started telling people I was her boyfriend. I was *never* her boyfriend. After another person asked me about her, I went to find her. She was standing outside the science building with a pack of girls. I should have pulled her aside to talk to her privately, but I was pissed. I'm not even sure why I was so angry, actually. I mean, now that I'm looking back at it, who *cares* if she thought we were together? I knew we weren't. I should have left her alone. I should have ended it by walking away. I didn't. Instead, I called her a whore in front of all her friends. I told her she was out of her mind for ever thinking that we were a couple. I told her that couples don't fuck and leave one another at the bluff."

"Scott—"

"I unleashed on her! Of course, all her friends started jumping all over what I said. They all started calling me a dick and an asshole; people were watching. Before I entered the main building, I turned and yelled, 'I may be a dick now, but she'll *always* be a slut.' I didn't stop there. I reminded her that no girlfriend of mine would ever give it up so easily.

Harp, we never did anything more than fuck. We had nothing. It was entirely incomparable to what you and I have. She cried hysterically after I confronted her. I could never do that to you! I can't even imagine how much pain I'd feel if I ever made you cry like that."

"Is that why you were so clear in the beginning that you wanted me as your girlfriend?" I asked, being careful to keep emotion out of my voice.

"It might have been." He shrugged. "You were the first girl I ever wanted *more* with."

"And you wanted me to know—"

"You were special," he interrupted. "You were different. You're better. I could *never* make you feel like I made Lindsay feel. It would kill me."

"Scott, I'm not better than anyone."

"I left campus with Brad. I couldn't deal with that." He continued with his story, dismissing my words. "I told him everything, and he decided to fix my situation. After a while, she started to think she was *with* Brad. He let her think that; he didn't care if people thought they were together. I didn't care, either; she was off me and onto someone else, and you know Brad—he can't even decide what Leigh is to him."

"Scott, that's exactly what Lindsay said about me," I said, panicking. "She said that I was a slut, and that I was being passed around between you and Brad. She said that's how you two work—you share everything."

He lightly played with my damp curls and nodded. He knew this already. Lindsay made her truth my rumor to hurt Scott. She used me to hurt him, and in the process, I was hurting. Scott's reiteration of his history with Lindsay was painful to hear, but it was more painful to watch. There was agony on his face throughout the story. He was distraught as he relived this painful part of his past. I knew, though, that his agony was entirely selfish. I knew him. If I wasn't in the picture and Lindsay had popped up with this, he wouldn't have cared. He would have carried on and told her to get over it. Because someone he had a vested interest in was being hurt, because a relationship he cared about more than anything was being impacted, his pain surfaced.

"I'm surprised she didn't start telling people you were pregnant," Scott continued.

"Scott!" I gasped.

"She'd been between Brad and me in such a short period of time that we had no idea which one of us was responsible, so we ignored her. I assumed she had figured out how to get it taken care of. Even if she didn't, I wouldn't have cared. At sixteen, I wasn't about to tell my parents about my possible role in the pregnancy of a girl they had never heard of, and I certainly wasn't about to entertain that conversation with Lindsay."

"Scott," I interjected before he could go on, "I don't look at you differently."

"You should."

"Why?" I barked. "The Scott I'm with isn't the same Scott from last year or two years ago. What's the point in holding the actions of Old Scott against you? I don't know that Scott!"

"I'm still that Scott," he raged. "You just don't see him! I don't show him to you!"

"And I don't care that I don't see him! I spend my entire day with you. Does that mean you're working double time to be two different people? I don't buy it!"

"Harper, I did those things, and things like them, to multiple people multiple times throughout high school."

"I don't recognize that Scott. I've never met him. The Scott I know has given me the absolute best experiences. My Scott holds my hand at school and gives me his away jersey to wear to home games. My Scott taught me how to drive his truck and essentially gave that same truck to me to use while he is away in the fall. My Scott won't stop talking about my two-hundred-meter race or hat trick."

Scott inched himself closer to me, draping one leg over the bed and pulling me closer to him. He continued to show that crooked smile I loved as he got closer to me.

"My Scott...Well, it goes without saying that he has unbelievable patience, and he is kind when we're intimate." I smirked. "He tells me he loves me over and over. He holds me the entire time, from beginning to end. He kisses me and asks me how I feel and if I'm alright. He knew I wanted to do it for the first time in a familiar space, a room that expressed how much we meant to one another. He took the time to put up all the pictures he had of the two of us to make my first time more intimate and romantic. I can't imagine the Scott that you describe. My Scott wouldn't do that to someone. My Scott didn't do anything like that to me—"

"I wasn't *your* Scott then," he whispered. "I wasn't anyone's Scott."

"I won't let you beat yourself up over something you did when you were sixteen. You're clearly sorry about what you did. If Lindsay is looking for an apology, give it to her. Don't give it to her because she'll stop saying things about me if you apologize, but because you are sorry. She looks back and remembers how you didn't want a girlfriend, and then she sees you with one now. She sees you with someone you love when you couldn't love her. That hurts her. That would hurt me if I were in her place. I would crumble if I saw you touching someone else, let alone talking or laughing with that person. We are all on the same track team together. That probably kills her. She sees you with me at every practice. She sees you being a proper boyfriend to me. She wants an explanation, and she wants to hear you apologize."

"Harper?" He scratched his head and leaned in very shyly. "You really think all she wants is an apology from me?"

"Scotty...." I nodded slowly. "She just wants to hear you say *something* about it."

"What about you?" He pulled himself against me and wrapped both hands around my waist. "I don't care about *her* right now. What about *you*? Do you forgive me?"

"I have nothing to forgive you for." I smiled softly. "You didn't do anything to me."

"Harp, you said I was at fault."

"I don't blame you now. I said that when I thought you'd slept with her while we were together. Those things happened before I knew you. You weren't my Scott."

"Harp, I can't believe you are being so understanding about all this."

"Fix it, and I'll be even more understanding!" I wrapped my arms around him. "Make sure she stops talking about me."

"Good as done!" Scott kissed me. "Harper, you are unbelievable!"

"Oh, you have no idea!" I laughed lightly. "I fought Barrett this afternoon."

"Harper!" He quickly pulled away. "What did he do?"

"Scott, I took care of it. I kicked him squarely in his chest."

"Tell me. What did he do?"

"Well, don't let this ruin your night. Promise? I mean, I handled it." I pleaded. "I just got back in a good mood, and I don't want you getting upset. So, promise?"

"I promise to not be pissed off tonight, but tomorrow might be different. If it makes you feel better, I'll even be pissed off tomorrow when you're not around."

"Alright, I went out to the truck after Lindsay spoke to me. Barrett was essentially waiting for one of us. He called me a slut, which upset me, but wasn't the reason I kicked him. I kicked him…Now don't get mad, Scott!"

"Harp, I won't get mad. Now tell me."

"Scott, he touched me."

I felt Scott squeeze my waist tighter than usual. He buried his face in my neck, breathing rapidly and heavily against my neck. I could feel the tension building in him as he clenched me tightly.

"Where?"

"It doesn't mean anything, so don't think I am somehow tarnished. He pressed his palm flat against the small of my back like you do."

I could hear Scott grumble—it was a low rumble emanating from his chest. He kept his head tightly tucked into my neck. His breathing continued at the same accelerated pace.

"He did the same thing you do," I told him. "He ran his fingers across my waist and touched my thigh before I could fight him off. He said he knew why you hang on to me."

"Harper, he's finished. I'm sick of him watching us! *You* can fight him for things he *says* to you, but once he touches you, he becomes *my* problem. And you're not tarnished. You're not even close to tarnished." He pulled my face close to his and kissed me roughly. "Barrett won't bother you again. He's done. I'll take care of him tomorrow afternoon."

"Scott, you can't get in a fight. You'll get suspended! I already heard about the incident in the locker room after practice today."

"That was nothing. That guy Justin decided to ask me about the rumors. I threw him against the lockers and told him to never talk about you again."

"Just don't fight Barrett. I don't want to see you get suspended and jeopardize your graduation." I slowly smiled as a thought formed, "Actually, get suspended. That way, you won't have to graduate, and you can stay in high school with me!"

"Oh, you'd love that!" His light laughter made me hopeful that this awful argument was over for the night. "I'll fight him tomorrow, but I'll do it off campus."

"Please, just let it go. If you fight him off campus, you'll get arrested."

"I won't get arrested." He laughed. "You think my dad would arrest his own son?"

"Scott...." I rolled my eyes.

He leaned over and kissed me, and I let him assume control. His lips traced the outline of my collarbone.

"Can we pick up with our plans for tonight?" I mumbled.

He continued kissing me, and I hoped it would lead to much more. I could feel how much more he wanted, and I wanted just as much, if not more.

"Babe, we need to continue our plans as scheduled." He laughed. "We need to make up for our fight! We should try to salvage as many of our original plans as possible. We've already lost too much time."

"I had a whole wardrobe for tonight," I sulked, "and I'm not going to get to wear it if we start up like this, already on my bed."

He smirked. "You said earlier you didn't think I enjoyed it with you. I'd like to have it on the record that I thoroughly enjoy being with you each and every time."

"I can tell," I smirked. "And I believe you, especially right now. Umm, did you notice—"

"Notice what?"

"I know that you are *really* into it, but I'm—"

"You're not into it?" He panicked and pushed off me. "Harper, I have to know if you're not into it!"

"Scott, I enjoy being with you." I popped on my elbows and tried to quell his near panic attack. "I enjoy being close to you and feeling you. I *really* enjoy kissing you. I just haven't had the big...."

"The big what?"

"You know!" I whined before my eyes widened, intensifying the message, and I mouthed, 'the big O.'

Time froze as he stared at me. I couldn't tell if he was angry or confused as he glared at me. He bent down, his hands supporting his entire body against the bed as he leaned over me. A small smile, almost a smirk, appeared on his face, and I knew he wasn't really upset. My lips formed a smile that matched his growing grin out of relief.

"I can tell you something right now, Little Harper Whitmore," Scott declared. "This is going to get fixed! My girlfriend *has* to enjoy having sex with me. I cannot *stand* the idea of you not enjoying it."

"I told you I enjoy it! Being close to you is enough."

"Not enough for me," he exclaimed, laughing. "You have to enjoy all of it. You have to get as much out of it as I do, if not more."

"So, are you saying that you're spending the night?" I slyly caught my fingers on his waistband and ran my fingers from his left hip to his right hip before pulling his waistband toward me.

"What's that, Scotty?" That mock-surprised look never left my face. "Did someone just say that something was going to get fixed?"

"Well, I have to now." He smirked. "I would leave you in a dangerous situation if I left now, Harp. You home alone, a crazed kid out there who wants to touch you...."

"Oh, I understand." I nodded. "This has nothing to do with needing to make sure Scott Pierce's girlfriend enjoys having sex with him, nor does it have anything to do with your three-week obsession with tonight's sleepover."

"Harper, I'm the only one allowed to touch you inappropriately!" He grinned. "Plain and simple!"

"I'll save my scandalous red number for our next night alone then, alright?"

"Fair enough." He smirked. "I'm already too close to wait around for a wardrobe change, anyway."

I smiled and ran my hands underneath his shirt. His skin was warm and soft. I loved feeling his lean, muscular figure. Even if we never had sex, it would be just as enjoyable to simply feel his skin against mine. Pulling his shirt off and reveling in his natural glow and muscular body was satisfying enough for me. He kissed me. I moved, my motion matching the direction his hand moved under my shirt. He ran his lips up and down my neck, lightly using his tongue. I raised my hands above my head, assisting him in pulling my shirt off. I could feel his breath along my chest, collarbone, neck, and ear.

"God," he breathed, "you are hot."

"You mean that?" I pulled his face so it was looking at mine. "You really think I am more than beautiful? Not just now, but—"

"Every time," he emphatically interrupted. "You are more than just beautiful—you are spectacular. Guys want you. You know that, right? Every guy wants *this* with you."

"I don't care about other guys. I care about you. Do you *want* me?"

"Harper," he announced, "I more than want you."

I released his face, and he returned to kissing my chest. His lips ran down my chest, past my breasts, and slowly down my stomach. His lips began to trace the line of my hips, and then he was past my hips and below my navel. My breathing became shallow, and there was a greater space between my breaths. I quickly flinched.

"Scott!" I gasped. "What are you doing?"

"Shh…Just relax." He leaned over me. His face was inches away from mine, and his lips gently grazed mine. "You'll enjoy this." He moved back to where he had been, his face inches from a place it had never been before.

"What are you doing?" I whispered, concern and near panic racing through me. He didn't answer me. I felt his kiss in a new place, a special place. "Oh, my God! Scotty!"

I began running my fingers through his dirty-blond hair. For the first time in my life, I moaned, and my mind went blank. I barely noticed Scott's hands following the shape of my body. I barely noticed that when I arched my back, Scott held my hips firmly between his two very large hands. I stared at the ceiling, trying to focus on the colored pattern of the pink crown molding. His hair was soft between my fingers, his forceful grip on my hips was enjoyable, and his dominance was appreciated. I could feel him from the inside out. His soft lips were in a place I never imagined they'd ever be. I had thought I was already close to Scott, but this brought us to a whole new level. My body was on fire at that moment, and my head was thrown back.

Whether I was doing it intentionally or not, Scott seemed to appreciate my hands as they pulled his head closer into me.

He collapsed next to me when I was done. His hands wandered my body for a bit before he took charge again and leaned over me. His lips journeyed over my body before he let them meet mine.

"I told you that I'd get you to enjoy it." He grinned. "I'm pretty sure you enjoyed that."

He was right. I hadn't realized that I could enjoy it that much. Each time we'd been together had been beautiful, amazing...spectacular, even, but I had never felt what I had just felt with Scott. At the risk of sounding naïve, I never knew it could feel that good in that way. I assumed there was only one way to achieve such a feeling, and that would happen only if you were lucky.

I gripped his jaw between both my hands and pulled his lips to mine. He tasted different—unusual and erotic. Our foreheads pressed together as his eyes pierced me. His smile was addictive. I pulled his glistening lips against mine once more. I couldn't do anything more than kiss him. It was clear that Scott wasn't finished yet, and I wanted him to feel the same thing I just felt.

"Ah, my Harper wants me. You've never been this ready." Scott kissed my neck and collarbone. "Tell me what you want, Harper."

"I want you, Scott," I breathed. "I've always wanted you."

"We're gonna go hard." His voice was hoarse, but it still had his usual smooth, caring tone in it.

"Alright."

I pushed deeper into my bed as he initially slammed into me. I felt his neck and hair between my fingers. I could feel him inside me. He was very deep, and I enjoyed everything. My legs wrapped around him, and Scott took that as he should have—he knew I was enjoying it. His smile was large; I could see the pride and fulfillment on his face.

"Harper," he cried out.

I didn't expect this to happen twice in one night, but it was happening. I felt alive; I felt different. All the while, Scott's long fingertips ran down the side of my body. I ran my fingers through his hair once more. I bit my lip, and my head flew back as the feeling raced through me again. He went at it hard again. A sense of intense passion overtook me. I was so sensitive that I wanted it to end. I was worried about what would happen if it kept going. I felt that if Scott kept going so fast, I would explode. He kept going faster and faster, and I did just that.

"I love you," I screamed. "My God, I love you."

That was it. We both finished at the same time. I had finally found sex enjoyable, just as Scott wanted it to be for me.

"Harper, you are unbelievable." He collapsed next to me, entirely out of breath. "I didn't think I was going to make it happen."

"Oh, Scott, I can't believe that," I panted. "It was unbelievable!"

"You enjoyed it, babe?" He smiled. "Just tell me again that you enjoyed it."

"I never thought I could enjoy it like that," I exclaimed. "I felt like I would explode if you kept at it. Scott, you have no idea how much I loved it!" I leaned over him with a giant grin on my face. "It was unlike any of the other times. I always enjoy being close to you, but this was something else!"

"Yes, well, you're welcome!" He grinned. "I'm proud of doing that for you, but I'm more proud of myself for caring enough. I've never cared as much as I did tonight. I fell in love with making you *feel*. It was a near-obsession to ensure you enjoyed being with me this time."

"Is that what that was?" I chuckled. "Obsession?"

"That was me being obsessed and pulling out all the stops."

"Wait, you've never done that?" I held his jaw between my small hands. "Scott, tell me! Have you ever done what you did *before*?"

"What are you getting at?" He smirked. "Why are you asking me?"

"I want to know if this is one first we shared."

"It was good?" he asked.

"Very!"

"Yes, that was the first time I'd ever done that. I was nervous about it because I didn't really know what to do. I was mostly going off memory."

"Memory?"

"Porn," he stated matter-of-factly.

"Ahh. Well, it was very good, Scott!" I smiled. "I mean, it was the first I'd ever…you know, but it was beyond amazing. I mean, it happened twice! I honestly didn't think it could happen more than once at a time."

"Keep talking, Harper! You are doing absolute wonders for my self-esteem."

"You should be proud!" I giggled. "There is something to be said for porn, apparently."

"I am," he boasted. "First time out of the gate, and it happened twice!"

Scott pulled me onto his body. I rested on his stomach, looking at him and tracing his smile lines with my index finger. He was wearing a much wider grin than usual; it had a great deal more excitement built into it. His hands followed the outline of my spine up and down my back, and the feeling of his fingertips was relaxing, calming, and enjoyable. I physically fell deeper into him and fell more in love with him as we lay there together.

"I'm getting up." I grinned as I pressed my hands along his upper chest and pushed myself off him. I quickly kissed his pouty lips. "I love you so much, Scott," I whispered. "I love you more now than I did a few hours ago."

I reached for Scott's oversized T-shirt. I was utterly immodest as I got dressed, not caring what he saw as I pulled my arms through the sleeves and my damp curls out of the collar and onto my shoulder. I caught Scott smiling as he watched me.

"What?" I whispered and smiled. "Why are you smiling like that?"

"I don't know…." He smirked. "No reason."

"You look like you're thinking about something."

"I'm just enjoying the view," he proclaimed. "I'll give you an equally enjoyable view."

With glee, he threw the comforter to the side of the bed, his exaggerated movements forcing it to fall entirely to the floor. He got out of bed and started moving boastfully. He stretched slowly from head to toe, forcing my attention to his relaxed state before he reached for his baby blue boxer shorts. It was then that it hit me.

My face went blank as I saw him. He'd done it again. I was partially to blame for not saying something sooner, but this was the third time he'd done it. He'd forgotten to put a condom on. I'd made it a point last time this happened to always remember and be responsible. I briskly walked over to my desk and looked at my calendar. I started counting, completely angry with myself for not reminding him. At that moment, it was too late to do anything except examine the upcoming Sunday circled in thick red marker.

"Harper, what's wrong?"

I swung around and leaned against my desk, crossing my arms.

"I'm not mad at you, alright, Scott? Trust me, I'm not mad at you, but you have to start remembering to wear a condom." I groaned. "And I know it's partially my fault for not reminding you, but come on...."

His head dropped as he walked toward me. I understood the meaning of "walk of shame" as he rounded my bed to meet me. His head stayed drooped, and his body was slouching. He looked down and saw the large red circle. He pointed to it and looked at me as he held his finger on it.

"This means you get your period on Sunday?"

"Yes," I mumbled.

He looked back on Sunday. "So, we're okay?"

"Scott...." I sighed. "We should be okay, but that just means we got lucky. You gotta start remembering, please. Especially when you go off to college! You don't want to return to the island because you found out your high-school girlfriend is preggo!"

"Harp...."

"No," I interrupted, "you were so good about remembering in the beginning. The last two months, you've completely abandoned the idea of remembering to wear one."

"Harper, I'll admit I gotta start remembering—I'll take complete ownership of that—but have you thought about telling your mom about us? You might consider telling her about us and getting on something."

"You really want my mom to know about our sex life?" I asked sarcastically. "You want her to think about *that*?"

"No!" He groaned. "No...Not at all. I don't *want* her to think about that, but babe, you gotta get *something*."

"Scott! I really don't want to have that conversation with her. I know she says that she'd be cool with it. She acts like she's cool with it, too, but I just don't want to have that conversation yet."

"Harp, do you have condoms in this room?"

I stayed silent. I didn't want this to somehow get turned against me. It seemed pretty clear that Scott was preparing to do just that.

"Harper, you knew I was going to spend the night tonight." He sighed. "I figured you'd be prepared for the main event."

"I figured *you'd* be prepared!" I rebutted. "I mean, I thought this was sorta *your* thing to remember."

"Why would this be *my* thing?"

"Well, because you're the one with the penis!"

"That's not fair!"

"A lot of things aren't fair," I added. "Most all those things have to do with you having a penis, in fact!"

"Well, if we are going to start doing it in your room, you need to be prepared for my forgetfulness by having condoms here to remind me."

"Scott," I pleaded, whining slightly. "Please?"

"No, Harper. You need to get them."

"I don't want my mom to find them," I whined, "and I'm too nervous about buying them."

"Harper! You can't have this both ways. You have to be responsible for this on some level. Either tell her or hope she doesn't find the condoms in your room. As for buying them, I'll buy them for you."

"You know what, Scott? Look who's talking. Don't you *have* condoms in your room?"

"Of course I do!"

"Really? Then how come we've done it without one in *your* room before?"

He stood looking at me, moving his hands to his hips as he

thought about how to best answer my question. He looked perplexed, and it looked like he was having trouble coming up with a reply.

"I'm going to lose this argument, so I am going to admit that we both need to be a bit more concerned about preventing a pregnancy," he admitted. "I'll buy condoms for your room until you decide to take the pill."

"I really don't think the issue is *having* them." I smiled. "The issue is getting you to wear one!"

"Alright…." He chuckled and shrugged his shoulders. "I deserve that one."

"Maybe this is why you're in freshman health as a senior. Have you thought about that?"

"Harp, I am a senior in health, not a senior in *freshman* health. I didn't take it as a freshman because it wasn't a requirement when I was a freshman. You know this because I have had this discussion with you numerous times."

"Exactly! That's the problem! You should have taken it. You seem to be a bit short in knowledge in some areas."

"Babe, I'm not short in anything!" He grinned wickedly before leaning into my ear and whispering, "But Harp, doesn't it feel *so* good without one?"

"Scott!" I pressed my hands against his bare chest and lightly pushed him away. "Do you admit you're intentionally not wearing one, then?"

"I didn't say that!" He laughed.

"Scott," I groaned.

"I think I got lucky when I got you. You seem to always know when your periods are and whether or not we are safe. *You* seem to be doing well in health." He looked away with a tease of a smile. "Maybe for my final project in health, I'll do a presentation on how responsible my girlfriend is."

I rolled my eyes, crossed my arms, and slouched against my desk, prepared to listen to Scott's rant.

"Yeah! I'll do a whole presentation on how the best way to avoid teen pregnancy is to get a girlfriend who knows exactly when she is scheduled to get her menstrual cycle...but then I'd probably have to mention that my girlfriend won't go on the pill because she's afraid of having that conversation with her mother."

"You know," I countered, "for *my* final project, I'll do a presentation on how difficult it is to be the only responsible one in a relationship. I'll mention how one would think having an older boyfriend would make things easier, but age doesn't really mean anything!"

Scott's wicked grin widened across his face, his smile lines getting bigger as his teeth started to show through his lips. In a few moments, he couldn't contain the laughter echoing through his chest.

"I can't be the only responsible one in this relationship," I whined. "I don't *want* to be a mother."

"Harper," he asked me, "why are we out of bed? I'd like to go back to bed."

"Scott, we are out of bed because I am starving! You didn't run six miles this afternoon and go through a large amount of emotional distress."

I spun around and exited my room. Scott quickly followed me down the long flight of stairs, lightly tapping my behind. I ran down the stairs rapidly, skipping stairs to avoid Scott's hands along my body.

"Hey Harp, you wanna skip school tomorrow? We can take a three-day weekend! We can sleep in tomorrow and just hang out."

"I really want to, but I can't. I have an algebra quiz tomorrow." I cringed. "We have a track meet on Saturday, and if we skip school on a Friday, we can't compete. Believe me, I'd like nothing more than to skip. I want to hang out with you, but I also don't want to hear any more about being a slut."

I hopped onto the kitchen countertop, and Scott quickly moved in front of me, wiggling himself between my knees.

"Harper, you're not a slut. You are far from it."

"I know that, and you know that, but the rest of the school doesn't. Even if you fix things with Lindsay, people will still believe the worst about me, and it's out there now."

"Harper, it's only high school. I know as a freshman, that's hard to understand. As a senior, I can tell you it will go by quickly, and what happens in high school won't really matter afterward."

"So, are you saying I am *just* your high-school girlfriend and after *your* high school experience, you'll forget about me and move on?"

"Absolutely! That's exactly how it works! I'm just getting what I can right now, and then I'll move on to college girls," he teased. "As soon as that diploma is in my hand, it's 'nice to know you, Harper'!"

"Not funny," I groaned. "Are we doing frozen pizza or delivery?"

"I think the answer to that is simple." He smiled. "Frozen pizza would require us to do some work. Delivery requires a phone call."

"Not calling!" I quickly called out.

"I'll call." He rolled his eyes. "Same order?"

"I have no cash on me." I winked. "And yes, same order."

"So not only did you forget to provide condoms for your guest, but you also forgot to get cash to feed your guest?" His smile reflected in his eyes as he reached for the phone, never taking the grin off his face or his eyes off me. "I got dinner tonight. You've given me more than enough. Grab my wallet."

"I did manage to get another pillow for my guest." I glowed as I left the kitchen. "My guest shouldn't complain too much."

I pranced down the hall, Scott's wallet in hand, and wrapped my arms around his bare chest when I got to him, smiling up at him. He looked at the calendar next to the cordless phone as he finished the order. His finger tapped the large blue circle around a Sunday three weeks away, and I shook my head.

"That's all," Scott said into the phone. "Yeah, fourteen Parker Drive...Yeah, the one with the circular driveway...Thanks."

I watched and waited until he hung up.

"Harper, does your mom know you're not doing the church thing?" he asked me.

"Yes." I nodded slowly. "She knows."

"And?"

"I told her it wasn't something I wanted to do right now." I shrugged. "We had a lengthy discussion about it, but when it was done, we agreed I was not doing it."

"What was involved in the *lengthy discussion*?"

"She suspected my relationship with you factored into my decision.

I think she's worried what *could* happen in our relationship is due to my decision to not get confirmed, but it doesn't."

"Harper...." He groaned. "I know our relationship doesn't factor in, but I think this is the sorta thing you'd tell me. I mean, you basically denounced your religion. That's kind of a big deal!"

"I didn't denounce my religion; I just opted out of being confirmed right now."

"Fine, at fifteen years of age, you opted to denounce your religion for the time being." He smiled. "I'm incredibly proud of you! I'm not religious, and this is a big deal to me."

"I really don't think it is." I lightly laughed. "I just decided that Confirmation wasn't for me."

"I don't care how you spin it; emotionally, you are literally the strongest person I've ever met." He smiled. "You live how you want."

"Thank you," I replied as I reached up and kissed him, "but I'm really not that strong."

Our first sleepover didn't start as initially planned, but it turned into a memorable night we managed to salvage. We ate Chinese food in my bed while watching television before he helped me with my algebra homework, and we did our health assignment. After, we talked for the rest of the night. I laughed hysterically at Scott, and Scott laughed at my laughter. We went to bed that night in my full-size bed, planning on sleeping next to each other the entire night. I set my alarm, and we lay next to each other. We faced one another, the light from my television illuminating my room, and I rested my head against his bicep and felt safe, secure, and happy under my feather-down comforter. It was just us.

I pulled the comforter closer to my chin and fell asleep next to him well after midnight. I only woke up once that night to shut the television off. He was asleep, but his hand still found my spine as I reached for the remote.

"Where are you going?" he whispered, half asleep. "Stay with me...." His hand crept along my waist, and he started tugging me to get me back into bed.

"Nowhere, Scott," I whispered. "I'm not going anywhere. I'm right here."

I tucked him in, pulling the sheet and comforter high up his torso. I let my hands wander along his body. I felt his warm, smooth, sculpted body, and I cuddled into him and slept soundly.

EIGHT

I SAT ON THE STAIRS OF MY PORCH, that internal cringing feeling returning as I saw Scott start the truck. I wanted to stay home and pretend that nothing else existed outside of Scott and me. I wanted to grab him and tell him to shut the truck off and return to bed with me. I wanted it to be just us again. Sitting on my porch, my stomach in knots and fighting off nausea, I wanted to skip high school and be the senior that Scott was right now—one who didn't care about rumors! Unlike him, I did care. I both cared about and feared what they were saying in the same breath. For some reason or another, all of this was important to me. I couldn't change that.

"Harper," Scott whispered, suddenly in front of me. "I need you to ignore it. I need you to remember that it's just us."

"I know."

"Every time it gets difficult today, I want you to find me, and we'll get right back into it being *just us*."

"I don't want to go," I whispered at Scott's large sneakers in front of me. I focused on how my size-six Vans were dwarfed by his shoes. I let my hair drape over me like a curtain, hiding my face and the embarrassment that ran through me.

"I don't want to go to class," I told him, "or walk around knowing people are saying things about me."

"Harper." His large feet moved and turned around as he sat down two steps above me. I closed my eyes and felt his fingers pulling my hair behind my ears. He traced the outline of my ear slowly, tucking my curls away tightly before reaching around and lifting my chin. "If it gets bad, we can leave campus. We'll go back to my house and spend the afternoon alone. If we leave, the rumors should stop. It will be an out-of-sight, out-of-mind situation. Let's give it until your fourth-period algebra quiz, though. If it is too much, then we split!"

"Alright...." I nodded. "Fourth period."

"Harp, I'll walk you to every class and pick you up afterward. If people see us together and happy, just the two of us, the rumor will fade away. People will start to not believe it."

He reached for my hand slowly, sliding his hand underneath mine and lacing all his fingers in mine before closing them tightly.

"Let's do this, Harp. We'll go to Starbucks for breakfast, and then we'll face this together."

We pulled into the parking lot at school slightly later than usual. The majority of the good senior parking spots were already filled. That didn't matter for Scott; he always had spot number twenty-two. No one ever touched it—until that morning, that is. He pulled into the parking lot and saw his spot filled.

"Who the hell parked in my spot?" Scott roared. "Who's fucking eighties piece-of-shit Camry is parked in my spot?"

The truck had tinted windows, but I felt the protective barrier wasn't enough. The groups had already formed around the parking lot, and they were all gawking at the Pathfinder as it pulled in and idled in front of Scott's parking space. I was sure that the gawking had everything to do with the rumor, but I suspected it also had something to do with the car parked in Scott's space.

"That's *her* Camry," I informed my boyfriend.

"Whose?"

The Pathfinder didn't move. It sat idling in the parking lot as if Scott were waiting for someone to get into that car and move it.

"What are you going to do?" I asked. "Should we get her?"

"Who?" He frowned. "Get who?"

"That's Lindsay's car."

"Bitch!" His palm pounded against the steering wheel before Scott dropped the gear into reverse and backed up. He made a hard left in a single motion and backed into the next available space.

"The bitch has too much time on her fucking hands!"

"Scott, I can't do this. I can't get out of this car." I panicked. My heart was racing, I was becoming flushed, and my hands fluttered around as I spoke. "They're all staring at me. They're all thinking the *same* thing!"

"Harp, I'll walk you to class and pick you up. Babe, calm down. Listen to me! I'll be there every step of the way today."

"They're already staring," I whispered.

"Harp, they are always staring! It has nothing to do with what people are saying and everything to do with how gorgeous you are. Lindsay is making a scene, and that is what they're staring at this morning. They want to see how I'll react to her car in my space. They want to see *something*. I'm not giving them what they want!"

"It's more than that—"

"No," he snapped. "It's not more than that. Every one of those seniors thinks the same thing: Lindsay Paul is out of control, and she's terrorizing a freshman. *That's* what they are thinking. Maybe some senior girls are on her side, but most of the seniors are against her!"

"Do you promise?"

"Harp, it's just us," he whispered as he lifted my chin. "It's always been just us. Remember that."

After a brief moment of silence, Scott lifted my chin and pressed his lips against mine. It was the sort of kiss we usually shared privately. He was blunt and forceful, and, like always, I embraced it. I'll even admit I enjoyed the slight force of his hand guiding my head to his and the feeling of his tongue forcing my mouth open.

"It's just us," he breathed after he kissed me.

He helped me out of the truck and held my hand as we crossed the parking lot. I let my bag hang from one shoulder. Holding Scott's hand put me at ease. I dare say that our walk turned into a stroll as we crossed between the cars. I caught him smiling at me periodically as we entered the central courtyard of our high school. He abruptly stopped smiling, and I knew it was coming. I knew immediately the scene everyone was looking forward to was about to happen. Scott's grip on my hand tightened as we approached the building.

"Harper?" Lindsay looked at me. "Harper Whitmore?"

There she was—my rumor. She seemed frozen in place directly in front of me. Scott tried to move around her, but she kept pressing.

"Harper," she continued, "how are you this morning?"

She sounded haughty and condescending. She didn't care how I was doing, and I didn't care to respond to her. I only cared about the growing tightness of Scott's hand around mine.

"You don't have to answer her, Harper," Scott reminded me, looking at Lindsay. "You don't have to speak to her."

Still trying to maneuver around her, Scott pulled me into his arms. For each step Scott took toward the main building, Lindsay took two as she blocked his path. She kept her eyes locked on me. She waited for her answer and continued to move so that she was inches away from Scott.

Scott coldly addressed the girl in front of us. "Let's get into this, then, Lindsay. What do you want from me?"

"I want the same thing from you that you gave me—nothing!" Her voice dripped with hostility. "This is between Harper and me!"

I stayed frozen as she looked directly at me again.

"Harper, how are you?" she boldly asked me. "It's rude to not answer someone's question, you know."

"I'm fine," I whispered. "Thank you."

"Really, Harper? You're fine this morning? Tell me, Harper Whitmore, did you learn anything interesting last night?"

"Harper, don't answer her," Scott spoke into my hair. "You don't have to. This has nothing to do with you."

"This has nothing to do with *you*, Scott," Lindsay retorted. "This is between Harper and me."

Her fingertip ran down my bicep as she spoke, trying to intimidate me. She didn't even look at Scott. She kept looking down at me, and I felt absolute fear as I clenched Scott's hand more tightly.

"Scott's not the one being called a slut, is he, Harper? Scott's never the slut."

"Quit it, Lindsay," Scott demanded. "Quit trying to intimidate her!"

Scott tugged at my hand, and we started for the building. Lindsay and her quick footwork blocked me. She stood before me and looked right at me, waiting for my response.

"That's *your* specialty, Scott—intimidating young girls." She kept her eyes locked on me. "Isn't that right, young Harper, class of 2001? Let me ask you this: Were you intimidated by that kiss Scott gave you in his truck? Let me guess, you thought that was for you. It was really for my benefit, though."

It all clicked when she said that. His backing into that spot, his glaring at the senior pack, and the kiss started to flood me. I looked up at Scott, who only shook his head. If I were being honest, I knew that even if the kiss were ultimately for her, it was for me at that moment. That's how I justified it for the sake of my own sanity. Lindsay was hurting me, and Scott knew how to hurt her.

"That's not true, Lindsay," I roared, my anger finally bleeding through. "That's not true at all."

"Oh, isn't it?"

"Scott told me! He told me everything. I am very sorry that happened; and I empathize with you, but Scott has never intimidated me."

"Harper, I do not need your sympathy."

"I understand that," I muttered, "but I would like you to understand *my* position. I had nothing to do with what happened two years ago, and I have nothing to do with it now. That is between you and Scott. I won't give an opinion because I don't have one. I would like you to understand that the Scott who existed two years ago is not the Scott I am with today. I am sure it is difficult for you to see that, but that is what I see."

"Harper, are you taking his side on this?"

She condescendingly reached up and tucked a stray curl behind my ear. She only had a second to touch my curl before I swatted her hand away.

"Because I just don't see you as a dumb girl," she continued.

"Do not touch her, Lindsay," Scott yelled. "Don't lay a finger on her!"

"Scott, please do not say my name," she asked of him as she glanced up at him. "Don't say my name ever again. Harper, are you a dumb girl? I used to be a dumb girl. I used to think Scott loved me, but he never loved me. He can't love anyone. Do you believe Scott loves you? If you do, you *are* a dumb girl."

"Lindsay, quit it," Scott demanded. "I *never* said I loved you! You made this whole story up."

"Lindsay, you're wrong," I asserted. "I am the exact opposite of a dumb girl. You are correct on one thing: Scott didn't love you. I am sorry you believed otherwise. Scott *does* love me, however, and I believe him." I felt him squeeze my hand. "I can't change how he felt or how he feels about you. I can only be concerned about Scott and me, not Scott and Lindsay.

"Harper, let me ask you something." She inched toward me and whispered, "When he's inside you, does he look into your eyes? Are his eyes even *open*? Does he kiss you?"

"That's enough, Lindsay," Scott interjected. "Are you doing this because she's a freshman or because she's *my* girlfriend?" He inched closer to her. "'Cause I have a feeling if Harp were a sophomore or junior, you wouldn't be nearly as pissed."

"Ah, *Harp*. That's adorable." Lindsay pouted and moved closer. "*Harp*, tell me something: Does he take all your clothes off, or does he just want your pants off?"

"Lindsay," Scott hollered. "Enough! This has nothing to do with her. Why are you doing this? What's the point? It happened *two years* ago."

"I told you not to say my name." She locked her eyes on me. "Harper, does he stay with you afterward?"

She reached up to touch another stray curl, but I swatted her hand away.

"Or does he leave you to get dressed alone in the grass overlooking the Sound?" she continued. "He's good at taking what he wants, isn't he? Oh, that's right; Scott doesn't see *Harp* as a whore, does he? *You're* someone he can love. The rest of us,...Well, we're not lovable, apparently. We're just whores! He even lets you in his truck. The rest of us weren't even good enough to be around his truck. You, though... You can drive it."

I looked up at Scott. His eyes were closed, and pain played across his face. He squeezed my hand tightly.

"Scott loves me, Lindsay," I told her. "It's entirely different for me than it was for you. I am sorry you had a horrible experience, but please work this out with *Scott*. Please do not take your anger out on me."

"Harper, I have no anger." She chuckled condescendingly. "I have hatred, not anger. There is an enormous difference between the two!"

"I *am* sorry," I told her.

"Good luck, Harper. I sincerely hope you don't get hurt. It appears that you can hurt him, though. Just be careful. I'll stop with the rumors, but I can't speak for the rest of the girls who might start screwing with you."

"What are you saying?" I asked, slightly panicked. "Are you saying this is going to keep happening?"

"Lindsay." Scott interrupted my questions. "If there was ever anything between us, you'll stop this! You'll make sure—"

"I'll make sure what, Scott?" she roared, hatred in her eyes. "There was never anything between us. You made that *abundantly* clear! The only thing between us is my memory of losing my virginity to an asshole on the bluff. *That* is the only thing between us. When you were done, you threw Brad a bone."

"That's not how it happened," Scott said, exasperated.

"Oh, it's not?" She chuckled. "Christ, Scott! That's exactly how it happened."

She walked away but stopped suddenly and said condescendingly, "Good luck trying to break the record at the meet tomorrow, Harp."

"Lindsay!" Scott called out.

She froze when Scott said her name. He let go of my hand and walked closer to her. She looked only at the ground.

"I *am* sorry—"

"No," she barked. "No, you don't *get* to apologize! You will live with this for the rest of your life, just like I have to."

The small crowd around us had seen what they had come to see. They all dissipated as the bell for the first period rang. Scott took my hand and tried to walk toward the main building. I didn't move. My hand angled out with Scott's movements, pulling him back toward me instead of along behind him. I didn't know what to say or how to convey my fear of this happening again. Scott didn't seem concerned this could or would happen again. I pulled my hand away and glared at him, waiting for him to speak, but he said nothing.

"How many, Scott? How many are there? How many more girls are going to come forward like this?" I panicked, thinking about it. "Just tell me."

"Harper...." He walked closer to me and held my face. "It won't happen again. Lindsay was the worst of them."

"How many?" I fought away from his grip. "Why won't you tell me how many?"

"Because I have no idea."

"Goddamn you, Scott! Goddamn you. I could handle one. I could understand one. I could even sympathize with you on one, but I don't know if I can do this again. How many more times will this happen? How many more stories will I have to suffer punishment for?"

His hands wrapped themselves around my shoulders, pulling me into a hug quickly; I think he was hoping it would be too quick for me to pull away. He was wrong; I pushed him away.

"I can't do that again! I won't be punished for things you've done. That's not fair!"

"Harper, it won't happen again. Lindsay is the *only* girl I hurt. She's the only one who genuinely hates me! The rest knew what they were getting into."

"No! You're wrong. She just said there are others, and I believe her. There are more, Scott. How many times will I have to defend you like that? How many times will I have to be told I'm a 'dumb girl'?"

I grabbed my bag out of his hand and stormed into the main

building, leaving him behind. I raced around the corner for the second flight of stairs up to my first class and almost ran into Leigh in my panicked state.

"Harper, you gotta ignore it. I just heard the rumor in the bathroom from some bitches, but I corrected them, Harper, right there. Those bitches won't repeat that lie!"

"I need a break from all this!" I fumed. "I need a break from *him*! It's so hard. From the beginning of our relationship, it's always been so hard! I've had to think so much since we started, and it's not fair—"

"Harper," Leigh snapped, "calm down! What's going on?"

I couldn't breathe, and I couldn't control my heart rate. I managed to get both of his truck keys off my key ring, even though my hands were shaking. I put them on the gold "Harper" keychain that Scott had given me on Valentine's Day. He had been beyond excited when he found something with "Harper" on it; giving it back would hurt him more than simply giving his truck keys back.

"Here." I handed Leigh the two Nissan keys on the keychain. "When you walk into health class, put these on his desk. You don't have to say anything; just set them down. He'll get it." I raced up the stairs to the third floor, not waiting for her response.

"Harper!" Leigh yelled up the stairwell. "I'm not doing this! You can't break up with him over a stupid rumor."

"Leigh, this isn't over a stupid rumor." I stopped at the top of the stairs and turned to her. "This is over Lindsay Paul. She called me dumb."

"Harper, you can't dump Scott because some chick called you dumb. That doesn't make any sense," she yelled. "Explain this! Who the hell is Lindsay Paul?"

Leigh quickly got quiet as she looked down the hall. I followed her eyes and saw him standing there. His hands were casually in his pockets, his elbows slightly bent. His beautiful face tilted in confusion. All of his handsome features weren't enough for me to forget earlier this morning, though. Leigh looked back at me for a moment before turning to him.

"Scott, tell me what's going on," she demanded. "Are you two fighting over a rumor? Is that what this is about?"

"Harper is very sensitive to rumors," he stated flatly. "She doesn't like to be talked about."

"Don't talk about me like I'm not here," I yelled down at him. "I'm done, Scott. I am *so* done! I am not doing this again! I will not have some senior bitch call me dumb and treat me like shit because of something *you* did. That's not fair!"

"Harp, think about everything we've been through. Remember everything I told you. You're willing to throw it away over gossip? Even after last night?"

"Scott…." I sighed. "You enjoy this, don't you? You *enjoy* hurting girls. You only kissed me in the truck this morning because you knew she could see us. That kiss wasn't for me. I am so upset right now, and you enjoy it!"

I knew what he was doing while talking to me, and I knew I'd fall for it. If I stayed, I'd spend the rest of my relationship with Scott as a victim of gossip. I knew that. I wasn't about to do that. I could feel myself giving in to him as he inched closer up the stairs toward me. I couldn't think of a single way to get out, to pull away. He was one step below me, towering over me with his hand cradling my jaw when I knew I had to do something. I could feel his breath and smell his masculinity. The smell of last night clung to him even after a shower. He smelled of power and control, and I could feel him pulling me in with that power.

"Harp, that's not true." His lips barely moved as he spoke. His eyes burned into me.

I didn't want to hear it. I didn't want to hear about how this would never happen again. I didn't want to be told that Lindsay Paul was just a one-off. I didn't want to hear that Scott hadn't had another Lindsay-Paul situation and that I'd be alright. I didn't want to hear anything. I did the only thing I could think to do. I ran. I pulled away, his fingers hanging in the air in surprise where they had been tracing my jaw just a moment before.

Between first and fourth periods, Leigh and I wrote notes about the demise of my first relationship. After first and second periods, I found Scott leaning against the lockers outside my classroom. Each time, I pretended I didn't see him. I walked by him, knowing he was behind me and following me to my next class. Then I didn't see him after third period. Just as I was about to walk into algebra, completely surprised by how easy it was to get to class on time if you didn't have a boyfriend, I felt his arms wrap around my waist.

"I need you to tell me what to do," he whispered into my curls. "Just tell me how to fix this, and I'll do it."

"Could you go back to when you were fifteen and decided to start being a dick to women?" I whispered. "Maybe if you could change the last three years of your treatment of women, this would be fixable."

"Harper, I need you to forgive me," he pleaded. "I can't go the rest of my senior year seeing you every day in the hallway and at track practice and knowing you want nothing to do with me."

"You did nothing to *me*." I reminded him. "I just don't like what you've done before me."

I sat at our usual lunch table after fourth period, waiting for Leigh. I knew because of some 'bro-code' that Scott and Brad inevitably had to follow, no matter how close Brad was with Leigh, he'd have to put his feelings on hold indefinitely. Brad would not be sitting with us. I sat at the lunch table alone for what felt like forever but was probably more like ten minutes in reality. Within those ten minutes, I heard a few "sluts," being passed around, but even those seemed to be overshadowed by the newest rumor about Scott and Harper no longer being a couple. I focused on my cafeteria tray, picking at my fries and reading the label on my carton of skim milk. Though I wouldn't admit it at that moment, I secretly hoped that Scott would walk through the double doors of our cafeteria and beg me to come back to him once more, so I could accept.

I was startled by the dropping of a backpack on the floor and someone sitting down across from me. I looked up and saw Barrett Hudson.

"Harper, my chest is killing me," Barrett said with a stupid grin.

"It should!" I sipped my milk with hostility. "What are you doing here?"

"Then you succeeded in your task." He smiled and nodded politely. "I want to apologize."

"Barrett, you are only sitting here because Scott and I broke up."

"I heard something about that. I'm sorry. I am sure it probably had something to do with Lindsay," he said. "She can be a tough chick sometimes."

"Sort of...." I picked at my fries, not going into an explanation. "How do *you* know about Lindsay, anyway?"

"I think that everyone in school but you knew about Lindsay Paul. Apparently, nobody told you until it was too late." He smirked and threw his head to the side as if I were dumb for not figuring this out sooner. "I really am sorry for everything between us. I did use you to screw with Scott once you two were together. I hate Pierce, which I am sure you know, but I really like you. Sometimes, you just got in the way."

"You've reminded me enough that he'll be gone next year," I mumbled as I picked at my lunch. "You should also consider yourself lucky that Scott and I broke up; he had plans to get you off campus this afternoon."

"Thanks for the tip. The irony is that I really wanted him to beat my ass on-campus." He frowned before shaking his head. "Is that what *you're* planning on doing?"

"I don't hate Scott," I snapped. "I don't hate him at all. Actually, I am not even angry with him, now that I think about it. I can't actually remember *why* I was angry at him."

I began scanning the cafeteria, hoping to see Leigh, Brad, or Scott before the lunch bell rang and fifth period began. I continued to study the cafeteria, looking for one of the important people in my life to appear. I knew Scott would probably have gone home for his free periods, but I had no idea where Leigh was.

"Well, after everything he's done to the girls in this school, I'd think you'd hate him," Barrett countered. "I hate him, and the only thing he did to me was take my chance with you away."

"Barrett, you didn't *really* know me until basketball season. That is reason enough that you didn't have a chance. You didn't know who I was until I was with Scott already."

"Not true! I knew who you were during tennis season. Everyone knew who you were because you made varsity soccer. Between sets, we'd hang out around the chain-link fence, watch the girls' soccer practice, and make comments about the really tiny freshman on the field." He chuckled quietly. "That was when I told the guys on the team I was going to learn more about you. Scott encouraged me to learn as much about you as I could. He seemed to really think I had a chance."

"Scott told you this? He encouraged you to get to know me?" I pressed. "I honestly didn't know who you were until basketball season when you made varsity and started hanging out with Brad and Scott. I'll admit, though, even after you introduced yourself to me, I kind of forgot who you were."

"Figures...Scott already had you."

"It had nothing to do with him."

"As soon as I tried to get to know you, Scott moved in." He pointed to the table where I sat with Scott for that first lunch nearly seven months ago. "The first day you sat with him in the cafeteria, I was sitting at this table, where you usually sat. I was going to get to know you that day. I wanted to talk to you about soccer, your winter sports plans, and why you were so tan when it was almost fall. I had my entire lunch planned, and I even ran it by Scott. I saw you walk into the cafeteria with Leigh, and then you went to sit with Scott."

"He asked me to sit with him."

The memory of that day rushed through me. He had remembered my name. He had noticed my curly hair and touched a curl. He had commented on my height and touched the small of my back. He had asked about being a freshman on the varsity soccer team, and he kissed me before fifth-period English in the middle of the courtyard.

"I left after I saw you sit down with him. It was bullshit, Harper. That was *my* day, *my* plan. Everyone knew I wanted to go out with you, and Scott had never said anything about you. He'd never said anything about wanting to be with you. That night at practice, we ended up getting out early—"

"I remember that! Because of the rain!" I smiled at the memory of our first date. "Your practice ended early because of the rain."

"What? No. If we quit practice every time it rained, we'd never play," he said sarcastically. "Scott and I got into a huge fight. I may have started the fight, but he started the whole thing by moving in on you!"

"So, Scott knew you liked me? He knew you wanted to go out with me? You're sure he *knew* this?" I asked with absolute distrust. "There couldn't have been any confusion? He knew you had planned on getting to know me?"

"He was partnered with me for doubles that afternoon, and we were losing forty to fifteen," Barrett went on as if he were ignoring my questions. "He commented about getting my head in the game, and I threw my racket and pushed him. I started in about him moving in on my classmate. I told him I'd get my head in the game if he stopped with you. He said it was too late, that he'd already kissed you and you were going out with him after practice. He moves fast; I'll give him that much!"

"It's because he has exceptional confidence," I said, my own confidence matching Scott's. "He always gets what he wants."

I looked up at the cafeteria again, scanning for Leigh. Lunch was ending soon, and I hadn't seen her. I figured she'd probably opted to spend her lunch with Brad. I kept looking for her, but I was really looking for Scott.

"He's not here, Harper. He took off toward the parking lot after fourth period," Barrett mumbled while he helped himself to my fries. "Ask him, Harper. He'll tell you what happened that day at tennis practice. He doesn't seem capable of lying to you."

I looked up and saw the double doors open. Scott stood there in the doorway with Leigh to his left. The bell was set to ring very shortly, and he strolled in. His hands were tucked in his pockets, his sleeves were casually rolled up, and he was confidently striding my way.

"I have to go, Barrett." I grabbed my backpack. "I hope your chest feels better, but if you ever touch me again, it will be a whole hell of a lot worse for you. Got it?"

I walked toward him, looking up at the clock and seeing that lunch was nearly over. I walked slightly faster toward him; Scott stopped, looked at me, raised his arm, and pointed to where I had been sitting. His face was pulled into a frown, and anger replaced any emotion he may have felt before walking through those double doors. Before I could figure out why he might be angry, I blurted the first four words that came to me:

"I want you back!"

"*Him*, Harper? You were sitting with *him*? You ran right to *him*?"

I turned my head and looked at Barrett, who was starting to get up and leave.

"It's not like that, Scott! He just sat down!" I panicked. "Did you hear me? I want you back! This was all a mistake!"

"Whatever, Harper! I was prepared to come in here and beg you to stay with me, but fuck that! I'm done." He turned and stormed out, yelling over his shoulder, "Do what you want. I should have fucking left after fourth period like I'd planned."

"It's not like that, Scott," I yelled after him. "He just sat down! What was I supposed to do?" I chased after him. "Scott!"

He spun around and looked at me, his hands in his pockets again, his casual stance. He looked incredibly handsome in the light blue cotton button-down shirt. His T-shirt showed underneath it. He was wearing his open-laced sneakers with his baggy jeans that were slightly faded. Looking at him, I knew I could put up with crazy senior girls if I could still say Scott Pierce was my boyfriend. He'd be the one holding my hand on campus.

"Harper, I walk into the cafeteria prepared to swallow my pride, and the first thing I see is you eating lunch with Barrett! What am I supposed to think? Why would you run right to him when things don't work out with us?"

Then I remembered we were in a fight. I hated how he thought he could win all our fights through guilt and tactical wordplay. He wasn't turning this around on me.

"Scott, don't you dare blame this on me! He sat down. I didn't invite him. Don't you dare stand there and act like you did nothing wrong," I yelled. "You think you know me so well? You think you've got me all figured out? You know what, Scott? I'm the one who has *you* figured out. You're the one who fucked up!"

"Everything I did wrong was before you and I were together or even knew each other. Harper, you were in sixth grade when I started doing everything wrong—"

"Exactly!" I threw my finger into his face. "And now *I* am getting punished for it."

"Harper, you really wanna have this argument in front of the entire school? Because I'll have it with you right here."

"Why not?" I spun around, my arms out. "They're already talking about us! No, wait, they are talking about *me*. They aren't talking about *you* or *us*; they're just talking about *me*," I yelled. "You know why, Scott? Because of *you*!"

"Don't you think this little scene is just adding to what they are already talking about?"

"I hate you so much, Scott!" I stormed past him, hooking my arm through Leigh's and marching toward the main building. "Let's go," I demanded of her.

"Harper," he yelled after me. "I can't *believe* I decided where I'd go to school based on you! Last night was the biggest waste of my time! I don't even know why I bothered caring!"

I turned around and stared at him, about to burst into tears. He had to know what he said had crossed the line. His face showed that he knew. I could feel my face getting red, and I was so saddened, so upset that I knew I could start crying at any moment. I looked down at my feet and let my backpack fall to the ground. My shoulders were shaking, and I desperately held back the tears that were threatening to escape. Scott didn't move from his spot immediately. He put his hands on his waist and looked around for a moment before slowly walking closer to me. He reached to pull me into a hug.

"Don't touch me, Scott," I whispered into his chest. "You don't get to hug me!"

"Just talk to him," Leigh suggested.

"He said he was done!"

"I'm not getting in the middle of this," Leigh yelled. "I just wasted my entire lunch period trying to convince Scott to talk to you instead of meeting Brad for lunch today! I'm not getting stuck in the middle of you two. I will not be forced to decide whom I want to keep as a friend, Harper or Brad. That's not fair to *me*. You two got yourself into this fight. No one will win this except some senior bitch! You have both said the worst things to one another! I'm not getting involved anymore. You need to fix this!"

"I'm not letting him win this one," I whispered.

"It's not a game, Harper! He's leaving in August," she reminded me. "Do you want to keep seeing him after August? Fix this, Harper! It's really not that big of a deal. There won't be any more Lindsay situations! He promised me in first period there won't be anymore!"

I stood, looking at her walk away. She left me standing in the courtyard with Scott. The lunchtime bell rang, and students were filing out of the cafeteria. I felt Scott's hand on my waist. While the crowd of students flowed around us, he pulled my hair to the left side of my head and kissed the right side of my neck.

"I am sorry I said I was done. I didn't mean it. You know I didn't mean it, Harper."

"Scott," I breathed, falling into him. I took a deep breath and whispered, "I know you didn't, Scott, but I also know how you knew who I was. I know why Barrett hates you."

"Harper…." He kept his lips near my ear. "That doesn't matter anymore—"

"You were only interested in me to prove that a freshman could get outplayed," I mumbled. "Just like this morning, when you only kissed me to hurt Lindsay."

"That's not how it happened," he breathed. "None of that is true."

Scott moved his lips up my neck until he reached my mouth and kissed me. His left hand guided my head as he kissed up my neck, while his right hand held tighter to my waist. He was full of confidence.

"Did you really think last night was a waste?" I breathed. "You don't care about last night?"

"I'd relive last night over again. All of it! Leigh didn't need to tell me how much last night meant; I already knew. Harper, I know you better than anyone!"

"Barrett never had a chance, did he?" I asked him, still upset at being used. "You used me because you were bored! You never wanted me, did you?" I pulled away from him. "You used me. That's what you do; you hurt girls."

"That's not true, Harper!"

"We're done, Scott."

NINE

I SAT ON THE LOCKER ROOM BENCH and stared at my empty locker. I had nothing to wear to practice. At the very least, I thought there would be a spare sports bra and an old pair of running shorts from the soccer season, but there was nothing. As I sat there contemplating my options, I arrived at the only sensible option left for me. I got up and knocked on the boys' locker room door, hoping nothing embarrassing would come from it.

"Harper!" Justin, a senior I'd never personally met but knew of through Scott, was on the baseball team and generous enough to open the door for me. He was tall, and though he wasn't wearing a shirt, shoes, or socks, he had managed to locate his pants.

"And what can I do for a *single* hot freshman like yourself?" he continued. "Anything at all…Rumor has it that Scott taught you well." He winked.

Despite being with Scott for nearly my entire freshman year of high school and knowing how he saw me, I still found myself slightly intimidated by innuendos and come-ons. The looming fear of the unknown permanently resided inside my brain.

"Um," I mumbled, "is Scott in there?"

"He is," the senior informed me, "but why is that your concern now?"

"Well," I grumbled and drew circles on the pavement with the toe of my shoe. "Maybe you could grab Scott for me? I need to ask him something."

"Scott," he screamed over his shoulder before turning his attention back toward me. "Is there anything else I can do for you? I heard you won't let Scott do anything for you—"

"Harper?" Scott exited the locker room and stood casually in front of me. His hands rested on his waist, and both his index fingers were lightly tucked into the waistband of his shorts. Neither one of his shoes was tied; it appeared that wearing a shirt in the boys' locker room was optional as he stood bare-chested in front of me.

"What's up?" He took a deep breath and watched another guy enter the locker room.

"I gave you back your keys."

"I'm aware."

"Yeah, I know you are, but I left my running bag in your car."

"Uh-huh." He nodded. "So, this is what you came to me for?"

"Well, what exactly did you want me to come to you with?" I mumbled. "I need my running shoes, or I can't practice today."

"This is my problem?"

"Scott—"

"The truck's unlocked," he snapped. "I know you left your bag in there."

"Well, why didn't you just give me my bag?" I felt shy around him as he towered over me, his confidence superior.

"Because I don't want to look at you," he stated flatly. "I want nothing to do with you!"

"Scott!" I gasped.

"The truck is over there!" He pointed. "Get your stuff."

I spun around and looked for the white truck, finding it in the sea of unglamorous high school transportation. It was clean and detailed. It was the only one without pink fliers tucked into the windshield.

"There were no fliers on your truck?" I whispered. "You don't have anything on your windshield."

"I'm aware. It would appear it's been resolved."

"What?" I pressed. "What's been resolved?"

"What's it to you, Harper?" he asked sadistically. "You're not my girlfriend anymore!"

"I know, but I figured—"

"You figured what?" he demanded. "You figured you were different? I hurt girls, *remember*? That's what you said. All I'm doing now is hurting a girl. Now, get your bag out of my truck!"

"We're not a couple anymore," I mumbled, "so you're going to hurt me?"

"Get your stuff, now!"

"This is how it happens, then," I breathed. "You pull them in and then cut them with your words. It's the easiest thing for you, isn't it?"

"No, Harper," he corrected me. "*You* cut *me* with your words!"

He spoke concisely, and before I knew it, he was gone. The door to the men's locker room shut. He *could* be mean if he needed to be. I had never seen it before. I felt hollow and confused at his words. I believed his words to be true and went on my way, destroyed inside that he was already onto his next conquest.

I intended to spend my entire practice working on my race. I wanted nothing more than to see Scott watching me and supporting me through my practice runs. The team sat in a large circle in the center of the field before practice; the team's senior captains led us in stretches. Unlike previous practices, I didn't sit next to Scott this time. I wanted to, but he seemed happy sitting beside Brad and laughing. He seemed content with having the seniors gravitating toward him, including many of the females on our team. The situation reminded me of the day we first met when his pack of senior friends acted so superior. He had it in him to be a jerk. He had the power to ignore me, forget about me and move on quickly.

He caused tremendous pain in me as he laughed with beautiful girls. He lay stretched out on the vividly green grass, his chest bare. Four additional girls with long, beautiful straight hair came over to him and smiled, sitting next to him and talking with him. He still caught my eye no matter how hard I tried to avoid looking at him. Our eyes locked, my eyes heavy with tears as I watched his long fingers casually graze the shoulder of one of the girls. His eyes burned through me while he delicately brushed her blonde hair off her shoulder with only the back of his index finger. His face remained emotionless as a single tear spilled over my right eye, and I was too embarrassed to draw any further attention to it by wiping it away.

He was hurting me, and he wasn't even speaking to me.

The circle broke up, and we all went to our respective events. Scott and Brad resumed their usual practice of wasting another afternoon of track practice. I was torn to shreds inside. He didn't speak to me; he didn't even acknowledge me. I was nothing but a freshman to him now. It was as if we never had anything between us. As I watched him walk in the opposite direction, I felt that everyone on the team had to know I was dying on the inside, including Scott. That wasn't fair. He may have given a lot to our relationship, but I gave just as much. Having him ignore me wasn't a reasonable option for me, I decided. He owed me more than that!

I started walking the straight-away of the track before upping my walk to a brisk pace. Soon I was lightly jogging, only a few steps behind him and within arms' reach. My right hand grabbed onto the outside of Scott's bicep, and I pulled on it, directing his attention to me.

"All I get is 'get your bag out of my truck'?" I asked condescendingly. "After everything we've been through, done together, and said to one another, you end our relationship with 'get your bag out of my truck'?"

"What do you want from me?" He spun around and yelled inches from my face.

"*What do I want from you?*" I parroted back. "I want nothing but a hint of decency. If we're over, act like I meant something to you; act like the last six months had some impact on your life! At the very least, pretend we're friends!"

"I'm just gonna...." Brad pointed over his shoulder toward the discus cage and walked off. "I'll see ya."

Scott remained standing in his usual stance: His hands were on his waist, his index fingers snuggly tucked into his waistband. He nodded at Brad.

"Is that what you think?" he asked me. "You think you actually meant something to me? You think the last six months had any influence on my life?"

"Did I mean anything to you?" I pleaded. "Was it all a lie?"

"It's not a lie if you believe it," he snapped. "It was a *game*, remember? You said it yourself."

"Barrett was right! You used me," I yelled. "You made me fall for you; you made me think you loved me. You're mean to girls, and I'm just another girl."

"Last night was all part of it...." He quickly turned away as his voice cracked.

"Oh my God!" I gasped. "It meant nothing? You played me—"

"Yup." His voice shook. He continued to keep his back to me.

"I was just some number, wasn't I?" I grabbed his jaw, jerking him toward me. "Look at me! I was just a number on your list of girls you've fucked before the real fun starts in college, wasn't I? Just one more virgin before college!"

"And you ate it up!" He glared at me until I pulled my hand away. "Easiest I've ever had!" He shrugged. "Sure, I had to play the bullshit role of the caring boyfriend, seeing shitty movies with you and telling you I *loved* you, but it paid off. I'd never screwed a freshman before, even when I was a freshman."

Oh, he could fight dirty. He *could* be mean, and it didn't bother him in the slightest. He'd not only perfected this craft, but he'd perfected hiding it from me until now, too. My brows pulled together tightly, and I bit my bottom lip out of fear that my rage-filled tears would make themselves present. I opted to not fight but simply walk away.

"I have to run." My voice cracked, and I slowly walked backward. "I'll leave you alone. I'll get your belongings back to you. I won't bother you."

I didn't want to hear anymore. I learned quickly and only needed to hear Scott say those things once. I didn't want to know what else he had to say or how he would say it. I imagined he'd pull out all the stops and dig deeper into our time together to hurt me. He'd use personal details of our relationship. I ran the straight-away of the track in the outer lane, pulling my stride faster.

"Harper! Shit!" Scott was yelling as his feet slammed against the rubber track. "Goddamn it! Please stop!"

I could hear his size-fourteen shoes skid against the rubber track. I could hear him getting closer. The gap between us was shrinking, and I forced myself to run faster. Soon it was too late, and his hands wrapped themselves around my waist and pulled me tightly toward him. He pulled my body against his chest and picked me up in a single motion. I instinctively wrapped both my arms tightly around his neck. I hated him then; I hated how mean he could be. I hated how he was also the only person I could cry on, and I suspected he was the only person I would ever be able to cry on.

"Why would you say that to me?" I sobbed onto his shoulder. "Of all the things you could have said, you had to say that you didn't love me! You had to say *that*!"

"Harper, I love you more than anything," he breathed. "I need you! You know that."

"Do you?" I sobbed. "You seem to have already moved on. You're already laughing with other people and telling me to get out of your face. You're already touching other girls."

"Laughing doesn't mean anything," he mumbled. "Being mean to you is hurting me."

"But the girls—"

"Touching that girl's shoulder meant nothing to me; it meant more to her."

"You're so good at it," I sobbed. "Last night meant nothing to you? It was just another night?"

"I feel like shit for that," he whispered into my neck as his grip got tighter. "I felt awful immediately after I said those things. I saw your face; I know you want us back the way we were. I know you were trying to fix us, and I was horrible to you. I want everything to be the way it was last night between us."

"You do?" I pulled away from his chest and wiggled down to the ground. "I want us back the way it was last night, too! I want us to eat Chinese food in my bed and laugh together. I want it to be like this morning when we were laughing in my bathroom. You made me forget everything."

"I *need* you to forget everything," he blurted. "I need you to forget how mean I was to you today! I need you to forget the gossip and Lindsay thinking that she beat a freshman!"

"Scott," I sobbed, "I don't care about the gossip. I want it to be just us again."

"I've always told you that," he reminded me. "It **has** to be just us."

"I haven't thought about anything except fixing this all day, and when you said you didn't want to see me, I felt so alone."

"Harper, I want everything the way it was."

"Like today never happened?"

"Like it never happened!"

"She thinks she won," I muttered, enjoying the feeling of his thumb wiping the tears off my cheek.

"Nobody won." he whispered.

"It was a game for her, but not for us."

He towered over me. He stood less than an inch from me, pulling me tightly to him. It was familiar, and it was easy. It was as if sixty other people were not running around the track that afternoon, and it was just us.

"Scott," I whispered as I pressed my forehead against his chest, "did you kiss me today to hurt Lindsay? Was that kiss for her or for me?"

"Both," he said honestly. "It was for you, but I knew she was watching. I wanted her to know there wasn't a chance that she and I would have had what I have with you. I wanted to hurt her. I wanted her to feel the pain she was causing you. I wanted her to see the pain of loving someone who was hurting."

"Scott, that was wrong," I breathed.

"You're better than her."

"Stop it," I blurted. "Stop it with that! I'm not better than anyone!"

"You are, and you know it!"

"Please stop," I pleaded.

"Harper," he breathed, "I need you to be with me."

"There are no other girls?" I mumbled. "You said—"

"No other girls," he interrupted. "I was asked out today while we were apart by a freshman and a senior, but I couldn't see myself with either of them."

"Just with me?" I pressed. "You can only see yourself with me?"

"Yes."

"And Barrett?" I breathed through my tears. I wanted an answer to that.

"Harper, I wanted to be with you since that first day I talked to you in PC. Barrett got in the way when he said he was interested, so I gave him his chance. I gave him three weeks to figure you out, and he did nothing. *He* could sit around and wait until his senior year to figure you out, but I didn't have that kind of time."

"It wasn't a game?"

"Not for me, it wasn't. I was being fair with him. I even suggested ways for him to be with you. He didn't take any of my advice and went after you when it was too late. He looked desperate when he was chasing you in the parking lot. Harp, you can't be with a guy like that. You can't be with a guy who throws himself at you!"

"I didn't ask him to sit with me today," I promised. "He saw me by myself and just sat down. He didn't ask."

"He went looking for you and got lucky that you were sitting by yourself." He sighed. "During health, Taylor asked me out. Before I answered her, I figured Barrett would probably do the same with you."

"Taylor asked you out?" I panicked. "That quickly?"

"Oh, Harper." He smiled and casually tilted his head. "I said no."

"Did she ask you out, or did she ask you to *prom*?"

"Harper," he sighed. "Does it matter?"

"To me, it does," I cried. "I wanted us to have that discussion! If you were discussing prom with other girls, I couldn't handle that."

He leaned further into me, lifting my lips to his. He was soft and gentle; he took his time and cradled my cheek with his large hand. He pulled away and leaned into my ear.

"Shh...Shh...Harper, calm down. I told her that I had my eye on a different freshman." He breathed deeply. "I just hope this girl likes getting dressed up for dances."

"Did you really say that?" I whined. "Seriously?"

"Yes!" He grinned as he took his right thumb and wiped a tear away. "She was surprised. She probably thought her gossip about our break-up came from a reliable source."

"Scotty," I whined, "when will you ask this freshman to prom?"

"I don't know." He grinned. "You know freshman girls better than I do; when do you think I should ask her?"

"Sooner rather than later!" I grinned. "If I know this freshman at all, and I think I do, I can assure you that she'll probably go crazy with dress shopping!"

"This freshman has a very good track record in picking out great dresses," Scott agreed.

"I love you, Scott." I smiled. "It's just us. It will always be."

"I love you, Harper." He grinned.

"What's so funny?" I exclaimed. "Why are you smiling like that?"

"Harper, can we leave practice early today? I'd like to get a head start on enjoying the *just us* part of our weekend."

He grabbed my waist and hoisted me up, wrapping my legs around him. I locked my lips to his again, letting my fingers get lost in his hair. I felt as though we were gliding back toward the locker rooms. I barely felt Scott walk the remaining distance. I only felt his hands on me.

"Am I too heavy?"

"Are you fishing for compliments?" he teased.

"I'm not fishing for compliments!" I laughed. "But I *am* suggesting that you never be that mean to me again!"

"I can promise you I'll never be that mean again."

"You better not, or there won't be any more *just us*."

"Harp," he groaned. "I was really upset at what you said today."

"What I said? Which part?"

"Are you kidding me?" he exclaimed. "All of it! You broke up with me, and you said I was mean to girls, which about killed me. **Then** you had lunch with Barrett and accused me of only asking you out because of him."

"Oh, Scotty," I exclaimed. "You have hurt feelings!"

"Harper," he said slowly, warning in his voice.

"I am sorry. That wasn't fair of me to say." I whispered. "As for Barrett, I shouldn't have believed him. I should have remembered how long we've been together, and I should have known that if this was a game, it wouldn't have lasted as long. I apologize."

"Thank you." He softly smiled as we neared his truck. "I am sorry for saying those things to you, too. I *was* mean to girls, and it hurt saying those things to you. It hurt to look at you as I said them."

"It was never a game…"

"Not with me," he informed me. "And I'll make sure you never hear about another girl."

Scott set me on the hood of his truck and kissed me. I continued to pull him closer to me; Scott did the same. It was the sort of kissing that you really only see in high school parking lots.

"Scott," I breathed against his lips, "I don't even know why we broke up! I can't even remember."

"Harp?" He ran his lips along my neck. "You know what we should do?"

"Yes, I do!"

"Is anyone at your house?" he breathed.

"Probably, but it's Friday night, so I don't have a curfew."

"Will you spend the night? Please, Harp." He pleaded. "We can hot tub at my place. My folks are probably out for the night." he declared while I continued to kiss him as he pulled me closer to him.

"Scott, we should leave now, or I'm liable to behave inappropriately."

Scott's hands wrapped around my lower back and pulled me toward him. He lifted me off the truck and set me down directly in front of him. He grabbed a fist full of my hair and gently pulled me toward him.

"I have absolutely no recollection of why we broke up," he told me, "but I do have a strong recollection of what I had planned for tonight."

"Give me a second to get my bag."

"Harp?" Scott didn't let go of my hand; he gently pulled my hand back. "I love you!"

"I know you do." As usual, I allowed him to pull me up off the ground and kiss him again. "And I love you!"

"Babe," he exclaimed as I briskly walked to the locker room. "Make it quick!"

I pranced quickly into the locker room with a significant smile. I was happy that Scott and I had fixed whatever it was that destroyed eight hours between us. Whatever it was, it wasn't worth it. I wasn't going to focus on it again. It was out of my mind. My Friday night with Scott had been actively restored.

There she was in the locker room. That vague memory of what destroyed us sat on the long bench, putting together her running bag. I said nothing to her. I pretended she wasn't there as I opened my locker, carefully spinning my dial until the combination was entered correctly. I had nothing to say to her and didn't want to speak. I imagined that the only thing I wanted to say to her was *better luck next time*.

"So the freshman is back with her boyfriend," Lindsay declared.

Apparently, *she* had something to say to me. I again avoided speaking to her. I knew that if I did, it would turn ugly, and she had enough ugliness in her life. I wasn't scared of her; I was tired of her. It saddened me to look at her. She was so beautiful and appeared so well put together in life, and she depressed me. That made me sad for Scott, too, and just then, I wanted nothing more than to be happy for Scott and his ability to change the course of his life with such discipline and dedication.

"Bye Lindsay," I responded.

I opened my locker, pulled out my track bag, put on one of Scott's oversized heavy sweatshirts, and started for the door. I had nothing to say to her. She wanted to use me to hurt Scott, and I didn't want to play. I had the confidence to have a battle of words with her, but I didn't want to waste any more time away from Scott that evening.

"I'll see you tomorrow, Lindsay," I added. "Good luck!"

"I guess she really is a slut," she groaned.

"What did you say?" I dropped my bag and walked closer to her. "Say it again," I dared her.

"I said that I guess you really *are* a slut, but you're first and foremost a dumb girl." She inched closer to me. "I thought you'd smartened up when I heard you broke up with Pierce. I thought you'd finally gotten it, but I guess that isn't the case now, is it?"

"Lindsay, you're the slut, and you're the dumb one."

"No, I *was* a dumb girl, but I'm not anymore, and I'm certainly not a slut, but you seem to not care that Scott was practically fucking you on the hood of his truck."

"That's right, Lindsay," I replied with a low grumble. "Scott doesn't care that people see his hands on *me*, but he made sure that no one saw his hands on you. *That* was something he never wanted anyone to know about."

"Maybe you should consider getting a room," she countered.

"We've done it in a room before, unlike you."

"You're a whore!"

"Lindsay, you're the one that continued to get used by someone who never said he loved you. You were the one that continued to get left alone up at the bluff to get dressed. You couldn't make it stop because you were dumb. That didn't happen to me," I said calmly. "To the best of my understanding, once a dumb girl, always a dumb girl…Correct?"

"Harper, Harper…Or should I say, *Harp*? I'll admit that I was a dumb girl, but I stopped being a dumb girl once I figured out Scott's game. You…You know Scott's game, and you continue to get played."

"Lindsay, did you figure out Scott's game before or after Brad?" I walked closer to her. "There is no game, Lindsay—not with me, at least."

"Harper, you may not see yourself as a dumb girl, but you are. You are a slut for giving it up to Pierce, too. You have to at least see *that* much!"

"If you see someone in a committed relationship as a slut, I guess that's what I am, but I'll remind you that you know absolutely nothing about what goes on between Scott and me. I'll tell you what: Call me a slut if it makes you feel better. Tell everyone, in fact; make signs for tomorrow's race, tell my parents, tell the sheriff who will be at the race tomorrow. Tell him that his son is dating a slut. Tell Marie Pierce also—she absolutely adores me. She might find it interesting to hear that her son's girlfriend is a whore."

"Fuck you, Harper," she whispered. Her voice was cracking, and tears were welling in her eyes. I could see her face shake. She'd lost her confidence. She'd lost everything she built up about herself—her ego and style had all vanished.

"That's it? *That* got you upset, Lindsay? Not the regret or my hatred for your actions? No...You wanted to be known as Scott's girlfriend. That's your biggest regret? You wanted to have dinner at his house, to stay the night in his bed. You wanted him to come over and meet your parents, to be friends with your siblings. You wanted that life with Scott?"

I knew her tears were borne of jealousy. She had wanted the kind of relationship with Scott that I had, and she never got it. I didn't care then; I was tired of always being the bigger person. I was angry at her for taking eight hours away from my relationship with him.

"Poor Lindsay didn't get what she wanted. She opted for the easy route. She *became* easy," I mocked her. "I'm sorry that your first time was with Scott on a bluff overlooking the Sound, and he thought it was meaningless. At least you had a beautiful view of the water."

"Stop it, Harper," she yelled. "You have no idea what you're talking about. You're just a stupid freshman."

"My first time ever was with Scott, too," I continued. "It was in his bed on New Year's Eve. I'll tell you about it if you'd like. I remember that you asked me about it. He told me that he loved me over and over, and if you're a relationship person like me, that is a very important thing to hear during the act, especially if it's your first time. I imagine you also thought of yourself as a relationship person, didn't you? I mean, you thought Scott was your boyfriend. You told people that you were together. All your friends thought you were together... Where are all your friends now?"

I nudged her over on the bench and sat down next to her. Condescendingly, I took her hand and held it. I pretended to console her as I wiped a tear away with my thumb and lightly brushed her blonde locks away from her face. I swept them behind her shoulders and tucked them behind her ears, ignoring her shaking shoulders and heavy sobs.

"He kissed me through the entire experience and asked me over and over again how I was feeling and if I was enjoying it. I'm sorry he didn't ask how you were doing. I'm also very sorry he didn't care whether or not you were in pain. I can't imagine getting dressed *alone* afterward. Scott insisted that I stay the night after our first time, he nearly demanded it, but I had a curfew... You're awfully quiet. You don't have anything to say?"

"Harper," she declared as she cried, "I have nothing to say to you."

"I figured you'd have *something* to say. All you do is talk!" I chuckled. "I mean, from what I've heard from Scott about your sophomore year and what I've heard you say to my face, it seems that you never shut up!"

I continued to hold her hand and lightly rub her back condescendingly. I knew the amount of pain I was causing her, and I didn't care. I wanted her to feel far worse than I'd felt the last two days. I wanted her to feel confused, angry, and desperate. I was able to overcome my emotions with Scott's help, but she didn't seem at all capable of removing herself from her own emotional carnage.

"I was so sad," she mumbled through her tears. "I hated it. I hated going through it, and I hated knowing how it was going to end. I loved him so much."

"That's sad," I agreed, continuing to rub her back. "That's it, let it out."

"He never loved me," she sobbed. "He never felt anything."

"I wouldn't know. I suspect that's something only a whore experiences."

"Harper, are you finished?" she snapped through her tears. "Have you finished forcing me to relive my pain?"

"Don't ever tell people I'm a slut," I told her. "My experience was nothing like yours. Think twice before you call me dumb, too, or next time we'll start reminiscing about your pregnancy."

"Harper, I'd heard you were a nice girl, that you were eager to make friends and always smiling. Everyone always has something nice to say about you. Even Maureen and April, who hate *everyone*, had something positive to say about you. Brad tells people how awesome a chick you are, and not just 'cause you're his best friend's girl." She spoke with deep sadness, making her words harder and sharper. "But honestly, I think you're just like Scott."

I gave a single grunt and walked away.

We did what we found ourselves to be good at together that night—we laughed. We laughed while he lightly wrestled me onto the sofa. I was already in my swimsuit. He teased and tickled me, and I squirmed in his light grip, trying to catch my breath.

"We're never going to make it to the hot tub if you keep this *up*," I declared, laughing.

"Is that a pun, Harper?" He laughed. "Are you making a joke?"

"Something is definitely *up*!" I roared with laughter as he tickled me. "And if you'd like it to go away, I suggest we make a move upstairs."

"Babe, not one person is in this house," he reminded me.

I pulled away from him, leaving him collapsed on the sofa while I skipped over fallen pillows, hopped over the ottoman, and ran through the living room and up the stairs toward his room. I felt his fingers lightly brush my bare waist as he tried to catch me and pull me into his grip. I failed to suppress my laughter. It got the best of me, and I collapsed on the stair I was standing on in a fit of giggles.

"What are you doing, Harper?" He grinned. "I'm not even touching you!"

"I know!" I attempted to breathe through my laughter. "You keep *trying* to tickle me, though!"

"Harper, babe, calm down!" He laughed while his hands continued to tickle all the places that made me squirm. "I'm hardly touching you. What is so funny?"

"Scotty," I screamed. "Stop it!"

"I'll give you something to scream about!"

"Let me remind you to be nice," I teased. "You seem like the kinda guy who needs to be reminded to be nice to his girlfriend!"

"Oh, Harp." In a single scoop, he picked me up and carried me the rest of the way up the staircase before making a hard turn into his bedroom. "You're asking for it now!"

"Too soon to make jokes?" I asked innocently.

"Harper!" He cried as he tossed me onto his bed. He tossed me against his mattress, and I bounced high enough that he had time to climb underneath me before I landed against his blue comforter.

"Scott," I breathed as I traced his smile lines, "I can't go eight hours without you again."

"We have to remember that it's just us in this relationship," he breathed into my ear. "We have to ignore everyone else."

"I know."

"I'm not ignoring the fact that I have my shirt off, and you don't, either," he declared.

"Scott," I screamed, "I have a *bikini top* on!"

"I'm taking it off!"

"You do that!" I encouraged him as I felt his hand move up my back and tug at the strings. "Just a forceful tug on that string, Scotty, and you've got it!"

"I got it, I got it!" He smiled as he tossed the top onto the floor. "Now for the bottoms… I'm at a loss!"

"Oh babe, let me show you," I exclaimed before pulling at his strings and tugging at his shorts. I laughed at Scott's astonished reaction. "Now, we'll be doing it a bit differently this evening. A special showing, if you will…."

"What are we doing?" He grinned. "The anticipation is killing me!"

"I've wanted to do this for a *very* long time!"

"How long are we talking?" He smirked. "More than three months?"

The feeling of power raced through me. His hands clamped onto my hair and locked me in place. I immediately fell in love with the power; I felt in charge. I loved the person I was becoming with Scott. He'd changed me in more ways than one, and I was better for it. I wanted this, and even though he never asked for anything oral, I knew he wanted it, too.

"Harper," he groaned, losing his hands further into my curls, "that feels *good!*"

I kept going. It was clear that he wanted this to continue, but he seemed hesitant about letting it continue. I feared my self-proclaimed sexual empowerment would whither if I halted. He was obviously enjoying what I was providing to him as he became more and more vocal about it, but then he pulled away and fell on his back, pulling me up to his chest.

"That," he exclaimed, "I never saw coming!"

He tugged and yanked my bottoms off, letting me continue to be in control. The power I had to make Scott feel as he did was exhilarating. I felt more powerful than I could ever have dreamed. At that moment, I had more power than standing up to Lindsay. I was becoming demanding about what I wanted as I leaned over Scott and enjoyed the control he let me have.

"Scott," I breathed out as our bodies pressed together. I could feel how hot his skin was. How the slight perspiration from his olive complexion pulled tightly against my already hot skin. "I think it's happening again!"

"Harper, you're amazing."

"I love you so much, Scott," I breathed, pleasure building quickly. "I am so sorry for today."

"Don't be sorry, babe," he breathed. "Be thankful we're back."

I broke the state record for the two-hundred-meter race late that Saturday morning. I finished it in twenty-four point nine seconds. Scott squeezed me tightly against his chest as we watched my banner get raised opposite his three-point shooting record in our school's award room.

"We're a power couple now, Harp," he informed me.

TEN

I WENT TO GREAT LENGTHS TO AVOID the topic of graduation. I hoped that Scott hadn't noticed I wasn't bringing it up, and when it was brought up, I'd politely excuse myself or intentionally change the subject in the hope that I wouldn't have to talk about it. I didn't want people to know about my disdain for Scott's graduation and the fact that he would leave the island in the fall. I had a feeling that my avoidance of the topic was doing just the opposite. Scott, being the understanding person that he was with me, had not yet brought it up. He'd allowed me this one selfish act of not congratulating him just yet on his impending graduation.

I kept my mind occupied with either my intense love for Scott or my intense love for dress shopping. I focused on the event that would require a phenomenal dress for my phenomenal date—prom. Scott knew it meant more to me than to him, and he took great care in planning to ensure that I had the best night possible. He even sent thirty-six red roses with a card detailing the date of the event. I carefully placed the roses on my dresser next to a framed picture of the two of us from Valentine's Day.

My mother had a very strong interest in shopping, so she didn't mind when I tried on twenty or thirty dresses over the course of four hours one Sunday afternoon in April. The only downer about the afternoon was that Scott had placed the topic of birth control back in my head. The topic itself wasn't the problem, but the promise I'd broken to my mom about being honest with her was bothering me. The topic had ruined my ability to pick a dress. I was filled with indecisiveness because of my sudden reproductive responsibility.

Recently, Scott had become the voice of reason when it came to birth control. I was suddenly becoming the irresponsible one in our relationship. All the times we failed to use a condom were not entirely his fault. I could and should have spoken up sooner and reminded him, and I did take responsibility for that. I was always the one who felt stupid afterward, while Scott never seemed to care until I freaked out on him. The pill seemed like our most viable option.

"Harper, when exactly is prom?" my mom asked. "If you can't find anything today, we can always go to Northgate Mall next weekend," she suggested as I tried on my thirty-first dress of the afternoon.

"It's in May, so I really want to make sure I get it today. I don't want to be one of those girls who freak out and settle on an ugly dress at the last minute."

I stood in the dressing room and stared in the mirror at the maroon dress I had on. It had a form-fitting corset top, spaghetti straps, and a tulle bottom that went past my ankles and puffed out about a foot around me. I loved the dress. I thought I looked adorable, and I hopped out of the dressing room and looked at my mom, who was sitting in an oversized leather chair and waiting for me.

"Harper, that is the dress! I'm not just saying that because we've been to fourteen different stores, and I'm starving, either. I really do love the color and the style. You look striking. Though your…Um, your *top* seems to be a bit…bubbly."

I smiled when she said I looked striking. I'd never thought of myself as striking. I always saw myself as cute or adorable. Girls that are short with big curls, cute smiles, and a slightly squeaky voice got called adorable, not beautiful—unless their boyfriend is Scott Pierce. Then they are called beautiful or "fucking hot." **Striking**, however, isn't a Scott Pierce word. As for her concern over my breasts being somewhat exposed, well...That was a concern I didn't share.

"You really think I look *striking*?"

"I do, Harper. You are beautiful," she stated. "You have no concerns about your.... *top* in that dress, though?"

"Not really," I mumbled. "I think I'm alright with that."

"Alright, then."

I saw her eyes roll at my acceptance of my body, but I knew that she wouldn't be the one looking at me all night. Frankly, I didn't care what she thought about my chest at the moment. I couldn't let this go on; the secret of my sexual relationship with Scott was eating me away from the inside. I'd made so many promises to my mom about this that I finally had to come clean with her, or I'd never be able to enjoy prom night with Scott. I was tired of drilling Scott on the use of a condom and feeling like I had to monitor our sex life with a red marker and calendar. I was tired of being in the moment and forgetting to ask him to put one on and then wailing on him afterward, only to be reminded that he enjoyed our lovemaking more without one.

"Mom, I have to talk to you about something important."

She sat up in the oversized waiting chair and leaned against her knees, waiting. I paced the small dressing room, running my words through my head before speaking them. At first, I figured it would be best to tell her like I told Leigh, but then I remembered telling Leigh was different. She wasn't shocked or surprised, and she encouraged my sexual relationship. Mom, despite being open-minded and realistic, was still my mom. I had to come right out with it, I thought.

"I've made a decision."

"And what's that?"

I started to pace the mirrored dressing room, looking down at the maroon dress I'd yet to officially decide on.

"Harper, what is it?" she pressed.

I spun around and sat on my knees, facing her. I kept my hands busy with the tulle as I spread it out around me, lightly patting it down, so it completely encased me. I caught a glimpse of myself in the mirror. Despite having my hair in a messy bundle of curls, I looked and felt gorgeous. I knew I'd feel even more beautiful the night of prom because Scott would remind me minute after minute of how attractive I'd look.

"Harper?"

"Mom, I broke a promise to you, and it's killing me. It's eating away at me."

I took a deep breath before I continued. Her face didn't change. She simply sat in the dark leather chair, waiting for me to come clean.

"I didn't tell you before because I was afraid of what you'd think of me."

"Harper, tell me now," she insisted. "You have me worried. I've never seen you this serious before."

"Mom, it's not bad! I don't think it's bad, anyway. I just feel bad for not telling you sooner." I kept my eyes and hands on the maroon dress and spoke to my mom, "I am afraid that when I tell you, you'll look at me differently. You'll see me as…I don't know …Not your daughter anymore? Like maybe I'm someone else's daughter or something."

"Harper?" She reached for my hand. "I won't think of you any differently, no matter what it is. Unless you are involved in hardcore narcotics, I highly doubt I'd think any differently of you. I'd probably look to Scott if you told me you were involved in something like that, but you'll always be my daughter." Her reassuring voice almost had me convinced. "What is it?"

"First, I think that, if anything has changed, I've grown from this choice. I think *we've* grown from it—Scott and me…Not the breaking of the promise—that I feel horrible about. I certainly don't feel horrible about my decision, though."

"Then tell me, what is your decision?" she pressed. "If you feel absolutely certain of your decision, my opinion shouldn't matter in the slightest."

"But when have I *not* cared about your opinion?" I sulked.

"I promise." She gave a reassuring smile. "I won't think differently, but remember, my opinion shouldn't matter in any decision you feel confident about."

She had a point. She always had a fantastic way of making sure that I understood her. I slowly looked up and took a deep breath. I made sure to look right into her eyes as I addressed her.

"I'm not a virgin anymore."

She didn't say anything. She didn't move immediately, either. She simply looked at me, her hands holding her expensive Kate Spade handbag, her perfectly manicured nails and expensive gold jewelry glittering against it. She slowly leaned back in her seat. The only sound came from the leather seat as it adjusted for my mother. She gradually tucked her frosted hair behind her ears and spoke.

"I see."

"You're not mad, are you?" I whispered. "You're not disappointed in me? It took me a long time to make this decision and longer to act on it."

"No, no, no! Harper, I'm not disappointed, and I am certainly not mad. I wish I could say I'm not surprised, but I am. It's tough to wrap my mind around you engaging in that type of relationship."

"Mom—"

"I can only assume it's with Scott."

"Oh yes!" I affirmed. "It's with Scott."

"There's that," she said to herself.

"You think I'm too young?"

"It isn't a matter of age," she stammered. "I suppose that even if you came to me at twenty-five or thirty and told me you had a sexual relationship, I would still have a tough time digesting the news."

"But you," I mumbled, "knew this might happen, right?"

"I knew you'd eventually have a boyfriend and that you would eventually have a physical relationship. I wasn't ignorant of this; I think I wanted to pretend it wouldn't happen, though."

"Mom…." I smiled softly. "We're fine."

"You two have been together a while now."

"Since September."

"What happens after graduation?"

I slowly shrugged my shoulders and gave her a tight-lipped smile. "Mom, I love him."

"I assumed you'd stay together after he graduated."

"That's the plan."

"Alright, I honestly have no need to know what goes on between you and Scott in that aspect of your relationship, but I do feel that I have a responsibility as your mother to make sure that you are both safe. I want to make sure that *you* are being safe."

"We've been safe."

"Harper, he is older than you, and he has already been with—"

"He has," I interrupted her. "And he has been checked. Before being with me, he got a physical."

"And you've been safe?" she asked. "Of late, you said?"

"So far," I whispered.

"This was your decision?" she asked, concerned. "I am sure it was a joint decision, but you didn't feel pressured in any way?"

"I never felt pressured."

"I am happy for you, then. I'm not sure what else I should say to you except to reassure you that I am not disappointed or angry with you. I suppose I knew that this was going to happen. I mean, you've been together since September. I have to be honest—I never thought you'd last this long. You know, with all the differences between the two of you. I suppose since both of you are talking about staying a couple after this year, you both really love each other."

"You don't think differently of Scott, do you?" I asked.

"Not at all! I could tell very early in your relationship that Scott loved you, but I wasn't sure if you knew that or if he'd made a point of telling you."

"He made a point to tell me."

"I think at your ages, sex seems like a significant step in your relationship. At least, with you, I can tell it was a critical step. You, no doubt, spent a long time debating the decision. I can only hope when you both arrived at this point in your relationship, Scott knew it was a very emotional decision for *you*, and he handled it carefully."

I nodded in agreement. Everything Scott and I had discussed about my decision flooded my mind. I loved how he handled my choice, but I loved how he never pressed for the choice, either.

"Scott isn't exactly a mystery," my mom continued. "He's pretty easy to figure out. It also probably helps that I am good friends with Marie. I get an inside perspective that way."

She laughed, no doubt at some conversation she and Marie had shared. It was probably a conversation I would be happy to have no knowledge of.

"Harper, I'm not going to ask you how long you two have been... you know. I'm going to assume that it hasn't been long, so I will ask if you are willing to do *me* a favor."

"What is it?"

"Will you start taking birth control? I *don't* want to be a grandmother in my early forties." She smiled. "I'm not near Marie's age. Her being a grandmother is one thing, but me... I can't have that," she joked.

"That is the reason I told you." My head tilted, and a small smile of relief came to my face.

"I assumed so when you brought it up; I can't imagine you were looking forward to this discussion."

"I was dreading it," I agreed, "but I'd rather have this discussion with you than be caught standing in the condom aisle at Rite-Aid or worse, PC."

"Think of it this way, Harper: You can either be caught standing in the condom or the home pregnancy aisle. It's your choice!"

"True, except both are in the same aisle, and I don't want to be seen in that aisle at all!"

"You do know that Scott can go into that aisle, right?"

"Oh, I am aware," I exclaimed, "and he has been."

"Alright, I can see this is a paralyzing fear for you, and I sympathize greatly," she teased me and winked. "In that case, perhaps oral contraceptives are the best option."

"Yes," I exclaimed. "I couldn't agree more, and thank you. I don't like talking about this; outside of Scott, you're really the only person I've discussed this with."

"Really?" she exclaimed. "Leigh hasn't been pressing you? I'm surprised! That girl is the nosiest person. She can't stay out of anybody's business!"

"Leigh knows," I sighed, "but I limit the details."

"That's probably best with her."

"Mom, can we not tell Dad about this?" I pleaded.

"I'm not telling him anything," she assured me. "That is a conversation I'd rather not have with him, ever! If *you* want to, by all means, go ahead."

"No way!"

"Harper?" She leaned down and laid her hands on my bare shoulders. "Thank you for being honest. I know what you share with Scott is none of my business, and I am sure you didn't want to tell me but thank you. I'll make an appointment for you tomorrow, alright?"

"Alright." I nodded, stood up, and began twirling around. "I think I am going to get this maroon one. Do you like it?"

"I think it's perfect!" She smiled and fluffed my dress out. "I must tell you I am delighted that you aren't a cliché!"

"What do you mean?" I stopped twirling and faced her.

"You're not losing your virginity on prom night." She stood up and twirled me around before unzipping my prom dress. "I think now I have a better understanding of why you're not too concerned about your chest showing," she declared with a twinkle in her eye.

"Mom!"

She smiled an all-knowing grin. "Harper, I do your laundry. I have a general idea of the recent changes in how you view your body!"

"Oh, my God," I groaned.

"I knew *something* was going on."

Like any other Monday, Scott dropped Morgan off at her elementary school before continuing down the street toward the high school. Before we dropped her off, we went to Starbucks, where Scott bought Morgan a tall hot chocolate and let her pick a donut. As this was a standard Monday, Scott and I walked together toward first period after we got to school, stopping and kissing passionately in the main hallway outside of my classroom.

"Harper, let's skip practice today and go to my house," he suggested, kissing me again. "We can grab take-out and hot tub the entire afternoon. Come on, we don't have a meet until Thursday."

"Let's skip after fourth period, Scott," I breathed. "I can't skip algebra."

"Even better!"

We continued to kiss while passersby told us to get a room. I slowly pulled away and headed toward my class. He patted my butt. "I love you, Little Harper Whitmore," he yelled before we walked into our respective classrooms.

My first-period class, U.S. History, was a bore, but we were informed during an intercom message from the principal that there would be an assembly during fourth period. This had me very excited. I'm sure it had Scott just as excited. While we were both in different classrooms, I knew we were both thinking the same thing—we could skip fourth period now, giving us the entire afternoon to hot tub, make out, watch television, and probably do much more without the interference of parents. I tapped my pencil against my forehead as I waited for first period to be over. I wanted to run across the hall and discuss what I knew would be our shared idea.

"So, we're skipping fourth period also?" Scott asked me as soon as the first period was over.

"Yes we are!" I nodded and grinned.

I tugged on his T-shirt and pulled him toward me. Scott forced us against the lockers, causing them to rattle and cause onlookers to stop and look at us, but it wasn't enough for me or Scott to dial back our intensity.

"I could easily skip right now," he informed me.

"I want to, believe me," I shot back.

"We're skipping today?" a familiar voice asked. We looked over at Brad and Leigh, standing next to each other.

"Um…." I pointed at Scott and me before answering, enjoying the feeling of Scott's fingers running circles around the small of my back. "No, *we* are."

"You two can do whatever you want, but we are skipping," Scott added. "This is just *us*."

"Harp, what do you two plan to do this afternoon?" Leigh asked. "Could you write me a note in second period that details exactly what you want to do with Scott this afternoon?" she teased. "Those notes are *so* hot!"

"Harp, I gotta read these notes," Scott demanded. "Come on, just those ones!"

"Wait," Brad interjected. "You're skipping the assembly? We get our caps and gowns during the assembly, Scott."

"Harp," Scott sulked. "We can bail afterward, but I gotta get my cap and gown."

"That's alright." I smiled and nodded. "We'll leave right after the assembly."

"Are you sure?" Scott pressed. "I can pick up the cap and gown later if you'd rather."

"No, you shouldn't push that off. It's a big deal."

"Harp, I can have Brad grab it for me," he suggested. "Then we can get lunch and hang out at my place."

"Scott," I ordered, "get your cap and gown. It will be alright."

I instantly became aware that a bad mood could prevail if I didn't control my emotions, so I did my absolute best to change my demeanor and save the turmoil building inside me for later. The discussion of caps and gowns, graduation, and diplomas was a touchy subject for me, and hearing it discussed so casually was annoying.

I heard my name announced on the intercom and felt relieved because I could pull away from the discussion, and Scott would not be able to press me on my emotional state. If he pushed me, it would be a quick trip to sob-town for me. I always got this way as soon as he mentioned graduation.

"I gotta go, guys." I reached up and kissed Scott goodbye.

Before I made it out of the main hallway, I felt his long right arm drape over my shoulder and his left arm wrap around my chest. He turned me around, lifted me off the ground, and pulled me tightly against his chest. He whispered clearly into my ear. He must have seen the emotion on my face before I left.

"We'll be alright," he affirmed.

I looked at him, tightly pressing my forehead against his cheek. I breathed him in and enjoyed the smell I had learned to cling to nearly eight months ago. I could only give him a fake smile and hope he wouldn't notice the difference.

"I know."

I wiggled out of his grip and began walking to our high school's main office. I did everything in my power to push out thoughts of graduation, but walking through the main hallway made that virtually impossible. The walls were now decorated with words like 'congratulations' and 'class of' 98.' I wanted this hallway to be decorated with fliers for prom festivities or perhaps pages torn out of the many magazines devoted to that subject. I even contemplated redecorating with the store ads, giving girls ideas about where to buy their prom accessories. Unfortunately, the hall was screaming graduation, and I was screaming on the inside.

"Hi, I'm Harper Whitmore. I was called down," I announced when I got to the main office.

"Yes, Ms. Whitmore." The school receptionist began fumbling through the notes on her desk and handed me one. "Your mother is picking you up before the start of the fifth period for a doctor's appointment."

I read the note and realized that my mother had been quick about getting me to a gynecologist. There was no other explanation. She must have been thinking about my sexual relationship with Scott, which made me slightly uncomfortable. No matter how open and honest my relationship was with Julie Whitmore, the idea of her thinking about my sexual experiences made me somewhat uncomfortable—even if it was the responsible approach to the situation. It occurred to me that my fantastic afternoon with Scott was busted. There would be no skipping classes. Spending the afternoon in a hot tub was not in my near future.

My thoughts were interrupted by the receptionist, who reminded me that I should be getting to second-period health. I nodded and slowly walked to second period. My good mood had disappeared in the span of thirty seconds. I entered health and waved my standard-issue note to Ms. Tierney, which explained my tardiness to her class. I took my seat and began to write a note to Leigh about my quick mood change and how I'd become a responsible individual, just as Scott saw me and was finally going to be taking an oral contraceptive. I explained the irony that I did not feel as liberated as the pill was supposed to make me feel.

We handed in our health assignments and started our class discussion on the potential long-lasting emotional dangers of abusive relationships. I decided to mentally check out of this discussion and not pay attention to class. I sat, eagerly anticipating the bell that would declare our dismissal. I exited the classroom quickly to find that Scott was waiting for me. He knew my smile was anything but genuine, and he knew there was something up. I knew he needed to fix it and make me feel like he knew he could.

"Scott!" I lightly pulled away from his kiss. "My mom is picking me up before fifth period for *the* doctor's appointment."

"Oh, Harp, that just killed my buzz. We haven't skipped since February." He leaned his back against the hall lockers and pulled me close. "I have to spend the rest of my afternoon alone now."

"You could continue your day as originally planned," I suggested. "Go home without me and go to track practice."

"Harper, I hate track and field," he sulked. "This is the first year I enjoyed it because of you. If you're not there, I will not enjoy it."

"You always know what to say," I smirked.

"It's only Monday; we can skip tomorrow and chill at my place!"

"I'm running out of Mondays," I sulked.

"Harp," he sighed, "I'll look for you at the assembly!"

That is precisely what we did. Each student sat with his or her respective class, except for one student who had been under the influence of her much older boyfriend. He'd had enough courage to sneak his freshman girlfriend over to sit with him for the entire hour as faculty handed out awards to seniors who were overachievers in their scholastic endeavors. Scott was a solid student, but he didn't anticipate winning an award for it.

"Are we going to talk about this?" he whispered to me in the back row of the auditorium. He leaned over, his elbows on his knees, and looked very serious as he asked.

"I don't know what you're talking about," I whispered. I didn't mimic his actions. I sat tall and pressed my palms against my knees as I looked him in the eye.

"Yes you do."

"Nope." I shook my head.

"Harper...." His tone was annoyed and frustrated.

For the remainder of the hour, Scott and I stayed silent. He slouched back in his seat, pulled his feet onto the seat in front of him, and rested his elbow on his thighs, resting his head against the tips of his fingers. He was angry with me. Once the tension between us was enough to slice through, I slid my hand along his thigh and reached for his hand. I feared he'd refuse to take my hand or simply place it back on my leg, but he held it. I casually slid back into my seat and pulled my knees to my chest while he draped his left hand over my knees and held my right hand with his. I smiled, tight-lipped, as we continued to sit in silence.

The faculty asked the seniors to get into alphabetical order to claim their caps and gowns and any other applicable décor for their graduation day after the assembly. He stared at me as we remained frozen in our seats in the large auditorium.

"Harper—"

"There is nothing to talk about."

"I know you hate it."

"I'll meet you outside," I whispered in a flinty voice that wasn't mine.

I did my best to regain composure on my way out of the auditorium, but as I was sitting at the flagpole and watching freshmen, sophomores, and juniors march off to the cafeteria, I couldn't help but grow slightly angry that Scott had put me in this position. I was, no doubt, the only freshman who was not looking forward to becoming a sophomore. I would stay a freshman forever if Scott stayed a senior. I wasn't *just* a freshman at this school; I was Scott's girlfriend. I didn't have the typical freshman experience as others. I got one hazing experience from Morgan and April, but those never materialized into anything further purely because of who my boyfriend was. I never was pushed around, and all of Scott's senior friends adored me. My struggles this year weren't typical, as they directly resulted from my unique relationship status. I should have considered myself fortunate not to have the *typical* freshman experience, but part of me grew increasingly discontent with my freshman "glory days." I couldn't help but wonder how my sophomore year would do.

"Harper!"

I stood up and saw Scott lightly jogging in my direction. He had his cap and gown in his right hand and a small plastic bag in his left, a tassel with the dreaded '98 hanging from it.

"Sorry," he told me. "I really didn't think it would take that long."

"Your last name is Pierce. It's not quite Whitmore, but it's close enough to the end of the alphabet for it to take some time to get to."

"Is this how it's going to be?" he asked.

"Whatever." I rolled my eyes. "We only have a little time left before my mom gets here."

"Did you eat?" he asked. "We could grab something quick."

"No, I'm not really hungry," I mumbled.

"I'll keep hounding you about this until we have this discussion."

"What discussion?" I pressed. "You keep asking me about it. What do you want me to say?"

"I'm going to come by your house after your doctor's appointment, and we'll discuss this for the first and last time."

"Scott, don't tell me what to do," I voiced. "Don't tell me what's going to happen in my life, either!"

"I'm not, but I'm also not going to be the only person in this relationship who's excited about my graduation," he barked. "That's not fair!"

"I'm happy for you," I roared. "Are you happy now? I said it! I'm happy that you're getting a diploma!"

He sighed deeply, and we slowly walked toward my mom's now parked Lexus. Scott reached for my hand. He laced his fingers with mine, and the discomfort I felt vanished. I was back to being enamored with Scott. I realized that I was only questioning my high-school identity when I was away from Scott, and then I remembered I would be away from him for the next three years.

"Harper," he breathed so my mother wouldn't hear, exasperated, "we're discussing this later."

"I know." I begrudgingly nodded.

Scott casually kissed me on the forehead and opened the passenger-side door, pretending everything was absolutely fine between us.

"Hey Julie!"

"Hello, Scott," my mother exclaimed. "I just had breakfast with your mother. How are you? I see you got your cap and gown! Congratulations! I'm so happy for you. I know your mom is thrilled!"

That pessimistic part of me immediately thought my Mom was only congratulating him to cement the reality of his graduating into my mind. It took me only a moment to remember my mother didn't play that game; she adored Scott.

"Thank you, Julie," Scott exclaimed. "That really means a lot!"

"I can't wait to see Harper in her cap and gown." She gleamed.

"Julie, I think Harper can't wait to be seen in her cap and gown." He smiled at me.

"Hilarious," I informed him.

"See ya, Harper." He quickly kissed me and smiled, nodding. "Please call me!"

Not surprisingly, it turned out to be one of the worst appointments of my life. The cold metal clamps were painful when inserted, and the excruciating scraping of my cervix remains the most uncomfortable experience I have ever willingly gone through. Dr. Marquis was professional but exceptionally cold. She did not reserve her judgment of my boyfriend's age, either, and that was the most disconcerting aspect of the entire visit. After snapping her rubber gloves into the wastebasket, she informed me that we were finished. I couldn't get out of there fast enough. I walked into the waiting room, prescription in hand.

"Ready, Harper?" Mom set her magazine down and stood up.

"Mom," I whispered, "I hate that woman. Let's roll!" I stormed out of the waiting room and headed to my mom's car.

"Harper, you don't like your gynecologist?" she joked as we climbed into her car, and she laughed. "She's not your favorite person?"

"No, I hate her! That woman is judgmental, obnoxious, and an overall nightmare!"

"Harper, most women don't enjoy visiting their gynecologists," she informed me, laughter in her eyes. "Least of all for their first visit."

"I can imagine most women don't enjoy this type of visit, but she judged me. She asked about my *partner's* age," I exclaimed. "I gave her Scott's name, and she wouldn't use it. She preferred *partner*. But that isn't even the worst of it! She didn't like it when I said he was eighteen. That did not sit well with *her* at all. It's none of her business!"

"Harper," my mother sighed, "not everyone is as tolerant about Scott's age."

"What?"

"We don't have an issue with it," Mom assured me. "It is odd, though. We'll admit that. We've heard other parents talk about it behind our backs, and some even discussed it openly. They asked us if we would continue to let you see Scott after he graduates."

"What's it to *them*?"

"Some parents have different parenting styles. People are nosy, especially when you live on a small island. People think their opinions count for something," she stated calmly. "There was a moment when your father and I thought about not letting you see him anymore, you know. He'll be a freshman in college next year, and you'll only be a sophomore in high school."

"What changed?"

"You've been very honest about your relationship with Scott from the beginning. You were upfront about having a boyfriend and never hid his age or grade. You've never snuck around and never given us any reason to worry. Scott has always been very honest with us, as well. We decided if we put an end to you two, you'd probably start sneaking around, and we didn't want to force you into dishonest behavior." She hesitated as if she wanted to say something more.

"But?" I asked.

"But Harper, he's going to college next year. So far, you haven't been hurt by Scott. When he goes to college, he will meet new people and experience new things. You've recently started having a physical relationship with him. Adding some physical distance into the mix could cause unnecessary turmoil."

"So?" I stared her down. "What are you saying? Just say it, Mom!"

"I'm saying I don't want to see you hurt next year because you find out he's seeing someone else or doing something else and not with you."

She stopped talking and focused on turning into our driveway. It was as if my mom had realized she was speaking to an irrational fifteen-year-old girl who was utterly infatuated with her older boyfriend and nothing she said would get through to me correctly.

"He might forget about me? Is that what you're saying, Mom?" My fears about his graduation sprang to the front of my mind again.

She shut the car off, and we sat in the driveway, looking at one another. "Harper, I didn't say that."

"No, but you *are* saying it is all a waste of time because next fall I'll be old news," I screamed through my tears, placing my fears in her words. "You were saying the amount of time I spent debating on even being Scott's girlfriend, to begin with, was all a waste of time because he's just going to leave me when he starts college. You think the decision to have sex with Scott was something I should have skipped altogether because, in the end, Scott will start screwing someone else!"

"Harper, I never said that! I said your father and I discussed limiting your time with Scott because we wanted to prevent you from feeling the pain of something like that happening, but we decided not to." She reached over and wiped the tears away from my cheeks with her thumb. "Harper, we don't want to see you in pain because you won't see Scott every day. That is all."

"Mom, you have no idea how cautious I was at the beginning of our relationship. You have no idea how obsessed I was about not getting too close to him because I knew I could get hurt. I've always known I could get hurt. You have no idea of the reputation Scott's built and how I had to deal with it. I have spent a lot of time worrying about every aspect of our relationship—his reputation, how people will see me, how people will see Scott, and how Scott really sees me. I believe Scott when he tells me that he won't forget about me in the fall, but I don't know what will happen next year. I know very well we might break up. I get it! What I *wasn't* prepared for was hearing about how my parents have been trying to think of ways to keep us apart. *That* I forgot to worry about this year."

I jumped out of the car and ran into the house, straight to my room. I sat in my chair, my knees pulled to my chest, focusing on the rain against my window and the ocean in the distance. I thought about how much I wanted Scott, even though I knew all too well he would be leaving. I wanted to know why I felt this way. I wanted nothing more just then than to not be Scott's girlfriend. I wanted to go back to being the Harper who got out of my mom's car that first day of high school and had her entire high-school career planned out. I wanted to be the Harper who knew she didn't want a high-school boyfriend or a sex life but wanted to enjoy being her.

That Harper was gone. I couldn't even recall that Harper. I couldn't remember why she never wanted to have a boyfriend or why she didn't want to have sex. That Harper seemed so distant. The Harper I found myself to be now was a girl who wanted her freshman year to last forever. She wanted to have her boyfriend be with her every day. This Harper was deeply in love with Scott Pierce, and the idea he might lose interest in her caused her to cry hysterically and wish she'd never met him. I loved him so much that I wanted nothing more than to feel nothing. I didn't want to feel the pain of Scott graduating, the pain of him leaving me, the pain of him potentially forgetting me. Maybe I loved him more than he loved me.

We weren't breaking up, but the anticipation of us potentially ending next fall hurt just as much. I felt his long fingers run along my jaw, rounding my neck before landing on my collarbone. His touch forced me to look up, at which point he kissed me. With an ease only Scott could have, he stepped over the back of my chair onto the seat cushion and wrapped his long legs around me.

"Your flowers are beautiful," he whispered. "Someone must really love you."

"Does he?" My voice was sullen. "Does he love me?"

"Harp," he sighed as he buried his face deeper into my neck, "without a doubt."

"Scott," I breathed and tilted my head into his palm.

"What's bothering my little Harpy?" he mumbled as he buried his head further into my hanging curls. "It can't be so bad that she *needs* to listen to this much Fiona Apple."

"Nothing." I wiped my eyes and looked away. He continued to bury his face deeper into my curls. I could feel his breath along my neck. I started to forget about the anticipation of our potential break-up.

"Something is bothering Harper," he sang. "She's looking at the Sound like she's never seen it before."

"Mom and I got into a fight," I whispered.

"Why?"

"My mom thinks you'll leave me when you start college."

"Is that really what she said?" he pressed. "Word for word, Julie said that?"

"Yes," I snapped.

"I spoke with your mom just now," he informed me. I looked at him quickly, and he went on. "She's afraid it could happen but is more worried about your potential loneliness. She's afraid we became too close too quickly."

"She doesn't care about that," I rebutted. "She thinks you'll leave for college and start fucking other girls!"

"No, she doesn't." He sounded very calm. "She thinks you think that."

"I don't think that."

"Oh really?" His brows raised high before his face drooped into a heavy frown. "You don't think I'm going to graduate high school, start college, and start cheating? It seems to me that is your biggest fear of all."

"I don't think you're going to cheat," I mumbled.

"Then what do you think?" he pressed. "You're certainly not volunteering anything!"

"I'm not thinking anything."

"This entire time, I thought my girlfriend was one of those intellectual girls who overthought everything, but she doesn't really have a thought in her head?"

"Well, what can I say? You like 'em dumb!"

"That's right, I do!"

"Scott," I yelled, "I'm not dumb!"

"If that's true, you *must* have at least one thought in your head."

"Well, what do you want me to say?" I argued.

"What are you thinking?"

"When you finish high school—"

"*Graduate*," he corrected me.

"When you get a diploma, will you dump me?"

"First, say *graduation*," he demanded. "Then I'll answer your question."

"*Graduation*," I condescendingly parroted back to him.

"Thank you." He sounded sarcastic.

"You're welcome," I snapped. "Why the attitude, anyway?"

"Because, Harper, whatever anger you're dealing with about my graduation is taking time away from our relationship, and it's starting to piss me off. This is a huge deal to me. I'm finishing high school, and I finished near the top of my class despite everything that's happened."

"Scott—"

"No," he interrupted me. "I get it. I know you think this is it for us. I know you think once I finish high school, I'm done with you—I'm done with us—but I won't be!"

"It's hard to imagine you not being with me every day. The idea bothers me."

He sighed and dragged his fingers through his sandy blond hair. "Harper, I'm not going anywhere. I don't know how to make that any clearer to you."

"You are," I told him. "You're going off to college! You're heading off this island and to a place where I won't get to see you every day. There will be thousands of girls at the university!"

"I'm giving you my truck. I'm forcing you to become a better driver so you can get off this stupid island and see me as much as possible. You haven't thought once about how this is killing me, have you?"

"Is it?" I argued. "Is it killing you? I wouldn't know because you haven't said anything about it."

"I remind myself I'll be seeing you every weekend, during the week once you get your license, and maybe you'll be able to walk onto the ferry on a Tuesday, and we'll have lunch," he explained. "I trust we'll be alright; we'll make it."

"I sometimes wish...." I didn't finish the sentence; I didn't want to say what I'd been thinking. I didn't know how it would come out or sound.

"What?" He pulled my hair around my shoulder. "Just say it."

"I wish I didn't love you so much," I finished. "I wouldn't feel so angry about you graduating if I didn't. I wouldn't spend so much time thinking about how I've changed in the last few months. I wouldn't spend so much time examining how I let myself get wrapped up in this relationship to the point that I forgot about what I'd originally wanted out of high school."

He forced me to look at him. "Harper, do you regret us?"

"That's the thing! I don't regret any of it. I'd do it all over again, but if we'd never happened, and I was a normal, single freshman girl who was told that I could either have what we have right now or stay the Harper I was at the start of high school, knowing how I feel right now, I'd choose her over us. I don't want to feel so terrible about you leaving in the fall."

"Harp, you only lost who you *thought* you were," he corrected me. "You lost the chance to be the person you *thought* you would be. You became better than what you'd originally wanted for yourself. You discovered a part of yourself that you never thought you had."

"Do you really think that?" I questioned him. "Sometimes, I don't even see myself anymore. I just see Scott's girlfriend. I'm just the girlfriend of the hottest, most popular guy on campus. I'm just the girlfriend of the league leader in three-point shots. It's like I don't have an identity of my own."

"Not a chance," he responded. "If that's how you feel, then I must simply be Harper's boyfriend. I'm the boyfriend of the only freshman girl on varsity soccer, who just so happens to also be the only player in the league to do a hat trick all season. Now I'm the boyfriend of the girl who broke the state record in the two-hundred-meter race. I gotta tell you, I'm just fine with that. It doesn't matter how people see you or me; it only matters how we see each other. It's just us, remember?"

"Scott, I'll always be Harper Whitmore, Scott's first girlfriend."

At that moment, it occurred to me that I had no problem with that idea whatsoever. I will be known as Scott's first girlfriend; I was someone special; I was better than any girl in Scott's past or future because I was the one he fell in love with first.

"Okay," I acknowledged. "I suppose that isn't a bad title to have. It's a title I appreciate, especially when senior girls approach me and remind me I'm the first girl Scott's *ever* loved." I smiled and lightly shoved him. "I like being reminded nearly every day that my boyfriend is the hottest guy on campus, now that I think about it."

"See?" A small smile grew across his beautiful face. "I need you."

"We'll be together?" I asked. "I mean, we'll be fine?"

"Harper, we'll be fine." He returned to kissing me gently. His right hand slowly moved down the length of my arm and skipped over to my rib cage. He pulled his lips away gently, leaving our foreheads pressed against one another. "I graduate in May. It's April now, and I don't leave until August. Maybe you can stop living in the future and live in the present? I understand where you are coming from, and I can sympathize. I never thought I'd have a girlfriend. I never thought I'd care so much about someone other than myself, but I did. I have had to learn to cope with and accept the upcoming changes."

"Scott, do you love me?" I whispered. Scott's eyes rolled. "Please, Scott, just reassure me you do. I think if I can remember that when you leave in August, it will make the separation a little easier on me."

"Harper, I don't know how you could forget—I tell you all the time! I don't just throw that around, either. If I didn't love you, we wouldn't have been together as long as we have been."

"I suppose," I mumbled. "Especially after last month with Lindsay."

"Christ," he exclaimed, "don't remind me. She tried to apologize to me in physics."

"She did?" I asked, astonished. "You never told me that!"

"The apology happened probably a week or two after it all happened with us, and I didn't think you were ready to hear her name at that point. You had just glided back into being *just us* together, and I was worried hearing about her might rock you out of that."

"Did she upset you?" I pressed. "I mean, when she apologized?"

"I wasn't upset, no. I told her she didn't need to apologize to me, she should apologize to my girlfriend, but she dismissed that idea."

"She is such a bitch," I roared. "She said the most hurtful things about you and me! I had never even met the girl until that day after practice. She spread gossip about me, and she won't give me an apology? I can't wait to see *her* graduate."

He grinned. "That is another reason I'm so into you. You really believe in the idea of it just being us in this. You've been that way since the beginning. You hate it when anyone says anything about me or us."

"I don't want people gossiping about us, especially when we keep parts of our relationship so secret." I smiled. "I can promise you that no one knows anything about *that*."

"Even Leigh?"

"She knows very little," I assured him. "She knows the highlights, but I never talk about everything else."

"What happened last month…Was that a *highlight*?"

"She knows Lindsay was someone before me, but she doesn't know the details."

"Thank you." He smiled. "I love that you respect everything that happens between us as private."

"Of course I do!" I smiled. "That is how it works in relationships."

"No, it doesn't, Harper. Look at Lindsay; she *thought* she was in a relationship and told everyone!"

"We don't have to mention her anymore, do we?" I whined. "I'm sort of exhausted by her at this point."

"Absolutely!" He grinned. "She's gone."

"I mean...If you want to discuss her at any time, I'll listen," I mumbled. "I suppose if you want to talk about *any* of them, I'll have that discussion with you. I think she upsets me because she told me about being with you in detail, which was very hard to hear about."

"I've said this before, but I don't need to talk about anyone other than you." He grinned. "And I talk a lot about you!"

"Do you?" A large smile grew across my face.

"Everyone in the senior class was very aware of your two-hundred-meter race, weren't they?"

"Ah, so you're the one who drew all the attention to that race!"

"Harper," he breathed while leaning to my curls, "we'll make it. Trust me on this!"

"You really think so?"

"We'll have a great summer. We'll go to eastern Washington and hang out by the lake all day. We'll work on our tans." He smiled. "When August comes around, we'll deal with my departure. I honestly think we'll be fine."

"You really want me to go to eastern Washington with you this summer? Really?"

"Of course I do," he informed me. "Why wouldn't I?"

"I don't know! It didn't even occur to me you'd go this summer. I hadn't thought about what we'd do this summer."

"See? You've been so obsessed with my graduation that you completely forgot about the possibility of us having an awesome summer together!"

"Oh, my God," I screeched. "I'm so excited!"

I leaned in and kissed him, holding his face tightly between my small hands. He pulled me onto his lap and stretched his legs onto the ottoman – it was very clear from Scott's subtle moves what he hoped to happen very soon.

"I just gotta get out of going to Boston this summer," I told him. "Trust me, my parents will agree to the change in summer plans after the tantrum I'm going to throw! I've already been trying to get out of it. I'll get to buy new swimwear! Scotty!" I screeched.

"Unbelievable!" He smirked. "All it took to get you out of this graduation funk was to ask you to come to eastern Washington with me? I should have done this a month ago!"

"There are a lot of things we should have done a month ago," I told him, laughing.

ELEVEN

I SPENT THE ENTIRE DAY PRIMPING and prepping for my first prom, but I was still not ready for Scott when he arrived, as always, on time. For once in my life, I stood with my hair completely done and face completely together, wishing Scott was the sort of boyfriend who showed up late, providing me a little more time to obsess over final details. He made dinner plans in Seattle that evening before we headed to his prom.

I had been so consumed with preparing for prom I neglected to realize until Scott pulled into my driveway that my parents were going out for the night. Under normal circumstances, we'd have the house to ourselves, and Scott would never let an opportunity like that pass us by.

Scott snuck up behind me and pulled me against his chest. He whispered into my ear while I stood in the kitchen preparing myself a light snack before our dinner.

"Harp, I like what I'm seeing," he whispered in a low growl. "You smell really good."

"Yeah? If you like my bathrobe, you'll love my prom dress."

"Scott?" My father's deep voice broke our moment of intimacy. The familiar hands wrapped around my waist were quickly pulled away.

My father entered the kitchen, coming close to Scott and directing him toward the hallway. Perhaps because Scott and I had grown so close, I sensed Scott's fear of my father was growing. I watched Scott walk behind my father, his hands slightly fidgety. First, he had them in his pant pockets and then placed them on his waist. He put them in his back pockets, then crossed and uncrossed them before putting them back in his pockets. The two men were still within earshot. I wasn't sure if my father had intended it to be that way or if he simply didn't realize I could still hear everything.

My father reached inside his coat pocket and handed Scott a five-by-seven plastic card. "Here, Julie told me that you and Harper still plan on seeing each other next year, so you'll need this."

Scott gently took the card out of his hand and examined it. I looked at Scott as he slowly smiled and read the plastic card. Relief washed over his face, and he reached to shake my father's hand. My father lightly patted Scott's shoulder while he shook his hand firmly.

"Thank you, Mr. Whitmore," Scott stated happily. "I really appreciate this; you honestly didn't have to do this."

"Listen, Scott, I've seen the guys with whom Harper goes to school. They're all a bunch of burn-outs! Most of them don't seem like they are sober half the time. Their wide-legged jeans and long hair annoy me. I can't have *that* in my home. I can't have Harper with a boy with bleached blond hair, black roots, and a nose ring!"

Scott started to chuckle.

"I'll admit I was not a fan of the age gap initially," my father told him. "I hated it! Julie can elaborate another time on the earful I gave her about how much I didn't approve. I don't notice it anymore, though. If you guys decide to continue this next fall, I want you to know I support it. The age doesn't bother me in the slightest. Harper's a big girl who seems to know how to handle herself. From what Julie tells me, she appears to know how to handle *you*, too."

"Yes, she does, sir." Scott smiled.

"When you put that in your windshield, and they ask how you know me, please say that you know *Jay* very well. Quit it with that Whitmore crap!"

"Yes, sir." Scott lightly chuckled. "I'll try to refrain from being so formal."

"I've heard your truck is staying with Harper."

"Yes," Scott stated. "I told her she could keep it while I'm at school."

"That's generous of you," my father remarked. "It's evident my daughter means a great deal to you."

"She does, sir," Scott stated.

"Julie has said Harper feels the same—that *you* mean a lot to her."

"I am very aware of that."

"I can assure you that you mean a great deal to her. I never want to see her feel anything less than what she does right now," my dad warned my boyfriend.

"She won't."

"Well, in that case, flash the card when you get on the ferry, and you won't need to pay the walk-on fare. It'll save you a couple of bucks. I'm sure Harper will visit you often when she gets her driver's license, so I'll be sure the truck gets a permanent sticker on the windshield."

"Thank you, sir. I never expected anything like this."

"You can thank me, but quit it with the Mr.-Whitmore talk and the sir stuff. I see you nearly every day. That polite shtick is getting old."

"I'll try."

"Have fun tonight, and be safe," my father ordered him. My father patted Scott once more and walked toward the front door.

Scott stood still, watching my parents leave to enjoy their Saturday night. He didn't move. He didn't even acknowledge me when I locked both my arms around his waist.

"Harper, I can't believe your father gave me this," he whispered. "Did you know?"

"No, he never told me. I don't think it's a big deal, though. My mother has one in her car."

"Yeah, but she's your mom, Harp. She's your dad's wife. I'd expect *her* to never pay to get on the ferry. I'm not in your family, though, and this card is for family." Scott let out a heavy sigh. "I just think this is a huge thing, Harper. It's a huge deal to have your father give me this. I know he's said that he likes me—"

"He's always liked you, Scott," I interrupted him. "He's always really enjoyed seeing you around the house."

"I know. You've told me he likes me. It's one thing to sit next to him at a soccer game or stand in the driveway and talk to him about basketball; it's entirely different from being given a family pass to ride the ferry for free."

"Scott—"

"A part of me thinks he gave it to me because he really does like me and approves of us, but the other part of me, the cynical part, thinks he only gave this to me as a reminder to not hurt you next fall, especially after everything he just said about you—"

"Scott, that's not true," I exclaimed. "If anything, he wants you to have the pass so you remember to come back to the island regularly next fall. There is not an ulterior motive to this. He said he sees you every day, which means he notices you and doesn't mind seeing you."

"I was worried about the cost of getting on and off the ferry for the two of us," Scott told me as we pressed our foreheads against each other. "It means so much to me, Harp. It means he really likes me and accepts me as part of his daughter's life."

I groaned. "Scott, enough about the card, my dad, and the fact that I'm someone's daughter!"

"Harp, I know Julie really likes me, but hearing your dad likes me is a big thing for me. Now I know he likes me; I can never screw up."

"Quit it!" I laughed. "I don't want my only prom ruined with this sappy talk."

"I'm done!" He grinned. "I won't talk about it."

"Are you sure that you used to be an asshole? I'm just not seeing it. I don't believe you have one badass bone in ya," I teased. "You are very adorable when you get emotional, though."

"I'll be badass right now if you like," he whispered. "This house is empty, and I've gone over three weeks without you, babe."

"Oh, that's sweet, Scott," I teased. "It just so happens I would really like to feel the weight of a two-hundred-ten-pound man on me right now."

"Really? Any man?" He smirked. "Not one man *specifically*? Any man will do for my little freshman?"

"Well, I don't know any other two-hundred-ten-pound men but you." I smirked. "And you're standing right here."

"You know where I could find a ninety-eight-pound freshman?"

"There is one upstairs," I cried as I ran upstairs and into my room.

I rested my head against his chest and looked around at my messy, disheveled bedroom floor. Not only were the clothes we wore earlier today strewn across my beige carpet, but numerous purple University of Washington T-shirts, stuffed animals, and pillows were spread across my floor, reading chair, and bed. I sat on Scott's lap and continued examining my now almost-entirely purple bedroom.

"Scott, is there a reason I have all this University of Washington paraphernalia in my room?" I questioned. "I know you will be going there, but is there another reason you continue decorating my room with it? You continue to shower me in University of Washington garb!"

"*Garb*?" he questioned. "Have you been speaking to your grandmother Ethel recently?"

"Seriously, look around you!" I laughed.

"What are you getting at?" He tried to hide his smile as best he could. "I just want you to be prepared for basketball season this winter, that's all!"

"I've just been putting a few things together—"

"What things?" Scott interrupted. "Tell me what you've put together."

"You mean aside from me being your girlfriend and the absolute love of your life?" I lightly pinched his waist and laughed as he squirmed. "You seem to have a vested interest in my algebra grade and feel that anything less than an A-minus is simply unacceptable."

"Oh, Harp, I care! That's all!" He laughed.

"Uh-huh! You also continue to think we will be just fine being separated by a ferry ride next year. I am starting to feel confident, but you have this plan in place when you are away in college. It's a plan I am looking forward to as best I can, but your confidence is astounding!"

"Harp, I've always been very confident."

"Yes, you have!" In a quick motion, I pulled the comforter around my body and resumed my position on his lap. "Are you comfortable with me sitting like this?"

"Ninety-eight pounds never felt so good!" He continued to hide his smile. "Continue."

"For some reason, you are putting off getting recruited into the pros until your senior year. You claim it's because you want a college education, which is respectable, but I know you well enough to know that it might have something to do with the fact that I'm still in high school." I smirked. "You're not even trying to hide your grin anymore!"

"Neither are you, babe!" He grinned. "I just want to be intelligent, that's all!"

"You were also very focused on me breaking the two-hundred-meter. You were much more than just a supportive boyfriend in that case."

He immediately became serious. "That's just common sense. That and your soccer will look good on your college application. Your extracurricular activities will carry you right into a college of *your* choice. It's more than that, though, Harper. I have tremendous pride in you, and your breaking that record just added to my pride! Now please, Harper, continue."

"What universities are you interested in me being *carried* right into?"

"That's neither here nor there—"

"Uh-huh! Finally, Scott, we arrive at the Pathfinder. I know you want me to drive it around next year; the gift was that I could *share* the Pathfinder. I think you want me to tool around in it to remind the rest of the high school that Scott Pierce still exists and is still the boyfriend of Harper Sage Whitmore."

"But—" Scott interrupted. I immediately put my finger to his lips, signaling him to let me finish my well-organized thesis. "Continue," he told me.

"More importantly, Scott, you want me to visit you as much as possible. You want me to visit the *University of Washington* as much as possible."

"Say it, Harp. You seem to think you've got it all figured out. I'm just waiting for you to finish."

"You, Scott Pierce, want your girlfriend to *apply* to the University of Washington!" I yelled triumphantly. Scott gave me a round of applause.

"Well done, Harper, well done!" He continued to applaud. "You seem to have it all figured out. You are a sharp little freshman, aren't you? It is true that I do want you to *consider* applying to the University of Washington, and I am going to do my absolute best to sell the university to you. I would love to essentially redo this year. You'd be a freshman at Washington, and I'd be a senior. It is also true that I would hate to play pro ball and have a girlfriend who was still in high school."

"So you admit it?" I asked him. "You want me to apply to the same school you're going to?"

"I want you to do whatever you want. I'm not about to tell you what to do, but I *would* like you to consider applying to my university when you become a senior. To prove that I am not demanding that you attend the University of Washington, I'd suggest perhaps also applying to Seattle University." We both laughed. "I hope you've already dropped your interest in the University of Massachusetts?" His eyebrows rose. "Right?"

"So, you're open to me applying to any school within a specific radius of your school, then? The University of Massachusetts is not within that radius?"

"I didn't say that." He laughed. "I would be a little annoyed if you opted for Massachusetts, though."

"We don't need to be talking about this now," I told him. "It's trivial this year; I'm not a senior until 2000! We have plenty of time; anything could happen in the next few years."

"We might not even be here, with Y2K looming!"

My hair was pinned up. My beautiful curls draped over my thin headpiece, which boasted sparkling rhinestones. My exceptionally well-done makeup tied it all together. I flipped the visor down during the drive to my first prom and put on my finishing touches. I pulled out my retainer and placed it carefully into the plastic holder, smiling at Scott when he glanced over to watch me getting ready.

"No retainer tonight, Harp?" he teased. "You're not afraid that your teeth will get banged up again if you go a night without it?"

After putting on my final lip gloss coat, I smiled at him, flipping up the visor. "Scotty, I think I am put together as best I can!"

"Harp, you look gorgeous this evening," Scott said with assurance as he downshifted and made a right-hand turn into the only yacht club on the island.

"Really? Thank you! You are very handsome in your tux. I am impressed and slightly suspicious that you got a maroon tie to match my dress."

"Despite what you may think of my normal casual attire, I do know something about looking sharp when the moment calls for it. I knew you would be pissed if I showed up in a green tie, so you can just go ahead and be pissed that I looked at your dress."

I looked out the dark window and saw the yacht club parking lot entirely filled. I looked at the clock and saw it was a little before ten.

"Are you sure you're not pissed that we're *very* late to your prom?" I asked. "I mean, it is *your* senior prom."

"I am totally fine with being late to this thing," he exclaimed. "Harp, the real question is whether you will be alright with it."

"Scott, I have reevaluated my priorities in life."

"Oh, please, do tell." He smirked. "What fifteen-year-old priorities have you shuffled around?"

"Well, I think that lying on my bedroom floor for nearly three hours with you was probably a better pre-game to your prom than going to dinner on the mainland and showing up to this thing on time."

Scott found a vacant parking spot behind the yacht club, shut his engine off, leaned over, and kissed me unexpectedly.

"Harp, I swear it's like you're the female version of me."

"Highly doubtful!"

"Sit right here," he commanded me.

Before I could reply, Scott was already out the door and lightly jogging around the back of the truck. He opened the passenger-side door and stood there briefly, gathering his thoughts. I looked at him patiently, taking my seatbelt off and spinning around in my seat to face him.

"Harper, I bought you something. I almost gave it to you when we spent those three hours on your bedroom floor earlier today, but I wanted to give it to you tonight at the *actual* prom. I wanted you to have it while doing one of your favorite things—dancing in expensive dresses."

"Dancing in expensive dresses *is* one of my favorite things, Scott!" I reached up and pinched him on the cheek. "You know me so well."

With his right hand, he reached inside his tux jacket and pulled out a black velvet box.

"No! No! No! No way, Scott," I declared, jumping to conclusions. "Not a chance! I'm fifteen. Absolutely not! My father will kill you, and then he'll kill me, and then he'll kill my mom for letting us get this involved. After that, he might take his killing spree outside the family and kill Leigh if she knew something about it! Put that away right now! You have no idea what Jay Whitmore is capable of if pushed! You know he has a hunting license, right? Assume he has guns, Scott! Assume it!"

"Harp, calm down," he instructed me, exasperated. "I know your father has a hunting permit. My father is the sheriff, and he did a background check on your family when we started going out."

"Calm down?" I pointed to the velvet box. "This is not something to calm down about! Your father checked up on me?... I don't think I like that."

"You have nothing to check up on, but your parents do," he told me. "Yes, he checked up on your parents."

"Are my parents clean?" I asked with a suspicious whisper. "I mean, like, do they have anything to hide?"

"Nothing exciting at all." He smirked. "Your mom speeds occasionally. She's gotten nabbed a few times at the ferry docks—"

"Well, that's not exactly fair." I dismissed his words with a wave of my hand. "I mean, if the ferry is about to pull out, she's got to speed to attempt to make it."

"Exactly; not very exciting." He smirked. "Obviously, your dad has a hunting license and a handheld in the house."

"What is a handheld?"

"A gun."

"Wow," I exclaimed. "I had no idea!"

"Harp?" He handed me the small black-velvet jewelry box. I took the box gently out of his hand using only my index finger and thumb. I placed it on my palm and looked up at Scott with only my eyes. "Go ahead," he instructed me.

It was a silver watch; "Tag Heuer" was printed in the center, and there was a light pink shimmer on the face. The name stood out to me—it reminded me of Scott's watch. He had the same name in the center, but his watch was much larger and far more masculine. This one was delicate and sophisticated, not plastic or digital. It was a grown-up watch, just like Scott's.

"You bought me a watch?" The extreme shock came through in my voice. "You didn't have to buy me a watch!"

He didn't respond immediately. He gently took the watch out of the box. His large hands and fingers overshadowed the tiny links of my new feminine watch. He unclasped it with such agility that I barely heard the slight click it made when he expanded the clasp.

"September 1997," I read as I looked at the watch.

"I hope there is never an end date engraved in there." He smiled, "If you need to put an end date in there, just stop wearing it or something."

"Scotty," I gasped. "It's so beautiful! It's the most beautiful thing anyone has ever given me."

"I highly doubt that," he replied, "but I am very happy you like it."

"No, Scott, this is the nicest thing anyone has ever purchased for me."

"You gave me so much this year, Harp," he breathed. "You saved me...."

I dabbed a small tear away as it appeared just below my left eye. I watched him gently put the watch on my left hand, carefully turning my wrist and clasping the latch.

"Why a watch?" I asked.

"Despite what I say, you're always concerned with the time we have left together."

"I know." I nodded slowly, acknowledging that I got stuck in my own worries about our time together. "Scotty, I love it. Thank you!" I stood on the rail of his truck, standing eye-to-eye, and kissed him as he held his arms around my waist. "I promise to never have an end date engraved. I think that is an easy promise to make!"

He lifted me off the rail of his truck. He held me briefly while I thanked him as best I could in a public setting.

"Keep this up, Harp, and we're going back to your bedroom floor for another three hours instead of into the yacht club."

"We can leave early if the need presents itself."

"Amazing, Harp! You are simply amazing!"

We walked into the prom together. The people inside were already well into a night of dancing, and it seemed that only a few people managed to notice our tardiness. The reason for our delay was truly no one else's business, but it was startling to realize that I had gone from thinking that nothing was more important to me than this prom to having time with Scott at the top of my list of priorities in life.

Before Scott had the chance to realize what song was playing, I already had my fingers laced with his, and I was tugging him onto the polished dance floor.

"Harp, seriously, I really don't dig Mariah Carey!"

"Please?" I continued to pull him with both my hands. "Dig it for me."

Scott had never danced straight through the night with me before this. That night, I felt I wasn't just a freshman tagging along with Scott. When Scott removed his jacket and strutted into the center of a circle to begin break dancing to the Quad City DJ's, I felt the pats on my back and the cheers from the seniors. I knew at that moment that Scott was right all along—the age gap only mattered in high school. After a while, no one would really notice. They'd just see us as a couple.

After Scott strategically placed his maroon tie around my neck, I heard the DJ say that a song request and dedication had been made to Harper Whitmore and that it would be coming up. I was startled by the request. I looked up at Scott, who was not fazed by the recent announcement. He continued to move his hands over me as we danced.

"Did you hear the DJ?" I yelled.

"No." Scott remained focused on me and our synced dance moves. "What did he say?"

"A song was requested and dedicated to me."

"Huh," he grunted. "I'm sure he'll announce it again."

We continued dancing to my favorite songs, though to Scott, they were songs he'd learned to tolerate.

"And here is Harper Whitmore's song!" The DJ cheered.

"You heard that, right, Scott?" I yelled while we continued to keep our symmetrical but inappropriate dance moves going. "Right? You heard that?"

"Yes, *that* I heard." He pointed in the direction of the DJ. "It'd better not be a boy band, and it better have a solid backbeat. Maybe it's Beck! I could go for some Beck. Or Smashing Pumpkins! I'd even tolerate that Savage Garden stuff you leave in the truck," Scott teased. "I suppose it could be anyone who dedicated a song to you. It's probably Brad!"

"If it was Brad, it would be something by ODB or Warren G as a joke." I smiled.

It wasn't Beck, nor was it a boy band with a danceable backbeat. It certainly wasn't a dedication from Brad to his best friend's girl, either. I knew immediately who the dedication was from: A girl I thought had moved on and gotten over me. She'd most certainly moved on from Scott. I danced with Scott, feeling his hands along my waist and wrapping them around my stomach. I kept my back to him. I felt him move his lips across my neck as we danced exceptionally close. I glared at Lindsay Paul, standing with her usual group of senior girls, her arms crossed and anger burning under her pale skin. Her anger showed through her eyes as we listened to the lyrics of Lauryn Hill's "Doo Wop (That Thing)." She glared back at me while I enjoyed Scott's public display of affection.

It wasn't a game that she and I were playing, but for some reason, as I listened to the song and mouthed the lyrics to her, I felt as though I'd won a game. The prize was Scott as a boyfriend. She'd wanted Scott as a very public boyfriend at one time, and I had him now.

"Girls you know you better watch out/Some guys, some guys are only about/That thing, that thing, that thing."

I had my fill of looking at Lindsay, attempting to ruin my prom with her ongoing anger. She was complacent when she knew Scott wasn't with anyone, but that all changed her senior year. I could only imagine the memories of her sophomore year of high school would haunt her forever, and her own poor choices entirely drove it. I spun around in Scott's arms, smiling broadly at him, teetering on a giggle of happiness. I stood on my tiptoes in my heels, reaching for Scott's lips. I met his kiss and gripped his biceps for support. I held his kiss longer than usual. I was ever-so thankful that I had opted to keep my heels on, bringing our height difference to a reasonable gap.

I knew how to kiss Scott to gain the response from him that I wanted Lindsay to witness. I smoothed my hands down his biceps and traced a line down his torso before latching onto his waistband. I knew where his hands would end up soon. As if on cue, both his hands arrived on the small of my back, pulling me closer.

I pulled away slowly and revealed my perfect teeth and a large grin. Our faces were only inches apart.

"What's so funny, Harp?" Scott asked me.

"I know who made the song request!" I laughed. "Your senior gal pal requested it. I think Lindsay still likes you—better yet, I think she *loves* you."

"That sucks for her." He leaned down and returned to kissing me. "I already apologized to her a few times. I'm not sure what else she wants from me."

"Oh, I'll tell you what she wants from you...Well, she doesn't actually *want* it, but she'll take whatever she can get because of her low self-esteem and deplorable self-worth." I pulled away from Scott quickly, and he tilted his head and smiled. "It's true, Scott," I told him. "She'll take whatever you give her. That's why she apologized to you. She hopes you'll bring her back into your good graces."

"Harp, are you saying that if I walked over there right now and said something about being sorry and wanting to fix our past, I could get laid within an hour?" Scott absentmindedly ran his fingers under the strap of my dress, slowly going further under the fabric at the front of my dress while staring off into the distance. "Would it be that simple?"

"You're wrong on one count," I told him. "You could have it in the bag within thirty minutes." I quickly snatched his finger before it moved any further along my breast line. "But don't even think about it," I hissed between my teeth.

"See, Harp?" He smiled. "That's one of the problems I'd have. I'd have to wear a bag with her because that girl has been around. You… Well, I know where you've been, Little Harper Whitmore. You're clean as a whistle!"

"One of the many perks of being with a fifteen-year-old freshman," I joked. I smiled quickly. "Seriously, don't even think about it!"

"Oh, Harp," he promised, "I'd never. It just never occurred to me until now that I should—or *could* be chasing after girls with low self-esteem." He was unable to contain his own laughter. "I'd have to wear a bag with those girls, though, and the days of wearing those are long gone for me!"

"Scott, I'll let you in on a secret." I leaned into him and whispered in his ear. "That is exactly what you did before me. It was unintentional, but you went after girls with atrocious self-worth and horrendous self-esteem before you met me."

"Maybe that's why I *intentionally* went after you—you have such high self-esteem! I just wasn't used to it."

"Really?" I held my grin and laughed. "You think I have a high self-esteem? I'm not sure about that. I am sure I don't have low self-esteem—I have a healthy self-esteem, I think."

"No, you don't." He shook his head and lightly pouted his lips as his smile lines very delicately showed through. "You intentionally put that image off to the public, but deep down inside, you have a very high self-worth. You know exactly what you are and what you look like, which gives you a demeanor that scares many people off. Lindsay, for instance, is an eighteen-year-old senior, and she's terrified of you."

I spun around, leaning into Scott's chest and feeling his hands around my waist as they slowly wound around to my stomach. His lips brushed against my neck again. I continued to mouth Lauryn Hill's lyrics until Lindsay had had enough and stormed out of the ballroom.

Our fingers laced as we walked an arm's length from each other, swinging our linked hands in bliss. We were heading through the long hallway, away from the loud, pounding music, strobe lights, and beautifully dressed seniors. I pulled myself toward him, standing on my tiptoes, and quickly kissed him before heading into the women's room. His smile was small and tight-lipped as he leaned against the wall and patiently waited for me to finish.

I freshened up my face, rolled a new application of gloss across my lips, and checked my teeth quickly. I fluffed my curls out and pinched my bobby pins deeper into my full head of curls. I felt beautiful enough to be on Scott's arm that night. I flashed a beautiful smile at myself and left the restroom to return to Scott's arm.

I looked up and down the long-carpeted hallway for Scott. I saw him talking to the tall, thin, blonde female who had dedicated a song to me. A large crowd began gathering behind her. She wore a royal blue silk dress with spaghetti straps. It was backless, and the fabric gathered at a scoop on the small of her back. She was so thin that even from a distance, I was able to make out each vertebra on her back. The dress included a very long train, which she held in her left hand. Her hair was cheap looking, done up in an over-curled up-do and tied together in a sparkly headpiece. Lindsay Paul was making *my* Scott upset.

I watched Scott's gestures, his hard, firm hands working and his fingers tightly pulled together as he directed the conversation with his hands. Scott was a man who hardly ever used his hands to speak unless he was angered or made a concerted effort to understand something. He was now directing an entire conversation with Lindsay with his hands. He seemed annoyed, and he was quickly becoming frustrated; he ran both his hands through his short dirty-blond hair before forcefully putting them into his pockets.

I inched closer to the crowd gathering in the hallway; I kept a somewhat safe distance but moved closer. I began to hear Lindsay raise her voice and saw her press both her hands into Scott. I didn't want to interrupt a conversation that no doubt had very little to do with me. I suspected it had more to do with 1996 and the events that took place then. I inched closer, and I was shocked to hear her voice crack.

"I was never asked, Scott! No one ever *asked* if I wanted it! Your parents just came into my life and told me what would happen!"

"I didn't know that. I didn't know my parents took care of anything," he yelled. "This has nothing to do with *me*. If you have this animosity over the abortion, you should go to your parents or my parents, but not me!"

"That's right," she shouted at him. "Scott hides behind his parents! He knows they'll take care of everything," she yelled. "Whatever trouble Scott gets into, his parents will bail him out. He gets whatever he wants, whether he knows it or not. You got me because you wanted me. That's how you work!"

"I have no idea what you're talking about. I didn't even *want* you. I just had you because you were throwing yourself at me, and I certainly never told my parents about us."

"Fuck you, Scott," Lindsay nearly screamed. "I was never good enough to be introduced to your parents; I knew you never told them about me, unlike your precious Harper!"

"Leave Harp out of it," he screamed. "She has nothing to do with this!"

"Oh, I forgot that she's Harp to you."

"She has nothing to do with this and I don't appreciate how you've tried to ruin her name this year. I nearly lost her because of your shit!"

"Oh, heaven forbid that Scott should have to suffer through anything."

I stepped forward, fighting my way through the crowd that was forming behind Lindsay. I wedged myself through two large senior guys. One of them was Brad, who placed his hand around my shoulder and looked down at me out of concern and the need to protect me. I looked over at Brad's left and saw Leigh mouthing precisely what I was thinking: "What the hell?" While she inched closer for a better view of the drama unfolding.

"Harper," Brad whispered as he pulled me back, "you don't need to see or hear this."

I didn't say anything. I looked up at him, noticing how well-groomed his hair was for once, and fought against his motion to move me back through the crowd.

"Are we done here?" Scott asked Lindsay. "Harp will be here soon, and I really don't want her evening ruined because of your shit! She'll probably have to hear about it since you've invited the entire senior class to watch you bitch me out!"

"Heaven forbid that Harper find out what kind of guy her boyfriend really is."

"Harp knows all about me," Scott calmly informed her. "You can stop trying to inform her of anything else."

"Really? Does she know that Scott's parents showed up at my house, ready to write a check for the abortion and money for any pain caused?" she yelled. "I guarantee that if this happened to Harper, things would have been a whole hell of a lot different. Harper is not someone the Pierce family would ever think to buy off, is she?"

"When you're right, you're right, Lindsay," Scott confirmed. "Harp isn't trash, and neither is the Whitmore family. If this ever happened to Harp, I can guarantee that nobody would ever find out."

"Scott, I loved you, and you shit on that," she yelled. "I really don't care if the class knows."

"You don't know what love is. I never loved you! How could I love you if I didn't know anything about you? How could you love me if you didn't know anything about me?"

"You knew me. I just wasn't good enough for you!"

"Lindsay, what we did—what you thought we had—I did with about twelve other girls that year alone. None of them dragged it out for two years, either!" The crowd started to immediately mumble simultaneously.

"God, Lindsay, I am tired of apologizing to you for what happened. The only person I should ever have to apologize to is Harp, and she doesn't need an apology. It seems that I've apologized more to you just this year than anyone in my entire life. It's exhausting. I'm tired of being beyond nice to you and feeling like shit for what happened. The only person I really care about in this whole situation is Harp; it's impacted her life because you've managed to drag her into this. She doesn't deserve that; she's too good for that."

I'd never heard Scott be harsh to another girl before. I'd only heard about how he was from others; I'd never imagined what it would be like to witness Scott like this. Even during track season, when we had our falling out that one day, his words hurt, but I knew they were only words. There was nothing material behind them. Hearing Scott's words now were like hearing another person speak, a person I didn't know. I'd assume it was another person if I hadn't seen him with my own eyes. I watched Scott as he ran his hands through his hair and put them back on his waist before casually placing them in his pant pockets.

"That's right," Lindsay countered. "Apparently, she is the only girl good enough for Scott."

"I guess every guy has to spend a little time in the gutter before he knows exactly what he doesn't want."

"That's why I wasn't good enough to be your girlfriend? I was from the gutter?"

"Was?" Scott repeated. "You still are!"

"Scott." I stepped forward and shook my head. He looked directly at me, his face calming. "Don't," I warned him.

He looked slightly ashamed but also relieved to see me. He shook his head and looked at the floor before he looked back up at Lindsay. He wiped his face with his hand before running his fingers through his now-disheveled hair.

"That's why the abortion?" Lindsay asked. "Your parents didn't want trash to be brought into this world that they'd somehow be associated with?"

"I didn't want you as my girlfriend because I didn't want a girlfriend," he calmly told her. "I just wanted what I got. I can't account for the abortion, but I can tell you that my parents have already been through one teen pregnancy with my brother. Another would probably throw them over the edge. I suspect it had nothing to do with where you came from, how they perceived you, and everything to do with their sanity."

I slowly walked toward Scott and slid my hand into his pocket, locking my fingers with his. I kept my eyes on his as he looked down at me, firmly holding my hand.

"Lindsay," I whispered.

"Harper, I don't know what to say to you, except that the Scott you are with is not the real Scott. I hope you know that."

"Lindsay, it doesn't matter which Scott I'm with. This Scott is with me, not you."

He let go of my hand and wrapped his arm across my torso, pulling me in front of him. Her eyes followed Scott's motions, examining each of Scott's routine movements before settling back on me. This time, I knew that his movements were not for her and not for me. They were for him.

"Lindsay," I reminded her, "you don't want the last memory people will have of you to be your outburst at the prom."

She glared down at me. I locked my eyes with hers as I slowly stepped back into Scott's chest.

"Are we done here, Lindsay?" Scott politely asked. "Did you get everything you needed here?"

"Harper, your curls look fake," she told me. My mouth dropped, and I gasped, both astonished and horrified. "And another thing," she continued. "You'll always just be Scott Pierce's girlfriend. There is absolutely nothing special about you. You are as ordinary as a freshman could be."

All I could do was gasp.

"I told you to keep Harp out of this, Lindsay," Scott warned her. "Why the hell would you say that?"

"Oh bitch, I tried!" I pulled away from Scott's light hold on me. "If you want to get into this, we can. I'll start by ripping out that nasty hair piece you got tangled up in that horrible bleach job, followed by removing that ridiculous tiara you're sporting – I imagine it's lodged in those unnatural, permed curls because you'll never be Prom Queen, and you've desperately wanted to feel some form of admiration since Scott left you a shell of a person."

I felt Scott pull on my bicep. The crowd was loudly erupting in cheers. I knew the cheers were less for me and more for the potential for a senior-freshman fight, but I didn't care. I wanted Lindsay to fight back, but she didn't. She stayed silent and took in everything I said, offering no defense.

"You better watch your back, doll face," I continued, "because these curls are natural! Try to remember before you start running your mouth with its banged-up teeth that this ordinary freshman is told routinely by her boyfriend that he loves her. That was something you couldn't even get Scott to lie to you about!"

The rage I felt toward her picked up where Scott's anger had left off only moments prior. I recognized how angry she could make someone; how antagonistic she could be. Any remnants of my usual calm, rational perspective were gone as I stepped toward her, untangling my arm from Scott's grip, and pushed her backward with all my strength.

"You better think twice before discussing the authenticity of my curls! You'll probably have time to think about it next fall while I'm tooling around in the Pathfinder, which you weren't even good enough to be seen around!"

I watched as Lindsay attempted to not trip over the train on her dress. I wanted her to fall backward in front of her whole class. I attempted to push her again, but I was quickly stopped by Scott's long right arm wrapping around my waist and pulling me to his chest.

"Scott! That bitch called my curls fake!"

"Harp, no one thinks your curls are fake," he whispered into my ear as he walked us backward out of the crowd.

"Oh, and Lindsay, I appreciated your song request," I yelled. "I wasn't sure if you were finally admitting something about yourself, though!"

"Harper." Scott's one word of warning entered my ear.

"That bitch just tried to ruin my one prom with you!"

"Fortunately for you, you'll have two more that she won't be able to ruin! I think you may have destroyed her night, though."

Scott set me down at the edge of the dance floor. The dark ballroom prevented me from seeing his face clearly. The only light in the room came from the strobe lights streaking across the ballroom. We looked at each other as best we could. I focused on the pattern of green and blue lights that streaked across Scott's face before I spoke.

"Scott, I won't have another prom with you! She got you upset at the only prom we'll ever have together."

"Harp," Scott sighed, "I'll go to your proms."

"You will?" I exclaimed. "You will really go to my proms?"

"After watching you defend me like that and knowing you didn't tear into me for what I said to her, I think that's the very least I can promise you. I never wanted you to see or hear that. Overall, I've done a pretty solid job hiding my old self from you."

"O-o-oh, you're even promising!" I gloated. "I don't care what I saw or heard. I get it—she can't let go. She is spiraling down quickly and trying to take you with her. Please do tell me about the twelve girls just that year, though," I teased. "Wow!"

"Rough estimation," he joked. "There is only one right now, though, and I hope to keep it that way for a long time."

"Oh, Scotty...."

TWELVE

"ENJOYING THE LAST FEW MINUTES of your high-school boyfriend, Harper?" Barrett said as he approached me.

I was standing on the green grass of our high school's football field, watching Scott interact with classmates for the last time on high school property. I watched as he had pictures taken. He laughed, knowing his minutes were numbered on campus greenery.

"You better take it in," the now-sophomore continued. "He won't be here anymore after today."

I spun around and glared at Barrett as he towered over me. He was alone, and he was confident. He didn't care that Scott was only a few feet away. In fact, it seemed as though he would embrace a last violent moment with Scott.

"I'm now enjoying being the girlfriend of a college freshman," I responded.

"He's not in college yet."

"Why are you here?" I pressed.

"My cousin just graduated."

"Then why are you not with your family?"

"I wanted to wish Scott well." He leaned in to whisper into my ear. I could smell him. He smelled plain and boring. Generic bar soap was what I sensed as he moved his lips against my hanging curls. "I also wanted to remind him that it will be just you and me next year, and I will try my best to get you to like me."

"Barrett!" Scott's voice carried as he crossed the field and grabbed me to him. "Are you bothering Harp?"

"Not in the slightest."

That summer was the best summer of my life. I fought hard to get out of going to Boston with my family, and I prevailed. My parents and Morgan continued with their two-week travel plans, and I journeyed to eastern Washington with the love of my life for two weeks in June and three weeks in August.

Crystal Lake was just as Scott described. We stayed in a beautiful two-story house with a wraparound deck. The house sat alone, high up on the shore of the beautiful blue water. Every morning, I would walk down the overgrown path that led to a private and somewhat sandy shore. I would lie in the sun in my new hot-pink bikini, wearing my black shades and drinking iced tea until noon. Scott would bring Rainier Beer with him at noon, and I would drink that and lie in the sun in the afternoons until I fell asleep due to extended sun exposure. I'd always wake up to Scott running an ice cube from my collarbone to my cleavage. I loved Scott's dark skin, his muscular build, and the fact that he never wore a shirt with his board shorts. We even had matching black Ray-Ban sunglasses. He was always willing to make me laugh, which made me love him more.

Our last day in eastern Washington was a Friday in late August. We were prepared to start the fall apart. Instead of being upset together that Thursday night, we opted to celebrate Scott's nineteenth birthday a few days early. We slept outside that night. I screamed "Scotty" multiple times. I woke up that Friday morning clinging to Scott, desperate for our summer to continue.

"We'll come back next June, Harp, and we'll do it again."

Scott left for school the following Monday. It was a gray day. There were heavy clouds over the Sound and a fog rolling in off the shore.

I hugged Scott tightly, feeling his long arms wrap around my waist as he picked me up off the ground. I buried my face in his neck and cried, leaving his shirt soaked. My father held the ferry until Scott boarded. Nothing felt worse than Scott going that day. I cried for three days straight.

I locked myself in my room, sitting in my reading chair and staring at the white Pathfinder in my parents' driveway beneath the basketball hoop, already waiting for my sophomore year of high school to end.

Made in United States
North Haven, CT
27 February 2024